Nova Terra: Greymane

SETH RING

Nova Terra: Greymane

This book is a work of fiction. Names, characters, businesses, organizations, places, events and incidents either are the product of the author's imagination or are used fictitiously. Any resemblance to actual persons, living or dead, events or locales is entirely coincidental.

1st Edition

Contents

CHAPTER ONE

Despite the overcast sky, work in the quarry was dangerously hot. Wiping the trickling sweat from his face for the umpteenth time, Thorn felt the rough scrape of stubble on his cheek. Dirt, caked on his hands and covering his rough shirt, left streaks on his large face. Adjusting his grip on the sledgehammer, Thorn rechecked the large stone he had picked to crack open next. Hot to the touch, the stone he was splitting had a good chance of containing Fire Iron, the primary product of this quarry.

Infused with fire energy from the magma flows underneath the quarry, Fire Iron was a bright orange ore found encased in sedimentary rocks. Sought after for its higher than the average melting point, Fire Iron was often used to create armor and weapons as well as tools for trades involving high temperatures like forging and smithing.

Because of the fire energy contained in the Fire Iron, mining it was a hot, arduous process and the only option was to set up open-air quarries to extract the ore. Still, very few miners had any interest in frying while working, so most of Angoril's Fire Iron came from mines that used convict labor.

Thorn had been here for four weeks already, smashing rocks for days on end. With three grueling weeks to go before his [Criminal] title would expire, there was no relief in sight. Splitting stones was a hard, tedious business that required a surprising amount of precision and patience. First, the stone had to be dug from the hillside and cleaned off to determine if it contained Fire Iron ore. The process for guessing if a stone had any was rough, at best, since most of the stones radiated heat after being pulled from the ground.

Resting his hand on the stone for a couple of minutes, Thorn tried to judge if it was still as hot as it had been when he first pulled it out of the hole he had been digging in the side of the hill. By pulling the stone from the earth and letting it sit for a couple of minutes in the open air, Thorn had a rough idea whether it contained Fire Iron ore based on how hot it was. If it contained no ore, the stone would cool to the point that he could leave his hand on it indefinitely. On the other hand, if the stone started to warm his skin, then there was a good chance it contained the precious ore.

Looking around, Thorn did not see anyone paying attention to him so, holding the hammer like he was hitting the stone, he grabbed the stone with his other hand and squeezed it into gravel. For the first week, he had been stuck in the quarry, he had used the hammer and chisel to peel back layers of sedimentary rock one chip at a time, revealing the Fire Iron ore underneath. He soon learned, however, that the sedimentary rock was not as tough as the Fire Iron ore. With the correct amount of pressure, he could separate them with a little squeeze from his massive hands.

Of course, not everyone had the luxury of being an eight-foot-nine-inch giant with endless strength, evidenced by the fact that the other prisoners gave him an extra wide berth. A bit of rubbing took the excess stone off the Fire Iron ore, revealing a nice piece about the size of a fist. A normal fist of course, not one of Thorn's.

Thorn tossed it into the basket with the rest of his ore and started digging for another stone. Within seconds, sweat was once again dripping from his face. Ignoring the droplets, Thorn settled into the rhythm of the work. This was the first time he had ever done any sort of heavy manual labor and, to his surprise, he found himself enjoying it. There was something wonderful in the repetitive motion of digging through the earth, hunting for ore.

Even though none of the features of Nova Terra that were designed to keep players comfortable were working, Thorn was having the time of his life. After his emotionally-intense interaction with Ouroboros and the rest of the group, the hard work was cathartic, washing away much of the stress and mental turmoil he felt.

The days spent cracking open stones had blunted the edge of Thorn's anger. It was monotonous work, which gave Thorn plenty of time to sort through his emotions regarding being forced into spending his Destiny points on someone else by people he thought were his friends. Combined with the silence brought about by his disabled messaging feature and the guards who discouraged interaction among the inmates, Thorn was starting to decompress.

While his initial reaction was to be furious with the group, continued thought on the matter had left Thorn unable to maintain his anger. If Ouroboros had explained the situation, there was a good chance that Thorn would have helped him anyway, giving his Destiny points to help Ouroboros acquire the Exalted Devil Blood Berserker class. Plus, because the game did not enforce a specific morality, it was quite difficult to say that what they did to him was "against the rules". It had happened so it felt like, on some level, the game was approving it.

By the time two weeks had passed, Thorn had lost any desire to get back at them, helped a bit by the fact that he had taken out some of his anger on Jorge. They had done what they wanted to do, and he was going to do what he wanted to do. Freedom lay in accepting reality and making courageous choices despite the actions of others.

Giving in to his anger and trying to hunt Ouroboros and the group down was admitting that they were able to control him and to dictate his actions. Thorn had had quite enough of others restricting his actions and wasn't about to give himself over to the desire for revenge. Without question, what they had done had hurt Thorn, but he could choose to bear that pain with dignity, not losing sight of the way his aunt Julia had raised him.

Thorn had been raised to be a hero, but so far, he had not been doing a good job of it. After entering this new world, he had gotten lost in the freedom of it, forgetting that the only thing that happened when one lost their boundaries was getting lost. It had taken a very painful experience to wake him up, and it was time to return to his path.

Plus, the loss of Destiny points was nothing compared to what he had gained.

"Status."

Name: [Thorn]	Race: [Titan]
Health: [100%]	Mana: [100%]
Titles: [Battle Mad], [Wolfsbane], [Lord Greymane, the Moon Wolf], [Friend of the Earth], [Criminal]	Conditions: [None]
Abilities: ~~[Wolf Lord's Howl]~~, ~~[Avatar of the Wolf]~~, ~~[Call the Pack]~~, ~~[Blessing of the Moon]~~, ~~[Presence of the Wolf Lord]~~	

His Criminal title had locked all his abilities, but Thorn still had five of them, even without a class. From what he understood, that was five more than most people. Having his Destiny points taken from him was terrible, but as a result, he had met Hati, the Moon Wolf, the god of the night, and become Hati's avatar. The trade-off was enough to make even the best players jealous.

Looking at his status, Thorn struggled to resist the smug smile that tried to sneak onto his face. While he had to be very careful what kind of class he took since he would never be able to change it, he was starting way ahead of almost everyone else. Having faced a fatal medical condition his whole life before entering Nova Terra, his experience in the game thus far had been beyond anything he had ever dreamed. While he did not know what the future held, Thorn was confident in facing it. And even if his status as the Avatar of the Moon Wolf could not solve the problem, he always had his strength to fall back on.

The conversation with the Moon Wolf had broadened his vision of the game, but Thorn was still unsure what he wanted to do. So far, he had been meeting his goal of living freely, but he was starting to wonder what the point was. For a time, his goal had been to continue adventuring with Ouroboros' party and join the super guild Ragnarok, but that path was destroyed after they decided to dump him for a class upgrade.

His encounter with Jorge after he got back to Berum had given him plenty of time to think about what his new goals were. Over the last four weeks, a rough plan had emerged. The first order of business was to get out of prison, after which, Thorn decided he would pick up a class. Once he had a class, he was going to go complete the requirements tied to his [Lord Greymane, the Moon Wolf] title. According to the description of the title, he needed to clear a castle or something. It had been a while since he had been able to access the description since almost all his player features were locked while he was in jail.

He could still think about classes, and after a couple of weeks of mulling it over, Thorn had settled on the sort of class he wanted. Of the five classes, Combat, Support, and Production were off the table while Utility classes were still too combat focused for Thorn's taste. He had excessive amounts of strength and no need for abilities to augment his already formidable martial arts. He had decided on a Leadership category class. With the title [Lord Greymane, the Moon Wolf], Thorn was confident he could find a Leadership class that would fit with the direction his life seemed to be moving in Nova Terra.

His [Presence of the Wolf Lord] ability was ideal for interacting with Wolfkin, and from what Hati had said, there were still groups of Wolfkin that were not corrupted. The rough shape of an idea had started to form in Thorn's head. While it still lacked definition, getting a Leadership category class was a must. As he was thinking about this, a loud bell pealed, signaling the end of the workday.

With a satisfied sigh, Thorn shook the packed dirt off his shovel and picked up his hammer and chisels. At the end of the day each of the tools needed to be checked along with all the ore he had collected. Nearby, other prisoners were groaning under the weight of their ore bags as they made their way toward the checkpoint at the end of the quarry. Running his eye over them, Thorn smiled.

When he first arrived, the sound of the quitting bell was a difficult and dangerous time, as those who had not met their quota for the day would rush to take ore from those who had. Thorn had put a stop to that. Now, each prisoner spent their day working hard to meet their quota since there would be no chance to take someone else's hard work with Thorn around.

Lining up to have their ore weighed, the convicts chatted quietly, looking forward to the evening meal and resting. At the back of the line, Thorn stood holding a sack four times the size of any of the others. The rate at which he unearthed ore was monstrous, so the guards had found him a larger sack to prevent him from having to make multiple trips each day.

Seeing him towering over everyone else, one of the guards pointed him out to the guard beside him.

"That is the prisoner I was telling you about, the giant. Ever since he came, things have been quiet. Practically don't need us anymore."

"He is huge." His companion could not stop staring.

"You think? Nice guy, though. Pretty quiet and really calm. Which is good, since we couldn't stop him if he wanted to walk out of here."

"Why is that?"

"Haha, when he got here, a couple of the other prisoners thought that they would put him in his place, so they cornered him and tried to intimidate him. He laughed and kicked them into a pile. Then he flipped one of the ore carts upside down and trapped them under it."

"One of those things?" The guard pointed to the massive metal and wood carts perched on a rail line into which the convicts were emptying their bags.

"Yeah. It took ten guards to get it off them when we found them the next morning. But other than that, he hasn't caused a stitch of trouble. Actually, he has been keeping everyone in line for us. Someone tried to pull one of the usual stunts that first night and swipe another person's ore, and the big guy smacked him so hard he couldn't walk right for two days."

"That is awesome. What is the big guy in for?"

"Umm, I'm not one hundred percent sure. I think he is in for assault."

"Assault? I thought you said he was calm?"

"The story is that he killed some traveler in a town north of here. You know how travelers are. Everyone expected him to be a terror when the transfer came in, but it turns out he volunteered to come work instead of sitting in a cell. And I'm glad he did. He's made things much easier on us. But he only has three weeks left, so the warden is starting to get worried. I'm sure the bad bunch will be right back to their tricks when he leaves. After all, they're going to be in here for a long time."

"What about sticky fingers the third?" asked the guard, nodding toward a slight figure who had approached Thorn.

"Hah, he's got a week left. Seems he knew the big guy before he got sent in. Not friends or anything. He tried to lift something from the big guy's room and got thrown out a second story window. Cook over at the cafeteria was telling me he has been trying to butter up the big guy ever since he arrived. Probably needs help lifting something that is nailed down after they get out."

CHAPTER TWO

"Hey, Thorn, how was your day?"

Oblivious to the two guards talking about him, Thorn looked down at the slim figure of Oberlin Danihoff, III, the self-proclaimed master swiper he had caught trying to lift his goods back in Berum.

"It was about the same as every day, Oberlin." Thorn's deep voice echoed through the quarry. Even without projecting, his voice was almost as big as he was. "After all, we do the same thing every day."

"But each day is a fresh new chance, isn't it? At least, that is what people tell me." Oberlin flashed his trademark smile as he poked Thorn's large bag of ore. "How'd you do? Looks like quite the haul today."

"It was not too bad. I hit a pocket before lunch and managed to clear most of it out before the bell." Seeing the guard motion him forward, Thorn upended his bag onto the table to be sorted. The guard gave each piece a cursory look before tossing it onto a scale where a clerk recorded the weight. Never once in the four weeks that Thorn had been mining here had he tried to sneak a piece of slag into his pile of rocks, so the guard focused more on speed than on rigorous checking. After all, the pile of ore Thorn had brought over was massive and the guard was as excited to get to dinner as the convicts.

After the clerk recorded the total weight, Thorn and Oberlin joined the rest of the convicts queued at the cafeteria. Like most of the buildings in the quarry prison, the cafeteria was comprised of open-air seating and two small buildings where the food was cooked and served. As always, when Thorn arrived, the hum of conversation quieted, and everyone busied themselves with eating.

"You certainly make an impression." Still smiling, Oberlin looked around at the convicts eating.

"So, you've told me."

"Well, it never fails to astound me. This is one of the roughest crowds in Nova Terra, and they act like lambs around you." Oberlin paused for a moment, looking at Thorn sideways. "Then again, one can imagine why they would behave like that."

Dinner consisted of a big bowl of porridge, bread, a piece of fruit, and strips of meat. Because of the intense heat, the prisoners all drank massive quantities of water, and the cooks provided a sweet lemonade at each of the meals.

"Evening, Thorn." One of the cooks pulled out an extra-large bowl from below the counter when it was Thorn's turn. Next, to him, his assistant put two loaves of bread on a tray, along with four apples, and a small mountain of meat strips. Thorn's hands were large enough that he could balance the bowl and tray with one hand while he used the other to take a pitcher of lemonade from another assistant. "Come back if you need more. We have plenty."

Like most of the guards, the cooks loved Thorn. The gentle giant solved their problems with difficult prisoners by being around, and any convicts that tried to make trouble in line were quelled when they felt his burning gaze. There was something about Thorn's hungry face that seemed to terrify the prisoners into submission, and for that reason alone, Thorn had made himself a favorite of the staff in the prison.

"Thanks." With a smile, Thorn accepted the huge quantity of food and walked to his customary spot. Despite the outdoor eating area consisting of benches and tables, Thorn had learned very that they were not made for someone his size. His first attempt to sit at one of the tables had tragic consequences for its bench.

Instead, he sat at the far end of the cafeteria on a large stone that marked the boundary of the eating area. At least a stone would not collapse when he sat on it. Over time, the table closest to him had moved to a convenient spot within reach, so Thorn put his food down and waited for Oberlin to sit.

"Thank you for waiting." Oberlin joined Thorn, and they dug in. Wiping his mouth, Oberlin glanced around and then spoke in a low voice. "Have you given any thought to what I talked to you about yesterday?"

"Stealing is wrong, Oberlin." Thorn did not even look up from his meal.

"Look, I am not asking you to steal anything. I need someone I trust to cover me when I go talk to the merchants. You don't understand how dangerous it can be. I'm telling you, Nova Terra has a dark side."

"I'm well aware of Nova Terra's dark side. But stealing is wrong, and so is selling stolen goods. Why don't you listen to what I told you before? You are a talented guy. Why waste your talents on stealing?"

"Ha. Easy for you to say." Defeated by Thorn's calm but final tone, Oberlin's shoulders slumped. He had been trying for almost two weeks to convince Thorn to team up with him once they were both out. However, every time he broached the subject, he always got the same answer. “What could I do? My only skills are going unseen and opening locks. The only people I know are other crooks and fences. My class is locked, and all my abilities only work for one thing. Believe me, I’ve tried. I’m on my last class, so there is no more changing.”

“I don’t think you ever mentioned what class you have.” Thorn looked at the small thief with interest. “I’ve been thinking about what class I want to get, but I haven’t decided.”

“What do you have now?”

“I don’t have a class.”

“You don’t have a class?!” Oberlin spat out his porridge as he turned to stare at Thorn. “How did you get so big without a class? I thought you were a Mountain Barbarian or something?”

“Nah, I’m naturally tall.”

“Somehow, I don’t think eight feet, nine inches counts as ‘naturally tall’, Thorn. You must be a giant in real life as well. Why don’t you have a class, though? You should be able to get one almost as soon as you come into the game. You can get them almost anywhere you can get training. There are general class quests littering the starter cities.”

“I’m not sure. No one told me about them, so I don’t think I ever found one.”

“What do you mean, you never found them? You told me you trained at the Training Hall, right? Didn’t you see the giant stone pillar with the warrior on it? You have to go up and touch it.”

“Oh, I thought that was a sign for the training hall.” Thorn blushed. Thankfully, his face was dirty enough that Oberlin did not notice.

“The fact that you missed all the class change stones is almost impressive. At least it would be if it was not so ridiculous.” Oberlin shook his head and licked his spoon clean before pointing toward himself. “I have a special utility class called Master Locksmith. It gives me an ability that lets me bypass almost any lock and lets me know the best route for sneaking. It is useful for one thing and one thing only, which is why I ended up here.”

“Interesting. I noticed that, when I got here, you were not chained up.”

“Yup. There is not much of a point, so the guards don’t worry about it. I’ve been in and out of this place so many times, you wouldn’t believe it. I’m not sure why they even bother bringing me in. It’s not like they can stop me from getting out.”

“Can you open magic locks? I saw someone break a magic lock once. Looked quite complicated.”

“Any lock means any lock. Arcane, mechanical, puzzle, doesn’t matter what it is. If someone has seen it and wants to get through it, I can open it. Some might take more time, but they all crack eventually.”

“Classes are so interesting. Is Master Locksmith an Ancient Inheritance?”

“No.” Oberlin frowned and changed the subject. “Look, Thorn, I appreciate what you are trying to do, but at this point, my options are set. I’m in a hole, and there is no way to get out, even if I wanted to.”

“That isn’t true. There are plenty of things you could do. You could be an explorer. With your stealth, you could map places no one has ever been before. You could be a security consultant. You know, get people to pay you to break into their place, and then tell them how it was done.”

About to continue listing ideas for the depressed thief, Thorn saw a clerk making his way. A few weeks ago, the clerks would not have dared to walk through the crowd of convicts without a full armed escort, but after Thorn had tossed a few of the convicts into the large pots of porridge in the cookhouse, they were able to walk about unmolested. Ignoring the dark looks he was getting, the clerk walked up to Thorn and handed him a form.

"You're out tomorrow, Thorn."

Confused, Thorn looked at the paper. It had the warden's signature and looked very official.

"What do you mean he is out? Doesn't he still have three weeks?" Oberlin cut in. "How can he get out early?"

"What does it matter to you?" the clerk asked, annoyed at Oberlin sticking his nose in Thorn's business. Turning back to Thorn, he said, "The warden would like to see you in thirty minutes. He'll be waiting for you in his office. No, no, you can finish your meal." Seeing that Thorn was about to get up, the clerk hurried to stop him. "He is in no rush."

As he ate, Thorn wracked his brain for possible reasons that the warden would let him out early. According to the books, his crime was assault. Attacking another player in a town was considered taboo, and if the guards caught you, the penalty was seven real days in prison, which meant seven weeks in jail, if you spent that time logged in, due to the game's time dilation. A first-time offense would have let Thorn sit in a comfortable cell, but he had volunteered to come out and work for the experience.

As an alternate reality, Nova Terra mimicked the real world in many ways, including there being a list of crimes that, if you were caught, could get you tossed in jail. The sentence for killing another player was one of the lighter ones, at least for the first few times. Still, it was curious that he was being let out early. Maybe he was being let go for good behavior?

After Thorn finished his food, he patted Oberlin on the shoulder, taking care to be extra gentle, and followed a guard toward the warden's office. The prison camp was situated in the bottom of the quarry and consisted of four sections. The cafeteria and the bathhouse were large outdoor areas, while the prisoners' bunks were under large pole buildings without walls. The last area was a compound set aside for the guards, clerks, and the warden.

When they arrived at the compound, Thorn had to stifle the urge to chuckle. A seven-and-a-half-foot wall surrounded the compound, more than enough to keep out the convict's prying eyes. All but Thorn's, of course. The first day he had come here, the sight of his head appearing above the wall had given the guard watching the gate into the compound quite the fright.

Once the guard opened the thick log gate, Thorn followed the clerk into the compound, down a paved sidewalk, up two flights of stairs, and into the elevated office of the warden. Large glass windows on each side gave the office a 360-degree view of the quarry, and four guards stationed around the office kept a constant lookout for prisoners making trouble.

Ducking and turning sideways to squeeze his bulk into the room, Thorn was glad that he could straighten up. Many of the other buildings in the quarry had regular eight-foot ceilings, forcing him to duck. The warden's office had a full ten-foot ceiling. Smiling at the guards who were all watching him come in, Thorn settled himself in the middle of the room, ignoring the creak of the floor as he shifted his weight.

"Ah. Good evening, Thorn." The warden turned around, placing his drink on the large desk.

"Good evening, sir," Thorn replied, dipping his head.

"I'm sure the clerk informed you that you'll be getting out soon, so I wanted to take an opportunity to have a bit of a chat with you before that."

"Yes, sir. He said I was getting out tomorrow."

"A welcome surprise, I am sure." The warden smiled, adjusting his glasses. "Though, all of the staff here will miss you. I'm sure I speak for all of us when I say that it has been a pleasure having such a peaceful and hardworking resident over the last month. You have been a model inmate, and we will miss your good example." The warden paused for a moment to take a drink before continuing. "You were assigned your prison term due to the assault of another player in a city, is that right?"

"Yes, sir." Thorn nodded.

"Your sentence was extended if I understand the situation

because the player you attacked died as the result of your attack. Attacking another player should get you a week in jail, but that goes up if the attack was lethal. Quite surprising that you could kill him before the guards got to you."

"That is correct, sir. I threw him against a wall. Sometimes I have trouble controlling my strength."

"Well, despite the nature of your crime, the powers that be have decided to reduce your sentence due to your good behavior over the last month. However, all of this is contingent on you being willing to accept a parole task."

"Parole task?"

"Yes. Rather than have you stay in prison, I have a task for you to do outside of the quarry. Do you think you are up for it?"

"Do you mean a quest?"

"That is exactly what I mean. If you are willing to accept this quest, you are free to leave tomorrow. The rest of your sentence will be waived and, so long as you complete the quest, your criminal title will be removed. Don't break any other laws, and it will be as if none of this ever happened."

Taking a deep breath, Thorn nodded.

"What do you need me to do?"

CHAPTER THREE

"The task is simple." The warden straightened his glasses. "I need you to help solve a problem at another quarry."

ding

Trouble at the Embersplit Mine
The miners at the Embersplit mine have been having trouble meeting their monthly production quotas. Figure out what is causing them to fall behind and help them solve it. Successful completion of this quest will result in the termination of your sentence. Failure to complete this quest will result in serving the entirety of your sentence. Title Removed: Criminal

"South of here, there is another Fire Iron ore mine that is having a bit of trouble. I'd like for you to head down there and see what you can do to sort it out. Once you have finished, your criminal title will be removed." Seeing Thorn's furrowed brow, the warden smiled at him. "Do you have any questions?"

"No, sir." Thorn put his thoughts in order. "I am appreciative of this opportunity and will do my best to complete the quest. "

"Excellent, I am glad to hear that. Alright, you are free to go. Report to the administration station at the breakfast bell tomorrow."

After leaving the warden's office, Thorn paused a moment to stretch. Standing in-doors made him feel quite cramped. As he made his way back toward the bunkhouse where he slept with the other inmates, Thorn's mind wandered back to the event that led him to prison.

***

Thorn had just arrived back at Berum. After walking around the city for a while, he found himself at the temple, where he sat down for a moment of peace after the emotional turmoil of being betrayed by his friends. Yet his moment of peace was soon shattered. Just as he had settled into his breathing routine, he caught sight of a familiar figure coming up the steps of the temple. Looking over, eyes hardening, Thorn saw Jorge. At the same time, Jorge caught sight of Thorn's large figure seated on the steps and stopped dead in his tracks, his eyes going wide.

“Hey, Thorn,” Jorge said, watching him. “Looks like you made it back. Haha.”

Thorn had expected to be furious if he ever encountered Ouroboros, Mina, Velin, or Jorge, but all he felt was cold. Cold and unnaturally calm.

Seeing that the cold look in Thorn’s eyes had not receded, Jorge took a small step backward, his hand resting on the pommel of his knife. “Thorn, I know what Ouroboros did wasn’t cool, but you have to understand there is much more at play here. You benefited by following us, but there was a price for it. Don’t do something you’ll regret.”

Slowly, Thorn stood, towering over the dwarf, who put up his hands nervously. “Whoa there, big guy, let's be gentlemen about this. That business before was just business. Besides, if you draw a weapon, the guards will be all over you.”

Looking at the small figure in front of him, Thorn frowned, his brain working a hundred miles a minute. A glance showed a few guards looking over at them.

Jorge saw Thorn’s glance and laughed. “Let me give you some advice, kid: don’t even bother thinking about revenge. If you do, don’t blame me for putting you down again. Haha.” With another smirk, he turned to go, only to feel a brief sensation of motion before his screen turned black and he disconnected.

Stunned, he stood in the familiar white space, the words [You've Died] floating in front of him, accompanied by a timer, counting down.

[24:00:00]
[23:59:59]
[23:59:58]
[23:59:57]

Thorn had watched as Jorge turned away and, for the briefest of moments, all the cold rationality that enveloped him burned away under pure rage. With a big step forward, his hand shot out, and he grabbed the dwarf, his hand wrapping around Jorge's shoulder. With a swing of his arm, he sent Jorge flying at a nearby wall, watching in satisfaction as the dwarf hit the wall with so much force that his armor deformed.

ding

You Broke the Law
You have attacked another player in town and have been seen by the guards. If you turn yourself, in you might be given a lighter sentence. Would you like to turn yourself in? [Yes]

[No]

Feeling quite a bit better, Thorn pressed [Yes]. Though it took a while for the guards to find chains that fit him, Thorn stood calmly waiting to be taken away. After a struggle, chains were fitted around his wrists by two perspiring guards. As his vision faded to black, the last thing Thorn saw was a notification.

Temporary Title Earned: Criminal
They say the only thing wrong with a crime is getting caught, which you have.

When Thorn awoke, he was in a prison cell, complete with graffiti and a sketchy bunkmate. Though he had taken out his anger on Jorge, the flash of satisfaction that had come from smashing Jorge into a wall crumbled quickly, leaving Thorn upset. After a few days of incarceration, Thorn had volunteered for the quarry, where he had worked until now.

***

The morning sun rose hot, and the bright rays poked Thorn awake even before the morning breakfast bell rang. Most of the other inmates were sprawled on their hard beds fast asleep. Countless days of back-breaking labor was a sure recipe for deep sleep, and it was with groans and grumbles that they dragged themselves up at the ringing of the bell.

As usual, Thorn was the first one out of bed. A hard day breaking stone and collecting Fire Iron ore hardly tired Thorn at all, so the seven hours of sleep he had gotten was more than enough. Gathering up his few belongings, Thorn made his way over to the administration post, accepting three loaves of bread and two sausages from one of the cook's helpers on his way. While he could do without sleep, his gargantuan form needed food regularly.

"Hello, Thorn. Here to check out?"

"Yup. Warden said I'm getting out today."

While the prison guard in charge of the checkout procedure stamped his papers, Thorn took the opportunity to look around once more. There was a little fondness in his heart for this place. Everything in the quarry was simple and clear cut. There was no confusion or indecision, and most of all, there were no messy relationships. "Well, maybe one," Thorn thought to himself as he spotted Oberlin hurrying over.

The thin thief was panting by the time he got near the administration post. One of the guards gripped his spear tightly, dropping the point in Oberlin's path. Stopping, Oberlin's hands went up, and he took a step backward, eyeing the guard warily.

"Are you being discharged, Thorn?" A faint anxiousness could be heard in Oberlin's tone.

"Yeah, good behavior." Thorn smiled blandly.

"Well, congratulations." Oberlin flashed a smile of his own at the giant.

"Thanks. See you around." Thorn picked up the paperwork the guard was holding out and collected the gear he had been wearing when he was arrested. With a wave, he walked through the quarry's large gate.

ding

Title Advancement: Criminal (parole)
You have been let out on parole. The terms of your release are to complete the quest [Trouble at the Embersplit Mine]. Some of your disabled player features have been enabled.

Accompanying the title update was a storm of notifications as his messaging system was unlocked, practically burying Thorn in messages from his aunt. Grimacing, Thorn flicked through them, before dashing off a message. His allotted solo playtime wasn't up, but he could not blame his aunt for worrying after not hearing from him for four weeks of in-game time.

After answering messages from Dovon, Jarvis, and Hamm, Thorn continued scrolling through the notifications as he walked. The quarry was a few miles from the nearest town, so Thorn headed that direction. Thankfully, his inventory had been unlocked, so he had plenty of food, as the bread and sausage he had eaten on the way out of the quarry were not very filling.

About to toss a pastry into his mouth, Thorn froze, his eyes locked on a blinking notification. He had not seen it in the initial flurry of messages, but there it was, blinking before his eyes. A message from Mina.

It took a full two minutes before he could react, and when he did, it was just to put away the pastry. Sitting down on the side of the road, Thorn stared at the blinking message, all sorts of feelings trampling across his heart. Hesitating for a moment, Thorn's eyes hovered over the button to open the message before he sighed and minimized it without opening it.

Lying back, he put his hands under his head and stared up at the cloudless sky, beginning to breathe as his master had taught him. Thorn had assumed that the fading of his negative feelings toward Mina and the others meant that he had gotten over their betrayal. His reaction when he saw the message from Mina indicated otherwise. The tumultuous emotions that rushed back were still quite strong, proving that time had only buried them. After a few moments of calm breathing, the pressure in his chest faded, and Thorn got back up to continue on his way. He would worry about the message from Mina later.

His distance-eating stride carried him over the hills, and he soon saw the towers of a town peeking over the trees. The quarry where he had served his time was due west of Berum in a mountainous area. On his way to the quarry, the prison wagon that carried him had stopped in the walled city that lay before him. Since his map had been disabled, he had not been able to identify it but, according to his re-enabled map, this was the bustling city of Narthil.

The gates of the city were patrolled by guards who looked at Thorn with distrust. Having played Nova Terra for a while, Thorn understood that they were reacting to his [Criminal] title, so he did not take it to heart. Rather than find an inn, Thorn restocked his supplies and looked for a map shop.

After his ignorance had brought him so much trouble, Thorn had taken full advantage of Oberlin's experience and willingness to talk while they were together. While he could not claim to be an expert, he was not a beginner anymore. One of the things Oberlin had mentioned in passing was that there were shops where maps could be purchased to make travel easier. As Nova Terra did not include any sort of fast travel system, knowing where you were going was essential, so many people sold maps of the places they had been.

Once he found the map store, Thorn purchased a general map of the area as well as a map of Narthil. Looking at it, he soon spotted what he was looking for, and a quick walk found him in front of a beaten-up bar. While he was in jail, he had talked to Oberlin extensively about Nova Terra and had picked up numerous tidbits of information.

One piece of information that Thorn had found very interesting was that most people did not use map stores for unlocking new sections of their world map and, instead, tried to find pathfinders. A Pathfinder was a Utility class that specialized in exploration and discovery. They could share their maps with other people for a price. Often found hanging around bars and other areas players gathered, pathfinders were the best way to get an accurate map.

A faded sign showing a jack of diamonds creaked as it hung from a post, one of the supporting chains hanging limp. Cracked and peeling paint suggested that the bar had once been red, but time and dirt made it hard to tell.

Pushing the door open, Thorn ducked inside. As he straightened to his full height in the bar area, silence spread out from him in a wave. Already an eye-catching figure, the dark armor granted by his ability [Avatar of the Wolf] added an air of danger to Thorn and combined with his [Criminal] title to create an imposing aura, causing those who filled the bar to look at him carefully. Used to such reactions, Thorn did not bother with them and instead walked to the bar. After eyeing the stools that stood in front of it, Thorn rejected the idea of sitting and placed a massive hand on the bar.

“Hello, what can I do for you?” The bartender wiped the bar in front of Thorn.

“I’ll take a double pint of your special.”

“Sure, sure.”

Watching the bartender fetch a tall glass from under the counter and head toward the taps, Thorn looked around the room. As one would expect from a bar in a run-down part of town, the room was filled with a variety of dangerous looking characters. A thought flashed through his mind as he looked around, causing Thorn to smile. If he had walked in here a month ago, he would have been nervous.

But after his experiences in the quarry, Thorn had gained matter-of-fact confidence that put him at ease. Thanking the bartender for the beer, Thorn took a sip and grimaced before putting it down. Truly just as bad as Oberlin had mentioned.

“I’m looking for someone who can show me around,” Thorn spoke to the bartender quietly, causing the rag wiping the bar to pause. Setting the rag down, the bartender placed his hands flat on the bar, his fingers spread for a moment, before picking the rag back up to resume his wiping. Thorn stacked up ten silver behind his tall glass.

“Third table along the wall.” Speaking just as quietly, the bartender did not look up as he smoothly grabbed the coins.

With a nod of thanks, Thorn turned around and took a step before stopping with a sigh, destroying the mysterious air that had just been built up. There was no way he would be able to squeeze through the tightly packed tables, let alone sit in one of the booths along the wall. Helpless, he could only turn around to ask the bartender for help.

Eventually, Thorn found himself in a small back room the bartender lent him, facing the robed and hooded figure who had been sitting at the table along the wall. Catching glimpses of leather armor beneath the robe when the figure entered the room, Thorn was pretty sure this was the person Oberlin had described.

“What do you want?” Despite the roughness of the question, the figure’s voice was pleasant to the ear and pitched higher than Thorn had been expecting.

“Are you a Pathfinder? I need information.”

“Maps or log info? I don’t guide, and I won’t join your party. I only take gold as payment.”

“I’m looking for a map and as much information as you have regarding this region.”

“The whole region?” The pathfinder’s voice lightened, showing her surprise. “That’s expensive.”

“Yes. As much as you have.”

“Okay, no problem. Give me a second.” Pulling out a large, blank piece of smooth leather, the Pathfinder held a slim hand against it for a moment. Spreading from her hand, trails of ink curled across the surface of the leather, leaving detailed markings. The whole process took almost seven minutes, and when she was done, the Pathfinder flipped the map over and began to scribe in tight script on the back.

“I’m combining all the log information with the map. That will allow you to highlight a place you have not visited and see the info you have received as a popup. Since you are a big customer, I am also adding some rumors I’ve heard. They are probably nothing, but if you are bored, you can check them out.”

CHAPTER FOUR

His wallet four gold lighter, Thorn left the bar. The map had been more expensive than he thought it would be, but Thorn did not mind. His long discussions with Oberlin in the quarry had made him realize just how important exploration was in Nova Terra. While it would be possible to stay in one place doing the same thing, in-game character growth relied on learning more about the world. Thorn had caught glimpses of this through his interactions with Ouroboros and his group, but it was not until Oberlin began to describe his adventures that it clicked.

Ouroboros had been right about one thing, knowledge really did equal power in Nova Terra. The more one knew, the more they could do. After all, Nova Terra was just as complex as the real world. The system rewarded players who could creatively apply what they knew about the game world and seemed to adapt itself to those who treated it like the real world.

While the map shop in the city could sell maps of the local terrain, the real prize was the map that Thorn had purchased from the Pathfinder. Her personal experiences with the region would be invaluable as he began to explore. The day was ending by the time Thorn left the city, the wall casting a long shadow that met up with the forest.

A few minutes after he left the gate a small group of strange figures left the city, looking in the direction he had walked. The leader scratched his red beard as he watched the group's ranger looking around for signs of Thorn's passing.

"You sure he's got money?"

"I'm sure, boss." A nervous-looking warrior rubbed his hands together as he reassured his boss. "He paid in gold coins. I saw Emilia spending one and I know that she didn't have any before."

"And you said he is big?"

"Yeah, the biggest guy I've ever seen." the nervous warrior shrank as he remembered Thorn's imposing figure.

"That's alright," the red-bearded warrior spat on the ground, resting his hand on the large axe at his waist. "The bigger they are, the harder they fall."

Oblivious to the danger following him, Thorn walked to the

southwest. According to the map that he had purchased, his destination was almost a day's travel south of Narthil, tucked away in the same mountain chain as the quarry where he had spent the last month. Much like the area surrounding Berum the countryside was forested with rolling hills.

After night fell Thorn set up his camp and rested. Truth be told, he was not tired, and he had been eating on the move, so he was only slightly hungry. Instead, Thorn wanted to take a moment to deal with the messages that had piled up during his jail time. Opening his messaging function, the first thing he saw was the message from Mina. Ignoring it, Thorn answered his other messages one by one. Once he had cleared most of his inbox, Thorn dialed up his Aunt Julia. The call connected almost instantly, a video chat opening in front of Thorn's face.

"Xavier! Finally! Where have you been? Why haven't you been answering my calls? I've been going nuts over here thinking something happened to you! Are you okay?"

"Yeah, I'm fine." Thorn rubbed the back of his head. "I've just been out of touch for a while."

"Seriously, what's up with that? What has you so preoccupied you can't even respond to a message? Wait, why is your tag red? You're a criminal? You are a criminal!?"

"Uh, yeah. I might have attacked someone in a town accidentally."

"What do you mean accidentally?" Julia's eye narrowed as she glared at her nephew. "You have been incommunicado for a full month. Fighting in town is max seven days."

"Umm, maybe more on purpose, actually." Thorn scratched his cheek, embarrassed. "And I might have killed him. I'm actually out on parole right now."

"Wow, I let you start Nova Terra and you go straight for the criminal behavior, huh?"

"Well, a lot of stuff happened."

Seeing the mixed look on Thorn's face, Julia's gaze softened.

"Yeah? Why don't you tell me about it?"

For the next twenty minutes, Thorn recounted his adventures since arriving in Nova Terra. He told his aunt about how he fumbled around the game at the beginning, and how the trainers at the Training Hall had taken him under their wings. About Mina and Ouroboros, Velin and Jorge. About his encounter with the Blood Hunter, Gargish and battling the elementals in the Elemental Gorge.

His expression heavy, he spoke about the group's encounter in Hati's Ascent. How they battled through the dungeon, arriving at the final boss. And how, after beating Karrandras himself, the others turned on him, stripping him of his Destiny points and leaving him for dead.

Julia fell silent as he finished telling her his story. From Thorn's tone and downcast expression, she could tell how very deeply wounded he was. And no wonder. It made Julia's heartache to hear about his first friends threw him aside for benefits, and she could only imagine what Thorn must have been feeling.

"Do you want me to find them for you?" While her tone was even and her face calm, Thorn could tell from the cold look in Julia's eyes that she was furious at what he had experienced. With the fifth strongest guild in the game at her back, finding Ouroboros and exacting revenge on Thorn's behalf was not out of the question.

"No, thanks though."

"It wouldn't be hard, Xavier. The Society of Roses has a great network and it would not take much to find them."

"I appreciate the intent, but I think I want to handle this on my own." Thorn shook his head.

"Alright," Julia fell silent. Despite the heaviness on his face, she could see the quiet resolve underneath it. "Listen, kid. I am so sorry for what you went through, but remember, suffering sucks, but..."

"Suffering is the foundation of success." Thorn finished the statement she often told him. "You are right." With a big sigh, Thorn felt the last of the pent-up emotions leaving his chest. The remaining anger, frustration, bitterness, and pain disappeared with the cool night breeze.

"Thanks for listening." Smiling at his aunt, Thorn felt much better. "Besides, it isn't all bad. I'm stuck with a single class, but I got a pretty sweet title out of it."

"That's right." Happy to see her nephew perk up, Julia changed the subject. "You never told me what happened after they left you. How did you make it back to the city?"

"Well, I thought I was dead, but it turned out there was a bit of a glitch. I pseudo-died but there was an issue with the pod that they are fixing. So, I did not respawn in the city, instead, I woke up in the dungeon. Anyway, I met Hati, the Moon Wolf."

"Wait, the god? The god of the night?" Seeing Thorn's nod, Julia flipped out. "Are you serious!? Do gods still exist? This changes everything! We assumed they had all been killed! If Hati is still around, then I bet there are other gods hiding as well! What was it like?"

"Pretty intense. Hati is a giant wolf, obviously, but by giant, I mean like as big as the world. Anyway, Hati gave me a title, which combined with another title I have, so now I am [Lord Greymane, the Moon Wolf]. I'm the Avatar of the Moon Wolf and the leader of the Wolfkin, though I think I still have a lot to do before I can assume that position."

For a moment silence reigned as Thorn's unflappable aunt stared at him in undisguised shock, her mouth hanging open. Taken aback by her reaction, Thorn could barely resist poking the screen, wondering if it had frozen.

"WHAAAAAT!"

Startled by Julia's scream, Thorn jumped.

"You are the avatar of the Moon Wolf? And what is with that five-word title?! Titles like that are insanely rare. As in, I only know of two other players in the entire game who have a five-word title."

"Yeah, Hati said something about sending me down a different path since I could no longer take multi-category classes. After thinking about it, I think they meant that I could use a title to make up for it. The title comes with four different abilities, all of which can grow and get more powerful. As I've been considering their application, it seems like the title is a mini-version of a quad category class. The abilities fit under Combat, Support, Utility, and Leadership."

"Hold on, it is a title? Not a class? This is starting to make sense. Old legends talk about the god's avatars, but all this time people have been searching for them as if they were classes. To no avail, I might add. It has been assumed that you could become an avatar if you found the correct class combination, but from what you experienced, that is not the case. You said Hati picked you?"

"Mmhmm. Hati was watching me and liked my character or something like that."

"You keep saying they. You don't know if Hati is male or female?" Julia looked at Thorn skeptically.

"Haha, no," Thorn chuckled. "I only saw the top of their nose and eyes. A bit hard to tell by that, and I don't want to get struck by lightning for getting it wrong."

Julia smiled, happy that her nephew was able to be in high spirits despite his situation. A few minutes later she waved goodbye after making Thorn promise to contact her more frequently. They were almost halfway through Thorn's one-year free range wandering agreement and she was starting to think about how he would fit into her guild.

Thorn, on the other hand, was not thinking about the future at all. While he had been stuck in prison, he had spent almost all his time thinking about the future but right now he was just taking a break and enjoying the soft crackle of his fire and the cool night air.

snap

The faint sound of a cracking tree branch woke Thorn from

his daze. Someone was coming. Ever since his encounter with Hati, the Moon Wolf, Thorn had found his sense sharpening, allowing him to instinctively judge how far away the broken branch was and in what direction.

Staying seated, Thorn flipped over his hand, pulling his tetsubo out of his inventory and placing it across his knees. Running his fingers over the metal protrusions on its end, Thorn couldn't help but wonder where Master Sun was.

Slowly the sounds grew louder as the group coming got closer to his camp, coming to a stop about fifty feet away from the fire. Thorn had chosen to settle in a natural clearing where the ground dipped, providing a bit of protection for his fire. Since Thorn carried ready-made food in his inventory, the fire was not used for cooking, so Thorn let it blaze merrily.

After a slight pause, the group made their way forward, soon stepping into the light of the fire. Thorn counted four people, making a mental note that there was probably an assassin of some sort sneaking around. Watching Ouroboros' team operate had been quite the education for Thorn and after experiencing Jorge's backstab, Thorn had vowed in his heart never to forget about assassins.

The most eye-catching of the group was a large man with a full, red beard and scars across his right eye. Almost 6' 5", the bearded man was covered in chain mail and carried a large bladed axe at his belt with a buckler on his left forearm.

Next to him stood two yellow-robed, bald-headed figures, one holding a four-ringed khakkhara staff while the other held a golden vajra. Both monks held their weapons in front of them, staring at Thorn as if he was a great demon. Peeking out from behind the rest of the group, a brown-haired warrior watched Thorn, his hands rubbing together with nervous excitement.

“Good evening.” Since they remained silent, Thorn decided to open the conversation. “Welcome to my camp. I’m happy to have you join me.”

Having looked around the camp and seen that Thorn was alone, the red-bearded man chuckled to himself and rested his hand on his axe. Waving his other hand, he signaled for the two monks to spread out, surrounding Thorn from three sides. The nervous warrior stayed behind the red-bearded leader, his eyes flicking to the forest behind Thorn.

“Let's make this short and sweet. Hand over all your gold and credits and you won’t get hurt,” said red beard, his eyes narrowed.

“You are robbing me?” Thorn was stunned.

“Yeah, and if you don’t play along, I don’t mind sending you back to spawn.” Red beard spat.

“Oh, wow. Well. This is a novel experience.” Thorn, seeming unperturbed, wrapped his hand around the tetsubo’s handle and stood up. And up.

As he stood, the two monks on either side of him tightened their grip on their weapons, each taking a small step back. One began to chant to himself in a low voice, the other just gawked. The red-bearded robber in front of Thorn looked up at him before whispering to the cowering warrior behind him.

“I thought you said he was big?”

“He is big.”

“That’s not big, that is giant! Forget it.” Turning his glare back on Thorn, red beard pulled out his axe. “I guess you want to play the hard way, huh?”

“Whoa, wait. Hold up.”

Seeing Thorn’s hand go up, red beard paused.

“I don’t even know who you are. Don’t you think you should introduce yourself?”

“Actually, he’s right,” nodded the monk with the mace. “I’m Mali, the Enlightened Buddha, and that is my brother, Jamir, the Evil Monk over there,” he motioned with his mace, pointing at the other monk who was still chanting.

“Hi.” Jamir paused his chant long enough to nod his head.

"Nice to meet you, I'm Thorn."

"Enough!" For some reason, seeing their friendly exchange made red beard furious. "My name is Pulen Blood Beard and it'll be the last thing you'll hear!" Roaring this out, he raised his axe and was about to jump forward when Mali, the Enlightened Buddha yelled out, "Wait!"

"Oh, for crying out loud, what is it now?" Pulen turned his glare on the yellow-robed monk.

"If you say it that way, the last thing he will hear is you saying, 'it'll be the last thing you'll hear'. Shouldn't you say it the other way around? Like, 'the last thing you hear will be the sound of my name, Pulen Blood Beard!' Then, whoosh! Slice him with your axe."

"But then they will hear the axe, right?" Taking interest in the conversation, Jamir stopped his chanting to chime in. "So, the actual last thing they will hear will be the whoosh of the axe."

"Ah, that is true." Mali nodded sagely.

CHAPTER FIVE

Amused, Thorn watched the monks toss ideas back and forth. Before they could come to a consensus on the best way to deliver the line their boss flipped out. Thorn had been keeping an eye on him from across the fire, so he was ready when roaring in rage, Blood Beard launched himself forward.

"Wave Crossing Chop!" He yelled. His jump brought him across the fire and he landed steadily in front of Thorn, bringing his axe down in an overhead chop. At the same moment, a faint twang sounded, like the string of a guitar being plucked and an arrow shot from the darkness toward Thorn's back.

Startled by their boss' sudden move, the two monks dropped their discussion and raised their weapons, striking from the side. Despite the four rings banging around on the khakkhara staff, the weapon made no sound as it struck at Thorn's feet. Rather, it was the mace that let out an evil wail as it struck toward Thorn's right shoulder. From how smoothly the attacks came in it was obvious that the group had practiced this attack often and they were quite proficient ambushers.

Thorn planned on meeting the axe head on, but the arrow shooting toward the center of his back made that a dangerous gamble. While Thorn was wearing armor, who knew if the arrow had any special ability. Instead, Thorn lifted his tetsubo in a smooth motion, jabbing it at the mace-wielding monk on his right while twisting his body to the side to move out of the way of the arrow.

The abrupt shift caused the arrow to miss and Mali to step back, but the other two attackers adjusted their weapons' trajectories, continuing to smash toward Thorn. With a slight smile, Thorn took a large step forward, his massive stride taking him well out of the reach of Jamir's staff and Pulen's axe. Mali was still moving backward as Thorn pressed forward, his maces trying to ward off Thorn's tetsubo which was thrusting forward like a spear.

Aware that another arrow was probably on its way, Thorn changed directions. Turning his body toward Pulen Blood Beard, he stepped forward again, lashing out at the chain-mailed warrior with a horizontal strike. The red-bearded warrior was in the middle of an attack himself and could only brace himself as he saw the blur of the tetsubo coming toward him.

With a loud bang, the steel-wrapped weapon smashed into Pulen's side. Shock flashed across his face as his body turned into small motes of light that drifted up into the sky. For a moment there was silence as the other attackers stared at the place where Pulen had stood in utter astonishment. Had he just died from a single hit?

The warrior who had been following Pulen was the first to react, giving off a high-pitched scream and running away as fast as he could. Mali backed off a few steps as well, his eyes extra wide. On the other side, Jamir put his hands together and started chanting again, though it was obvious how nervous he was from the sweat that had started to bead his brow.

Keeping an ear out for the sound of the archer in the woods, Thorn glanced at the two monks. His one strike seemed to have knocked the fight right out of them.

"So, are we going to keep going or what?" He asked, spinning his tetsubo in his hand.

"There is no need, no need." Mali's maces disappeared and he waved his hands at Thorn. "As the Buddha has said, 'let's not fight' and 'it is better to show mercy than to build a ten-story pagoda."

Ignoring Thorn's puzzled look, Mali rushed over to stand next to Jamir who was still softly chanting.

"Benefactor, we will not bother you anymore. Come Jamir, let us leave this wise man to his thinking." Mali bowed his head repeatedly toward Thorn and, grabbing the other monk by his arm, pulled Jamir into the woods as fast as he could.

Thorn watched till they were out of sight before using the end of his weapon to poke through the few things that Pulen Blood Beard dropped when he died. Apart from the small number of coins, there was a set of bracers and a half-used sharpening stone. Pocketing the coins, Thorn tossed the armor and sharpening stone into his inventory. The bracers were much too small for him, so he did not even bother examining them.

Sitting down by the fire again, Thorn stretched out and closed his eyes. It was obvious that Pulen Blood Beard had been the motivating force behind the attempted robbery and since he would not be able to log in for twenty-four hours Thorn was not concerned that they would be back to try again.

The next morning found Thorn well on his way to Embersplit Mine. He woke while it was still dark and started on his way after cleaning up his camp. Because it was night his ability [Blessing of the Moon] activated, granting him excellent night vision, so walking in the dark was no problem.

It was mid-morning when he arrived at the sprawling town. Unlike Berum and Narthil, the town of Embersplit had no wall. The buildings were largely wooden, hastily constructed and in danger of tumbling down at any moment. Making a mental note, Thorn swore to be extra careful as he walked around. It would be an utter disaster if he were to accidentally knock most of the town down.

The mine was located on the north-west side of the town, tucked in between two mountains. Unlike the quarry, the mine was not open-air. Instead, it dove deep into the mountain range through a series of twisting tunnels.

ding

Calling up his notifications, Thorn saw that he had a chat request from Oberlin.

“Hey, Thorn! How is it going?” Oberlin flashed his trademark smile.

“Aren’t you supposed to be in prison still?”

“Eh, details.” Oberlin waved dismissively. “I heard you are headed to Embersplit. That is quite a coincidence because I happen to be there right now.”

“Yeah, what a coincidence.” Thorn rolled his eyes. There was no doubt in his mind that the thief had peeked at the documents in the warden’s office before breaking out of the quarry.

“We should meet up. I am at the Green Goblin in the center

of town."

Knowing that Oberlin would not let him go, Thorn sighed and agreed to meet him. As he closed the call, Thorn could not help but wonder if he was forever cursed to be hounded by over-enthusiastic people.

The Green Goblin was a squat building situated in between a general goods store and the local surveyor's office. According to the sign hanging crookedly on the wall, it was the oldest inn in town, having been established when the Embersplit mine was first discovered. Staring at the doorway skeptically, Thorn called up Oberlin.

"There is no way I am fitting inside this place. How about you come out?"

"Huh? Oh, right. Yeah, sorry. I did not think about that. I'll be right out. We can stay somewhere else."

"I'm planning on camping out near the mine anyway. I am pretty sure that if I touch any of the buildings in town they are going to collapse."

"Haha, that would be quite something." Oberlin walked out of the inn and patted Thorn on the arm. "Good to see you again buddy. So, do you need any help with your quest? Since we're both here, why don't we team up and help each other?"

“Will you allow me to refuse?”

“Haha, no, probably not.” Oberlin gave a small smile. “You are pretty much my only shot at completing my quest so I’m afraid I’m going to keep bothering you until you say yes. But I’m happy to help you with whatever you need to do first. Don’t you have a quest to get rid of your criminal status?”

Sighing, Thorn decided to give up trying to shake Oberlin off. If their time in prison had taught him anything it was that the thief was persistent.

“Alright, you can help. Step one is gathering information. I want to go scope out the mine and talk to the mine supervisor, so let's head that direction. According to the quest, the miners are not meeting their quota, which could mean any number of things.”

“That doesn’t tell us anything.” Oberlin’s brow furrowed as he read the quest description that Thorn shared with him.

“Actually, it gives us a couple of useful pieces of information. First, the problem is solvable. And not through mining. That is, I don’t have to do the mining work. The quest is expecting me to clear whatever obstacle is keeping the miners from being productive. Second, because something is keeping the miners from being productive, we know that whatever the problem is, it is not an issue of the miner’s attitudes. And even if it is an issue of attitudes, it is likely that there is a simple and direct solution.

"After all, the quest is expecting me to be able to clear it in a short amount of time. Third, I did a bit of research about Ember Iron, which is the mine's primary mineral. Unlike normal iron, Ember Iron is a type of coal used to increase the temperature of smith's forges. It allows for more efficient smelting and is in high demand. However, Embersplit mine is known to be one of the smallest Ember Iron mines already, so the fact that the production has fallen is not a serious issue. This leads me to believe that the reason I was dispatched to the mine is less about the actual production levels and more about resolving a different issue. The production is just being used as a cover."

As the two walked out of town they talked about possible problems the mine could be facing that would cause production to slow down. After concluding that there were way too many possibilities, they began to talk of other things.

The mine entrance was a quarter of a mile away from the town of Embersplit, so it did not take them long to reach it. A wooden fence surrounded the naturally formed cave entrance and a guard dressed in rusty armor sat near the door, dozing in the sun. Opening his eyes as Thorn's shadow fell over him, the guard was so startled he fell backward off his stool.

"We are here to see the mine supervisor." Just as Thorn was about to speak, Oberlin stepped forward and stared down at the guard.

“O... okay.” Recovering from his shock, the guard got to his feet and opened the fence door. Thorn and Oberlin followed right behind him, stepping into the fenced-in area in front of the cave mouth. Oberlin looked around with interest while Thorn examined the cave before sighing with relief. It looked big enough that he would not have to duck.

After a few minutes of waiting, a frazzled-looking man stumbled out of one of the buildings, still trying to tuck his shirttails in, without much luck. Unkempt hair pointed this way and that and one of his suspenders had fallen from his shoulder, making one side of his pants sag dangerously low. The man slowed down as he got close and took in Thorn’s staggering height.

“Hello, are you the supervisor here?” Thorn spoke in as friendly a tone as he could manage. “My name is Thorn, I’ve been assigned a parole quest to help you determine why your production has fallen in the recent months.”

“Hello, hello. Welcome.” Nodding his head repeatedly, the mine supervisor invited them into his office. “I am Supervisor Hobson. I oversee day-to-day operations here at the mine. Thank you for coming out to help us figure out the issue.”

“Why don’t you tell us about what is going on. When did you notice something wrong?”

“Of course, of course. So, everything was normal until three months ago. Production was normal for the first half of the month, but it dropped due to a small cave-in. After that, it recovered but then it dropped back down by the end of the month. It has been sporadic ever since."

"How do you measure your production? Is it by the weight of the Ember Iron you pull out?"

"No, no, we only weigh them to verify the number of pieces that we bring out of the mine." Supervisor Hobson opened a cabinet and pulled out three pieces of orange and brown ore. "Ember Iron is a strange mineral in that all the pieces are uniform in size and density. See, the variation on them is tiny. This is one of the advantages of Ember Iron as a consumable, it makes for a controllable fire.

"It also means it is easy to determine the mine's production. We used to count the number of Ember Iron pulled out of the mine each day and then weigh them to verify, but these days we mostly just weight them and then pay accordingly. Recently, though, we have been finding that our monthly totals have been lower than they should have been. Part of that is due to losing one of our best miners, who quit. I'm worried that when the end of the year comes, we will be so far behind that the mine will be closed down."

"We'll need to see your books." Stepping out from beside Thorn, Oberlin smiled his best smile.

"And you are?" Supervisor Hobson looked at the thin thief warily.

"This is Oberlin, he is my partner. He will be helping me with the investigation." Thorn rested a big hand on Oberlin's shoulder. "We will not only need to see your books but if you have a list of your employees and schedules for the last couple months, that would be helpful as well."

"Of course, of course. Please give me one moment." After pulling the documents out, Supervisor Hobson left the two of them alone, saying, "I have to go see what the miners have produced today. If there is anything you need just come get me."

Watching the supervisor leave, Oberlin had a strange look in his eyes. Turning to Thorn who was looking through the schedule he hesitated for a moment, before saying, "He is lying you know."

"Hmm?" Thorn looked up, a large finger marking his place on the page.

"The supervisor is not telling the truth about something. He is nervous for some reason. In my line of work being able to spot lies is important and I would stake my reputation that he was concealing the truth."

"Is that so." Thorn couldn't help but smile. This was getting more and more interesting. "Do me a favor, go find out where this Margo Talern is. Try to do it without alerting anyone though."

"Margo Talern?"

"Yeah, he is a miner. According to this schedule, his last week was the week that there was a sharp drop in production. I'm going to keep looking over the books."

"Got it, leave it to me." Nodding his head, Oberlin left the office as Thorn busied himself with the account books.

CHAPTER SIX

After poring over the books for almost two hours, Thorn straightened and stretched his arms. The numbers were tedious but important and he was starting to get a clearer picture of what had happened since the initial drop in production. Now to see what Oberlin had dug up.

Thorn found Oberlin hanging out by the front gate, chatting with the guard who had been lounging there when they first arrived. Seeing Thorn coming, Oberlin coughed and pretended to be in a serious conversation with the guard, even producing a pad of paper as if he was taking notes.

“Thanks for your help Charles, I'll let you know if there is anything else we need.” Oberlin pretended to have just seen Thorn as he put the pad away. “Oh, I didn't see you there, sir. I just finished up the last interview with Charles here. He was very cooperative.” Oberlin threw a poorly concealed wink at the guard.

"Good, follow me back to camp," Thorn commanded, running his eyes over the guard's rumpled uniform. With a bit of a sniff, he walked out the gate and left the mine. After a few steps Oberlin caught up and Thorn shortened his stride so the thief did not have to run to keep up. In silence, they proceeded until they were well out of earshot of the mining camp.

"You were onto something," Oberlin said, his voice laced with excitement. "Officially, that Margo guy was let go and moved to another region to take care of his sick relative. But I got a look at the mine's sign-in sheet. You know, where the miners sign in and out of their shifts? His signature from that date was forged. Pretty crappy forgery too. Looks like someone tried to use a tracing method to make it look like he signed out of his shift midweek and did not come back the next day. He went in on a Wednesday morning and never came out. At least, according to the sign-in sheet."

"That means we need to get into the mine."

"Exactly. Chances are he got whacked while he was in the mine."

"Whacked?"

"Yeah, you know, killed?"

"Right. That is a possibility."

“Look at you being so calm. Did you find anything else in the books? You were in there a lot longer than I thought you would be.”

“They were interesting. Not only do they record the total amount gathered, but they also record the individual collection rates of the miners. About two and a half months ago they had a low production day because there was a reported collapse, right? After that, Margo Talern ‘quit’ suddenly. I looked through the individual records and he was one of the highest producers in the mine. What is especially fascinating is that the miner with the next highest production record, Reeve Hewet, has been having a lot of low production days recently.

“We need to get into the mine and talk to Mr. Hewet. We also need to check out the ore they are pulling out of the mine. The weights do not match up. If we add up all the weight that the individual miners get credited with, the number is much higher than the amount stored. Somewhere between the collection point and the storage, they are losing the weight. Which means something that is being brought out of the mine is being removed before the monthly collection.”

“You want to go back after dark?”

“No, I want you to go back after dark. Stealth is one area where I am not naturally gifted. Two months ago, the night guard was replaced with a Jonas Hewet who, I'm guessing, is related to Reeve Hewet. I need you to sneak back in and check what is happening after dark. Tonight would be the night for them to get rid of any evidence of what is going on."

"You got all that from reading some records?" Oberlin looked at Thorn from the corner of his eye. "Are you sure you have never been a criminal?"

Not bothering to respond Thorn stopped once they were halfway between the mine and the town and began to set up camp.

"We will camp here. Once it gets dark you can head back."

A few hours later, Thorn sat watching the flickering flames of his campfire, thinking about the strangeness of his life. Oberlin had gone back to investigate the mining camp, leaving Thorn to finish his dinner. Now, sitting by the fire as the cool night breeze blew past, Thorn had to chuckle. So much had happened in the last few months.

He had gone from naivety to heartbreak. From extreme discomfort to physically unstoppable. From law-abiding to incarcerated. And now he was investigating the potential murder of a bunch of data by another bunch of data. What a strange, strange world.

With a long sigh, Thorn decided to stop thinking about it and just go to bed. Better to face what was in front of him than try to avoid it. Just as he was about to climb into his oversized tent, he froze, remembering the message from Mina that he still had not opened. He had tossed it to the bottom of his messages, resolutely ignoring it.

But wasn't that just avoiding the difficulty? Wasn't his refusal to deal with the message a refusal to deal with the messiness of his relationships? Thorn knew deep in his heart that the correct way to handle the distress of a broken relationship was to face the reality of it head-on. Only then could he make the choice to either try and fix it or cut it loose. By hanging on to the unopened message, wasn't he just prolonging the pain it caused?

Glumly, Thorn sat back down by the fire. If he was going to face life head-on, then he was going to have to face this relationship head-on as well. Thorn opened his messages and pulled Mina's message up to the top, his finger hovering over the button to open it.

"Thorn, Thorn! You were right, they are moving something!" Abruptly Oberlin's shadowed face appeared in front of Thorn in a video message, startling him badly. "You've got to get over here! Don't worry about being quiet. I'll give you the details on the way."

"Alright, I'm on my way." Standing, Thorn waved his hand, collecting the two tents to his inventory and kicking the logs in the fire apart so they would die out. Within moments he was thundering toward the mine. "What is the situation?"

"Wow, is that you thumping? You were not kidding about being unsuited for stealth. I can hear you from here!" Oberlin looked surprised.

"You told me not to worry about it." Thorn was annoyed. His long stride ate up the distance, each footfall leaving a deep impression in the ground. "I'll be there in 30 seconds or so, you better tell me what is going on."

"Nine players showed up and started arguing with Supervisor Hobson. They almost came to blows but it is obvious the players are elites. They have not spotted me, but it was a close thing. They are loading up a cart full of some sort of ore that doesn't look like Ember Iron. I can't tell what it is from here, but they took it out of the storage shed. Are you sure you are not accompanied by a herd of elephants? I'm literally shaking." Oberlin held up his hand that was vibrating.

Ignoring him, Thorn hit the gate of the mine with his shoulder, smashing through it like it was not even there. Splinters peppered the ground around him as he slid to a stop in front of a large carriage that was being loaded with boxes. Cloaked figures stood around the carriage as a couple of miners loaded the boxes of ore into it. Three detached themselves from the group, rushing toward Thorn, weapons drawn.

His eyes taking them all in, Thorn noticed that two members

of the group had bows. Making a mental note to watch for arrows, Thorn brought his focus back to the three enemies in his face. In perfect coordination, the three players attacked. Activating some sort of ability, the two players on the sides slid forward, their swords slashing out at Thorn's arms while the player in front of him stabbed forward with a thin blade.

Without panicking, Thorn stepped forward to break their momentum, his tetsubo flicking across his body toward the player on his left who was forced to jump back. With a twist of his body, his weapon cut through the air, forcing the player in front of him to pull his thrust back, before smashing into the last attacker's back.

Without even looking, Thorn knew that player wouldn't survive the strike, so he stepped forward and grabbed the player with the thin sword, his massive hand covering their shoulder. Squeezing, Thorn heard a yelp of pain and the clatter of their weapon falling to the ground. He tossed them aside while aiming an overhead strike at the last attacker. Unable to block the force, the cloaked figure disappeared into lights to join his companion and Thorn stood facing the rest of the group.

Six cloaked figures stared in shock at the giant in front of them. His moves were smooth and well-practiced, a strong blend of power and grace. After a moment of silence, the two with bows pulled out arrows and the rest of the players drew their weapons. Just as they were about to rush forward, a voice came from behind the cart.

"What is going on here?" A handsome young man in red leather armor with a silver trim walked forward, two figures in cloaks behind him. "Who is he?"

"Who are you?" Thorn asked, his voice overlapping with the red-armored man's.

"Were you hired to stop us?" The man's voice gained a cold edge as he saw that two of his nine men were dead, and another was wounded. "Who hired you? Theropholi? Alexander? Ouroboros?"

Taken aback, Thorn looked at the players in front of him carefully. Their well-coordinated movements had reminded him of Ouroboros and his team, but he had assumed that it was because they were elite players.

"How do you know Ouroboros?" Asked Thorn, his deep voice rumbling around the compound.

"How do I know Ouroboros? Are you kidding?" The man was confused. "You were not hired to stop us? Then why are you here?"

"You are stealing. I'm here to stop you."

In the pregnant silence that followed the sound of Oberlin facepalming could be heard from the darkness where he hid.

"Haha, is that right?" Once he recovered from his shock, the red-armored leader laughed. Gesturing to the two people behind him, he smiled at Thorn. "In that case, you will not mind me getting rid of you."

Throwing off their cloaks, a man and a woman moved forward to stand in front of Thorn. Dressed in the same red armor that their leader wore, each had a shield and a scimitar. From their confident gaze and steady gait, Thorn knew they were going to be trouble. Both the man and the woman walked like Hamm, the sword trainer in Berum, setting off alarm bells in Thorn's head. He had never managed to win a fight against Hamm which did not bode well for his chances here.

Nervous energy blossomed in Thorn's mind as he stared at the two players in front of him. Yet the increasingly familiar burning excitement in his chest soon drowned it out. Ever since he had faced Gargish, the Blood Hunter, Thorn had found himself drawn to combat, no matter how dangerous. Now, facing two expert fighters, Thorn could feel that excitement growing, making his hands itch.

Just as the man was about to open his mouth, Thorn couldn't help himself. A long step forward put him directly in front of the man and his fist flew out, punching forward. Startled, the man showed his training, managing to get his shield up before Thorn could hit him. Taking the blow on his shield, the man was thrown off his feet, flying backward.

His partner, seeing Thorn strike, slashed toward him with her scimitar, its edge lit by a sickly green glow. Thorn caught the scimitar on his tetsubo, frowning slightly as the scimitar bit a chunk out of his weapon.

“Telis, get back!” The leader shouted, looking hard at Thorn before calling out, “Formation three.”

Instantly, the remaining players split up to surround Thorn while the female warrior who had jumped back went to assist her male companion who was still struggling to his feet. Seeing his shield arm hanging uselessly she couldn’t help but gasp. Thorn’s punch, which had looked rather casual, had contained enough force to dislocate the man’s arm.

Gritting his teeth, the red-armored warrior mumbled under his breath. A thick red glow seeped from between his lips as he spoke, surrounding his shoulder and healing him. Within a few moments, his arm was back to normal and he and Telis joined the rest of the players in surrounding Thorn.

Watching the eight players around him, Thorn could tell that he was in a lot of trouble. It was obvious from their movements that they were well trained and that spelled danger. He had taken the initiative to surprise attack the red-armored warrior and had not even been able to deal any permanent damage. While it looked as if he had the advantage, the swift response from the female warrior and the handsome man in the back had destroyed any edge Thorn had gained.

Now, surrounded by eight players, Thorn knew his chances were plummeting. "Then why don't I maximize my value." Thorn thought, his eyes locking onto the handsome man standing in the back. Feeling Thorn's gaze settle on him, the hair on the back of the handsome man's neck rose instantly and a cold chill ran down his spine.

"Get him!" He screamed, pointing at Thorn.

Thorn measured the distance. 50 feet. Obstacles include four players and a carriage of ore. Doable.

As the other players reacted to the yell, Thorn threw back his head and howled, the cry echoing eerily around the mine compound.

Stunned, the players surrounding him stumbled as his [Wolf Lord's Howl] ability activated. At the same time, Thorn activated [Avatar of the Wolf]. Streaks of silver flew from the moon, surrounding Thorn's gauntlets, as razor sharp claws formed on his fingers. Taking advantage of the chaos in the formation around him, Thorn dashed forward, heading straight for the leader standing next to the carriage.

CHAPTER SEVEN

Seeing Thorn's charge, the handsome man growled and muttered under his breath, the same thick red mist seeping from his lips to surround him in a swirling red shield. At the same time, he pulled a scepter from his waist and pointed its barbed tip toward Thorn. Another muttered command sent a scarlet bolt of energy shooting toward Thorn!

As soon as the scepter appeared Thorn instinctively knew he could not face it head-on. Angling his body, he dashed diagonally, putting the carriage between them. Undeterred, the bolt of energy punched through the wall of the carriage, searing a deep line across Thorn's arm. Hissing in pain, Thorn braced himself and grabbed the carriage. With a heave, he lifted it from the ground and tossed it at the players charging from behind him.

The carriage trembled as it flew, the sheer surprise of the situation making several the chasing players forget to dodge.

With a tremendous crash, the carriage came back down to earth, crushing four of them. Amid the splintered debris anguished screams sounded from those under the carriage's broken bulk.

Not even bothering to look at his handiwork, Thorn resumed his dash toward the leader, whose face was white as a sheet. As he charged, Thorn felt the bite of an arrow in his shoulder. Gritting his teeth to ignore the sting, Thorn focused his attention on getting to the red-armored leader. Another scarlet bolt lanced forward, this time hitting Thorn in his side, cutting through his armor and leaving a massive smoldering wound along his ribs.

"Two more steps." Thorn thought, narrowing his focus even further. Readying his weapon, Thorn crossed the last twenty feet in two of his massive strides. Smashing down with all the force he could muster, Thorn brought his iron-bound tetsubo down on the shifting red magical shield.

Horrified, his target broke into a hurried mumble. A deep stream of red mist poured from his mouth, reinforcing the shield. With a crack that shook the ground, the tetsubo landed on the shield, causing a massive amount of the mist to dissipate but not managing to get through. Seeing the thin layer of mist still swirling in front of him, Thorn tossed his weapon into his inventory and reached out his massive clawed hands, grabbing the bubble of mist and squeezing it with all his might.

With an ominous groan, the shield warped as Thorn's claws pushed into it. The shield thinned at a visible rate, the stream of mist pouring from the leader's mouth unable to reinforce it quickly enough. Just as the silver claws were about to pierce through, Thorn felt a stinging pain. The other players had caught up, burying their blades in Thorn's broad back. Ignoring his dimming world, Thorn gritted his teeth and redoubled his efforts, pouring all his strength into breaking the shield.

With an ear-rending crack, the mist shield shattered into nothingness, causing the leader to stagger in pain as the feedback hit him. Thorn lashed out, his claws connecting with the leader's chest. Yet just as he made contact the red-armored woman landed a strike to his neck, causing the strength to drain from his hands. Still, the weight of the blow could not be stopped and as Thorn fell to the ground, he could feel his claws ripping a furrow through the front of the leader's red armor.

Still trying to fight off the encroaching darkness, Thorn grinned. This was the first time he had used any of his new abilities and despite not managing to get his main target, he was quite pleased.

"We'll try this again another time." Thorn's deep voice sent chills down the leader's spine.

Hearing Thorn's defiant statement, Telis readied her scimitar for another strike, only for Thorn to turn into motes of light, drifting off to the ether.

Scrambling to his feet, white-faced and shaking, the leader looked around and let out a string of obscenities. Seven of his eleven subordinates were dead, and he was badly wounded. The carriage lay in shambles, the wheels and walls splintered beyond repair. In the distance, he could hear the shouts of the town guards on their way to the mine.

“Koral, get the chests, we’re leaving,” he snarled. Who was that monster? And why had he shown up tonight?

“Um, boss?” The red-armored warrior looked up from where he had been searching through the wreckage of the carriage, his voice panicked. “They’re gone.”

“What!” The leader screamed, the veins on his neck popping out.

A hundred feet away Oberlin smiled at the sound, patting his belt.

As the world faded to black, Thorn found himself standing in the now familiar login area. As before, Myst stood in front of him holding her tablet.

“Hello, Myst,” Thorn greeted her warmly. “It is nice to see you again.”

“Hello, traveler. You seem quite cheerful for having just

experienced your first death. Would you like to talk about it?"

"Haha, I guess I am. I knew pretty much right away that I would not be making it out of that situation alive. There were twelve of them after all. But I think I did pretty well."

"You seem to have adapted to Nova Terra's light-hearted treatment of death quickly. Why do you think that is?" Myst asked, jotting something down on her device.

"That is a great question, Myst." Thorn paused and watched for a reaction. Faced with Myst's impassive face he sighed and continued. "I had a good, long think about it. And, ultimately it seemed a bit silly to care too much about it. Since death is impermanent, why not use it to your advantage?"

"What do you mean by 'use it to your advantage'?"

"Think about it. If the worst that is going to happen is that I'll have to spend twenty-four hours in Fantasia, then it is easy to weigh death against my objective. In this case, it was worth it to try my hand at killing the leader of my opponents. While I wasn't successful, I learned about my abilities and I think that next time I will do better. Trading that knowledge for a day of rest seems like a pretty good deal to me."

"You traded your death for understanding?"

"It would be more accurate to say I traded a time-out for

understanding. After all, I'm not dead, am I?" Thorn smiled.

"Thank you for answering my questions, traveler. Unless there are extenuating circumstances, you will no longer meet me upon death. You will find the entrance to Fantasia behind you. Please enjoy your stay," Myst finished writing on her pad, giving Thorn an appraising look. With a small nod, her figure faded into the air, leaving Thorn alone.

The door to Fantasia was an oversized affair, just right for Thorn. "Nice of them to take my height into consideration," Thorn thought as he walked through. As soon as his foot crossed the threshold, Thorn found himself in a futuristic city. He was joining a large crowd of others in exiting what looked at first glance to be a railway station.

Overhead levitating cars and buses zipped by, stopping on platforms to let their occupants head into the floating bullet trains. Around him, people rushed about their lives, not even sparing him a glance. At first, Thorn found it strange, until a dragon-headed individual brushed past him, jabbering away on his communications device while he tried to sip a scalding beverage.

A closer look showed that the people around him were of all races and shapes and sizes, having brought their in-game race with them into Fantasia. Walking to the side of the road, Thorn gingerly sat down on a wall. After being sure that it would hold his weight, Thorn opened his menu and called his aunt. Rather than wander around Fantasia as he had when he first entered Nova Terra, he was looking forward to saying hi.

“Xavier. How are you, hun?” Julia’s excited face popped up on the screen.

“I’m well. Have I called at a bad time?” Thorn asked, noticing the sheen of sweat on her face.

“No, no, this is great. I just finished my morning practice. Hold on one second.” Taking a towel, Julia wiped her face and her neck. “Ah, much better. So, what’s new? Did you complete your quest?”

“No, not yet.” Thorn shook his head. “I ran into some more people from Ragnarok and ended up dying. I’m in Fantasia now.”

“Oh, again? Are you sure you don’t want me to get the girls to pay them a visit?”

“Yeah, really. I want to take care of it myself,” Thorn’s heart burst with warmth at his aunt’s concern. “I was hoping to meet up with you if you are free.”

“Of course. Why don’t you meet me at our offices? I can show you around.”

Agreeing to meet up, Thorn pulled up the address that Julia sent him and walked over while looking around at the city. All the traffic on the ground was either foot traffic or small scooter-like devices while the levitating cars flitted around between the tall buildings above everyone. Since he had entered the city Thorn had seen almost nothing but skyscrapers, each uniquely designed.

After twenty minutes of walking, Thorn reached the center of the business district. Despite housing almost half of the world's 11 billion people, Fantasia did not seem overly crowded. Where the five and a half billion people who used the city were, Thorn was not quite sure. According to what he had read, the city of Fantasia was almost another game in and of itself.

Stopping, Thorn looked up. Rising over six hundred stories, the building in front of him was truly massive. At its base it took up four city blocks, dwarfing all the nearby buildings. A wide-open walkway took Thorn up to the huge glass entrance, exotic plants hanging from levitating planters. At the door stood uniformed greeters, welcoming the people streaming in off the street. As soon as Thorn stepped inside a familiar figure made its way over.

“Welcome to Fantasia, Master Xavier.” Henry, the head of Atlas' security team bowed his head slightly to Thorn.

“Hello, Henry. It is nice to see you again.”

“Thank you, sir. If you'd come this way, we will take the private elevator up to see your aunt.”

Following Henry, Thorn could not stop looking around. The building was truly magnificent. A masterful neomodern structure, the smooth curves, and quirky edges blended peace and energy. Thorn had seen pictures and even video walkthroughs of the Atlas headquarters, but he had to admit that being here in person was completely different.

Standing comfortably in the elevator as it rapidly rose, Thorn could feel the care that his aunt gave him. One of the features of the massive buildings that sparked much attention when it had first been built was its scale. 'Scaled for a giant' some of the articles had said, unaware of how right they were.

"Xavier!" As soon as the doors to the elevator opened, Thorn's aunt rushed in and gave him a big hug. "I've missed you."

"Hi, Aunt Julia, I've missed you too."

"Come on in, I want to introduce you to some of the girls." Taking Thorn's large hand, she pulled him out of the elevator. "We practice here when we are not in the game. The facilities are better. Our practice room is state of the art. Oh, that reminds me. Before you go, set your home to this location. This floor and the two above it is the private residences. I hope you don't mind but I have been letting the girls use it since there are so many rooms."

"Of course, I don't mind. You can use it however you want. It is your home too."

"I know, I just feel bad because it is your building and here I am making all the decisions about it." Walking through a wide doorway, Julia let go of Thorn and pointed to a large staircase on the right. "Up that way is the living space. You'll find your room in there. You can set that as your login point for Fantasia and use it to get back to the game when your lockout is up. Come this way though, I want to introduce you."

Julia led Thorn into a spacious lounge with comfortable-looking sofas spaced around a round fireplace in the center of the room. Three women in their late twenties or early thirties were sprawled out on the couches chatting quietly. As soon as they spotted Julia coming in, they rose and came to greet her.

"Xavier, let me introduce you to Esmire, Bluefire, and Odele. They are the Society of Roses' management staff. Esmire is our COO, Odele handles our PR, and Bluefire oversees combat and training. Girls, this is my nephew, Xavier. He just started playing a little while ago."

A few hours later Thorn lay comfortably on his bed for the first time since he entered Nova Terra. Relaxing on the mattress that could easily fit a family of five, he put his hands behind his head and stared up at the aquarium overhead. Countless exotic fish swam through the water above him, yet they failed to catch his attention as Thorn's mind was drawn back to Nova Terra.

After spending less than a month of real time in the game, Thorn could easily see why this alternate world had become so important. He could hardly wait for the 24-hour lockout period to be over so he could dive back in.

But before he went back in, Thorn had something to do. With a deep breath, Thorn opened his panel and stared at his messages. About to open the message from Mina, Thorn paused and looked around. His room was quiet and empty. "Hmm, must just be my imagination," thought Thorn. The last few times he had been about to open the message something had interrupted him, making Thorn wonder if the game did not want him to read it.

As Thorn had played Nova Terra, everything seemed to fall into place, allowing him to progress from one adventure to the next. Yet, despite the apparent randomness of everything that had happened to him, Thorn wondered if there was a guiding hand behind it. Fortifying himself, Thorn pressed the button.

> Dear Thorn,
>
> First, and most importantly, I'm sorry. I'm sorry for

betraying you. I am sorry for trying to kill you. I am sorry for lying to you. I was pressured into doing it by someone else, but at the end of the day, I did it. I am so sorry.

I know I don't deserve forgiveness for betraying you, but I hope you would be willing to give me a chance to make it up to you. What we did was terrible and has hurt you, but if it is at all possible, I'd like to make it up.

Ever since that day, our party has broken up. Jorge was really scared after he died in town and has not been playing. Ouroboros has gone back to set up his faction in Ragnarok but Velin and I did not go with him. Something about him has changed. I haven't been able to sleep well because I feel so bad about that day.

Velin is helping me write this message because I am terrible with words. I know she feels the same way I do (haha, she didn't tell me to write that).

Please give me a chance to make it up to you.

Sorry,

Mina

CHAPTER EIGHT

Reading over it twice, conflicting emotions bubbled in Thorn's chest. The message reopened the painful memory that the last four weeks had dulled. Still, it was not as painful as it had been at first. At least now, Thorn felt like he could think about the situation clearly without being consumed with hurt and anger.

Part of Thorn wanted revenge, wanted to crush them into pieces over and over again. But another part of Thorn remembered how much fun he had with the group and longed to restore that relationship. Restless, Thorn looked at the timer. Still another ten hours before he could go back into Nova Terra. Getting up he headed to the gym. Maybe moving would help him think.

The workout room was an entire floor of the massive building and housed two pools, multiple tracks, an obstacle course, training dummies of all sorts, and a weight training area.

Taken aback by how huge it was, Thorn paused at the door. In the distance, he could see his aunt practicing with one of her guildmates on a large square platform. If he was remembering correctly, she was named Bluefire.

Wandering over to them, Thorn looked on in admiration at Julia's skillful use of her halberd. He had trained a bit in using a spear with his taijiquan master, but Julia's weapon was a bit different. With a longer, wider blade, she could cut more effectively, creating a whirling storm of blades that served as an offense and defense at the same time.

As he got closer Thorn noticed that, despite her skill, she was still struggling against her opponent, Bluefire, who was armed with tonfas. The silver weapons were fast and unpredictable while providing Bluefire with an impenetrable defense. The two women struggled back and forth, sending slashes and strikes at each other without any regard for safety.

Bluefire slipped through the silver net Julia was weaving and, flipping one of her tonfas around to increase her range, landed a solid strike on Julia's solar plexus, launching her backward across the room. Seeing her hurt, Thorn was about to run to her when she threw down her weapon angrily and shouted, "I concede." Instantly, her tired, sweaty figure was refreshed, and she stood up, restored to a perfect state.

"Hey, Thorn, coming to train with us?" Julia had seen her nephew come in, creating a slight gap in her concentration that Bluefire had taken advantage of.

“I’m just checking everything out. I still have about ten hours, so I thought I’d work off some steam.”

“You want to try sparring with Bluefire? She was just saying how she wanted to go for a couple of rounds with you.”

“I’d be happy to spar with you,” affirmed Bluefire, tightening her blond hair into a ponytail.

“I don’t know, I’m not super great at controlling myself yet.”

“Oh, come on, give it a try. Bluefire is one of the best PvP players in the game. You are not going to hurt her. Plus, this room is special, it allows us to use our abilities and skills from Nova Terra. And when we’re done it will heal everyone. Just like the sparring rings at the training halls.”

After a bit more prodding, Thorn stepped up onto the training ring. As soon as he did, he realized he could summon his weapons and armor again. A glance at Bluefire showed that she was not wearing any armor, so Thorn only summoned his tetsubo and got into his stance. Across from him, Bluefire bounced in place. Seeing that Thorn wasn’t moving, she smiled and flexed her fingers.

“Watch out, I’m coming,” Bluefire warned him. Accelerating, she dashed toward him, her body weaving unpredictably. Startled by her speed, Thorn swung his tetsubo in a long arc to try and force her back. Undeterred, Bluefire lowered her body until it was almost parallel with the ground and accelerated even faster, darting in under Thorn's swing and using the force of her dash to smash one of her tonfas into Thorn's side.

Unable to respond in time, Thorn could only take the blow. Since he couldn't dodge, Thorn decided to aim for mutual destruction. Switching his grip on his tetsubo, Thorn struck back at Bluefire with the back of his hand. Though confident in her attack, Bluefire still raised her other tonfa to block Thorn's counterblow.

Seeing the situation, an involuntary cry escaped Julia's lips. Yet the scene she had imagined never manifested itself. As the blow from Bluefire's tonfa impacted Thorn's side his body barely shivered. Feeling her blow connect, Bluefire was horrified to realize that her impressive strength was not that impressive next to Thorn. The attack she used was enough to send anyone else stumbling back, but Thorn simply grunted.

The rebound from the blow left her hand feeling numb, almost making her lose her grip on her weapon. Dumbfounded she forgot to dodge Thorn's counterattack, taking it solidly on her tonfa.

crack

A loud sound echoed across the ring as the silver tonfa

broke in half. Under Julia's stunned gaze Bluefire broke apart into little lights, disappearing into the air. A blue light shot down from the ceiling to reveal Bluefire, as good as new, outside the ring. Impassive, Thorn put his weapon away and stepped down out of the ring, sighing as Bluefire flinched back.

"Did...did you just die?" Julia asked Bluefire, barely able to get the question out.

"Yes." Bluefire sighed, depressed about how the fight had ended.

"But didn't you block?"

"The force was overwhelming, activating a crushing blow." Eyeing Thorn contemplatively, Bluefire asked, "What is your class, Xavier? My weapons give me significant damage reduction, but you smashed them like they were nothing."

"I don't have a class." Admitted Thorn sheepishly. "I'm just naturally strong."

"Naturally strong might be the understatement of the century. Naturally strong doesn't let you break a defensive weapon and one-shot a melee class. I mean, my defenses are not the best in the game, but they are not shabby."

"Haha, I think you were so stunned that your attack did not do anything to him that you forgot to dodge." Julia laughed, remembering Bluefire's stunned face.

"Please, you would have been crushed too. I hit him with everything I had, and he didn't even feel it." Bluefire stared accusingly at Thorn. "I want another round."

Five hours later, an exhausted Thorn threw himself down on the platform causing it to shake. After sparring for hour after hour he was spent and covered in bruises. While Bluefire had never been able to deal any significant damage to him, every one of her strikes left Thorn aching. It had been hard to keep up with her speed, but Thorn found his reaction time getting better and better as they fought. Already quick for someone his size, Thorn found it easier to respond to Bluefire's sudden movements as they practiced together.

Standing to the side, Julia waved her hand and a white light fell on Thorn's giant figure, filling him with energy and healing his bruised body. She had always thought that Thorn would do well in Nova Terra, but the last five hours had completely upended her view of the game. Thorn was like a mountain, immovable. Against a blunt weapon like Bluefire's, Thorn was invulnerable.

"With good enough armor, he would be invulnerable against bladed weapons too," Bluefire seemed like she was able to read Julia's thoughts. "If he had a bit more training and experience, he very well could be the most dangerous melee fighter in the game. Even without a class. I just can't get over how solid he is."

"How are you feeling, Xavier?" Julia asked as Thorn rose to his feet.

"I'm feeling pretty good. It is convenient that the system can reset us so we don't have to wait for the bruises to heal. Plus, I feel like I am getting a better grasp of how actual combat works. So far, I have done a lot of brawling, but all of my fights end quickly so it is hard to practice."

"Well, I think you are just fine." Bluefire tucked a strand of her hair behind her ear. "You have the most ridiculous advantage in strength, reach, and stability. You just need to practice anticipating your opponent's movements. Even though I couldn't do anything to you, remember that I am one of the better melee combatants in the game. Most other people are not as quick as I am."

"Hah, listen to her." Julia rolled her eyes. "You just spent five hours attacking him without dealing any real damage."

"What, you want to give it a try?" Bluefire sneered. "I bet you wouldn't last more than ten seconds."

"I was wondering, is there a place to train against abilities? Or magic?" Thorn asked. "I ran across some players who had some pretty crazy abilities. I don't know if I would have any chance against them."

"Sure, let's give it a try. Bluefire, do you want the first

round?" Julia asked, looking at her blonde friend.

"Yeah, why not. Maybe I can get some of my honor back." Bluefire joked, stepping onto the platform and readying her tonfa again. With a low shout, she summoned a blue flame that covered her weapons. "Watch out, big guy. These things are dangerous," she warned Thorn, waving her flame covered weapons.

The mystical fire dancing along the edge of the tonfas radiated danger so he readied himself, watching them carefully. Bouncing on the balls of her feet, Bluefire tapped her weapons together rhythmically before dashing forward. Each footstep left a burning imprint in the ring's floor as she moved forward.

Within half a second, she was right in front of Thorn, a strike flying at him. Startled by her increase in speed, Thorn fell back half a step, raising his weapon to block. With a loud clang, the weapons impacted one another, and the two players bounced apart. His hand numb from the force of the blow, Thorn estimated that the mystical flames had tripled Bluefire's attack speed and doubled her strength.

Under his watchful gaze, Bluefire chanted some arcane words, causing the fire that flickered along the edges of her weapons to burst out, forming blades that extended almost two feet beyond her hands. Warning bells started ringing in Thorn's head as he looked at the flickering blades.

“Those look dangerous.” Thorn blurted out, as Bluefire began to bounce again.

“You have no idea,” Julia smirked at Thorn’s nervous tone.

Focused, Bluefire sprinted forward again, her blades slashing out with ever increasing speed and ferocity. As he warded off the first few blows, Thorn felt that the attack was manageable, but that quickly changed. The attacks came in faster and faster, causing Thorn to retreat. Every time he blocked an attack a chunk of his weapon would break off, carved out by the mystic blades. Fed up with his passive position, Thorn gritted his teeth and struck out, ignoring a stab coming toward his side.

Her eyes flickering, Bluefire abandoned one of her strikes to deflect Thorn’s counter-attack while her other blade continued toward his chest. Feeling her blade bite into Thorn, Bluefire smiled in triumph. Once her blade connected, it was over. Yet the fight failed to follow her predictions as Thorn’s counter-attack continued toward her despite the growing stab wound in his side.

The moment his attack approached her weapon, she knew she was in trouble. Before it even connected, she could feel the compressed air from the tetsubo pushing her back. “If that hits, I’m dead.” Bluefire thought. Decisively abandoning her attack, she yelled out an arcane command and disappeared in a flash of flame, reappearing a moment later twenty feet away.

Losing his target, Thorn stumbled to the ground, falling to one knee. The flame blade that hit his side had cut deep and the blue flames continued to lick at him. Grimacing, Thorn clapped a hand over the wound as he stood to his feet. Despite patting the burning area a couple of times, Thorn found that the flames did not go out, instead of continuing to burn.

“Poison Flame doesn’t stop burning unless you get magical healing,” Bluefire remarked as she watched Thorn try to put the flame out.

“Huh, really? That is cool. Do they go out if you are defeated?”

“Um, yeah. I guess. They go out if I unsummon my blades. But how are you still standing? Most people who get hit with them are rolling on the ground within seconds.”

“Oh?” Thorn looked at Julia who was doing nothing to conceal her utter amazement. “It’s just a stinging feeling. Sort of like a hot electrical shock. I mean, it hurts but it is manageable.”

“Ah. Forget it.” Bluefire shook her head in defeat, unsummoning her blades. “I don’t want to fight anymore. You’re ridiculous. A total cheat. This is so unfair.”

“Haha,” Julia laughed as she waved her hand, restoring both

combatants to peak form. “Isn’t he amazing? Xavier, I knew that Nova Terra would suit you. Not everyone can force Bluefire to put her blades away.”

“Hmph. I could have won, it just would have taken a bit.” Bluefire grumbled.

“Thank you very much for sparring with me.” Thorn clasped his fists in a traditional martial arts salute, bowing his head toward the complaining lady. “It is very helpful for me to face such skilled opponents.”

“No problem, Xavier. I noticed that you were surprised when you saw my blades. Have you not had much experience with magic?”

“I haven’t. I’ve seen people use it, but I have not fought against it before.”

“Well, why don’t we change that?” Bluefire turned to Julia, “Xavier still has a few hours before he can go back into Nova Terra, why don’t we call Odele and Jasmine so he can get some practice in? It would be good for them too, they have been getting pretty lazy.”

“That is a great idea! Thorn, Odele, and Jas are two of our best casters. I’ll call them over and they can give you a rundown on how to fight against a caster as a melee combatant. Though you better get some armor on, their attacks pack a serious punch.” Julia pulled up her messaging interface as she spoke, sending a quick text.

Excited, Thorn equipped his armor as he waited. He had been feeling a bit depressed about his loss to the group at Embersplit Mine. Taking a deep breath as two women walked into the gym, Thorn greeted them and got into his stance. A deep excitement burned in his chest. He had never felt more alive.

CHAPTER NINE

An armored guard leaning against the wall of the temple nearly jumped out of his skin when Thorn's massive figure appeared right in front of him. After a few hours of practice against the two mages from the Society of Roses, Thorn felt like he had a much better idea of how to fight against a magic user. In fact, that knowledge was carved deep into his skin. He had been burned, frozen, shocked, and impaled over the course of the fight, each spell giving him a painful reminder of what he should have done.

The fight had evened out when, in a moment of frustration at his inability to close the distance, he had pulled out his large arbalest and dispatched one of his opponents with a massive bolt. He had still lost that fight, quite brutally in fact, but he felt as if he was on the edge of figuring out how to deal with casters.

The repeated losses had taught him that his body was

largely impervious to damage due to its density and overwhelming strength and stamina, a trait that only increased as he added armor. However, direct blows to his head or neck were just as deadly to him as they were to other players. While he could take more damage than the average player, he still had the same weak points.

This explained why he had fallen so fast at the mine. The female swordswoman had targeted the back of his neck, paralyzing him before finishing him off. Thorn had been so engrossed with crushing the red magical shield that he hadn't bothered to protect his neck. While armor could help with some of that, Thorn had no desire to cover himself in metal since that would further reduce his already low mobility.

While his blunt force damage was high, excessive even, the repeated fights against the ladies from the Society of Roses demonstrated the value of piercing force. Every time he died, it was because of some magical damage that ripped straight through his defenses. Thorn did have his immense strength on his side, often allowing him to trigger a [Crushing Blow], but that did not help against magical defense that negated all the force, or at least, cut it down significantly.

Bluefire's magical blades had been eye-opening. She used them for both defense and offense, combining blunt force with sharp, piercing damage to great effect. The more Thorn thought about it, the more he realized that this was what Master Sun had been trying to get him to achieve. Combined offense and defense that flowed into each other without warning.

In hand to hand combat, Thorn was close to unbeatable. His excellent taijiquan training, combined with his inhuman strength and weight made it almost impossible for him to lose. At melee weapon range his training with Master Sun and his impressive force was enough to give most fighters fits. Even his long-range combat abilities were higher than average due to the raw damage his City Defender arbalest granted him. However, once magic entered the equation all his advantages evaporated.

No matter how tough he was, he couldn't block a chaos bolt or avoid the slowing effect of an ice arrow. No matter how strong he was, he couldn't punch his way through an invulnerability bubble. Just like the fight against the spirits in Hati's Ascent, magic needed to be fought with magic. Rather than discouragement, Thorn felt renewed energy after losing to the Society of Roses mages. After all, it gave him something to work toward.

Nodding and tossing two silver to the gaping guard, Thorn sauntered off toward the inn where he was going to meet Oberlin. He had re-spawned in Embersplit since it was the last town he had been through before his run-in with the players at the mine had gotten him killed. He had just stepped out of the temple courtyard when he saw three familiar red-armored players standing in the middle of the street.

“There he is, boss. I told you he would log in.” The female warrior who had killed Thorn pointed a well-manicured finger at him.

“I can see that Telis,” the handsome man in red armor narrowed his eyes as he glared at Thorn’s massive figure. Planting himself in Thorn’s way, he rested his hand on his sword. Having started a fight in a town before and paid the significant cost, the gesture almost caused Thorn to laugh out loud. Thankfully for the red-armored man’s blood pressure, Thorn was able to stifle the chuckle, turning it into a cough.

“Hello, nice to see you again.” Thorn smiled down at the three players blocking him. Seeing that they were not about to move, he stopped. “What can I do for you?”

“What did you do with our boxes?” The red-armored warrior Thorn had nearly killed in the fight at the mine stepped in front of his boss and pointed at Thorn’s chest.

“Sorry? I’m not sure what you are talking about.” Thorn raised his eyebrows as he stared at the finger.

“Korith, stand down.” The red-armored leader called the warrior back. “I think we might have started off on the wrong foot. My name is Angdrin, Ragnarok’s fourth seat. I lost something during our scuffle last night that is important to me and I want it back.”

"Nice to meet you, Angdrin. My name is Thorn, and believe it or not, I have no idea what you are talking about."

"Hmph. I hope, for your sake, that is the case. If I find out otherwise you will suffer for it."

"Oh yeah?" Annoyed at the threat, Thorn stepped forward until he was almost on top of Korith, his eyes hard. Reaching out a huge hand, Thorn picked Korith up and put him to the side without any visible effort. Staring down at Angdrin, Thorn smiled, "It has yet to be decided who is going to suffer. We still have to settle our fight from before."

Shocked by Thorn's aggressive move, Angdrin stepped back before he could stop himself. Realizing that he had just backed down, he flushed, the anger in his eyes growing.

"Hmph. Watch yourself." Angdrin spat before turning and leaving, Korith and Telis trailing behind him. He could not start a fight in the center of town and from the look in Thorn's eyes, he had no idea what this exchange was about. Frustrated, Angdrin could only lead his followers away.

Watching them go, Thorn had a contemplative look on his face. Oberlin had not mentioned anything regarding this, only telling Thorn to meet him at the Green Goblin when he logged back in. Despite his silence, Thorn was positive that Oberlin had something to do with the missing items.

The Green Goblin was just as small and rickety as it had been the first time Thorn had visited so he did not dare squeeze in. Waiting for Oberlin to come out of the inn, Thorn thought about the encounter he just had with Angdrin. He had mentioned something about being one of Ragnarok's seats, but Thorn did not know what that meant. Was it some sort of leadership position? Like a council? Resolving to ask Oberlin, Thorn's thoughts drifted to Mina's message.

According to what she wrote, the party had broken up after Ouroboros got the Exalted Devil Blood Berserker class, due to the mixed feelings over their actions. Thorn still did not know how he felt about trying to restore his relationship with Mina and Velin. Part of him was revolted by the idea, but another part of him longed to go back to those fun, hopeful days before he was tossed aside.

As he was musing on these things a commotion in the inn caught his attention. Shouts, the sound of things breaking, and a flurry of voices drifted out of the inn's doors. Concerned, Thorn crouched down and stuck his head inside the door gingerly. The inside of the inn was just as sketchy looking as the outside and Thorn's gaze settled on a large group of players surrounding Oberlin's thin figure.

At first, no one noticed Thorn, but he coughed, catching a few of the player's eyes. Shocked, they nudged their neighbors and soon silence fell as the patrons stared at the giant head poking through the doorway.

"Oberlin, are you coming?"

"Yes." Like a slippery fish, Oberlin wiggled his way through the crowd and made it to Thorn's side. "Let's go." At first, Oberlin tried to squeeze out before Thorn pulled his head out of the doorway. Getting halfway out, he realized that Thorn's body was blocking the door. After some awkward shuffling, Thorn managed to back out and stand up without knocking against the inn. Seeing Oberlin's curious gaze, Thorn explained that he was worried about knocking the building over.

"Haha, you have to worry about the weirdest things. Still, it would serve them right." Oberlin remarked. "They tried to scam me out of three gold! Can you imagine? The nerve of some people!" As he spoke he hurried Thorn along.

"Oh yeah? And how much did you swipe on your way through the crowd just now?"

"Hmm? 6 gold, 54 Silver, and 19 copper," Oberlin said, patting his belt pouch. "You make a great distraction. I'm telling you, we should work together. We could be the best heist duo Nova Terra has ever seen."

"Speaking of swiping things, I met that red-armored man again today. Angdrin was his name. He mentioned that he was missing something. Do you happen to know anything about that?" After arriving at the edge of town, Thorn led the way toward Embersplit Mine.

"Yeah, while you were being your normal, distracting self, I swiped a couple of crates that had fallen out of the carriage you threw."

"What do they hold?" Thorn asked, looking at Oberlin.

Looking around to make sure there was no one nearby, Oberlin pulled out a crate and sat it on the ground. Opening the lid, Thorn could see an ornate box inside the crate. Magical runes, etched along the top and sides, pulsed weakly. His brow furrowed, Thorn looked at Oberlin who shook his head.

"I haven't had time to open them. It will probably take me a couple of hours to crack the magic lock, and maybe half that for the mechanical lock on the box. I need a quiet environment. There are six boxes, so we are talking at least a day."

"They look expensive."

"Expensive? They are priceless. I don't recognize the runes at all, which means they are not from the second or third era. If they are from the first era then we've got a huge time bomb on our hands."

"Time bomb?"

"Let's leave that for later." The thief's face turned serious.

“What are your plans after this?”

Thorn stared at Oberlin for a moment. The thief was rarely so serious, so Thorn knew that the content of the boxes was a big deal. After a little consideration, Thorn nodded and continued toward the mine.

“I want to wrap up this quest and then head back to Berum. I need to find a place called Greymane Castle, so I was planning on doing some research there. I’ve already gotten a map of this region and it doesn’t look like the castle is nearby.”

“What are the chances you want to help me with something?” Oberlin looked at Thorn.

“I told you, I don’t want to get involved in anything illegal. I’ve had enough of prison.”

“And I’m telling you! It is not illegal. I just need backup when I’m talking to a couple of people.”

“Tell me about it later and we’ll see. For now, I’m going to deal with Supervisor Hobson.” Having arrived at the gate to the mine compound, Thorn strode in. For a brief moment, the gate guard considered stopping him, but that idea was shelved when the guard saw Thorn’s determined face.

“Where is the Supervisor?”

“Uh...Super...Supervisor Hobson is...he is in his off...office.”

“Thanks.” As Thorn walked toward the mine office, his eye caught a flicker of movement in one of the windows. Smiling grimly to himself, Thorn did not bother knocking. Two steps brought him to the desk where he stared down at the cowering supervisor.

“Wha... What do you want?” Supervisor Hobson stammered, his hands clenching his armrests.

“I was sent here to fix a problem and it is time to do exactly that. Your mine is not producing the required amount of Ember Iron ore, I need to know that you plan on fixing that within the next two weeks or I will have to take drastic action.”

“B... but.”

“No buts. There are only two options. First, you increase your production of Ember Iron. Or, second, you inform your superiors that you found an ancient ruin at the bottom of the mine. Those are the two paths you can take. Well, there is a third one where I get involved, but I don’t think you would like how that ends.”

“Huh? How did you know?” Horrified, Supervisor Hobson recoiled further in his seat.

“It doesn’t matter how I know, what matters is what you are

going to do about it?"

"But if I tell anyone, those red-armored players are going to kill me!"

"You don't need to worry about them." Oberlin cut in, sitting on Supervisor Hobson's desk. "A mine supervisor will be the last of their worries. Look, you don't even have to tell your boss that you pulled a bunch of chests out of the ruin."

At Oberlin's words, Hobson's face drained and he slumped down in his chair, defeated.

"Alright, what do you want me to do?"

"Simple, just tell the mine owners that you found the ruin. Chances are they will be way too busy with that to worry about you. In fact, if you play it right, you may be able to keep your position here. Chances are, this will be turned into a dungeon launch point. Who knows, you might even end up running the dungeon."

Listening to Oberlin trying to convince the supervisor, Thorn's brow furrowed. Somehow, this ending did not sit well with him. After a moment of thought, he interrupted the other two, asking, "What happened to Margo Talern?"

"Ah, poor Margo." Supervisor Hobson shook his head. "He was the one who found the ruin. He had discovered it about a week before he died. He sold the information to that guild,

Ragnarok, who dispatched that group to explore the mine. Margo got greedy and tried to extort their leader who killed him off without batting an eye. After that, we could only cooperate. We pulled a bunch of stuff out of the ruin, hiding it under the Ember Iron ore. At night we would load it up into a carriage and the travelers from Ragnarok would take it away."

"You should not have any trouble reporting this to the mine owners." Thorn fixed Supervisor Hobson with an intense gaze. "Now tell me about the chests you loaded last night."

CHAPTER TEN

Supervisor Hobson took Thorn and Oberlin's advice and contacted the owner of the mine to inform them that they had broken into a ruin deep in the mine. At first, Thorn had a bit of interest in seeing what was in the ruin, but he dismissed that idea when he looked at the size of the tunnels. So far, Thorn had been lucky that all the underground spaces he had gone into had been able to accommodate his size.

That was not the case at Embersplit mine. While the entrance was large and Thorn could walk through most of the mine without issue, the tunnels that Margo had discovered were small to the point that even Oberlin had to squeeze through as he explored. Oberlin had gone down with Supervisor Hobson to look at the ruin, and when he came back and told Thorn that it looked like an old dwarven ruin, any motivation Thorn had felt went right out the window.

Within a day the mine owner, who happened to be the local

Count, sent soldiers, workers, and more miners to try and open the path to the ruin. Just as Oberlin predicted, the count had his men build a large number of buildings around the entrance to the mine, changing the signboard to read [Embersplit Ruin]. Annoyed by the constant banging and yelling, Thorn left the mine entrance and walked to the edge of the nearby forest to watch the frantic workers. He had not been sitting for more than two minutes when a young boy ran up to him.

"Sir traveler, the Lieutenant would like to see you." The kid stared at Thorn in undisguised awe.

"Alright," Thorn rose to his feet. "Can you show me the way?"

A makeshift canopy had been slung just inside the gate of the compound to provide shade for a table covered in papers and blueprints. Standing behind it, a harassed-looking military officer was barking orders to the various scribes, soldiers, and workers rushing past. Supervisor Hobson, as nervous as usual, hovered nearby. Seeing Thorn walk up, the Lieutenant threw down the paper in his hand.

"Hello, traveler. The supervisor tells me that you were instrumental in driving off the bandits that came to attack the mine compound. Do you think you could help me identify them? The Count is not pleased with the idea that someone was foolish enough to try and rob him."

“Of course, Lieutenant.”

“Ah, sorry for my breach of manners. My name is Tormand Tyeful, First Lieutenant of the Third Corps. I’ve been assigned from the Imperial Army to help the Count.”

“Thorn.” Taking the offered hand, Thorn shook it as gently as he could. “Identifying the culprits will be simple. They wear a very distinct red leather armor and have the symbol of the guild Ragnarok. Their leader is named Angdrin and his two main henchmen are Korith and Telis.”

“Oh, is that right.” Lieutenant Tyeful seemed to deflate, the aggression bleeding right out of him. “Well, maybe it is not so important after all. Ragnarok is not a group to be taken lightly, and they are not a group that the Count will be interested in pursuing. Anyway, why don’t we put that aside? Do you have any interest in helping us? We are still transporting material in and could use all the manpower available. The job is paid.”

“Sure.”

Two days later Thorn stood outside the gate of the mine compound. Taking a deep breath of the sweet night air, he looked at the notification that had just popped up a few moments ago.

Trouble at the Embersplit Mine: Completed

The miners at the Embersplit mine have been having trouble meeting their monthly production quotas. Figure out what is causing them to fall behind and help them solve it. Successful completion of this quest will result in the termination of your sentence. Failure to complete this quest will result in the extension of your sentence. Title Removed: Criminal

Free of the [Criminal] title, Thorn's abilities were back to one hundred percent and his titles were all active. Happy to be back to normal, Thorn pulled up his status.

Name: [Thorn]	Race: [Titan]
Health: [100%]	Mana: [100%]
Titles: [Battle Mad], [Wolfsbane], [Lord Greymane, the Moon Wolf], [Friend of the Earth]	Conditions: [None]
Abilities: [Wolf Lord's Howl], [Avatar of the Wolf], [Call the Pack], [Blessing of the Moon], [Presence of the Wolf Lord]	

Still classless, Thorn was not in a hurry to get one. His recent fights had shown him that he was proficient enough in combat to at least hold his own. While he was not unbeatable, anyone who wanted a piece of him was going to suffer. Not that he would turn down a good class if it came along, but finding a class was not his priority. After thinking for a moment, Thorn selected his [Lord Greymane, the Moon Wolf] title.

Title: Lord Greymane, the Moon Wolf
Chosen of Hati, the Moon Wolf, you have earned the title of Lord Greymane, rightful ruler of Greymane Keep and the Lord of the Wolfkin. To take the first step in being recognized as the rightful ruler of the Fang Forest, you must take Greymane Keep back from the corrupted wolfkin who inhabit it.

Avatar of Hati, Lord Greymane. While Thorn had not figured out the full significance of these titles he had the feeling that his path in Nova Terra would revolve around them. In order to unlock the combined title, he had to retake Greymane Keep. Which meant, first and foremost, he had to find it.

After getting the map of the region, Thorn had scoured it to try and locate Greymane Keep, but to no luck. In frustration, he had almost called Velin since she always seemed to know something about everything but had stopped since their relationship was tenuous at the moment. Still, he had been leaning toward replying to Mina's message and this would be a good excuse.

One of the main reasons Thorn had hesitated to reply to Mina was the anticipated awkwardness. Truthfully, he did not have any idea what to say. Sighing to himself, Thorn bemoaned his lack of experience with relationships. Thorn had known a good number of people, though most of them were employees of his or his aunt. This left him woefully short of experience dealing with disagreements and conflict, particularly with regular people.

He had read some books on conflict as part of his education, but nothing had prepared him for the emotional and mental turmoil that interpersonal conflict caused. Should he just pretend that nothing had happened? That seemed disingenuous. After all, Mina and Velin had both participated in Ouroboros' plan. In fact, Velin might have even helped plan it.

But what was the point of trying to get back at them? Mina was obviously trying to restore the relationship on some level, so responding angrily would undermine that effort, creating an even bigger rift. Thorn sighed again. Relationships were so complicated. Opening the message, Thorn read through it again before hitting the button to reply.

Staring at the form for a long time, Thorn eventually entered two simple sentences and hit the send button.

Let's meet. I'll be back in Berum in a week.

Rather than worrying about what was going to happen, or what could happen, or what the result would be, Thorn figured he could just take it slow and see where things ended up. He had written off those relationships weeks ago so if they never improved it wouldn't be too much of a bother. Still, there was part of him that longed for a better resolution to the situation.

"It is all so complicated." Thorn mused to himself as he glanced back at the mine where Oberlin had just finished talking to the gate guard.

"So, what now?" Oberlin walked up to Thorn, his hand patting his belt pouch.

"Next thing on my agenda is to head back to Berum. From there I need to find a place called Greymane Keep."

"Huh, I've never heard of it." Oberlin looked around at the quiet forest. Thorn could tell from his fidgeting that the thief had something to ask but did not know how to broach the subject.

"If there is something you need, just spit it out, Oberlin." Thorn's tone was even.

"Look, I know you have turned me down a bunch of times, but I need your help." Oberlin pleaded, clenching his fists and taking a deep breath. "A while ago I fell in with a bad crowd and they will not let me go. You are the only person I know who might be able to do something about them."

"You want me to kill them?"

"What? No, no. Do I look like someone who would ask you to kill people!"

"Yes."

"I mean, if you wanted to, I wouldn't stop you." Seeing Thorn's frown, Oberlin waved his hands and changed the subject. "Look, that isn't what I am asking. I just need someone big and threatening who can help me have a reasonable conversation with them. You fit both the requirements, and most importantly I know you are not going to sell me out."

"Where are they?"

"They have contact points all over the place. The nearest is a small town called Vermin. It is southeast of here."

"Vermin? Like, rats?"

"Yup. It is one of the red towns. Wait, don't tell me you don't know what a red town is?" Oberlin shook his head at Thorn's blank stare. "Sometimes I wonder if you grew up under a rock. Players in old MMOs used to get red names if they killed other players. A red named player could be killed by other players without penalty and it also meant that the guards would attack them on sight. Players with red names either had to wait for a certain amount of time so their name would fade or go to specially designated towns where criminals and player killers were welcome.

"Nova Terra is way more nuanced than that, so it does not use the whole red name thing. But the concept of towns for criminals has carried over. Vermin is, as you can imagine from the name, one of those towns. No matter how bad your record, you can still get services in the town. People buy and sell stolen goods, set up bounties and gangs, and do whatever they want.

"As you can imagine, it is not an environment conducive to one's health. Especially for a thief like me. I'd feel a lot better about going if you came along. Plus, once I am out from under these guys I can come with you and help you with your quest. You know, finding that castle and doing whatever you need."

Oberlin's hopeful face was almost enough to make Thorn agree on the spot, but, taking a deep breath, he suppressed the feeling. The last time he helped with another person's quest it had ended poorly.

"What are you not telling me? There is no way it is as simple as walking in and telling them that you are no longer working for them. If it was, you would have done it already and would not need me." Just as Oberlin was about to rush to explain himself, Thorn held up a hand. "Think this through, you only have one chance to explain."

Lapsing into silence, Oberlin bit one of his fingers. It was becoming obvious to him that Thorn was not as naive as he looked. Thorn did not rush the thief, just watched calmly as he paced back and forth.

“Okay, fine. I’ll spill the whole thing. I signed a contract with a specific secret society to provide intelligence. You know about Avalon, right? Just like them, except secret. I thought I was signing on to give them market prices and other economic information, but over the last year, the focus of the information they are asking me to gather has shifted into more serious stuff. Military intelligence and other things like that. I did not like the way the relationship was headed so I decided to leave. They did not take kindly to my intentions and I’ve been hiding ever since.

“The situation is further complicated by the type of contract I signed. Instead of a paper contract, I had to drip some blood on a statue and now I’m plagued every night with terrible nightmares that sap my willpower. I think they are trying to control me. My quest says that I need to break the statue in order to reclaim my soul. A bit melodramatic, I know, but that’s how quests work. I was in a desperate place when I agreed to join them and if I don’t find a way to break the statue, I’ll never be free. I have a plan for getting the statue away from them, but I don’t have the confidence to do it myself. With you there my chances of success increase quite a bit.”

“You want me to upset a powerful secret society so you can

sleep well at night?" Thorn asked, his gaze heavy.

"No, look. I mean, yes. But it is more than that. You would also be doing a great service for the empire since I am almost positive that the organization comes from the south. The far south."

"Demonkin?"

"Yes. From the research I've done, their methods are the same as the spirit magic that Demonkin use. I don't have direct confirmation of that since my main point of contact is human, but I am 90% sure that the organization is based out of the Southern Continent. Most of the information they were after was pertaining to military matters along the border."

"All the more reason for me to stay out of it, right?"

"No, you don't get it. Your quest is to become the lord of some castle, right? Greymane Keep? That means that as soon as a war starts you'll be dragged in. The situation has been escalating by the day and with the Demonkin side digging for military secrets war is inevitable. One of the requirements of being a lord is supporting the Empire when wars start so there is next to no chance that you will not be part of the conflict. Not only is this a great chance to strike a preemptive blow against your eventual enemies, but you will be helping me out.

"Look, am I willing to help you with your quests once I'm

free, but I'll give you the six chests we took from Ragnarok and help you open them. Each chest is worth a fortune. If that is not enough just tell me and I'll think of a way to make it work."

Watching Oberlin plead with him, Thorn's heart was moved. It was obvious how much the thief valued freedom, a feeling that Thorn understood well. His main motivation for playing Nova Terra was freedom so seeing Oberlin in this situation sparked Thorn's sympathy. Plus, if what Oberlin said was true, it was likely that war was on his horizon. Even Thorn's aunt had mentioned the increased activity near the capital during one of their casual conversations.

"The six chests, opening them, and everything you know about the organization," Thorn stated his terms.

"Are you serious?!" Oberlin looked up, excitement plain on his face. "Of course. Thank you!"

"Let's talk about your plan as we move. The sooner we get there, the sooner we are done.

CHAPTER ELEVEN

A wretched hive of scum and villainy. At least, that is how the forums described the town of Vermin. A decaying slum or cramped, dirty, squatter's camp would be the terms most would use to categorize the sight in front of Thorn. The town was a tangled mess of buildings, linked together with no semblance of order. The lack of unified planning had led to a rotting maze of streets, many simply ending where someone decided to put up a building.

The closer Thorn and Oberlin got to Vermin, the more agitated Oberlin became. Seeing Thorn's concerned look, the thief smiled wanly as they stood on a ridge overlooking the town.

"See that one-story building? The one on the edge of town there?" Oberlin pointed at a small shack on the western side of the town. "That is the entrance to the shrine. For this plan to work, I need to get in there. But there is no way to get past the guards. I need you to create a distraction."

"Your plan is to have me create a ruckus in the middle of town and then you will go in to steal the statue?"

"Pretty much. It is simple, but it should work. You're big enough to create a ruckus and I'm good enough to get in and out."

"That seems a lot like stealing."

"Are you serious? Why are you so worried about this? It is the same as looting a mob!" Oberlin half yelled at Thorn.

"Hey, calm down. It is not like I won't help, I just think your plan is silly." Thorn remained unperturbed in the face of Oberlin's outburst. "First, if I make a scene in the middle of town I'll attract way too many people's attention which is a good way for me to get killed. Plus, what are the chances that the guards in the shrine will leave? Pretty much zero.

"Second, if you could have snuck in, you would have done it already. That tells me that you are not as confident as you are letting on. I'm guessing that is because they have some means of detecting your stealth or determining your location. Chances are, whatever is letting you identify the location of the statue will act as a two-way tether. This means it is almost impossible that they are not expecting you. Making it even less likely that the guards will leave the shrine.

"Third, from what you said, the statue is not going to be easily accessible. Which means your plan is to destroy it on location since you can't steal it away. But doing that will alert the guards, making it hard for you to escape. Yeah, you could just die, but you have not embarked on a suicide mission before this which means there is something keeping you from doing it. Do I need to keep going?"

"No," sighing, and shaking his head, Oberlin shared a quest screen with Thorn.

Master Locksmith: The Pinnacle of the Craft
You have gained mastery of your dual category class, [Master Locksmith]. To take the next step you must complete the impossible, stealing your soul back from the Ordo Serpentes. Having given up your soul for safety at the beginning of your journey to mastery, it is time to take it back. Find the Blood Binding statue that holds your Soul Piece and reclaim it. Dying while this quest is active will result in the quest's failure. Reward: [Infinite Key Master] class upgrade

"You know, you are way smarter than you look. I mean, it isn't like you look stupid per se, but no one expects critical thinking out of someone with the constitution of an elephant. The reason I am so concerned about this is that I cannot die before completing the quest."

"See," Thorn smiled widely, "you should have just started from here. This is a class upgrade quest? Interesting, I've never seen one before. Okay, why don't you start at the beginning?"

"Fine. You might want to sit down." Oberlin crouched, his eyes never leaving the town. "When I first entered the game I thought I would get a clean break from my real life. I had money, nothing drastic, but enough to live comfortably while I played Nova Terra full time. I was hoping for a change of pace, something different. Nut, life had other plans and the first four classes I picked did not work out. I dabbled as a caster for a while and then switched to an agility-based fighter. I even tried being a chef after I realized I was unsuited for combat, and when that was too boring I fell back on my old real-life profession, thi...er...Locksmith.

"I had no desire to ever get into that again. I mean, I started playing Nova Terra to get away from my past. But it is the only thing I know. And I am good at it, really good at it. Good to the point that it took me less than a month to master the class and upgrade to Master Locksmith. I scraped out a living in the capital city opening locks for other players. All legal stuff. You know, chests and dungeons and stuff like that.

"Everything was fine, if a bit boring when one day one of my customers brought in a box for me to open. That was normal, but the box ended up being cursed. To make a long, complicated story short, in order to remove the curse I pledged myself to serve the Ordo Serpentes. That is the group we are about to go up against. I thought they were a group that dealt in intelligence, like the Children of Avalon, but it turned out that they are an offshoot of the Demonkin Empire's intelligence bureau.

"The bit of my soul they extracted was the part that carried the curse, but they soon started giving me outrageous requests, so I have been on the run from them for almost a year now. You were right about the statue though. If we are within a certain distance, the statue can sense my general location, and vice-versa. I am sick and tired of being chased around and even though my combat strength is zero, I have to try this."

"But it is not all bad, right?" Thorn patted the downcast thief on the shoulder lightly. "You have a quest for a triple class upgrade, right? And it is a natural upgrade, so it is even stronger than an
Ancient Inheritance, right?"

"Sure, but I have to live to enjoy it."

"No problem. Come on, let's go." Standing and brushing his pants off, Thorn set off, his large strides carrying him down the hill.

"Wait, what about our plan?" Oberlin scrambled to his feet and ran after him.

"First, we'll go talk to them. Then we'll break the statue. Last, we'll leave. I've got to get to Berum to meet someone and then find this castle."

"Are you crazy? We are just walking right in? Does that even work? Don't I have to sneak in for the quest?"

"Why would you have to sneak in?"

"The quest says I have to steal my soul back."

"There are lots of ways to steal stuff." Thorn stopped and looked at Oberlin squarely. "Every lock has a key, and all the keys are different. You wouldn't try and open every lock with the same approach, why would you assume that your quest has one approach? Genghis Khan stole lots of stuff and he never snuck anywhere."

"So we're going to burn the place to the ground after murdering everyone in the town?"

"Okay, so it was a bad comparison." Thorn rolled his eyes and continued walking. "My point is that you are too caught up in your identity as a thief. I'm assuming that has something to do with your past, but you do not have to live your life that way. Just because you did that in the past, doesn't mean you have to do that now. Right now, at this moment, you are a locksmith, a great locksmith. And it just so happens that you found the right key for this situation.

Me."

Stunned, Oberlin could only stare at Thorn's back as he walked confidently into town.

Vermin was occupied by players and natives that lived on the wrong side of the law. Murder and theft were common here and the law of the jungle was in full effect. When Thorn and Oberlin first appeared on the edge of town many eyes glanced toward them. After all, fresh meat was rare in Vermin.

Yet, those same eyes went back to their own business after seeing Thorn's size and large weapon. Most of the players here made their living preying on their fellow man, but as cruel as they were, few of them were stupid. Thorn's confident stride, his shining armor, the large tetsubo resting on his shoulder, and the glinting claws on his fingers all combined with his excessive height to intimidate the fight right out of the townsfolk.

Parting like water in front of him, the crowds hurried to the side, allowing Thorn to walk through the maze of streets to the building that Oberlin had pointed out. While it did not look like much on the surface, Oberlin had explained that it was only the entrance to an underground temple compound. Seeing no guards, Thorn pushed open the door and ducked inside.

The whole building was a single room, empty except for a

small shrine and a priest in a shimmering green scaled robe who was meditating to the side, his eyes closed. Thorn looked at Oberlin who stepped into the building behind him.

“Entrance is under the shrine,” Oberlin whispered. “If we are negotiating, we need to talk to the High Priest.”

“Excuse me. I’d like to talk to the High Priest.” Thorn walked up to the priest and looked down at him.

“The High Priest doesn’t see...Uh...okay.” Halfway through his refusal, the priest opened his eyes and immediately thought better of it. “Let me ask if he is available.”

“Thanks.” Thorn smiled, turning to Oberlin. “See, sometimes you just need to ask.”

“And be twice their height.”

“Sure, that can help.”

“Um, sir? The High Priest will see you. Please wait while I open the passage. You’ll want to head down the hall and take your first right.” The priest was very respectful as he pushed a button and the altar slid to the side, revealing a large passage down into the earth.

“Thank you. Come on, Oberlin.” Thorn began walking down the passage, pulling Oberlin along with him.

"Are you sure about this, Thorn? This seems like a really bad idea."

"Relax, it will be fine. All we are doing is asking for a bit of your soul back."

The passage they traveled down was smooth, reminding Thorn of the skin of a snake. After winding through the earth for a while a passage opened on the right. Thorn and Oberlin turned and found themselves facing a large door. Without a sound the door slid open, hiding in the wall.

Past the door was a vast hall lit by flickering candlelight. At one end there was a large altar, covered in small statues of a half human, half snake Naga. Each statue held a flickering pearl in outstretched hands. To the left and right were larger statues of snake people, armed with a variety of weapons, creating a sinister atmosphere. A robed figure stood in the center of the hall, leaning on a cane with a snakehead.

"Come in. I've been expecting you." The robed figure had a bizarre voice, it's cold tones seeming to slither uncomfortably around the room. "No doubt you are here in a futile attempt to reclaim yourself."

ding

Curious, Thorn opened the notification he had just received, a wide grin stretching across his face as he read it.

Hati's Honor
You have found yourself in a Temple of Salliish, the Shadow Serpent. Disgusted by the snake's sly sliminess, Hati has commanded that you, the Avatar of the Moon Wolf, show the serpent who is boss by destroying the temple. Destroy all the statues of Salliish and the main altar. This quest is your first [Avatar Challenge]. As you adventure around Nova Terra, it is your responsibility as the Avatar of Hati to represent Hati in challenging other Avatars to contests of strength and feats of valor. And occasionally, petty acts of vandalism. A challenge will be generated when you come within a certain distance of another Avatar. For a challenge to be recognized as legitimate, it must be openly announced to the Avatars involved. Reward: Increase Hati's Favor Failure: Decrease Hati's Favor

Agitated at being ignored, the robed figure stepped forward aggressively, lifting its staff.

"Whoa, hold up." Thorn raised a hand to stop the High Priest as he dismissed the notification. Stepping forward, he came to a stop in front of the robed figure, unaffected by the creepiness of the room. "Why don't we drop the good guy, bad guy act and talk this through? I'm sure we can come to some sort of agreement. My name is Thorn and I will be representing Oberlin. Our goal today is to retrieve the statue that contains a piece of his soul. How should I address you?"

The High Priest froze for a second. After a moment had passed, the hood flipped down with a deep sigh, revealing long chestnut hair and a stunning face.

"My name is Josephine, High Priestess of the Ordo Serpentes. Please have a seat." With a brilliant smile, she gestured to the side where a couple of carved stone seats were placed along the wall.

"Thank you, but I don't think that would go well for your chairs," Thorn smirked. Following Josephine over to the seats, Thorn squatted down as Oberlin took a seat.

"Now, you said that you want to negotiate for a soul piece? What makes you so confident that we will consider your offer?" Crossing one shapely leg over the other, Josephine propped her chin in her palm and stared at Thorn.

"Otherwise you would not have met us without a guard." Thorn's advanced sense of smell had failed to pick up any other people in the room when he walked in.

"Hah. I don't know if it is a pleasure to talk to an intelligent person or if it is annoying. Since we are being straight-forward, why don't you lay your cards on the table? What can you offer for the statue?"

“Honestly, I’m not sure. I haven’t really thought that far ahead.”

“You are trying to tell me you walked in here expecting us to just give you the statue? Don’t insult me.”

CHAPTER TWELVE

The sinister air of the Temple grew heavier as Josephine's words echoed around the room. Her voice took on the slithering quality that it had when they first walked in. The flickering torchlight seemed to splutter and dim as the deep pools of inky black shadow deepened. Shivering, Oberlin shrank back in his seat, throwing a frightened glance at Thorn who still looked calm.

This was not what he had in mind when he had recruited Thorn for the quest and he was becoming worried that the situation was getting out of control. About to try and mediate, he had barely gotten his mouth open when Thorn spoke again.

"Not only do I expect you to give me the statue, I'm pretty sure you'll give it to me for free." Without standing, Thorn reached out his hand to one of the stone chairs and squeezed the armrest.

BANG

Under his incredible strength, the armrest exploded into a cloud of dust, startling Oberlin. Josephine's eyes widened in surprise momentarily, but her expression was back to normal so fast Thorn almost missed it.

"Ah, you are threatening me." The Head Priestess stated, no change in her tone.

"Think of it less as a threat, and more as encouragement. A fight wouldn't be in either of our interests. What would be better is if you just gave Oberlin here his cursed soul back. He has done some work for you, you've hunted him up and down the region, seems fair to call everything square and let it go at that."

"Surely you have more than that. There is no way you would walk in here without something else to rely on." Josephine uncrossed her legs and stood, looking down at Thorn. Or rather, she tried to. It was difficult to look down on someone who, crouching, was at eye level.

"You were not joking about being straightforward, were you? Do you really want me to lay everything out? Okay." Thorn rose to his feet, stretching out to his full 8' 9" height and gazing down on the robed High Priestess. "The truth is, I have a quest to crush your altar and all the statues."

"Ah ha, the truth comes out. I thought I felt a familiar aura on you." A wide smile spread across Josephine's pretty face as she backed up to get out of Thorn's reach.

"Can someone please explain what is going on?" Oberlin complained. When the other two ignored him he sighed and got up as well, moving to the side of the room. The air grew thicker as Thorn and Josephine confronted each other. Without warning both turned and walked out to the middle of the large hall, as if they were of one mind. Summoning his tetsubo, Thorn planted the end in front of him.

"Why don't we start this over," Josephine spoke calmly, lifting her snakehead cane.

"I am Thorn, Avatar of Hati, the Moon Wolf."

"Greetings Thorn." Josephine gave a slight bow, her left hand on her chest and her cane held up. "I am Josephine, Avatar of Salliish, the Shadow Serpent. Is this your first time participating in an Avatar challenge?"

"Yes." Thorn was frank. "Would you mind explaining how this is supposed to work? I get the feeling that killing you is not the point."

"That is correct," Josephine eyed Thorn's massive figure. "Thankfully this is not a duel to the death. While some Avatars do go that far, an Avatar challenge is more of a duel for supremacy. Contrary to the commonly held understanding, the gods never left, instead of hiding for reasons unknown. Yet they never stopped their grand game. Ever since the first era, Avatars have continued to seek each other out to compete against each other.

“Challenges can come in all shapes and sizes; the only constant is that they are triggered when two or more avatars find themselves near each other. Avatars must state their challenge to activate it and will be penalized or rewarded with the favor of their sponsoring deity based on if they fail or succeed. You can think of favor like a currency that unlocks reward tiers from the deity. When you walked in I was notified that you were an Avatar and that I was to challenge you to a contest of strength. Since you are here for your friend’s soul, why don’t we make this simple? If you can beat me, you get his soul. On the other hand, if I win you have to do something for me.”

Thorn shook his head, “I don’t agree to unspecified favors.”

“Then what do you suggest?”

“Since we are dealing in souls, why not keep the currency consistent? If I win you let him go. If you win, you let him go but I’ll join your organization.”

“What!? No way!” Oberlin shouted from the side.

“Now that is a deal I like the sound of,” Josephine spoke at the same time as Oberlin, as if afraid that Thorn would take back his words. "You for him. The battle will go until someone admits defeat. What I mean to say is, make sure you give up before you die!" As her last word rang out Josephine lifted her cane and thrust it forward.

With lightning speed the cane stretched out, the snake head on the end growing larger and coming to life. Thorn had been watching closely so he was able to get his weapon up in time to deflect the thrust. Still, the snap of the snake head's mouth next to his shoulder made him sweat.

Seeing her attack fail, Josephine jumped backward and raised her hands high overhead, a purple glow gathering in the mouth of the serpent head. Loud chants began to roll out of her mouth as the purple light grew stronger and stronger, bathing the room in strange slithering shadows.

Tightening his grip on the handle of his weapon, Thorn was about to charge forward when warning bells started going off in his head. Shifting his momentum, Thorn threw himself to the side, dodging just as the tail of a giant snake landed where he stood moments before. The marble floor cracked under the impact of the blow, chips of stone flying through the air.

Focusing on this new enemy, Thorn faced the massive snake. Almost fifty feet long, the snake was as thick as a barrel, with jagged black and purple scales running along its sides. Wicked fangs were visible as it hissed toward Thorn, its cold, yellow eyes staring unblinkingly at him. As the purple light fell on the snake's skin it seemed to fade in and out of existence, melding with the dark shadows.

Josephine stayed still, her hands raised, continuing her chant. Seeing how the snake seemed to fade out as it left Josephine's purple light, Thorn narrowed his eyes. As if feeling Thorn's glance at Josephine, the giant serpent shifted to put itself between them, defending Josephine from a possible attack, further reinforcing Thorn's assumption.

"Let's test the theory." Thorn thought and stepped forward.

Lashing out with his tetsubo, Thorn aimed for the snake's side with a light probing strike.

tink

The hardened purple scales deflected the blows with ease. Thorn, borrowing the momentum swung his weapon again. And again, the blow was deflected. Unswayed, Thorn continued to lash out with increasing speed. Unable to react to the speed of the strikes, the giant snake stayed curled up, weathering the storm of blows.

In between the tiny gaps in the coils, Thorn could see the snake's eyes watching for the slightest break in his rhythm. Its attention was fixed on Thorn. Just as Thorn and the snake locked eyes, its head shot out from between its coils, forcing Thorn to abandon his latest attack and block in front of his chest.

With a crash the serpent rammed into Thorn, sending him flying backward into one of the Naga statues. Coughing, Thorn scrambled to his feet. As he did the snake struck again, this time biting at Thorn and forcing him to tumble out of the way. Missing by less than an inch, the snake did not pursue Thorn, instead of withdrawing back into the protection of its coils.

Staggering up, Thorn wove on his feet as he got his bearings. The snake was still in between him and Josephine who was watching the fight with much glee, her staff still shedding purple light on the fight.

"Haha, how do you like my pet? She is pretty strong, isn't she?" Josephine gloated.

"Eh, not too bad." Rolling his shoulders Thorn did not seem overly impressed. "Let's start round two." Charging forward, Thorn once again threw out a storm of attacks. His weapon blurred, raining down blow after blow on the scaly skin of the giant snake to little effect.

To the side, Oberlin stared at Thorn, a huge frown on his face. He had never intended for Thorn to get so enmeshed in his issue and he felt terrible that Thorn was fighting on his behalf. As he continued to watch his breath caught. Once again, Thorn had been sent flying into the wall, this time bringing down a bow-wielding Naga statue.

Yet, as this cycle continued, Oberlin's frown turned to confusion. Repeatedly Thorn was struck, tumbling through the air to smash into the wall, destroying the room spectacularly. However, what was strange was that Thorn always seemed to hit a new statue each time he went flying. Soon, it wasn't only Oberlin that was confused.

Josephine seemed to have caught on that something was wrong. Thorn was flying around like a human bowling ball, smashing into everything. Yet each time he hit the wall he bounced back up, no worse for wear. His attacks were as persistent and quick as if he was using up no energy. Growing frustrated, Josephine bit her bottom lip before shouting a command to the giant snake. Uncoiling, the snake slithered back, wrapping itself around her.

"What are you playing at? I can't believe an Avatar would be so weak. Especial44 an Avatar of the god of night. You should know that failing a challenge brings serious penalties." Josephine warned Thorn.

"But I'm not failing. I only have the altar left." Thorn pointed at the altar behind Josephine.

"What?" Looking around, realization mixed with a sense of horror dawned on Josephine's face. "You tricked me."

"I told you I had a quest to crush your altar and all the statues." Thorn smiled. "According to the rules you listed, an Avatar must state their quest and give their opponent a fair chance to prevent them from achieving it. I did that. I told you that I had to smash the altar and all the statues."

"And I assumed you were talking about the statues on the altar. Very tricky." The High Priestess narrowed her eyes as she glared at Thorn. "Well, I'm afraid you'll pay for that." Whispering an arcane word, the purple orb in the mouth of her cane flashed, forcing Thorn to squint. When the light cleared, the giant snake was gone. Instead, Josephine rose in the air, her body growing larger, a snake tail replacing her body from the waist down like the Naga statues.

"No one can trick me and get away with it! The glory of Salliish, the Shadow Serpent cannot be maligned!" As she grew, her robe fell away, revealing a tight-fitting armor that grew with her. Jagged claws grew from her fingers and her hair began to wave as if it was alive. Her eyes pulsed with purple light and she roared, shaking the room. Flecks of stone and little bits of dust and dirt fell from the ceiling.

Her eyes fixed on Thorn, Josephine shot forward, her snake tail sending her sliding around the floor as she advanced. Her unpredictable movement made her hard to pin down, but Thorn was not worried. To Oberlin's surprise, Thorn even put away his tetsubo and stepped back heavily, his feet hitting the stone floor so hard they left cracks in it. Spreading his hands Thorn dropped into a martial arts stance, a wide grin spreading across his face.

"Haha, I'm finally facing something I can use my training on!"

Thorn thought to himself. Every single fight he had participated in to this point was with people or creatures much smaller than him. Josephine's Naga form was much more his size. In fact, with her tail extended she was taller than he was. Plus, her upper body had grown larger to account for the tail so she was the perfect target for Thorn's Taijiquan.

With a piercing scream, Josephine lunged forward, her large claws outstretched. Rather than bracing himself, Thorn stepped forward, his front foot sliding across the floor smoothly as his hands came up to intercept the attack. With a twist of his torso, he deflected the attacking Naga, tossing her to the side.

Furious, she tried to knock Thorn back with her large tail, only for Thorn to accept the blow head on. Her tail hit Thorn's large figure and bounced off, unable to move him in the slightest. With a screech of pain, Josephine slid backward, out of Thorn's reach.

"What did you do?" Her pretty eyes were aflame with anger as Josephine glared at Thorn.

"What do you mean? I'm not sure I am following."

"Why can't I knock you back? My summoned serpent could throw you all over the place!"

"Oh, that. Yeah, I'm not jumping anymore." Thorn shrugged.

"I'm pretty heavy, so I am not easy to move. However, I've noticed that the game compensates for my weight when I jump, otherwise I'd never be able to get off the ground. So long as I intend to jump right before something hits me I'll move. But I don't have any more statues to smash so there isn't a reason to let you toss me around."

"This is stupid! How am I supposed to beat you in a contest of strength! You're as dense as a mountain!"

"So are we done?"

"In your dreams!" Chanting, a purple mist gathered in Josephine's hands, quickly solidifying into a bow. Hissing, she drew back the string and a purple arrow with a two-pronged arrowhead appeared, aimed at Thorn. "Die," she hissed, releasing the arrow straight at Thorn's heart.

For a brief second, Thorn considered trying to block the arrow, but seeing how fast it was coming in, he gave up that thought and dove to the side. Too fast to completely dodge, the arrow cut into Thorn's side, punching its way straight through his armor and ripping a gash along his ribs.

Grunting in pain, Thorn dashed behind a pillar, barely dodging the second arrow. Feeling the burning of the wound, Thorn looked down to see the edges of the cut slowly taking on a purple hue. Poison. He needed to end this fight fast.

CHAPTER THIRTEEN

Darkness dominated the edges of the room, allowing even Thorn to hide. Torchlight cast long shadows against the walls of the underground temple. The stone floor was cold to the touch, and the pillar at his back was hard. Despite the chill, Thorn was happy to have solid stone between him and Josephine's poison arrows.

The arrows themselves were not that dangerous. Thorn's massive body was much too dense for that. Despite their sting, they did very little damage to him. The purple poison coating her arrows was a different matter. Thorn could feel the poison numbing him and slowly draining his health. He did not know if it would fade over time or if his health would continue to drain until he died, and he was not about to risk his life experimenting with them.

About to peek out from behind the pillar, instinct made him jerk his head back in time to avoid another arrow. That same instinct prompted him to dive away from the pillar as Josephine's massive snake tail smashed through it, showering him with fragments of stone.

Scrambling behind another pillar, arrows clipping at his heels, Thorn thought frantically. "I need to close the distance, but those poison arrows are no joke."

"Ha, not so tough now, are you?" Near the altar, Josephine's Naga form swayed from side to side as she released arrows at Thorn's hiding place. "That's right. Keep hiding! Like that craven god of yours!"

At Josephine's words, something in Thorn's chest began to burn, sending hot adrenaline straight up into his brain. Without thinking about the consequences, Thorn grabbed a large chunk of stone from one of the pillars that Josephine had smashed and stepped out from behind his cover. His eyes burning, Thorn glared at the Naga, his teeth clenched in visible rage.

ding

Wolf's Rage Unlocked
A wise wolf chooses when to fight and when to run. But when they choose to fight, they do so with unmatched fury. Due to meeting the conditions for [Wolf's Rage] in advance, you have unlocked the ability out of order. Unlocking the [Wolf Hide] ability will require increased

favor from Hati.

[Wolf's Rage] may now be used three times a day to grant increased Stamina, Strength, and Speed for 1 minute per [Avatar of the Wolf] ability unlocked. While in this state, the player will have a strong desire to confront problems aggressively, even if it would be to their detriment.

Dismissing the notification without reading it, Thorn's gaze was fixed on Salliish's Avatar. Gone was the gentle, unassuming aura that Thorn normally projected. Under the effect of [Wolf's Rage], Thorn resembled a smoking volcano more than a peaceful mountain. His tightened muscles seemed to stretch his chainmail to the edge of breaking as if it were containing a monstrous pressure waiting to rip free.

Something about the titan's gaze pierced into Josephine's soul, unnerving her. Sneering to hide her discomfort, she pointed an arrow directly at his heart.

"You think you are the only one with powerful abilities? My poison won't take long to bring you down. Why don't you give up this pointless fight? Salliish crushed Hati in the past and no matter how you struggle you cannot escape the coils of the god of Shadow."

"Coil around this." Taking a sudden step forward, Thorn wound up and threw the large chunk of the pillar that he had picked up with as much force as he could muster. With a tremendous ripping sound, the stone cut through the air toward Josephine. Horrified by the force and speed of the rock, Josephine froze, forgetting to release the arrow she was pointing at Thorn.

Blurring through the air the stone passed Josephine's head, the force of the air ripping out a few strands of her waving hair as it went. Cursing his lack of practice throwing things, Thorn stormed forward, protecting his head with one arm while getting ready to smash out with his tetsubo.

It took Josephine half a second to snap out of her shock and when she did, Thorn had already crossed half of the distance toward her. With a hiss of fury, she slid back on her giant snake tail, shooting a poisoned arrow at the advancing titan. Not even bothering to dodge, Thorn took the shot directly in his chest. Feeling the sting as the arrow sunk into his chest, Thorn ignored it and continued pushing forward, focusing on getting into melee range.

Continuing to kite backward, Josephine was able to release one more arrow before her back hit a pillar. In her haste, the arrow cut past Thorn's shoulder, disappearing into the darkness behind him. Seeing that Thorn was only a few steps away, she turned and curled her body around the pillar, slithering up it as she readied another arrow. Undeterred by her escape, Thorn drew back his tetsubo and, with a tremendous bellow, smashed at the pillar.

BOOM

Massive chunks of stone rained down, pelting the floor and walls as the pillar exploded. With a terrified shriek, Josephine lost her grip, falling to the rubble-littered floor. Having lost her concentration, the bow she had summoned disintegrated into a purple mist. Reaching through the scattering mist, Thorn grabbed Josephine and lifted her into the air.

“Concede, or I’ll crush you,” Thorn growled through clenched teeth.

“Hah,” regaining some of her wits, Josephine wrapped her giant tail around Thorn, squeezing for all she was worth.

His eyes narrowing, Thorn stood unmoving as the coils tried in vain to crush him. The fury in his chest built and it was all Thorn could do to not smash Josephine into the floor. Controlling himself with effort, he wrapped a large hand around her tail and pulled, separating himself from her coils.

“Enough, let's be done with this, or so help me I will end it.”

For a moment, Josephine was silent. Then she sighed and her body shrank, separating from the giant snake who faded into the shadows.

“Yes, we are done. I concede.”

ding

Altar Smashing
You have successfully beaten the Avatar of Salliish, the Shadow Serpent in their own temple, Hati is pleased. It is about time someone put that slimy snake in their place. Reward: Hati's Favor

Looking at the quest popup, Thorn confirmed that his quest had completed. His rage still had not faded but, keeping it tightly under control he put Josephine down.

"Do you have an antidote for this poison?"

"Yes." Sullenly she pulled a vial out of her inventory and handed it to him.

"Thank you." Gulping down the antidote, Thorn felt the burning sensation fade from his wounds. Josephine stared, completely dumbfounded as he, without flinching, pulled the two arrows that were stuck in his chest out, ignoring the spurt of blood that accompanied each one.

The red-hot fury in his chest was starting to fade, leaving behind an empty, tired feeling. Looking around at the utter ruin around him, Thorn could not help but wince. He had always been a careful, controlled person who tried his best not to break or hurt anything but that restraint had steadily evaporated after coming into Nova Terra. He was not the only one looking around the room in dismay.

"You are like a human wrecking ball!" The Avatar of Salliish was ready to pull her hair out over the state of the underground temple. Rubble from the broken statues and demolished pillars littered the room, and only a few torches had survived the frenzied struggle.

With a smile, Thorn turned to Oberlin who was still cautiously waiting to the side and gestured him over.

"You can go ahead and get your statue."

"Uh, that's okay. I might stay over here." Oberlin shook his head while he nervously patted his belt pouch, not wanting to get anywhere near Josephine who had resumed her High Priestess look, cloak and all.

"No problem. I can get it for you." Thorn looked back at the altar. "Which one is it?"

"I think it is one of the ones on the front corner."

"You mean one of these?" Thorn walked forward toward the altar while pointing.

"Wait for a second, would you consider taking a different prize?" Josephine stepped in front of Thorn, blocking him from the table.

"What are you trying to do?" Thorn's eyes narrowed.

"I can provide you with all manner of things that are better than a silly statue. After all, the statue is of no use to you. It is only useful to the cowardly thief over there. Salliish has informed me that he thinks highly of you and is willing to give you magic items or wealth, even a high position in our organization if you are willing to give up on the statue."

"The Order of Snakes, or something, right?"

"Ordo Serpentes."

"Right, that. I wouldn't have to pledge myself to Salliish would I?"

"No, serving Salliish is not required. Though, the Shadow Serpent is a gracious Lord and would bless you greatly if you wished to submit to him."

"Nah, not interested." Thorn waved his hand dismissively.

"Don't be so quick to turn me down, Thorn. Even if you do not want to serve Salliish, there is room for you in the Ordo Serpentes. The benefits are fantastic and the pay is generous. Especially for someone with talents like yours."

"Isn't the whole point of the Snake Order to sneak around? You know, shadows and stuff?"

“It’s the Ordo Serpentes!” Struggling to put a lid on her temper, Josephine’s eyes narrowed. “The Ordo Serpentes does have a covert operations branch, but that is only a small part of the organization. While we have an intelligence organization that rivals even that of Avalon, our force can be compared to the largest of guilds.”

“Hmm. Then why haven’t I heard about you before?”

“For one, most of our forces are focused in the southern continent. While we gather intelligence in the north, we are short staffed among the human lands. If you were willing to join us, it is possible that you could grow to control an entire army here in the northern continent. Imagine, a full army of players who would jump to obey your every word!”

“Players?” Thorn’s eyebrows rose in surprise. “The Ordo Serpentes is a player organization?”

“Like most of the larger organizations in the game, it is mixed. We have countless natives that support us, but players make up the majority of the foot soldiers in the Ordo Serpentes.”

“This all sounds interesting but too restrictive. Plus, I don’t think Hati likes your god so much.”

“Please, what does that matter? They don’t have to like each other for us to work together.” Josephine rolled her eyes.

"What is important is what you can get out of it."

"So far, you have not told me what I can get out of joining you. And don't give me that talk about becoming a leader in the north. There is no way that you would hand me an army."

"As I said earlier, it is nice talking to intelligent people," Josephine giggled. "Of course, like any title or class, you would have to work for authority. But the Ordo Serpentes does have several classes and titles available. There are even triple category classes that you can trade merit for. In the shorter term, you would gain access to the information network, supply points all over the northern and southern continent, access to specially crafted gear, and much more."

"And what would I have to do for all of these things?"

"You would be assigned a quest every two months. The rest of your time is yours to do what you want. The only exception is that if a war were to break out, you would have to participate. Oh, did I mention that you would get paid?"

"You pay?"

"Of course. It is a standard non-disclosure, employment contract. You would be hired as a professional player and we provide a generous compensation package based on your level in the organization. With your raw power, it would not surprise me if you were making six figures soon."

"That is a very kind offer, but I think I'm good. I'll take the statue now." Thorn shook his head.

"You really are dense. The statue is useless. Why not take the..."

In the middle of Josephine's question, Thorn's eyes flickered and without waiting for her to finish he took a large step forward, a large hand shooting out and pushing her to the side. With a short scream, the High Priestess flew, tumbling to the ground when she landed. Two large steps brought Thorn to the altar where he saw some of the statutes had lost their glow. More and more of the glowing orbs held by the statues were fading out by the second, leaving dim, lifeless orbs behind.

Gritting his teeth, Thorn pulled his tetsubo and swung hard, smashing straight through the still glowing statues. The blow smashed the statues into pieces, sending shards of stone pinging off the walls. As each statue broke, the glowing orb in its hand dissipated, a sigh rising into the air.

The first blow cleared three-quarters of the table and the reverse swing cleared the rest. Many of the statues along the edge of the table had already gone dark when Thorn attacked, the orbs shattering along with the statues. The statue that Oberlin had pointed out fractured and broke, the pieces scattering across the floor. Furious, Thorn turned to glare at Josephine who was staggering to her feet, white-faced. The now broken statues lay scattered across the floor.

“That was not part of the deal.” Her voice trembling, Josephine faced Thorn.

“Neither was whatever you were doing,” Thorn growled. “Pulling the souls out of the statues before we retrieve the one we want is not playing fair.”

“I’m sorry, I don’t have any control over what Salliish does.” Josephine couldn’t help but take a step back under Thorn’s glare.

“But you do have control over what you do.” Thorn’s anger burned hot in his chest and he forcefully restrained it. “The things I hate most are people lying to me or trying to trick me.”

Furious, Thorn turned back to glare at the altar. Reliefs along its sides showed a giant serpent that seemed to be moving in the flickering light. The shadows danced, growing larger and larger. Behind Thorn, Josephine gasped.

With a whoosh the few flickering torches flared brighter, the rising flames causing the shadows in the room to jump. Streaming together, the shadows intertwined, forming dark, twisted cords, meeting over the altar. As Thorn looked he could see glittering scales forming as the pillar of shadows grew.

"Um, Thorn, something is happening, and I don't think it's good." Oberlin pointed nervously at the shadows gathering on top of the altar.

CHAPTER FOURTEEN

Grim-faced, Thorn watched the growing shadows as they solidified into the form of a massive snake. Even larger than the snake that Josephine had summoned, this snake was black as night, it's dark scales seeming to absorb the last remaining light in the room.

[FOOLISH MORTAL] boomed a voice, seeming to come from nowhere and everywhere. [CROSSING ME WAS THE WORS…].

BANG

The voice cut off abruptly as Thorn stepped forward and slammed a fist into the altar, sending a massive vibration through the room. With a tremendous cracking sound the altar split straight down the middle and the materializing snake rippled before shattering into shards of shadow. Josephine froze, shock painted on her features. She watched in growing horror as Thorn kicked one of the halves of the altar away, grabbing the other and hoisting it over his head with a grunt. She flinched as Thorn smashed it into the ground, sending shards of black stone flying across the floor.

As the echo reverberated around the chamber, Thorn stood for a moment, his breathing growing calmer. After a moment he turned, all signs of anger gone from his face. Ignoring Josephine, Thorn looked toward the side of the room where a figure detached itself from the shadows and gave him a grin, patting the belt pouch at its waist.

“Big enough distraction for you?” Thorn asked Oberlin while brushing shards of black stone from his greaves.

“Yes, sir.” Oberlin’s grin widened. “I don’t think I’ve ever seen a better one. Seriously though, how freakishly strong are you? Those snakes were huge!"

Thorn ignored the question, turning to look at Josephine, who was still in shock. He gave her a slight bow.

“It was very nice to meet you, Josephine. Thank you for explaining how the Avatar challenges work and for entertaining us all this time. We must get going now. Sorry, we can’t help to clean up, but I’m sure we’ll run across each other again.”

“Yeah, I’m sure we will,” Josephine said, her bright eyes fixed on Thorn.

Uncomfortable being stared at like that, Thorn waved to Oberlin and they left the underground temple. As they made their way up to the surface, Thorn heard a notification.

Friend Request: Josephine - High Shadow Priestess - Avatar of Salliish	
Accept	Reject

Taken aback, Thorn hesitated for a moment before he hit the accept button. At his side, Oberlin chatted away, obviously in a good mood. Pushing the door to the outside open, the thief froze. Standing in front of the building was a half circle of rough looking players, all staring at the door. Thorn, seeing Oberlin stop, frowned and moved him aside, stepping past him to face the other players.

“Excuse me, do you mind moving? We are headed out of town.”

“Oh, are you?” At Thorn’s words, a tough looking human with a scar running across his lips stepped forward. “You haven’t paid the tax though. You can’t come into our town and not pay the tax.”

“Tax? For coming into town? Are you serious?”

“Do I look like I am joking?” Despite facing Thorn’s imposing bulk, the scarred man spat on the ground in front of his feet.

"It doesn't matter how big you are if you don't want to die, you better pay up."

"And how much is the tax?"

"Haha, that is a better attitude," growled the scarred man. "Five gold for the thief, ten gold for you since you are oversized."

"And if I don't pay?"

"Then you can enjoy some time in Fantasia. And when you come back, we can have this conversation again."

Feeling a tug on his arm, Thorn looked down at Oberlin.

"We'll respawn here since this is the last town we've visited."

"Oh," realization dawned on Thorn's face. "So if we don't pay the tax they'll kill us and then keep killing us when we respawn."

"Yup. That is why most people don't visit red towns." Oberlin nodded, not seeming worried.

"Huh, I can see why."

Annoyed that he was being ignored, the scarred thug stepped forward. Unfortunately, that brought him closer to Thorn, making the difference in their size more pronounced.

He quickly took a step back.

“Fork over the gold or face the consequences!”

“Oberlin, you said that there are no town guards?”

“No, there are guards, but they don’t really come out. And if they do, it's only to extort people. They are always absent when a player breaks a rule that would get them locked up in another town. But the benefit is that they will not stop you so long as you don’t mess with the native in charge of the town.”

“Good.” His voice turning flat, Thorn’s eyes locked onto the scarred thug. Stepping forward, his hand shot out like lightning, swatting away a vain attempt to block and grabbing him firmly by his chest armor. Lifting the thug, whose face had paled, Thorn turned and launched him with all his strength.

BOOOM

A nearby building, unable to withstand the force of a human smashing through its walls, collapsed in a storm of splinters and plaster.

The rest of the thugs, who were in the middle of drawing their weapons, paused. As one, their eyes fixed on the now collapsed building that Thorn had thrown their leader through. They looked at Thorn, then at the building, then back at Thorn. With a clang, they put their weapons back in their sheaths and turned to walk away.

“Hey,” Thorn had barely gotten a single word out when the bandits broke into a mad dash, disappearing before he could get his second word out. “Aren’t… Okay, I guess not.” Thorn looked at Oberlin who shrugged. Shaking his head, Thorn walked out of Vermin.

“You know, Thorn, you could make a pretty awesome warlord,” Oberlin announced as they walked.

“Sorry, not interested.” Thorn shook his head, changing the subject. “Did you get your soul back?”

“Yes, thanks to you keeping the High Priestess busy.” Oberlin pulled a glowing orb out of his inventory.

“Wow. I have to say, that is impressive. I did not see you take it and I was staring at the table pretty much the whole time.”

“There is a reason my class has ‘Master’ attached.”

“Did you get your new class?”

“Yup, [Infinite Key Master]. Makes me even better at opening locks. There are a couple of other bonuses, but it is pretty focused on getting into things that other people want to keep you out of.”

"Well, I know who to call if I lose my keys. Does this make you the only person in the game to have mastered a dual category class?"

"Possibly." Oberlin was not as excited as Thorn imagined. "It is pretty much impossible to know. There are a lot of players that don't talk about their game time. Unless you are getting the information from Eve herself, I would take everything you hear with a grain of salt. For example, I have no idea what that business about avatars was about. I thought all the gods fell to the dragons. Everyone has their own secrets."

"What are your plans now that you have gotten your soul back? You're free to go anywhere now, right?"

"Helping you of course. I only got the orb back because you helped me. There is no way I would have managed to sneak it out otherwise. For now, you're stuck with me." Oberlin grinned, looking happier than he ever had. "I am still working on the chests, it seems like the locks require specific quest items to open. As soon as I figure out what we need to find I'll let you know. Until then, I am going to walk around behind you since you make about the best shield there is. You threw that guy through a building. Isn't that cheating or something?"

Continuing to chat, they made their way toward Berum. Nova Terra had no fast travel system so Thorn expected it to take more than a day to make the trek. If he had been by himself he could have run, shortening the time it would take, but Oberlin lacked Thorn's stamina so he set the pace.

As they camped that night, Thorn spent some time looking through his messages, replying to his aunt and a note sent by his *sifu*. Mina had gotten back to him as well, setting up a time and place to meet, her excitement and nervousness obvious by the tangled tone of the message. Thorn was still not sure what he was going to do when he met with Mina and Velin, but he felt that he should at least try to restore the relationship.

As he stared up at the stars Thorn knew that they were fake and yet, he could not help marvel at their grandeur. There was a feeling of freedom in his heart as he lay under the stars that Thorn had never experienced before. Before the dark expanse of space, how small he felt, and how wonderful that was. As his appreciation of the beauty of the night sky grew, the problems in his heart melted away.

It took two days for Thorn and Oberlin to travel to Berum. Oberlin was so happy that they were done walking that he nearly cried. Ignoring him, Thorn nodded to the city guards who were looking at him with suspicion. Though completing the [Trouble at Embersplit Mine] quest had cleared the [Criminal] title, the last memory the guards in Berum had of him was trying to find chains that would fit around his massive wrists.

Much like regular people, the natives of Nova Terra had long memories. Just because he had been cleared of his crime, they did not forget that they had thrown him in jail not too long ago. Already nervous when they had to arrest Thorn, they were even more nervous now that he had gotten out and returned to Berum. Thorn, on the other hand, barely thought about it at all. He walked past them into the city, leaving Oberlin sitting on the ground where he had collapsed in exhaustion.

“Hey, wait up.” Oberlin dragged himself off the ground and chased after Thorn’s massive back. “You are meeting up with some of your old party members, right? When?”

“Tonight. We are meeting at a bar near the courthouse at six. Still, a couple of hours, so I am going to get something to eat.”

“Sheesh, do you ever stop eating? You were eating almost all morning as we walked.”

“There is a lot of me to keep fed.”

“Fair point.”

The last time he had been in Berum, Thorn had been a regular at an inn called the Speckled Hen. As he walked in that familiar direction, Thorn began to realize that the townsfolk were staring at him. Every time he turned down a street the players would move out of his way, but otherwise ignored him. On the other hand, the natives were much more concerned about him, pointing and whispering to each other.

"You are pretty popular." The attention was so obvious that even Oberlin noticed.

"I'm not sure why. Last time I was here no one paid any attention to me."

"Sure, but you also were not a violent criminal. Killing someone in town is not common. And who knows when you'll snap and kill someone else. Haha," Oberlin laughed at his own joke. "But seriously, the last thing the townsfolk remember about you is that you were arrested. Your size makes you easy to remember. Don't be surprised if your reception is less than friendly."

Arriving at the Speckled Hen, Thorn ducked through the door, Oberlin following him. Thorn had picked this inn because of the tall ceilings that let him stand freely. As they entered, the innkeeper hurried up a big smile on his face.

"Thorn! It is great to see you! It's been a long time. Were your charges dropped? There were some terrible rumors going around about you, but I know you. There's no way they could have been true."

"Hello, Gerald," Thorn smirked at Oberlin who was standing next to him, his mouth hanging open in shock. "Yeah, I was able to get the confusion cleared up. Is Elsie still cooking lunch? I know I'm a bit late, but I'm starving."

"Of course, of course. You go get a seat and I'll let her know you are here!" Gerald pointed them to an open table in the corner that had a large tree stump instead of a chair and bustled off toward the kitchen.

"What was that?" Oberlin was still confused as he pulled up a chair to the table. "Are you related to him? He treated you like his long-lost son."

"Haha. No, this is where I ate when I stayed in Berum last time." Thorn waved at one of the waitresses who recognized him.

"So? I eat at lots of places...oh." Realization dawned on Oberlin's face. "You mean this is the only place you ate? And they are still in business? Your appetite must have been smaller back then."

"Yeah, my meals generally cost me about a gold a day. Half a gold on days I am getting food to go."

"Sheesh. No wonder he likes you. Really shows the power of gold, huh?"

Soon, steaming plates of food arrived, filling up the table and half of another table that Gerald pulled up. Watching the food rapidly disappear into the bottomless pit that was Thorn's stomach, Oberlin could only shake his head and do his best to get food before it was gone.

Once the food was gone, Oberlin leaned back and looked at Thorn.

“What next? You said you need to do some research to try to find the location of a castle, right?”

“Yes. Greymane Keep. I need to meet someone tonight who, depending on how the meeting goes, may be able to give us a hand figuring out the right location. If not, I was planning on digging through the library to see if I can find any references.”

“Library is good. There are some groups that specialize in game knowledge, but that can get expensive fast.”

“Money won’t be an issue,” Thorn stated with certainty.

“In that case, we’ll want to talk to Avalon. They have the deepest understanding of Nova Terra. Most expensive, of course, but if you have the coin there is almost nothing they can’t find.”

“How do we get in contact with them?”

“You’ll need a referral.” Oberlin fished around in his pouch for a minute, pulling out a silver-bordered card with a large embossed A. “They have people all over. Look for a shop with this symbol on the sign and then have a former customer introduce you. I’ve picked up info from them before so I can make the introduction."

"Shops?"

"Yeah, The Children of Avalon are one of the biggest merchant guilds in Nova Terra, though their primary business is information."

"Alright. Then I'll rely on you if this meeting doesn't work out." Thorn nodded and rose to his feet, dropping a gold coin on the table.

A few hours later he found himself standing in front of the bar where he was going to meet Mina and Velin. All day he had been able to remain calm, but now, faced with the reality of having to see them again his stomach was in knots. Oberlin had noticed how tense Thorn was getting as the time for the meeting approached and had slipped away, leaving Thorn alone. Taking a deep breath, Thorn pushed the door open.

CHAPTER FIFTEEN

The interior of the bar was bustling, filled with players and natives drinking and talking. In contrast to the rowdy atmosphere, the table where Mina and Velin sat was quiet. Velin was as expressionless as ever, though there was a tension beneath her calm exterior. Mina, on the other hand, could not stop fidgeting nervously.

“Do you think he will come?” Mina clenched her cup.

“Probably.”

“But what if he is still mad?”

“We’ll have to see.”

“I want to apologize, but I don’t know how I am supposed to face him.”

"Mina, I'm sure it will be fine." The table lapsed into silence.

"But what if he doesn't forgive us?"

Not bothering to respond, Velin closed her eyes. Mina had been a bundle of nerves ever since she got Thorn's short response. And Mina was not the only one. While it might not show on the outside, Velin could feel the tension in her shoulders. They had done something terrible and she could feel the weight of it. And who knew if Thorn was going to forgive them.

Her eyes still closed, Velin could feel the moment Thorn walked into the room. The general hubbub died down as people glanced over at the sound of the door, their voices pausing at the sight of the giant. Taking a deep breath, Velin opened her eyes, looking first at Mina who was so nervous she had forgotten to breathe.

Thorn crossed the room, his big strides putting him in front of the table within a few steps. Moving the extra chair out of the way, he gestured to the table.

"Mind if I squat here?" Despite his initial butterflies, Thorn found it as easy to interact with the girls as before.

"P... Please do." Mina obviously did not.

"Thanks." Thorn pulled a large rock from his inventory and sat down on it. As he did so Velin pulled out a small pyramid and activated it, creating a bubble around the group. For a moment the three of them sat in silence, looking at each other.

“Thorn...” Mina’s courage evaporated as Thorn’s eye’s turned to her and her voice died out. Panicking, she looked at Velin who took a deep breath.

“Thorn, what we did was terrible and unkind and cruel. They say that there is no medicine for regret but both Mina and I deeply regret our actions and we hope that you will someday forgive us. If there is anything we can do to make it up to you, please do not hesitate to say.”

Time seemed to pause for Thorn as his mind and emotions raced. His chest was a giant ball of conflicting feelings and it took him a moment to gather his thoughts. He had rehearsed this conversation so many times in his head, but he was still not prepared. Now that he was faced with his betrayers his mind was a jumbled mess.

Velin and Mina had both abused and abandoned him once, what guarantee did he have that they would not do it again? They tossed him aside for profit, yet here they were asking for forgiveness. All the raw emotion that Thorn had worked so hard to get under control during his time in the mine threatened to bubble up and it took a few moments before he was able to get it under control.

Thorn’s head grew clear and his emotions calmed. They did

not deserve his forgiveness, but that did not mean he couldn't forgive them anyway. As Thorn examined his heart, he found a desire for reconciliation. His goal in playing Nova Terra was to be free and if he allowed himself to be bound by what they had done he would never reach it. Others might see his choice as weakness, but he thought differently.

"Let's make one thing clear."

Hearing his solemn tone, Mina paled.

"I forgive you."

"What?" Both Mina and Velin exclaimed at the same time, unable to believe their ears.

"I forgive you." Thorn breathed out, his chest feeling much lighter. "I've thought a lot about this and I am going to make the choice to forgive you. What you did sucked and it hurt me and don't you dare do something like that again, but I am not going to let it define who I am and what I do. If we can, I would love to restore our relationship. I'm sure there was more to the situation than I realized and on some level, I was in the wrong place at the wrong time.

"You did not do me any permanent harm, so let's move past it. I'm not saying that everything will magically go back to normal because it won't. But I think we can work on it. I would enjoy questing with you and I think that with time and effort we can repair what has been broken."

“But we stole your destiny points!”

“Sure, I understand.” Thorn nodded at Mina who was almost hyperventilating. “But destiny points are not necessary for playing the game. And I still think you are my friends, otherwise, you would not have sent me that message last week.”

“Thorn, I’m sorry. I was the one who came up with the plan.” Velin, who had been quiet, suddenly spoke.

“It’s fine.”

“No, it’s not. It is kind and generous of you to extend forgiveness, but I need to take responsibility for my part. I am sorry for hurting you, and I will try my best to see that it doesn’t happen again.”

“Yeah, me too,” agreed Mina, nodding her head. “I’m sorry that I killed you like that.”

“Thank you for your apology, you are forgiven. And Mina, I didn’t die.”

“What do you mean you didn’t die?”

“You only knocked me out. Due to a technical issue, the game did not recognize me as dead, so once you left, and combat ended, my body healed and I woke up.”

"Oh, wow. I thought since you met Jorge on the stairs to the temple that you had respawned. He was going there to check if you logged back in."

"Ah, yeah. I was there to be healed. We had some words."

"I don't think 'had some words' covers it. He has barely logged in since then. What did you do?" Velin asked, her eyes narrowed.

"Um. Well, I got a bit angry and might have thrown him at the wall."

"You threw a player at the wall so hard you had to go to jail for multiple weeks? So that means he died? How did you get past the damage reduction?"

"Damage reduction?"

"In towns, all players have pretty severe damage reduction applied to them. This is to prevent accidents and make it hard to assassinate other people. The most that should have happened is that his health would have dropped and you would be fined by the guards."

"Ah, I did not know about that." Thorn smiled. "No wonder everyone looked at me like I was a monster while I was in jail. As for how it happened?" Thorn reached over and picked up Mina's metal mug, tossing it in his hand a couple of times. Then, without any effort, he crushed it into a little ball and dropped it on the table. "I'm pretty strong."

"Well, no wonder he has not logged back in. I imagine that was quite a traumatizing death. Plus, I imagine that he is worried he might meet you again."

"If you talk to him, you can tell him I don't hold it against him. Oh, and I'm sorry for killing him. If he is willing to call it even I can let it go."

For a moment the table lapsed into silence.

"What happened with Ouroboros? Where is he?"

"I don't know." Mina looked upset thinking about the former party leader. "Ever since he got his new class he has been totally different. I don't like him anymore. We are not speaking!"

"Our group broke up." Velin looked down at the table, her voice low. "Something about his class, Exalted Devil Blood Berserker, has brought out the coldness in him. I'm not sure what it is, but he has become much more ruthless than he was in the past. Even with us. He has returned to Ragnarok to fight for a position in the leadership. I'm afraid I had a part to play in goading him into it." Velin looked down.

"Maybe, but you are not responsible for his actions. We all have to make our own decisions, and it sounds like he is making poor ones."

"Yes," Velin sighed, "but I understand why he is making those choices. He is under a lot of pressure from his family to succeed and the person who controls Ragnarok will have incredible power, authority, and wealth. The temptation to run over everyone or everything that gets in your way is strong when so much is on the line. Still, we did not come here to talk about Ouroboros. We are here to find out how we can make up for our own poor decisions."

"I told you, I forgive you. There isn't anything you need to do." Thorn waved dismissively. "I do have a quest that I would love help with, but I won't have any hard feelings if you don't join me."

"No, we'll do it!" Mina slapped the table and declared before Velin could say anything.

"Of course we will." Velin nodded. "What do you need?"

"Okay. In that case, let me call our other team member. Once he gets here we'll set up our plan of attack."

Oberlin must have been hanging out right outside the bar, because almost as soon as Thorn sent him a message he popped up next to the table.

"Velin, Mina, this is Oberlin. I met him before I got to know you and we got re-acquainted over the last couple weeks.

Oberlin, Velin and Mina." Thorn made the introductions.

After a round of hellos, the group got down to business. Thorn explained that he had to find Greymane Keep for his quest but that it did not appear on any map that he had seen. The information that he obtained from the Pathfinder in Narthil had not contained any hints either.

"Hmmm. It is rare that a quest would not give any supplementary details. Can you describe the process through which you obtained the quest?" Velin asked.

"I actually got it after I woke up in Hati's Ascent. I have to free the castle from werewolves."

"Ah, that helps quite a bit." Seeing the other's confused looks, Velin pulled out her notebook and flipped open to a blank page. Writing as she spoke she began to explain. "One of the basic rules of Nova Terra is that everything is connected. In fact, it is speculated that if an individual makes a connection that is false, the game might create the connection so as to give players a heightened sense of achievement. Eve is smart enough to make this impossible to abuse, but it means that there are connections everywhere.

"What that means for us is that everything surrounding a quest is a clue. Take, for example, the place where the quest was activated. Hati's Ascent was a temple to the god of the night, Hati, the Moon Wolf. Hati was worshiped by those corrupted wolfkin that we fought in the dungeon. We also ran into regular wolfkin before we got to the dungeon. They were trying to gain access, just like us.

“Based on the composition of their group and the fact that we had never encountered that sort of creature, we can tell that they came from a good distance away. They did not have any pack animals though and none of them were players, so they could not have come from too far away. This puts them between two and five days away.”

“Wait, why do pack animals matter?” Mina cut in, confused.

“No inventories.” Oberlin and Thorn said at the same time.

“Exactly. Since they were natives they did not have inventories which means that they had to carry everything in packs. They had no tents which means that all their pack space was probably food and other vital supplies. That means that they probably traveled for less than a week. Which would also make sense considering the shape their clothing was in. They would have been much rattier looking if they had been traveling for a long time.

“So, that gives us two pieces of information. First, the wolfkin at the temple that fell became werewolves, and the castle is in the hands of werewolves. Second, wolfkin that had not fallen were trying to get to the temple. This means that it is unlikely that the wolfkin came from the area around Greymane Keep. They may know where it is, however, so let's keep that in the back of our minds. Next, we know that the temple was situated in a wolfkin city. So it is likely that there is information in the city regarding the location of Greymane Keep."

"Oh no." Mina put her head in her hands.

"What is wrong?"

"That whole area is under Ragnarok's control right now. One of the leaders has taken over that area to loot. Getting in and finding the right information will be difficult, if not impossible," Velin spoke calmly.

"Aren't you part of Ragnarok?" Oberlin asked.

"We were. Suffice it to say, we are no longer part of the guild. So we may have some trouble. Angdrin, the officer in charge of this area is not known for being helpful."

"Angdrin? Is he..?" Thorn looked at Oberlin who was nodding his head.

"Yeah. That is the guy from the mine. Haha, small world. Thorn fought him and his red-armored goons two days ago. And we swiped a bunch of stuff from them. So, I'm pretty sure that they will be even less helpful if they see us."

"Granted, that makes the situation easier, right? We can bust in and not worry about it. Since we're already enemies I mean." Thorn smiled.

"I don't think that is a good idea." Mina frowned. "The Crimson Snakes are really tough."

"Haha, they did not look that tough. Thorn killed six or seven of them in their last fight. He probably would have killed all of them if he hadn't tried to break a magic bubble with his bare hands."

"You what?" Flabbergasted Mina stared at Thorn. Angdrin's personal guard, while not being the absolute best of Ragnarok's fighters were elite players. It was inconceivable that someone could wipe out so many of them, especially fighting all of them at once.

"Did I say that he *tried* to break a magic bubble? That's wrong. He *did* break a magic bubble with his bare hands. Cracked it open like an egg. You should have seen Angdrin's face, Haha! Anyway, he also crushed five of them with a large carriage full of ore." Oberlin bragged.

"Alright, I get the picture." Mina shook her head. "To hear you brag, I almost thought that you were the one to fight them."

"Nah, I don't do that direct confrontation stuff. But I did pick up six boxes that looked pretty important while everyone was distracted." Oberlin smiled smugly.

"Alright, let's focus. Avoiding conflict is a smarter bet since there are more of them than there are of us. What other avenues do we have for getting information, Velin?" Thorn waved for Mina and Oberlin to be quiet.

"We have the library here in town. We may be able to find a reference somewhere if we look through ancient legends. Because the quest is tied to the era of the gods our chances are best if we find a story about the wolfkin specifically. We could also look for old maps and compare them to our current world map. That is how we found the entrance to Davyos' Fall, the city where Hati's Ascent was. That is time-consuming though. We could also go talk to Avalon. Are you familiar with how they work?"

"Yes, Oberlin introduced me."

"Really, if we can't access the library from the city where we found the temple, our best option is to go find the wolfkin and see if they have any information. Unfortunately, they were hostile the last time we encountered them."

"Okay, then it looks like we're going to have to contend with Angdrin and the Crimson Snakes." Thorn picked up the balled up the cup.

CHAPTER SIXTEEN

As the early morning light broke over the horizon, the forest awoke. A curious wren landed on a branch, its head cocking as it looked down at Thorn's prone figure. Stretched out along a hill, Thorn peeked over the top, looking down at the entrance to the canyon leading to Davyos' Fall. Even in the early morning hours, two red-armored players stood guard, watching for anyone who might disrupt their guild's operations.

"Do they really just stand there? What a strange way to play a game." Thorn spoke quietly to avoid alerting the guards.

"To them, it isn't a game. It is a job. They play Nova Terra for a living, so it is the same as any other work. They get benefits, get paid by the hour, it is like working in the real world. So, if their employer tells them to spend some time standing guard, they stand guard." Velin lay next to Thorn, looking down toward the canyon. "They might be elite players, but they are on the low end of the totem pole."

"I guess that makes sense."

"When you two are finished can we get started?" Oberlin's voice drifted over from somewhere nearby. Thorn could not, for the life of him, tell where Oberlin was, but he knew he was in the vicinity.

"Yeah, let's get going." Thorn scooted back down the hill far enough that his head would not be visible over the top when he stood up. "Everyone remember the plan? We don't have much room for failure here. Once they are alerted it will be much harder for us to get through, so no messing around, okay?"

"What? Why are you looking at me?" Mina complained, adjusting her pointy hat. "I'm an elite player, I know what to do."

"Great." Thorn ignored Mina's pouting. "Velin, when you are ready."

Nodding, the elven War Priestess pulled her staff out and walked over the hill toward the Crimson Snake guards, Mina by her side. As they came down the hill the two guards perked up, lifting their swords and shields. After a moment of staring at the approaching girls, the guard on the left, a middle-aged man with a mustache, motioned for the other guard to put down his weapons when the two girls got closer.

“Miss Velin.” Mustache bowed respectfully as they got closer.

“Morning. Do you know me?” Velin greeted him, her face impassive.

“Yes, Miss. I worked a shift at headquarters last year and saw you with Lord Ouroboros. Congratulations, on his advancement.”

“Mmhmm. Why are you on duty here?”

“Lord Angdrin ordered that we guard this location to prevent anyone from other guilds from exploring beyond this point. There is an abandoned city and a dungeon in the canyon!” The younger guard chimed in, excited to be talking to someone as famous as Velin. He lapsed into silence as he caught a glare from mustache.

“My apologies, miss, but you can’t go beyond this point,” Mustache said, tightening his grip on his sword and shield. “Our orders are that the location is to be completely locked down. So no one can get in.”

“Even if I’m doing research in the tunnel? There is a magic door that I wanted to examine in more detail.” Velin’s cold face did not change expression at the guard’s refusal.

"I'm sorry, orders are orders." Mustache shook his head, suppressing a shiver. He had always heard that Velin was cold, but he could swear that the actual temperature had dropped.

"Hmm. Shame." Velin shook her head and stepped to the side, revealing Mina with a silly smile on her face and a fully charged wand in her hands.

"[Avalanche]!" Mina shouted, causing a massive flurry of snow to appear, burying the two guards before they could move. Stunned for a moment, they could not respond as a giant crossbow bolt flew down the hill, instantly sending the younger guard out of the game. Before the stunned state had worn off, Velin channeled a beam of pure energy into her staff, shooting it through Mustache's chest. He did not even have time to change his expression before he turned into motes of light.

With both guards gone, Thorn hurried down the hill to the canyon entrance, meeting Oberlin, Velin, and Mina outside the tunnel that led to Davyos' Fall.

"Okay, that could have gone better, but we did account for having to kill the guards. This means we are on a clock. We have less than an hour before we start seeing reinforcements. So, we cannot waste time if we meet other guards inside." The War Priestess was all business, hurrying them into the tunnel.

Not worrying about stealth, the group burst into the room with the magical door in time to see it click shut. Someone from the other side must have been alerted by the players that died and closed the door. At the sight of the closed door and active runes, Mina paled.

“It took us an hour and forty-five minutes to open it last time.” Mina shook her head. “There is no way we’ll be able to get through.”

“Hah, are you serious? It took you that long to open this thing?” Oberlin faded into view in front of the large bronze doors.

“What? You think you can do better?”

Oberlin smirked as his hands began flying, tapping here and there on the runic lock. Seeing his actions, Velin’s eyebrows rose. She looked at Thorn for confirmation and seeing him readying his arbalest, she gave a small smile.

“Mina get ready for another Avalanche. We need to make sure anyone on the other side of the door doesn’t have a chance to run.”

“Got it.” Still doubtful, Mina charged her wand.

For a moment the only sound in the tunnel was Oberlin’s tapping hands. Everyone else stood silently as they got ready for whatever was on the other side of the door. In three minutes the runic lock began to warp, dispersing with Oberlin's last tap.

"There you go," said the thief with a flourish.

"Thank you." Thorn stepped past him and pushed the door open violently, his arbalest leveled.

On the other side of the door stood three more guards in the red armor of the Crimson Snakes. Two held swords and shields while one had a bow on his back. With a start, they scrambled to get into position, but it was too little too late. Almost by reflex, Thorn sent his bolt at the archer, who exploded into motes of light while Mina dropped her icy stun on the two shield warriors.

Whether by luck or simply chance, the flurry of snow only caught one of them, the other managing to dive to the side. Yelling a war cry, the warrior who escaped the snow rolled forward, his shield in front of him as he attacked. Sadly, it did not go well for him. As he rose from the ground to approach Thorn, a massive foot lashed out, kicking the center of his shield.

[CRACK]

With a tremendous sound, the shield snapped in half and the dumbfounded warrior was launched backward, tumbling head over heels until he came to a stop almost twenty feet away. For a moment, his body lay still and then peacefully faded. The stunned warrior fared no better and soon joined his companions in Fantasia.

"It will take us ten minutes to get to the city if we run, so let's get going." Velin did not dwell on the fight, instead moving the party along.

To her surprise, Thorn put his arbalest away and scooped her and Mina up, one in each hand. Telling Oberlin to climb onto his back and hold on, Thorn began running, his strides growing longer as he sped up. Perched upon Thorn's broad shoulder, Mina giggled with glee at the landscape flying past.

"Who said this game doesn't have fast travel?" She joked. Velin ignored her, holding on tightly.

Each pounding footstep sent Thorn almost a dozen feet forward. Within less than a minute the city came into clear view and within three they were at its edge. With a smile, Thorn let the ladies down as Oberlin jumped down from where he had been holding on to Thorn's armor.

"That works too." Velin took a moment to fix her hair that had blown out of place during the mad dash. "Let's look for the library. We are aiming for speed over stealth. Oberlin, you keep an eye out. Thorn, you'll be in charge of blocking anyone we come across with Mina. I'll find the library and look for our information."

Sure enough, they had only traveled three blocks when

Oberlin sent a message saying that there was a group of five red-armored players heading for them. Nodding to Velin, Thorn and Mina split off from the War Priestess and went to meet them head-on. At first, Mina wanted to try and ambush them, but after remembering the way Thorn manhandled the previous group she shrugged and followed behind him.

The two groups met at a crossroads and immediately closed for combat. One of the Crimson Snakes had bows and one was wielding a staff. The other three held the familiar scimitar and round shield that Thorn had seen the others with. Charging forward, Thorn lifted his gauntlets to protect his head and neck.

Seeing a giant thundering toward them, the shield-wielding Crimson Snakes paled. The message they had gotten only said that someone had breached the large doors to the valley, it said nothing about a giant.

Two of the shield bearers braced for impact. The third, wanting no part of Thorn's charge, jumped aside. Lowering his body, Thorn sent two palm strikes into the center of the shields, blasting both players back. Not slowing at all, he continued to close on the archer who had started shooting arrows. Lifting his hands, Thorn knocked the first out of the air but missed the second, grunting slightly as it punched through his pauldron.

Next, to the archer, the staff-wielding caster was chanting, crimson mist spilling from her lips. As she started to raise her staff toward Thorn a long, eerie howl rang out, echoing off the surrounding buildings.

[Wolf Lord's Howl]

Taking advantage of the caster's momentary pause, Thorn suddenly accelerated, crossing the last few steps and ramming into her with his shoulder. With a sharp crack, her staff broke as she tumbled backward. As he charged, Thorn had pulled out his tetsubo which he smashed sideways into the archer. Both ranged fighters dealt with, Thorn turned to the remaining Crimson Snakes.

The warrior who had dodged Thorn's charge found himself on the wrong end of a cold, sharp ice spike, leaving the two that Thorn had knocked aside scrambling to their feet, their pale faces a testament to how hard the palm strikes had been. Seeing that they were the last of their group alive, one of the warriors gritted his teeth and, holding his shield up to stop the icy spikes raining down on him, charged forward.

"Get backup!" The warrior yelled over his shoulder as he swung his sword, trying to claim Thorn's attention.

"Nice try." Thorn grinned, appreciating his opponent's bravery. But appreciation did not stop him from backhanding him into a nearby wall. Dashing forward, Thorn was about to crush the last warrior with a strike from his tetsubo when the temperature suddenly plummeted. Shifting his weight to the side, Thorn threw himself forward in a roll, tumbling across the ground and smashing into some rotting barrels.

“[Sub Zero]!” Mina shouted

Behind him, the Crimson Snake warrior who had been fleeing froze solid and a flurry of ice spikes quickly ended the fight. Getting to his feet, Thorn glared at the short witch.

“Careful where you throw your spells!”

“It’s area of effect, it's not my fault you are so big that pretty much everything hits you.” Mina rolled her eyes as she moved to loot the bodies.

“I thought you were supposed to be an elite player. Friendly fire is not elite player behavior.”

“It didn’t hit you did it?”

“Yeah, but only because I jumped out of the way.”

“Oh, stop complaining. You sound like a big baby. A really really huge baby. Like, ginormous baby.”

“Alright, I get it.” Thorn shook his head, opening a message from Oberlin. “What’s up?”

“More enemies incoming. Looks like the main force. 23 Crimson Snakes, a mix of all sorts of classes. Angdrin is with them, along with the other two who you nearly killed last time. We should probably leave soon."

"Alright, sit tight. Let me check in with Velin." Switching the message to hold, Thorn added Velin to the call. "Hey Velin, I have Oberlin on the line. He says we have the main group of Crimson Snakes, including Angdrin, on the way. What is your time frame?"

"I'm not sure. I have not found anything yet." Velin's voice was laden with frustration. "I'm trying a different building next to the library and then I will be back."

Surprised at the rare emotion, Thorn's brow furrowed.

"What is wrong? It sounds like you ran into a problem."

"Problem? I'd say. I went to the library but it is gone. Completely gone. The books I mean, the building is still here. It looks like a group recently moved the entire library. All the shelves are completely cleared out. They did not leave a single book. Even the scroll racks have been cleared. Which means we probably have no chance of finding out what we need to know."

"Wait. You mentioned all the books are missing?" Thorn asked, his voice slow.

"Yeah. Who would waste their time moving so many books? Most of them are probably useless anyway, so it is a ton of dead weight hanging out in their inventory. But whoever did it ruined any chance we have of getting a clue from here. I'm doing one last check to see if I can scrounge up anything of value." Velin paused, hearing only deep silence from the other side. "Thorn? Thorn? Is everything okay?"

"Hahahaha!" Mina's laughter came over the call. "Velin, you have got to see this!"

Standing in the middle of the street, a mortified giant was standing next to a large stack of books that he had just pulled from his inventory.

CHAPTER SEVENTEEN

"You did what?"

"Um." Carefully watching the glaring elven War Priestess with one eye, while shooting a glare of his own at Mina who was still doubled over laughing, Thorn tried to choose his words carefully. "I picked up some books when we came through here the first time. Rember how we split up? Well… I ended up at the library so I thought I would take some books with me."

"Some books?"

"Well, I sort of kept putting them in my inventory. And my inventory is pretty big, so…"

"Oh my goodness." Velin put her hand on her face, defeated. "You have been carrying an entire library around with you this whole time? How are you still walking? Don't you know that weight decreases your movement speed and reaction time?"

"Ah, no wonder I've been feeling so sluggish." Realization dawned on Thorn's large face. "That makes a lot of sense."

"Forget it, let's figure out how we are going to get out of here."

"Right, we can go through the books later." Picking up the stacks of books he had pulled from his inventory, Thorn put them away and opened his messenger. "Oberlin, what is the situation?"

"You have been walking around with an entire library in your inventory? No wonder."

"What?"

"Back in prison I tried to pickpocket you a bunch of times to see what you had, but I only ever got books. I thought I had the worst luck ever. But it would make sense if you had thousands of books."

"You tried to rob me?"

"Yeah, but don't worry about it. We're friends now. Anyway." Oberlin coughed and changed the subject. "They're about two minutes away from the city. I'm on a rooftop at the southern end of the city. If you make your way over here we might be able to slip by. Wait, no, never mind. They are leaving guards to watch the path back to the tunnel. We are not going to get out of this without a fight."

"Okay, that is fine."

"Fine? What do you mean fine?" Oberlin protested. "I can't throw people through walls or shoot lasers like some people in this group."

"Let me know where they are going once they get into the city and we'll handle it from there." Thorn turned to look at Velin and Mina. "You ladies up for a brawl?"

On the edge of the city, twenty red-armored players moved forward in formation. In the center of the group, Angdrin looked around at the abandoned surroundings moodily. Ever since his encounter with that giant freak in Embersplit, his luck had been horrible. It had only been a couple of days but nothing seemed to be going his way.

"Telis, have you figured out who is messing with us here?"

"No, sir." Telis, responded very carefully, trying not to anger her boss any further. "Our teams have been going down too fast. We are estimating that there is a team of at least seven assassins, if not more."

"What is the last count of our losses?"

"Ten. Two at the canyon, three at the door, five in the city." Korith reported gruffly, his eyes never stopping as he scanned the quiet surroundings.

"Ten?" Angdrin could feel his temples throbbing from the stress. He had enough problems to deal with ever since that upstart Ouroboros had gone back to the guild headquarters. The last thing he needed was his Crimson Snakes being picked off in his own backyard. "Find out who is doing this and bring me their heads!"

"Yes, sir!" Shouting together, the group picked up speed, heading in toward the street where their dead members reported contact.

The long streets were silent apart from the well-ordered footsteps of the Crimson Snakes and the muted jingle of their equipment. The closer they got to the location of the reported fight the tenser the group got. A group of assassins could hurt anyone quite badly with a successful ambush. With well-trained precision, the Crimson Snakes spread out, creating space for Angdrin and his lieutenants to examine the scene of the fight, along with the help of a ranger.

"What is wrong?" Angdrin, watching the ranger scouting the area like a hawk, caught the faint frown on his face.

"Sir, it doesn't look like the work of assassins. It looks more like they got run over by a truck."

"What do you mean?"

"The traces show none of the blood splatter that you would expect from assassination techniques. However, we can see where multiple people went flying as if they were hit by a charge." The ranger knelt and pointed to some disturbed ground. "See, this is where someone in red armor struggled back to their feet. You can see the flecks of paint on these stones where they slide along the ground."

"So we are dealing with two groups?

Opening his mouth, the ranger hesitated for a moment, taking another look around. Before he could speak a loud sound rang out and a barrage of ice spikes shot from an alleyway, driving an unprepared Crimson Snake to the ground. Immediately shouts erupted from the rest of the groups and they swiftly formed ranks facing the mouth of the alley.

"Shields up!" Korith bellowed, while beside him, Telis stepped in front of Angdrin. Within seconds the group had formed a defensive half ring in the street, their backs to a building. Angdrin stood in the middle, flanked by Telis and Korith, glaring at the alleyway. Thanks to the quick response by his men, no one else had gotten injured by the ice spikes that continued to fly toward them.

"Squad 2, advance!"

Their shields up, a group of four Crimson Snake warriors left the protection of the half circle, dashing forward to the mouth of the alley where they split, two going to each side.

“Breach!”

Shouting a battle cry, the four warriors charged into the alleyway. After a moment the ice spikes stopped and everything went quiet. For a brief second, everyone froze, their eyes fixed on the mouth of the alley.

BOOOOM!

Without warning the stillness was shattered by a tremendous sound as the wall behind the Crimson Snake formation exploded into pieces, chunks of brick and mortar flying. Eyes wide at the sight, the leader of the Crimson Snakes stared at the debris flying past his shoulder. A sudden fear bloomed in his heart.

[Wolf Lord’s Howl]

Before he could react, an unearthly howl rang through the streets, stunning everyone who heard it. The long howl seemed to echo in Angdrin’s soul, shaking his confidence and causing him to lose control of the spell he had started casting. A titanic hand, its sharp claws gleaming, gripped Angdrin’s shoulder as he stood, frozen, the last echoes of the wolf howl reverberating in his ears. The sharp prick of the claws as they punched through his armor shook him from his stupor and he tried to begin a chant.

“I told you we’d try this again.” Thorn’s deep voice sounded by his ear, making him choke on his words.

Under the horrified gazes of the Crimson Snakes, Thorn casually lifted Angdrin into the air and smashed him onto the stone street, instantly killing him. Picking up the odds and ends that dropped, Thorn looked at the rest of the Crimson Snakes who were staring at him in shock. Flexing his fingers, Thorn grinned.

“So, are we going to do this or what?”

With a roar of rage, Korith dashed toward Thorn, his shield up in front of him. Warding him away with a palm strike, Thorn drew his tetsubo with his other hand and charged forward, striking out furiously. The commotion had drawn the whole group’s attention and they paid dearly for it when the furious barrage of ice spikes resumed.

No slouches, the Crimson Snakes sprang furiously into action. The melee fighters advanced, their swords swinging while the casters behind them began to pepper Thorn with all sorts of spells. Enraged by having lost their leader they threw themselves at Thorn with wild abandon.

Telis and Korith were particularly troublesome opponents. Both were highly skilled and coordinated their attacks well with the casters. Using their shields to protect themselves, they would dash towards him at the same time, creating openings for the casters to launch their spells at Thorn. Finally, annoyed by their pestering, Thorn abandoned his defenses and latched on to Telis' shield, using his tetsubo to deliver a hard strike to her that sent her out of the game.

Feeling the bite of Korith's blade, Thorn grit his teeth and snapped a kick sideways, sending the warrior flying once again. This time though, Thorn drew his arbalest, finishing the job with a massive bolt that pinned the Crimson Snake lieutenant to a nearby building.

As the fight continued, Thorn could feel his health rapidly dropping. Though his pain tolerance was significantly higher than the average person's and his endurance was monstrous, the game corrected for it to prevent him from being an unkillable monster. That did not stop him from being a regular monster, however, and in less than ten seconds he had already sent four Crimson Snakes out of the game.

A fiercely burning fireball impacted on his side, sharp pain lancing through his ribs. Gritting his teeth, Thorn tried to ignore it, but he could feel his control starting to slip away. There were simply too many stabbing blades and arcane attacks. As his vision started to darken around the edges a warm light fell on him and strength surged through him! Roaring with glee, Thorn turned and jumped, landing directly in front of the mage who cast the fireball, smashing him into motes of light with his tetsubo.

"He's got a healer!" Panicked cries rang out from the Crimson Snakes. "Find them! Take down the healer!"

Unfortunately for them, Velin was well hidden in a second story room, peeking from a crack in the shuttered windows. Since she was only casting healing spells on Thorn who was rampaging below it was nearly impossible for the Crimson Snakes to find her and by the time they gave up another six of them had fallen to Thorn's tetsubo or the vicious ice spikes that continued to pour out of the alley.

Every time Thorn's health got low, light burst around him, healing his wounds and filling him with energy. Unable to find the healer or bring Thorn down, the Crimson Snakes soon fell into complete disarray. It took only a few more moments for Thorn to finish them off and soon he stood, panting, in the middle of an empty street.

"Wow, that was crazy!" Mina came running out of the alley where she had hidden as she cast her ice spikes. "You took on all of them by yourself!"

"No, you helped. And Velin helped a lot too. I almost died twice." Thorn sighed. "That was pretty scary for a second."

"Still, you killed Angdrin like it was nothing. I bet he is super mad right now. Probably breaking everything in sight. Hahaha, serves him right."

"You know Angdrin?"

"Yeah, he is a total jerk. The Crimson Snakes were our primary opponents in Ragnarok. He is slippery and deceitful, but the Crimson Snakes are considered one of the stronger groups. Seeing you smash him into the ground like that was really satisfying!"

Watching Mina chat happily as she busied herself with picking up the odds and ends that the Crimson Snakes had dropped, Thorn could not help but smile. The strangeness between them had started to fade and he was relieved to see her going back to her old behavior around him. After a few moments, he saw Velin coming out of the building where she had been hiding.

"Thanks for the healing. That was amazing."

"Of course, that is what I'm here for." Velin smiled, her eyes bright. "Once we've picked everything up let's get back to Berum. Without a doubt, Angdrin is calling for backup at this moment. He will try to trap us here until he can log back in."

"Alright," Thorn grinned widely as he flexed his fingers again. "I think Oberlin said there were some guards at the gate so we might have to rush through."

Thorn's excitement at the prospect of getting to fight more Crimson Snakes was infectious, causing the girls to laugh as he swept them both up and took off running. As Thorn charged through the city, Oberlin sent him directions, guiding him to the spot where the thief was hiding. About to put the girls down, Thorn felt Mina smack his head in excitement.

“I just had the greatest idea! Why don’t you run past the bad guys and I’ll shoot them with my spells? It will be like a tank!”

“Or a two-headed Ogre!” Oberlin chimed in from a nearby balcony. With a jump, he landed lightly beside Thorn and skillfully scrambled up onto Thorn’s massive back.

“Who are you calling an ogre?”

“Thorn of course,” Oberlin shifted smoothly, ignoring Mina’s pointed look. “The Crimson Snakes that were left to watch the entrance are in a straight line from here to the door. Mina’s idea is a good one, though. If you run by, she can freeze them. We only need to delay them long enough to make it through the door.”

“Alright, let's give it a try.” Thorn nodded and crouched slightly as he got ready to charge. With a boom, he shot forward, his tree-trunk-sized legs carving divots in the ground as he launched himself forward. Each step sent him hurtling faster, his speed increasing quickly. The others held on tightly as he ran, afraid of being shaken off by his jarring steps.

As they approached the first of the Crimson Snakes watching, Mina cast her spell.

"[Sub Zero]!"

Instantly, the horrified face of the guard froze solid as he stopped in place. Thorn, unable to stop his momentum barreled right over the Crimson Snake warrior, smashing into him like a freight train. As the unfortunate warrior dispersed into twinkling lights Thorn nearly tripped and fell on his face, barely catching himself with one of his hands.

"Oh wow. That was... uh..." Mina stared, wide-eyed, at the spot where the warrior had stood.

"Yeah, maybe let's not do that again." Oberlin's voice was weak.

Agreeing on a slower approach, the four players made their way out of the hidden valley, soon emerging in the canyon. As they left the cave, they could see evidence of a massive fight littering the canyon floor.

"It looks like the kobolds came back and attacked whoever was guarding here. They must have cleared out the rest of the Crimson Snakes."

"Well, let's get going. We don't want to get caught up in any unnecessary fights. Besides," Velin glared at Thorn, "we still have to go dig through a library."

"Haha, yeah. Sorry about that." Thorn avoided her gaze

sheepishly. He really had forgotten that he had looted the library the first time he went to the hidden city. His inventory was so big that he honestly threw things in and forgot about them. As the group made its way back to Berum Thorn made a mental note to go through everything he had stored in his inventory and organize it.

CHAPTER EIGHTEEN

With a long sigh, Thorn stared at the massive piles of random loot heaped on the floor of the room he was renting. Over in the corner, Velin was poring over a stack of books that Thorn had pulled out of his inventory. While retrieving the books that he had picked from the library in Davyos' Fall, Thorn realized that he had never dealt with the various things he had picked up in the dungeon where he had met Hati.

He continued to pull books, skins, gems, weapons, and other random loot that he had stored when he was a porter from his inventory, causing both Oberlin and Mina to stare in utter astonishment. Mina knew that his inventory was large but the endless stream of loot was almost too much.

"Alright, let's sort all of this stuff," Thorn looked around at the haphazard piles, "and then we'll see what we can sell."

"What are we doing with the books?" Oberlin asked, gingerly running his hand across the top of a stack of books almost as tall as he was."

"Keeping them. We can store them in the bank." Velin called out from the desk, her eyes never leaving the page she was translating. "But the rest of the stuff can go."

After a few hours of sorting, the floor had reappeared and Thorn's inventory was organized into neat sections. A trip to the bank and a couple of different merchants made a massive dent in his pile of junk and added a nice weight to his wallet.

On the way back to the inn where Mina and Velin were waiting, Thorn was lost in thought. Following him, Oberlin stuck to Thorn's shadow. The crowded city streets were normally hard to push through but Thorn's massive figure seemed to have a magical effect on the crowds who naturally made a path for him.

A couple of blocks from the inn, Thorn slowed to a stop and crouched in the shade of a building. Seeing him stop, Oberlin stood close, waiting as Thorn continued to think quietly.

"How would you feel about helping me out with something?" Thorn's deep voice rumbled like thunder, even when he was trying to speak softly.

"You name it. I can't tell you how grateful I am for your help with the Ordo Serpentes."

"Don't worry about that. It turned out to be something good for me too. I want to hire you to do something. The job will be for at least a year, maybe longer."

"You want to hire me?"

"Yeah, formal employment. I'm thinking about building a team and I could use someone who understands how to find information."

"Well, I can certainly help with that. But I don't know if you realize the extent of what is required for building an official team. You have to pay the members of the team. And not just with in-game stuff, but with real money. And you have to provide health care and pay taxes and all sorts of other things."

"Yeah, I read a guide."

"It is a cool idea, but unless you have a sponsor, you'll go broke trying to get the funds together I don't mean to be a downer but putting together an official team is very costly and a lot of work." Oberlin shook his head. "I'd be happy to put together an informal team with you, but I don't know how realistic it is to expect anything of it."

"We have a sponsor." Thorn watched the crowded street as

he waited for his words to register.

“Getting a sponsor is the hardest… What?!”

“We have a sponsor,” Thorn repeated his words dully, pretending that he wasn’t thoroughly enjoying Oberlin’s shock.

“How did you find a sponsor? How big a team are they willing to finance? Are they willing to build a full guild? How much are they offering?” Excited, Oberlin blurted out a whole string of questions before his expression turned puzzled. “Who are they?”

“Atlas.”

“Atlas? Atlas Energy?!”

Opening his interface, Thorn sent Oberlin a message with a document attached.

“That is the employment contract. If you are interested you’ll be hired for a term of one year. While there are no specific roles in the contract, I currently envision your role being something like an intelligence officer. I am looking for someone who can assist me in collecting, sorting, and ranking intelligence while also helping me make contacts.

“I’m realizing that Nova Terra is way larger and more complex than I originally understood. This world is not a game, at least in the normal sense, and I think it is time to stop treating it as such. I have a quest that could potentially lead to controlling a region and I want to capitalize on it by putting a team together that will eventually transition into a guild that will use that region as a base. I don't know the specifics of where I am going to end up, but I can guarantee that I'm going to leave my mark on this world and I would love to have you join me."

For a moment Oberlin was silent, his eyes growing wider and wider as he read the document that Thorn had sent over to him. Seeing the official letterhead of Atlas, the thief's heart nearly stopped. As soon as he finished reading it, he signed it and sent it back to Thorn.

"Sounds good, boss. You got yourself an employee."

"Thanks. I know all of this is sudden, but we've got a lot to do. For your first task, I'd like you to head south to make some specific connections. I'll send you the exact details when you are on the road."

Saying goodbye, Thorn watched Oberlin vanish into the crowd. He sat in the shade of the wall for a few more minutes, watching people pass by. His whole life he had been an observer and it was finally time that he stood up and began to take control of his life for himself. Rising, Thorn smiled. He had a feeling that the next few years of his life in-game were going to be eventful. Laughing happily to himself, Thorn joined the crowds.

The girls were sitting together in the room when Thorn got back. Velin had finished examining the books and maps that Thorn had looted from the library and compiled all the new information into notes.

“Did you find out where the keep is located?” Thorn sat on the floor by the table.

“I did. It looks to be about three days east of here. The history of the region is quite complicated. We will need to tread carefully as the enemies will most likely be quite dangerous. May I ask how you got the quest?”

“It triggered after I got a title. Is that important?”

“Absolutely. Rather, it would be more accurate to say that is highly likely that it is important. Almost everything in this game is important. I’ll try to do a bit more research to see if it will influence our approach. If all you have to do is clear the keep we should be okay, but complicated areas like this one tend to generate a lot of quests which could put us into conflict with other players. High-density quest areas like this will be fiercely contested if there are any teams or guilds involved.”

“I’m sure we’ll be able to handle it.” Hearing a knock on the door, Thorn paused. “That will be the food. Let’s eat and chat about all this after dinner.”

Opening the door revealed four waiters straining under massive trays of food. On his way up to the room, Thorn had ordered enough food to feed an army. Or himself.

After the four servers carried the massive trays of food into the room, Thorn, Mina, and Velin ate their fill. As the girls chatted quietly, Thorn carried the mound of plates and bowls down to the kitchen. As he returned he heard the conversation die down. Ever since his transformation into the Avatar of the Moon Wolf, his senses had gotten much sharper, and while he could not tell exactly what the girls had been talking about, he knew that it wasn't a happy conversation.

Ducking through the door, Thorn saw Mina looking glumly at the floor. Velin's expression was neutral, but that did not mean anything since she almost always looked like that. Sitting down on the floor, Thorn organized his thoughts for a moment before he began to speak.

"I think it is time we had a serious talk."

"A... about what?" Mina looked up, the frustration on her face replaced with nervousness.

"About what we are going to do next." Thorn tried to smile reassuringly. "You can't follow me around while I do quests forever. I think that we need to define our working relationship. No, wait, hear me out before you say anything." Holding up his hand to prevent Mina from speaking, Thorn took a deep breath.

"I've been thinking a lot about Nova Terra and what I am hoping to achieve in this world. I won't pretend that I have everything figured out, but recent events have started making my path clearer. I want to lay out my thoughts and then hear yours. No matter what conclusion we come to, I want to remain friends, but that does not necessarily mean that we have to quest together. That said, I'd love to stay together. Sorry, I'm getting scattered.

"My eventual goal is to carve out a piece of Nova Terra for myself. I've been thinking about this a lot ever since we faced off against the Crimson Snakes. The way they play is very intriguing to me. Building up a territory, leading other people, growing influence. All these parts of the game really appeal to me but I am not naive enough to think that I can do all this by myself.

"I want to start a team. An official team like Ouroboros had before. Actually, I've already started a team and Oberlin has joined it. I'd love to have you two join the team as well. I have a sponsor already and I'm working out the details for it, but I think it would be really awesome for both of you to join."

"We'd lo..." Before Mina could finish her statement, Velin quickly covered her mouth.

"Thank you for your offer, Thorn. We would love to hear more details about this." Velin kept her hand over her short friend's mouth.

"Haha, sure. I've sent you the employment contracts. The team sponsor is Atlas Energy and the budget is generous. I'm not one hundred percent set on what the team's primary goal is at this point. Why don't you take a moment to read through the contract and I can try to answer any questions you have?"

For a few moments, silence reigned as Mina and Velin read through the file that Thorn sent them. At first, Mina looked over it casually, but the contents soon left her mouth hanging open in shock. Velin had brought out her notebook to write down her questions, but it lay forgotten at her side as her eyes widened in surprise. Neither girl said a word until they had finished reading over the document. Even after they finished, they simply stared at each other for a moment.

"Is this real?" Velin's voice was quiet.

"Yeah." Thorn frowned. "Why wouldn't it be?"

"You expect me to believe that Atlas is offering us a contract on their official team?!" Mina shouted.

"Ah, yeah. I know someone in the company." Thorn's face broke into a smile. "I mean, I think the conditions are pretty good."

"Pretty good is not even close. Generous pay, paid

relocation, a ridiculous benefits package that includes housing and a state-of-the-art pod for long term immersion? Team share options and living space in Fantasia? All attached to a self-defined contract period and a severance package? This is an offer straight out of a fantasy for a professional player." Velin's voice was flat.

"Ah," Thorn scratched his head. He had asked his aunt for a standard elite player's contract and had polished up a few of the areas he felt were not quite up to scratch to try and make it more attractive. On further reflection, maybe he had made it a bit too attractive.

"Honestly, this looks outstanding." Velin looked squarely at Thorn. "But it is only fair to tell you that we don't come without issue." Glancing at Mina, whose frown had returned, Velin smiled bleakly. "Ever since we got out of Hati's Ascent, things have gone terribly for us. At first, it was strained relationships inside the group, but over the last couple of weeks, it has gotten worse. A lot worse.

"When you met us, Mina and I were professional players registered to Ragnarok's third team, led by Ouroboros. That team was disbanded and our contracts, along with Jorge's, were terminated. On top of that, our housing contract was terminated as well and all our accounts were frozen, citing a criminal investigation."

"They said the building was being used for trafficking illegal substances." Mina's tone was hollow.

"Who said that?"

"The city inspectors who came to notify us that the building we were in was being condemned. We've been living in an Internet Cafe for the last two days but I think we are about to get kicked out." Velin sighed again. "So much has happened all in a row that it is pretty obvious that someone has it out for us. Someone with a lot of pull. I don't know if they are targeting us because of our former membership in Ragnarok or if it is because we were close to Ouroboros, but I don't want to bring trouble to you."

"This all started two weeks ago?"

"Two weeks in game, two days real time."

"Ah, right." Thorn nodded. Since he spent all his time in the game, it was easy to forget that time in the real world passed differently. "You don't need to worry about it, I am not afraid of trouble."

"This is serious, Thorn. Whoever it is has serious connections in our city government. I don't want to drag you into our mess. We have already ruined your life enough."

"I'm serious as well. Atlas is not afraid of anyone, no matter how many connections they have. You can have confidence that Atlas will have your back. I'm happy to add a protection clause if it will help."

There was something magnetic about Thorn's deep, calm voice that caused Mina to believe him completely. Without waiting for Velin, she signed the contract and sent it back to Thorn. Velin only took a couple of more quiet moments before she signed it as well.

"Welcome to the party." Grinning, Thorn stood up. "I've got to make a call, but I'll be right back. Our first order of business will be to come up with a concrete plan for our current quest. Excuse me one second."

Leaving the room, Thorn's grin changed to a frown. Mina and Velin's rapidly escalating situation was too coincidental. He walked down the stairs and asked one of the waiters for a private room. Though the furniture was too small for him to sit down, it was quiet and most importantly, sound-proofed.

"Hey, kid!" Julia popped up on his messenger app almost as soon as he hit the call button.

"Aunt, did you do something to that party I was with?"

"Uh, um. No?" Julia's eyes shifted for a moment until, unable to stand Thorn's stare, she threw up her hands in defeat. "Okay, maybe. I might have dropped a couple of hints here and there. But they deserved it. As far as I am concerned, they are getting off easy!"

CHAPTER NINETEEN

Frustrated, Thorn could only glare at his aunt. With the amount of power available at her fingertips, it was silly to expect that she would not leverage it to get what she wanted. It was even sillier for Thorn to pretend that he was not tempted to do the same. While he had ambitions of crafting his destiny with his own hands, he was not foolish enough to ignore the advantage that Atlas afforded to him.

Still, he was uncomfortable using the weight of the company to squash those that displeased him.

“I thought I told you that I would deal with it.” Thorn sighed, rubbing the back of his head.

“How could you deal with it?” Even thinking about what had happened to Thorn got Julia steamed. “What they did was unacceptable and there is no way I can let them off scot-free. No one is allowed to hurt you like that.”

Seeing that Julia was in full mom mode, Thorn held his tongue and let her vent for a few minutes. After it sounded like she had gotten most of the venom out of her system, Thorn smiled.

“Aunt, I understand what you are saying, but I would like it if you could let me handle this. I’ve been questing with two of them recently, and I was thinking of recruiting them to my team.”

“The girls, right?” Julia’s eyes narrowed dangerously.

“Yes. Mina and Velin are their names. Look, I feel loved knowing you have my back, but I don’t want to make a big deal about what happened. I’ve thought a lot about this and I think it would be best to get it behind me. At least, as much as I can.”

“You are forgiving them?! That’s it?! I don’t know that I can support that. Just because they are girls, it doesn’t mean you have to let them get away with murder. They tried to kill you and stole from you. I say you should make them pay.”

“Honestly, I would have agreed with you a couple of weeks ago.” Thorn sighed, rubbing his nose. “But then I started thinking about what I actually want from life and being consumed by anger, is not it. I know it sounds crazy, but when I started planning my revenge that is all I could think about. It took over my thoughts and made me angry all the time. That is not the type of person you raised me to be.

“Look, it isn’t like I am happy that they threw me under the bus, but I can’t deny that it helped me grow up. At least a little bit. My first foray into having friends of my own ended terribly, but I don’t have to let that define me, right? I am more than my pain, I am more than my body. You taught me that. My body bends to my will, not I to it.” Pausing to gather his thoughts, Thorn stared down at his hands as Julia waited quietly, watching him from the other side of the call.

“At the end of the day, my feelings are like my pain. They are like my body. Sometimes terrible things happen. And sometimes I’m an idiot and don’t see them coming. Or maybe I willfully ignore them because I really want friends. But I don’t have to let my feelings pick my path. I don’t know. I guess I’m saying that I want to try it again but on my own terms. Believe me,” lifting his head, Thorn looked his aunt squarely in the eyes, his voice taking on a hint of steel. “I will not let something like that happen again.”

“Alright, alright. I understand. I will take the pressure off.” Julia waved her hand, smiling fondly at Thorn. “Oh, wait. What about that Ouroboros guy. He got a four-category class at your expense. He is well protected by his family, but I was about to start putting the screw to them.”

“I’ll deal with Ouroboros myself.” Thorn shook his head. “I owe him at least a punch, but after that, I’m going to play it by ear. Besides, you can’t afford to be involved in this sort of stuff, Aunt. Atlas doesn't need bad press."

"Haha. You're cute. I've been doing this sort of thing for years, kid. I know what I can and can't do."

"I'll send you the contracts Mina and Velin signed. Can I trouble you with registering my team?"

"One sec." Julia scrolled through her contacts and sent one over to Thorn. "This is your lawyer's Fantasia avatar. Send them to him with a note and he can do everything you need. Have you decided on a name?"

"I'm thinking Titan or something like that."

"Titan is already taken. Honestly, most of the good names are taken." Julia looked at her nephew fondly. "You know, kid? I want to tell you how much I love you and how proud I am of you."

"Thanks, Aunt Julia. I love you too."

After the call ended, and Thorn had sent Oberlin, Velin, and Mina's contracts to his lawyer with a note, he sat for a couple of moments in silence. Meeting Josephine, the Avatar of Salliish, and butting heads with Angdrin of Ragnarok's Crimson Snakes had started an idea brewing in Thorn's head. To see other players treating Nova Terra as a world to be explored and conquered, he could not help but feel the bite of adventure.

If other people could take over territories, why shouldn't he? If others could set up massive, far-reaching, secret societies, why couldn't Thorn? He was not one hundred percent clear on what it was that he wanted to build, but the more he learned about his quest, the clearer his path became.

"One thing at a time." Thorn reminded himself before standing and heading back upstairs.

In the room, Mina was chatting away, a glimmer of hope shining in her eyes. The recent events in the real world had dampened her natural enthusiasm but she was bouncing back quickly. Velin, on the other hand, remained somber as she racked her brain for a solution to the issues that were plaguing her and Mina. Even though she had signed the contract, she did not want to involve Thorn if she did not have to.

ding

Mina froze, her face turning white as she looked at Velin. Seeing a message in her inbox from the bank she opened it, the slight trembling in her hands betraying her nervousness. The longer she read, the wider her eyes became as color came rushing back into her face.

"Ahhhhh! Velin, look at this! Look at this! The bank unfroze my account?! And they deposited the signing bonus! That means we don't have to stay at the cafe anymore!"

ding

“Wait, here is another message. It’s from the city inspection office! Our apartment has been unsealed! We can go home! Or buy a new home!” Mina was so excited she was nearly panting. “Can you believe how quickly things turned around? I mean, we signed the contract, like, twenty minutes ago! What a crazy coincidence for the inspection to be over too.”

“Yeah,” Velin could not suppress a sigh of relief. “Quite the coincidence. Mina, we will need to do our best in our new jobs, okay? No messing around.”

“Ha, when do I ever mess around?” Mina spun around as the door opened. Seeing Thorn’s large figure she pounced forward and hugged his waist as best she could.

Taken aback, Thorn looked the Elven War Priestess who smiled and shrugged.

“Thorn! You wouldn’t believe what happened! I’m so happy. Our accounts were unfrozen and our apartment building opened back up! We don’t have to stay in the cafe anymore! Ahhh!” Letting go of him, Mina danced around the room in excitement before collapsing on the bed that had been pushed against the wall.

“Thorn, thank you.” Once Mina had calmed down, Velin stood up and bowed slightly.

"No problem." Thorn waved his hand. "Not a big deal. I'm happy to help."

"We have both discussed it and we are going to take up the offer of relocation, so we'll be out of the game for a while. It should only take a day or so to move with a moving company, but we will not be able to log in during that time."

"Yeah, it will be good to move to a new place." Mina chimed in.

"Since you'll be out of the game for a week or so, I thought I could go ahead and scout the valley out. Oberlin will be meeting us there as he has a couple of things to do in the south." Thorn scratched his head. The whole-time dilation thing made it awkward for him since he was permanently logged in.

"Alright." Velin closed her eyes for a moment and took a deep breath. "Why don't we talk about the quest."

"What did you find out?"

"As I mentioned before, the area is about three days from here to the east. From the few records I could find, it seems that there is some sort of corruption that has established itself in the valley, making it relatively inhospitable. My recommendation is that you proceed with caution. Your quest aside, I think there is a high possibility that if we search the valley we might be able to find an inheritance quest. In fact, I would not be surprised if your quest is the introduction to a chain inheritance quest. I found six reported quests that match this schema."

"Schema?"

"Yes, since all the quests in Nova Terra are unique, it is impossible to find an exact match. However, over time, players have noticed patterns in the way quests are given, structured, and completed. This fits the bill for an inheritance quest, but it is distinct in that it is not a class quest, but a title quest. Most inheritance quests revolve around inheriting a class or a treasure associated with a quest. The six specific quests I found in Ragnarok's database that matched this were also based on a title and every one of them had to do with inheriting a place rather than a thing."

"You mean, like a castle?" Mina asked, sitting up on the bed.

"Yes. Though none of them gained anything bigger than a shop in the capital."

"How do you have access to Ragnarok's database?" Thorn asked. "I thought you left the guild?"

"I built the database." Velin flashed a sly smile. "Even without being in the guild they have no chance of keeping me out without rebuilding the whole thing. Plus, I have my own backups in case they do rebuild it."

“Ah. Gotcha. Sorry for interrupting.”

“No problem. As I was saying, the largest gain from the quests was a sizable shop in the capital and renting it out has made the player who completed the quest a millionaire in real life. In fact, all six of the players or groups who finished these quests have gained substantial wealth from their quest rewards. Owning property in Nova Terra is rare, and even rarer if we ignore the guild halls that cities make available to the guilds.”

“We’re going to get a castle!” Mina cheered.

“Well, we don’t know if this quest will actually lead to owning property, so we need to make sure that we find the quest that does when we are in the valley. Additionally, we have to find it before anyone else does.”

“Do you think there are other players in the valley?”

“Probably not at this point. The area is rural, but I’m worried about the Crimson Snakes. Angdrin is one of the three major power players in Ragnarok and is in control of this whole region. The top three forces in Ragnarok are currently fighting over the guild master’s seat. Angdrin controls the Crimson Snakes while Sylith, a Heavenly Silver Dragon Knight, leads a faction called the Silver Guard.

“Ouroboros has joined the fight recently by establishing the

Blood Guard using the class change stones that he gained from Karrandras. All three of the groups are competing for the guild leader's seat by comparing their gains in the game. All that to say, Angdrin is going to be on the lookout for any new area opening. If he can add it to his territory he will gain a huge advantage over the other two.

"This means that he has scouts checking out every possible new area that they can find. I'm guessing that he already has a hint about it, which would explain why he was locking down Davyos' Fall. He should be looking for the quest that will grant ownership of land in the valley, and if he gets it we'll have a serious fight on our hands."

"You keep talking about how controlling an area is really good. Can you talk me through the benefits?" Thorn felt like he was still struggling to grasp the whole picture.

"Of course. Let's say that we've formed a guild and we are going to set up shop here in Berum. Our first option is to rent space from the city. That costs us money, and while we can recoup those losses and even turn a profit if we are smart, we will always have the cost of rent to worry about. However, if we owned some land in the city, we would be able to build whatever we wanted, zoning permitting. Without having to worry about the rent payment, or having a landlord, we would have a lot more control and profit.

"Now, imagine that we owned the city of Berum. Not only could we turn it into anything we wanted, but we could also rent out the land to other guilds or groups who wanted to develop businesses in the city. When you start to factor in things like respawn fees, taxes on the citizens, tariffs on goods being brought into the city, and licenses for hunting or gathering material it can pile up quickly."

"Ouroboros used to say that if you controlled the castle you controlled the people." Mina got off the bed and walking to the window.

"He was right." Velin nodded. "The biggest advantage of ownership in Nova Terra is the relationship it gives you with the natives. For whatever reason, natives pay a lot more attention to players who have a stake in their community or authority granted by the game."

"So, owning property sort of legitimizes your existence to the natives?" Thorn mused.

"That is exactly right. And if we can get ownership in the valley we will have a large advantage over other teams and can maybe look at setting up a guild."

"What is the difference? I thought guilds were just large teams?"

"Not really. There are several different official organizations that the game recognizes. Each has a different function. Teams allow players to jointly accept any non-solo quest. Normal guilds are technically collections of teams that own a piece of property. Mercenary Corps are a specialized guild that takes part in player generated requests as well as native requests. Armies are a guild that works for a native who holds power. Finally, there are Merchant Groups, which are guilds based around trading, and Orders, which are guilds that focus on a particular set of rules. They could be religiously based or social groups. With only four of us, we'd be considered a team. We'll need to add more players or natives to our organization to make a guild."

"Natives can join guilds?"

"Yup. That is how Velin got her class." Mina nodded. "It was passed down from the Holy Crimson Cardinal that Ragnarok recruited. He is a native that teaches players related classes. He lives at the headquarters."

"Interesting. So what about an organization like the Ordo Serpentes?"

"Secret societies could be a native organization or they could be a player guild. The game does a good job of blending them so it can be hard to tell if a guild is owned by players or has been generated by the game."

"Huh." Thorn looked up at the ceiling for a moment, occupied with his thoughts. "If we want to build a guild then we'll need more people."

"Not just that." Velin sent Thorn a file. "Guilds need three things. People, Purpose, and Prosperity."

"Prosperity?"

"She means money. But money doesn't start with a 'P'." Mina chuckled.

"Prosperity is more than money." Velin protested, giving Mina a reproving glance. "Guilds need success in what they do. They have to motivate their members or they will fall apart. People and purpose are self-explanatory, but prosperity is probably the most important piece of the puzzle. Prosperity attracts new members while purpose will come as those players take on tasks in Nova Terra and begin to shape the world around them."

"Hmm. I'll have to think about this."

"There is no rush. As our group grows, I'm sure these things will become clear." Velin closed her notebook with a snap as she stood. "Now, we should log out and start our move. The sooner we move to our new place, the sooner we can be back to help clear the keep."

CHAPTER TWENTY

"Whew." Thorn wiped imaginary sweat from his brow as he looked back over the trees that stretched to the horizon. The forest was eerily silent, causing the sound of his footsteps to seem unnaturally loud. Since getting within fifteen miles of the valley the unnatural silence had grown noticeable as the sounds of insects and small animals disappeared. Even the wind seemed scared to approach, causing the air to have an unsettling stillness.

Glancing around at the trees that had been his only company for the last three days, Thorn couldn't help but miss Mina and Oberlin's constant chatter. Even Velin's stoicism would be better than this silence. He had almost started talking to himself to break the strange feeling that crawled up his spine.

The party had split up in Berum three days ago after their adventure in the abandoned city and their conflict with the

Crimson Snakes. To save time Thorn traveled toward the keep while Mina and Velin logged out to change their housing arrangements. Agreeing to meet up once they were back in game, they said their goodbyes and Thorn forged on ahead, arriving at this silent forest.

The terrain had been steadily rising for the last day and he could see that he was approaching a large mountain range. If Velin's conjectures were correct, then Greymane Keep was located in the valley on the other side of the mountains.

Breaking out into a jog he began to cover ground quickly and, feeling no drain on his stamina, kicked his speed up a notch. Soon Thorn was practically flying up the mountain, each stride carrying him almost a dozen feet. Trees flew by in a blur of greens and browns as his speed slowly increased.

Within half an hour he had covered most of the distance to the peak of the mountain and could see the snow-capped summit sticking up over the trees. Unfortunately, catching a glimpse of the snow peeking above the trees distracted Thorn enough that he wasn't watching his footing and, stepping into a small dip in the ground, Thorn lost his balance. He hit the ground rolling, smashing straight into a large tree so hard that it fell to the ground with a thunderous crash, its trunk directly broken off.

Groaning in pain and clutching his back Thorn tried to stand to his feet only to hear an odd chittering sound coming from under the tree that he had knocked over. Squeaks of anger and pain poured out from under the tree in an unrelenting torrent and, worried that he had hurt someone, Thorn pushed the pain in his back out of his mind, grabbed the tree trunk and lifted it up with one hand.

Greeting him was an absolutely furious little furry creature. It didn't look to be injured, but it was certainly angry, a fact it reinforced by jumping at Thorn with its teeth and claws bared. Despite being startled at the sudden attack, Thorn managed to catch the little creature with one hand where it scratched and bit furiously. Unsure at this sudden turn of events, Thorn was about to try and throw the creature off when he realized that the little monster wasn't hurting him as its teeth couldn't pierce his skin.

It was also quite cute, like a small red panda with multiple tails. A pretty pattern made up of three diamonds on its forehead made it look like it was wearing a small crown. Right now it was doing its best to chew through Thorn's gauntleted fingers. Afraid it would hurt itself, Thorn unsummoned his gloves, allowing the small creature to gnaw on his fingers to its heart's content.

When it became apparent that its efforts to remove Thorn's fingers was futile, the creature abandoned the attempt, instead climbing up onto Thorn's shoulder and shaking its little fist at his face while it scolded him. Moving carefully, Thorn pulled an apple out of his inventory and offered it. Snatching the piece of fruit and holding it in its mouth, the creature scampered down Thorn's tall body, jumping onto one of the trees he had uprooted in his tumble.

Sitting on its hind legs, it used its front paws to hold the apple while it munched on it, still grumbling in between bites while throwing Thorn dirty looks. Amused, Thorn brought out more food and sat down as well. Opening his messaging system, Thorn looked for someone who was online, finally settling on Mina's icon.

"Hey Thorn, did you find the castle yet? I just logged in and I am waiting for Velin before we come your way. Oberlin said he would be a couple of more days. Did he tell you?"

"Yeah, we talked. Hey, I have a question. Do you know what this is?" Thorn turned the camera to be forward facing, revealing the grumpy creature who had finished the apple and was now eating the rest of Thorn's food as if it was the most natural thing in the world.

"Oh, you found an Ailuridae! An uncommon royal Ailuridae at that!"

"Royal Ailuridae?"

"Yeah, it's like a red panda. But you can tell how rare it is by its number of tails. One tail is common, two is uncommon, three is rare. Do you see the symbol on its face? That is how you can tell it is a royal creature. You should bind it as a pet and then give it to me!" Mina's eyes glowed as she gazed at the fluffy creature. “It is so cute.”

Seeing that Thorn was looking over, the creature shook its fist at him again, obviously still mad.

“Haha, what did you do? It looks like it is mad at you. Look how cute it is!”

“Yeah. I might have knocked over its home. How do I bind it as a pet?”

“There are a couple of ways to tame creatures, the simplest being to pay an Animal Trainer to do it for you. You can also use Pet Cards from the shop to tame creatures. They are considered vanity items so they will appear in your inventory immediately. In theory, if you could make the animal like you enough it will offer a contract on its own, but that is really rare. I would use a Pet Card if I were you.”

After he located the cash shop interface, Thorn searched around and clicked on the pet shop window. A semi-transparent screen covered Thorn’s vision, asking him if he wanted to travel to the pet shop or open it in windowed mode.

“Mina, what does it mean about traveling to the pet shop?”

“You’ve never used the shop?” Mina’s mouth dropped open in an exaggerated manner.

"No, I've never needed to." Thorn ignored her mockery.

"Well, if you are outside of combat you can go to any of the vanity shops. It takes you there mentally, but your body stays where it is. But that way you can get your vanity items and equip them immediately."

"Isn't that dangerous? What if you get attacked or something?"

"Not really. I mean, I guess it could be. Don't use it while you are in danger. Plus, there is a little bell thingy that will let you know if something is happening in Nova Terra. The shops are in Fantasia so if you are worried you can log out of the game and go there. Or open a shop in windowed mode. You're the size of a mountain, Thorn, don't be a sissy."

"Thanks, Mina." Ignoring her banter, Thorn ended the call and clicked on the button to open the shop in windowed mode. The see-through window solidified, floating in front of Thorn like a virtual video screen. Inside he could see the shop.

It was empty except for a middle-aged woman sitting behind a glass case. Shelving covered the walls holding a massive number of cards, each with the picture of a different creature on it and a colored border.

There were red cards along the bottom of the wall, blue cards at about waist height and a line of silver cards at head height. In the case in front of the woman were gold bordered cards and two black bordered cards.

"Hello sir, how can I help you?" asked the woman, smiling at Thorn through the screen.

"I have an animal here I would like to register as a battle pet." Thorn pointed at the Ailuridae who was still muttering in between bites of food.

"Oh my," gasped the woman. "That is an Ailuridae. A royal Ailuridae!" Quickly she stood and placed a thin block of wood on the counter. "Put it in the containment field, quick!" The block of wood lit up with a circle of blue runes which projected a glowing sphere into the air.

Puzzled, Thorn looked at her through the screen and then looked at the small furry creature. Seeing his confusion the lady covered her mouth and laughed.

"Sir, you can put it through the window."

Curious, Thorn stuck his hand through the screen, almost immediately making contact with the wooden counter in the shop. Surprised he pulled his hand back and stared at the window. It was like two completely different realities were superimposed on one another, with only this square hole connecting them. Shaking his head he turned his attention back to the matter at hand, reaching out for the small creature.

Catching it proved more of a challenge than he expected, however, and after a few fruitless minutes of trying and failing Thorn stepped back. The furry creature, obviously pleased with itself, preened, and managed to look down its tiny nose at Thorn, despite the incredible height difference.

Smirking, Thorn pulled a pastry out of his inventory, crouching down to hold it out. Slowly he coaxed the furry creature closer, tempting it with the freshly baked smell. Once again, as he waited patiently for the Ailuridae to take the bait, Thorn couldn't help but marvel at the convenience of an inventory. It stored his food in a perfectly preserved state, which meant that it came out as perfect as it had been when he put it in.

Eventually, curiosity and greed won out and the Ailuridae slipped forward, jumping up onto Thorn's arm to snatch the sweet-smelling pastry. Lighting up after the first bite, it devoured the rest of the pastry and then held out a small paw, demanding more. Three pastries later, it was so preoccupied that it didn't notice when Thorn stuck it through the window into the pet shop.

Thorn moved his hand into the field, feeling that the Ailuridae ceased moving as it entered the area. Thorn took a moment to examine his hand but seeing nothing strange looked back at the shopkeeper who was staring at the Ailuridae floating in the field.

"Wow, this is the first time I have ever seen an uncommon Ailuridae!" Gushed the shopkeeper. "And a royal one at that. Look, look, see the tails? See the black stripes under its eyes? And the cute white cheeks? Ooooooh. It's just too cute!"

Thorn cleared his throat, reminding the shopkeeper that she had a customer.

"Oh, oh, please excuse me. I am Sondra, the Battle Pet Master of Fantasia. Did you want to trade in this pet for money?"

"Actually, I'm not sure. Can you explain how this whole Battle Pet thing works?" Asked Thorn.

"Of course. Ehem. The Battle Pet system is one that allows travelers and natives of Nova Terra to tame wild animals and monsters and take them as companions. Each person can acquire one Battle Pet. As you grow, there are various ways to strengthen your Battle Pet. Every Battle Pet is ranked by color, with red being common, blue uncommon, silver rare, gold epic and black unique. Gold level pets are boss drops and black level pets are one of a kind."

"What does it cost to get a pet?"

"That depends on what color pet you want. All new pets are adjusted to match the progression of their owner so they can grow with them. The lower your progression when you get the pet the cheaper it is, and the same is true for the color."

"What do you mean by progression? I thought Nova Terra didn't have a level mechanic?"

"Oh, it doesn't. Progression refers to how close you are to mastering your current class. Battle Pets grow based on how they can support your class. So, in this case, because Ailuridae function as a healer, as you progress through your class your battle pet will gain skills that compliment you. That means they might develop offensive buffs if you are a melee fighter, or defensive abilities if you are a caster."

"What if I don't have a class?"

"You don't have a class? Oh, in that case, your Battle Pet will take their standard growth path, growing slowly over time until you get a class."

"You mentioned selling?"

"Yes, you can sell animals you find so long as you tame them first or capture them in a Battle Pet trap. For example, an ailuridae is a silver ranked pet and can be sold for 100 gold whereas a royal ailuridae is a gold ranked pet and goes for 500 gold per level."

"Hmmm," Thorn scratched his chin. "What if I wanted to bind this Ailuridae as a battle pet? What would the cost be?"

"Let me scan it and see." Sondra pulled a small crystal wand out from her robe and waved it over the suspended Ailuridae and after a few seconds a screen popped up.

Name: [Akira]	Race: [Royal Ailuridae]
Health: [100%]	Mana: [100%]
Titles: [Royal Princess]	Conditions: [Stasis]
Abilities: [Royal Grace]	

"Whoa!" Gasped Sondra. "This is a unique Ailuridae! Having a name and a title makes it a black ranked pet!"

"And how do I bind it?"

"Oh yes, yes. You bind a pet by paying a binding fee or by using an equally ranked card. So if you want to bind Akira here you would need to pay me 10% of the sale price of a black ranked card which would come to 1,500 gold."

"1,500 Gold? You mean that the normal price is 15,000 gold for a black ranked pet?" Thorn was stunned at the price. "That's incredible."

"I mean, each black ranked battle pet is one of a kind after all. And a unique item or pet could be said to be priceless. In fact, you have really lucked out by finding a unique pet," Sondra looked enviously at the furry creature rotating slowly in the blue light.

“I think I want to have this pet bound to me,” Thorn converted a couple of UC in his Fantasia account into gold and pulled a stack of ten gold coins from his inventory. One of the perks of having wealth, he thought. Thorn’s aunt had showed him how to deposit money into his Fantasia account. He had not tapped into it yet out of principle, but now seemed like a good time to break his self-imposed restriction.

“Sure, give me a second.” With more wand-waving Sondra activated the wooden base and with a twinkle the Ailuridae disappeared only to be replaced with a black-edged Battle Pet card. Handing it to Thorn, Sondra pointed at a small device on the counter with a needle, “Please place a drop of blood on the card. This will bind your pet to you and you will gain the ability to summon your pet by saying [Summon] and your pet’s name. You can summon your pet for any length of time but if it dies you will have to wait at least 24 hours before you summon it again.”

Thanking Sondra for her help Thorn did as she said, watching as the card disappeared and a notification box popped up to let him know that he could now summon a pet. His mood high, Thorn activated it and grinned as a chittering Ailuridae appeared on his shoulder. Different from before, the Ailuridae now had three tails and a curious expression as it looked around at everything else.

"Akira Status."

Name: [Akira]	Race: [Royal Ailuridae]
Health: [100%]	Mana: [100%]
Titles: [Royal Princess], [Thorn's Companion]	Conditions: [None]
Abilities: [Royal Grace]	

'Master?! Master!' An excited voice rang out in Thorn's mind as Akira hopped up and down on his shoulder. 'Master, I'm Akira. I'm smart and soft and beautiful and the best! I can fight and hunt and do magic and tell people what to do and I'm the best Ailuridae!'

Bemused by the torrent of thoughts from his new pet, Thorn picked her off his shoulder and stroked her fur. "It is nice to meet you Akira, I am Thorn. Let's get along, okay?"

CHAPTER TWENTY-ONE

Later that day, Thorn stood under a large tree and looked down the length of a long valley. At the end he could barely make out a series of cliffs rising to the grey blob that was Greymane Keep. Between him and the castle was almost ten miles of thick woods broken by a meandering river. The relatively close forest he had been walking through seemed to give way to old growth in the valley and tracks of large wolves became common.

Despite the tracks he saw no wolves and even Akira, who had been talking non-stop, sensed nothing. Sniffing at the tracks, Akira wrinkled her nose and jumped up on Thorn's shoulder.

“Master, those tracks smell awful. There is no way I would allow such big stinky creatures in *my* forest.”

Getting down, close to the ground, Thorn tried to pick up a

scent. Ever since he had become an Avatar his senses had grown increasingly sharp but he couldn't pick up any smell apart from the heavy smell of dirt.

"Can you tell what sort of creature it is?"

"It smells like a timber wolf, but really sour and bitter."

"Hmmm. Like this?" Thorn pulled a corrupted wolf's tail from the depth of his inventory.

"Phew! Gross, gross, gross!" Akira burrowed into the back of Thorn's shirt. "Put it away! Bleh, bleh."

"Haha, okay, okay."

Putting the tail away, Thorn walked down into the valley. The forest was still quiet, though Akira's mental muttering provided a break from the silence. Curious at the lack of creatures, Thorn could only assume that it was due to the presence of the corrupted wolves. He continued on his way until the forest began to thin out a bit. Akira had left his shirt and bounded ahead, zipping from tree to tree faster than Thorn's eyes could keep up, and now she ran back.

"Master, master! There are people ahead. It looks like they are hunters! Should I steal their food?! Can I?"

"No, wait till I catch up. I want to talk to them and stealing their food will make them mad." Akira pouted on his shoulder but begrudgingly pointed him toward the hunters.

The group of hunters noticed Thorn about the same time that he saw them and warily readied their weapons. Dressed in rough leather and tattered fur armor the human hunters were dirty and covered in grime but despite their bedraggled appearance, it was evident by the amount of game at their feet that they had experienced a bit of luck in their hunt. Now, hard faced, they watched as Thorn walked forward until he was about 30 feet away, bows at the ready.

“Hold there, traveler. Who are you and what business do you have in this forest?” The lead hunter was obviously unsettled by Thorn’s size, nervously resting his hand on his sword.

“Hello, I’m Thorn, a traveler, and I’m looking for Greymane Keep. Would you be able to direct me there?”

“Greymane?” the lead hunter’s eyes narrowed and he shot a glance at his companions. “What business do you have there?”

“I need to go there for a quest.”

“I can direct you there but I must warn you, it is infested with werewolves at the moment. Have you received the quest to recover the Statue of Hati?”

“Is there a quest for that? I don’t know anything about a Statue of Hati. No, I was heading there for a different reason but I would love to get the quest if it is available."

"Hmmm, I think you could get it at the town hall." The lead hunter relaxed his guard a bit. "I'm Charles Mallard, Captain of the Watch in the town of Greymane. Follow us back and you can pick up the quest."

Walking back with the hunters took a couple hours and while at first they watched Thorn closely, by the time the wooden palisade of the village came into sight they seemed to have accepted that he was what he claimed. Akira was much to be thanked for this change as she lost no time in making herself acquainted with the hunters and within a short amount of time was trying to con them out of snacks.

The village was a shabby affair, comprised of one main street with houses on either side. In the center of the village was an empty forge, a tavern covered in peeling paint and a small building that housed the village leader's office and the jail, all arranged around a little town square. It looked like the village had been larger at one point, the broken remains of houses among the weeds giving evidence to this.

Charles brought Thorn into the center of town and stuck his head into the jail, calling, "Thomas, we've got a traveler who wants to challenge the castle."

"Huh, another fool?" responded a grumpy voice and the door pushed open to reveal an old man leaning heavily on a cane. "Ho traveler. I am Thomas, head of this pile of excrement they call a village. Want to challenge the castle, eh? Can't say it is a smart idea, but we all have the right to choose our own death."

Stomping over to Thorn he pulled out a weathered piece of paper from his breast pocket and shoved it in Thorn's face, growling, "Please, kind traveler, help our poor village. Our poor village has come under a curse because we lost the statue of Hati from our temple. Go to Greymane Keep and get it back from the evil werewolves that live there. I know it will be hard but our lives depend on it. Blah blah blah."

Hearing Thomas' totally out of character tone Thorn couldn't help but chuckle. "So, tell me. What do I get for clearing out the castle?"

"Our eternal gratitude." responded Thomas, a mocking look in his eye.

Greymane Village: Lesser Curse
Thomas, the head of Greymane Village, has asked you to retrieve the statue of Hati that once stood in the village Temple. The statue was stolen away during a raid by a group of werewolves, causing a curse to settle on the village. Returning the statue will break the curse, allowing it to be used as a respawn point.

After looking over the quest update that popped up in front of him, Thorn dismissed it and carefully considered his next course of action. According to the information that Velin had dug up on the area, Greymane was the only village in the valley, which made it strategically important. The village was located near the entrance to the valley, while the keep stood against the cliffs on the other side.

While his current goal was to clear the keep and claim the throne of the Wolf Lord, Thorn did not know what to expect after that. Undoubtedly, this adventure wouldn't end with assuming the position of the Lord. Thorn had not shared the specifics of his quest with Velin and Mina, but the more he thought about it, the more likely it seemed that this was going to be a quest chain. After a moment of consideration, Thorn looked at the old man and held up his hand, showing the ring he had gotten off Gargish.

"Thomas, I will not conceal my purpose from you. I defeated Gargish, the Blood Hunter, in battle and have come to claim the keep as my own. I can break the curse for you, but I need some information about the castle and the werewolves in it."

"Eh? You killed that monster?!" gasped Thomas. A flame sprang into his eyes as he looked at Thorn intently. The longer he looked, the happier he got. "Well, who knew? You might be able to do it traveler. Talk to Charles. He has some supplies for dealing with the werewolves that might be helpful. And before you go, come talk to me."

Charles was behind the faded inn, working with the other

town guard to clean and dress the three deer they had brought back from their hunt. Seeing that one of the deer was still waiting to be processed, Thorn offered his help. After the work was done, and everyone had washed the blood from their hands Thorn brought up his objective of clearing the werewolves from the keep and retrieving the statue of Hati.

“That is quite the task you are taking on, traveler. Hold on one second, I might have something that will help you.” Charlie rummaged around in his bag, pulling out two colored bottles. Shaking the blue one he said, “This is a scent neutralizing potion. It should help you get close to the keep. You’ll drink it and it should last around four hours. This green potion is the opposite. It will attract all the werewolves in a certain area. You pour a bit out on the ground and they’ll gather. Should be enough for five uses in there.”

“Thanks. Can I get more of these potions? I have some friends who are coming to help me, and it would be nice to get some potions for them.”

“Sure, we can make some more but you’ll have to collect the ingredients yourself. Here, let me write you a list. You’ll need three Blue Bells, one Wolfsbane, and a Zimph root for each scent neutralization potion. The attraction potion is a bit harder to make. For that you’ll have to find seven Silverleaf and one deer heart.”

“Thanks.” Thorn looked over the list he had been given.

"Would you be willing to sell the hearts from the deer you brought back today? I have three companions, four if you count Akira here. I'd be willing to pay well for them. Say, 10 silver per?"

"I think that should be okay. Let me check with the others, but I don't see why that wouldn't work."

"Excellent. Let me know." About to leave, Thorn turned back at the door. "Oh, I wanted to ask, do you know where I can get a map of the area?"

"Talk to Markus. He has the little general store at the end of the street."

The next task was getting a room for the night so after thanking Charles for his help, Thorn found his way to the front of the inn. The receptionist, a thin bespeckled elf, assigned him a room with the largest bed the inn had and invited him into the general room for a meal where he found the locals enjoying their evening repast. The food was hearty, if plain, and Thorn was careful to control the amount he ate, lest he eat them out of house and home.

After he finished his meal, Thorn retired to his room and sent a message to Velin, Mina, and Oberlin, letting them know that he had found the keep and they should all gather here when they logged in. The trip from Berum took about two days, so he had plenty of time to look for potion materials.

Thorn had a good sleep despite barely fitting on the bed. He uncurled and stretched as he got up, refreshed. One of the things he appreciated the most about Nova Terra was that any sleep was good sleep. Unlike the real world where he would often wake up throughout the night, he had never had a bad night's sleep in Nova Terra.

Eating a quick breakfast of ten eggs, two loaves of bread and a giant bowl of oatmeal, Thorn decided to visit the general store as his first stop. The valley was large so a map would be helpful if he was going to be wandering all over.

The general store was as run down as the rest of the buildings, but as Thorn squeezed inside he was surprised to find the small room meticulously clean and well organized. A bell on the door tinkled and an older man limped out of a back room and took a seat on a stool.

"Afternoon, sir. What can I do for you?" The old man eased his leg and scratched his grizzled chin.

"Hi, are you Markus? Charles sent me down here. I'm looking for a map of Greymane Keep as well as one of the surrounding areas." responded Thorn.

"Greymane Keep huh? That is a dangerous place. Quite a dangerous section of country in general. Try the second shelf up on the left. There should be a green scroll. Bring it here, would you?"

Finding the appropriate scroll which seemed to be made from dyed leather, Thorn brought it over to the shopkeeper who spread it out on the table next to him.

“This is a map of the land around the castle, though you’ll notice the castle isn’t filled in. Never made it inside you see. There is a ruined village right near there, about seven miles from here. The village was destroyed by the wicked werewolves who live in the castle. In fact, this whole area is dangerous because it’s their hunting grounds so I’d be careful if you have a quest over there. Maybe find a party before you go.” Sniffing at the map and scratching his chin again the shopkeeper continued. “Anyway, if you want it I can copy the map to you for 2 gold. Oh and 40 silver for a general map of the surrounding area between here and there.”

“Yes please.” Thorn pulled the money out of his inventory. “Did you make all these maps yourself? They have a ton of detail.”

“Heh, you bet I did.” replied Markus proudly. “I was quite the famous cartographer before I took an ogre’s mace to my left hip. But I don’t regret it. Those were good times, but certainly not comfortable times.”

After thanking the talkative shopkeeper again Thorn took his leave and headed out of town. Finding a rock to sit on, Thorn pulled out his updated map and beckoned to his battle pet.

“Alright, Akira, let's make a plan. We need to find 12 Blue Bells, 4 Wolfsbane, 4 Zimph root, 28 Silverleaf, and one more deer heart. I’m going to rely on you to help me scout for this stuff, okay?”

“Of course! I’ve got the best nose!” Akira jumped up and down in excitement before leaping into the branches and bounding off.

“And…” before Thorn could continue, she was gone, leaving him with his mouth open. With a shrug he put away his map and stood up, dusting off his pants.

ding

Accepting Mina’s call, Thorn walked after Akira while chatting.

“Hey Thorn! We’re on our way so don’t get too excited and run ahead without us! It is only Velin and I coming right now, Oberlin said he had something he had to do in the south. Something about a deal with snakes? I don’t know. He’ll probably send you a message about it. Velin dug up some interesting information about the keep, apparently it used to be something else? A temple? I don’t know, I wasn’t really paying attention. Haha. Here, let me add her, she can explain it to you.”

CHAPTER TWENTY-TWO

"The whole situation is pretty complicated." Flashing a brief smile as a greeting, Velin immediately launched into her explanation when her image appeared next to Mina's in the video chat. "I ran across a story that talked about a group called the Night Walkers. From what I could figure out, they were followers of Hati and were a monastic order based out of the area you are currently in. There was no mention of Greymane Keep, but there was a mention of the Temple of the Night, a monastery fortress from which the Night Walkers operated.

"The reason I say that this is complicated is because the leader of the fortress was also the Lord of the valley and held a position of political importance. Anyway, what I want to say is that there may be an opportunity to pick up a class or something related to the Night Walkers, and more importantly, a class related to the Lord of the valley."

"Why would that be such a big deal?" Thorn asked impassively, hiding his astonishment at Velin's conjecture. This lady was a bit too sharp sometimes.

"Land. Wolfkin are not currently a playable race, but we've seen this pattern before in Nova Terra. The game introduces a few players to the race, gives out a few quests specific to them, and then unlocks them as a playable race with a specific start area. There is huge economic advantage to controlling starter areas, especially starter areas that come with a unique race. It could turn into nothing, but if what I think is true, there are going to be a lot of guilds eyeing this area soon."

"Alright. Let's think of a plan. Mina said you are on your way, right?"

"Yes. We should be there in three days."

"Cool, come to Greymane village when you get here. I bought a map that I'll send to you."

Saying goodbye, Thorn could only shake his head. He had not told the elven War Priestess about his title or the content of his quest, but she had still dug up so much information it was scary. Even worse, if she could dig it up, it was likely that there were others who could do the same.

Thorn had not given it much thought, but in the back of his mind he was worried about Angdrin and his Crimson

Snakes. After two encounters that both turned out poorly for the guild, it seemed likely that Thorn had made an enemy. Combined with the fact that he was now running around with two former members of Ragnarok and a grudge against another one of their officers, Thorn could see himself getting into conflict with the powerful guild easily.

While he had not done much research on the subject, Thorn had suspected that his quest was going to end in opening this territory for players. According to what Velin had said, the primary means of making money for guilds was controlling territory. If his instincts were correct, this path would paint a giant target on his already large back.

Since all of this was only speculation at this point Thorn put these things aside and continued his search for herbs. The forest was quiet and Akira was staying ahead of him, jumping from branch to branch. Occasionally, Thorn would come across a plant that looked like an herb and would get out [The Complete Alchemist], a book that he had looted from the abandoned wolfkin city.

Comparing the plant against the pictures, he would try and determine if it was worth anything. If it looked like an herb of any sort he would carefully dig it out and store it in his inventory before continuing his search.

After six hours of walking through the woods, Thorn had found 2 Wolfsbane and 3 Silverleaf. He had picked up several other plants that seemed valuable as well, but he was a far cry from what he needed for the potions. It was getting into the mid-afternoon so he stopped to eat and then decided to venture a bit further out. According to his book, both Zimph root and Blue Bells liked more sunlight, so he thought he would have better luck along the edge of the forest where the valley started to rise.

The old timber of the forest was spread out enough that Thorn did not have any trouble weaving through the tall trees, allowing him to arrive at the eastern edge of the forest with plenty of daylight left. He scoured the edge of the forest, successfully digging out seven Zimph roots. Or at least, he assumed they were Zimph roots. While he had a book to compare to, he really had no experience with plants so he was sort of guessing.

As Thorn put away the last of the roots, Akira came zipping back, dashing from tree to tree until she was above Thorn's head.

"Master, master! There are big smelly wolves ahead! There are bunches of them! They have a gross cave and everything!"

"Whoa, calm down Akira. Where are they?"

"Up ahead, I can show you. You should bash them so they leave and stop making the forest smelly! Come on, come on!" Turning on her heel, the furry Ailuridae dashed off again, almost disappearing from sight as she rushed ahead.

“Hey, slow down. How am I supposed to follow you like that?”

“Master, you are too slow! What if they leave? Then you can’t bash them!”

Shaking his head, Thorn followed behind his battle pet. After walking for a few minutes, Thorn saw Akira crouched on a branch, peering around a tree. Trying to move as quietly as possible, Thorn moved up to the trunk of the tree, peeking his head around it. Ahead of him, three large corrupted wolves lounged in front of a small cave carved into the side of the hill.

“Master, there are six smelly wolves.” Akira scampered down the tree, climbing out on Thorn’s broad shoulder and whispered into his ear.

“I only see three.”

“I smell six different gross smells. I have the best nose so you can trust me.” Akira patted Thorn’s head comfortingly with her tiny claws.

“Okay, let’s sneak up on them.” Thorn whispered back, pulling his arbalest out of his inventory and loading it as quietly as he could.

“Uh, master, that doesn’t seem like it is going to work.”

“Why not? If we sneak up on them we might be able to take a couple of them down before they can react.”

“But master, you are too loud.”

“Huh?”

“You sound like an earth dragon when you walk, master. Even when you tiptoe.” Akira looked at Thorn innocently. “Or, if not an earth dragon, then maybe a whole herd of big deer. Really big deer. Or moose.”

“Wait, so they know we are here?” Thorn planted his face into his hand. “Then why are we whispering?”

“I’m not sure, master, but you were doing it so I did it too.”

“But why are those three not responding to us? Oh, wait. It is so the others can flank us, right?” Turning his head, Thorn could make out three large corrupted wolves stalking silently through the trees behind him. “Hah. Akira, in the future, if someone or something is trying to sneak up on us please let me know.”

“Okay, master, I can do that.”

Judging the distance, Thorn knew he would not get more than one shot with his arbalest so he readied his tetsubo in his other hand. He had been debating the effectiveness of the mace-like weapon versus fighting unarmed and had found it better when dealing with multiple enemies, but now was not the time to debate that.

The corrupted wolves, seeing him turn around, paused, the largest of the group taking an aggressive step forward to stare at him. Lifting its head it barked out a sharp command, sending its two companions further out to the side to flank Thorn's position.

"Master, the smelly dogs by the cave got up. I think they are coming over." Akira had jumped back up in the tree and was watching the wolves by the cave.

"Okay, I got it. Stay up in the tree and don't get near the fight, okay?"

Now completely surrounded, Thorn's eyes narrowed. This was the worst possible situation. These corrupted wolves were bigger than the ones he fought outside of Berum by almost fifty percent. The spikes growing from their shoulders were heavier and their claws longer and a faint rotting stench drifted from their panting mouths.

It was obvious from their attempted ambush that these corrupted wolves were smarter as well. They had neatly encircled Thorn, putting him at a serious disadvantage. Considering his options, Thorn knew that he needed to break out. His body tensed as he glanced quickly to each side. The wolves flanking him were both smaller than the leader by almost a foot so Thorn decided to go left. As he was about to launch himself forward a thought drifted into his mind, causing him to fix his eyes on the largest wolf.

If he went left or right, the three wolves closing in from the cave would be able to attack him from the side, while the large wolf leader would attack him from the other, putting him in the same situation he was in now. And if the wolf he targeted backed up or delayed him, he would still be surrounded.

If that was the case, it might be better to crush the biggest corrupted wolf in the pack, maybe that would intimidate the others. Settling on this new plan in a split second, Thorn launched himself forward, dashing straight toward the corrupted wolf leader. As he moved, his massive crossbow swung to the side and with a loud hiss, the bolt blurred through the air, burying itself in the chest of the corrupted wolf on the left.

Thorn's massive frame barreled forward, moving significantly faster than one would expect from something his size. The corrupted wolf leader, startled by Thorn's charge, was not interested in backing down and with a howl, charged out to meet him, its sharp maw opened wide.

The sharp howls of the four remaining wolves rang out behind Thorn, mixed with Akira's sharp chittering but he ignored all of it, focusing all his attention on the muscular bundle of razor-sharp teeth and claws in front of him. Before they smashed into each other, the giant corrupted wolf launched itself into the air, swinging wildly with its claws.

Thorn planted himself, his left foot driving into the ground as he got ready to swing, hitting the ground so hard that it sank into the dirt. Thorn swung his tetsubo with all the strength he could muster, smashing it into the leaping wolf's shoulder and side. With a yelp, the corrupted wolf changed directions abruptly, pinballing through the forest, smashing into trees as Thorn's blow sent it flying.

Using the follow through of his swing, Thorn turned around in time to see another corrupted wolf jumping at him. With a roar, Thorn let go of his tetsubo with his right hand and caught the wolf around the throat, smashing it into the ground. He hissed in pain as the flailing claws of the creature gouged his arm, mentally cursing himself for not having equipped his armor.

With no time to spare for his bleeding wounds, he smashed the wolf's head with the butt end of his tetsubo and stepped over the corpse to meet the three approaching wolves. Despite Thorn's show of force, the corrupted wolves showed nothing but madness in their eyes as they charged him. Fury, excitement, anticipation, and a whole host of other feelings began to build in Thorn's chest as he readied himself. There was something in this bloody, dangerous conflict that he loved.

Knowing that he was not going to get out of this fight

unscathed, Thorn threw caution to the wind and thundered forward, his weapon swinging. A few tense moments later, he had successfully crushed another corrupted wolf, but at the price of a wicked-looking cut along his ribs and back.

The last two corrupted wolves had learned nothing and lunged forward, their jaws snapping. Jumping to the side to avoid them, Thorn smashed through them, his tetsubo whirling as Master Sun had taught him. Locked in the deadly dance, Thorn focused on defending against the two corrupted wolves. As he had learned, he spun and blocked, smashing out with attacks when he was able.

The wolves snapped at him, dodging back as best as they could. Not letting up, Thorn pressed forward, breaking the neck of one corrupted wolf with a smashing blow. The last corrupted wolf stood no chance on its own and while it managed to maul Thorn's arm with its last desperate attack, it died soon after.

Breathing out heavily, Thorn stood amidst the scattered blood and torn up ground, his heart rate slowly calming down. The fight had been intense, but he had made it through mostly unscathed. Nothing that wouldn't heal with a bit of rest at least. The corrupted wolves had been unexpectedly difficult to fight. They were stronger and bigger than the corrupted wolves he had fought before and smarter as well.

If it had not been for his conversation with Akira, they may have succeeded in their attempt to ambush Thorn, which would have been even more dangerous.

“Master! Watch out!”

Snapped out of his thoughts, Thorn felt a sharp, piercing pain as the corrupted wolf leader sank its teeth into his back!

CHAPTER TWENTY-THREE

Grimacing at the pain, Thorn had never been more thankful for the game-like elements of Nova Terra. As the large teeth of the corrupted wolf leader sank into his back, Thorn twisted around, throwing an elbow behind him to try and dislodge the beast. Holding on with its massive jaws, the corrupted wolf leader ripped at his back and legs with its four paws, cutting deeply into his skin!

After two blows, he finally managed to get a hand around one of its legs and, summoning his strength, Thorn ripped it from his back, throwing it away. Blood gushing from his body, Thorn fell to one knee, trying to prop himself up as his strength flagged. He could feel his health draining from his body and the familiar darkness began to creep into the edge of his vision.

Struggling to its feet, its eyes radiating madness and corruption, the wolf that had attacked him growled menacingly. Its left shoulder was smashed almost beyond recognition, a dark, jagged bone visible through the gash Thorn's tetsubo had left in its matted black fur. Yet it forced itself to stand and limped toward Thorn again, blood dripping from its slavering jaws. A deep red aura surrounded the monster, reminding him of Amis' enraged form. No wonder the first blow had not killed it.

"Whew, these guys are tougher than I thought." Not used to having an enemy survive a hit, Thorn had been complacent, forgetting about the threat of the corrupted wolf leader after he knocked it aside. As the corrupted wolf circled, Thorn could not help but notice that its footsteps were completely silent, explaining how it had gotten so close.

A quick glance showed Thorn that his health was at less than 50% and it was dropping fast. Understandable, considering the amount of blood he was leaving on the ground. Still, he estimated that he had at least six seconds before his health bottomed out. But that meant he had to figure out a way to muster up the strength to stand. The corrupted wolf, despite its drive for blood had an uncanny awareness of his weakness and was staying out of range, pacing slowly back and forth.

"Master, master! Are you okay?" Akira's worried voice rang in Thorn's head.

"Not really. My health is dropping fast so get ready to be unsummoned." Thorn responded keeping his eyes locked on the corrupted wolf leader.

"I should use my abilities to help you fight, master! Royal Grace!" Akira squeaked.

Startled, Thorn saw a royal purple light wrap around him as Akira finished activating her skill. Miraculously his health stopped going down and even began to slowly fill back up as his wounds instantly ceased bleeding, his skin knitting itself back together.

"Akira, you can heal?"

"Of course I can, master. Didn't I tell you that I am the best?"

"Then why didn't you heal me earlier?"

"Um, I didn't think you needed it. Plus you told me to stay out of the fight, master." Akira pouted.

"Ah, that is true. Next time you have my permission to heal me." Thorn flexed his fingers as strength rushed back into them.

The corrupted wolf leader saw Thorn's expression perk up and immediately noticed that he was healing under his battle pet's spell. Furious, it howled with rage, lunging forward. Thorn met it head on, one hand clamping down on its throat, the other slamming into the side of its head, crushing its skull with an audible crack. Seeing that it was still twitching, Thorn threw the corpse down and stomped on the back of its spine, making sure that even if it was still alive, it would not be getting up again.

The sudden reversal was welcome, but the fight had exhausted Thorn mentally. Still, it was not quite time to rest. After looting the corrupted wolves' bodies, Thorn made his way to the cave where the wolves made their den. While the cave entrance was more than big enough for even the corrupted wolf leader to walk in and out, there was no way Thorn was going to fit, so instead he sat down to rest while he sent Akira into the cave to scout around.

A few moments later she bounced out of the cave, a handful of colorful flowers clutched in her paws, and perched on Thorn's knee.

"Master, the smelly wolves had a lot of flowers! Look, there was this shiny one, and this purple one. There was this yellow and green one and an ugly brown whiskery thing that I didn't bring because it was gross! There was also this glowing rock thing that was very warm. It is stuck in the wall and I couldn't get it out."

Carefully examining the flowers, Thorn's eyes lit up. The shiny flower that Akira had brought out looked like the flower that grew on Silverleaf. The others were not the plants that he was looking for, but he was not about to turn down more herbs. Still, since there was no way he would be able to go in and get the flowers himself, Thorn marked the cave's location on his map and decided to wait for Mina to arrive.

Finding some large logs, he blocked the entrance of the cave and continued his search for the plants he needed for the potions. Thorn had been thinking a lot about potions and their potential uses. He had noticed that fights in Nova Terra were much like fights in real life. Dangerous, painful, and above all, brief. Fights did not drag on the way that he had expected. Still, his race and larger size did give him a better chance of staying up while wounded, so maybe carrying some health potions would be a good idea. Plus, Thorn had found [The Complete Alchemist], so he was confident that he could develop his own potions if given time to practice.

By the time night had fallen, Thorn had picked up his last deer heart, a couple more Zimph roots, and three Wolfsbane. According to Akira, there were way more than 25 Silverleaf in the cave, so Thorn only needed to find a spot with Blue Bells. Deciding to ask around Greymane, Thorn made his way back to town and curled up on his bed at the inn.

The next morning, Thorn ate a big breakfast and resumed his search. He had asked various townsfolk if they knew a good place to find Blue Bells, and after encouraging a couple of people with a few silvers they marked some spots on his map. According to Akira, the corrupted wolves that he had killed were the only ones in the valley, so Thorn was able to relax his guard as he walked around.

The day passed quietly as Thorn wandered around the forest slowly, collecting the Blue Bells he needed. Thankful for his map, Thorn added as many details as he could while he walked. After all, if he was really going to be assuming the role of Lord Greymane, it made sense to know his territory.

A bit after dinner time, Thorn was sitting quietly on a hill outside of town, watching as smoke rose from the various homes and buildings, when he got a call from Oberlin. Accepting it, he saw Oberlin's face pop up. Other than a few streaks of dirt, the Infinite Key Master looked as dapper as ever.

"Hey Thorn." Oberlin's eye lit up with excitement when he saw Thorn's broad face. "You guessed right. Everything is going according to plan so far. I will need to stay down here for at least another week or two but after that I should be able to rejoin you."

"Awesome. Let me know if you have any trouble or need any backup."

"Thanks. So far, it has been pretty smooth but I will let you know."

After chatting for a few more minutes, Thorn ended the call and leaned back in the grass. Slowly, ever so slowly, a vision for his future was starting to come into focus. Much of the specific detail would depend on the outcome of his quest, but the general shape of his future was becoming clear.

Mina and Velin met Thorn the next day at the edge of town, both looking as neat as a pin, despite their two-day journey. The lack of fast travel in Nova Terra had been a point of confusion to Thorn until he remembered the 1:7 time dilation ratio the game employed. After all, that made three full days of travel in game a few hours of real time. Of course, that did not stop Mina from complaining about it.

“Why is your quest so far out in the boonies, Thorn? We had to walk forever! It took us so long! We need to get mounts. I can’t believe this stupid game has not made mounts for everyone yet. It isn’t fair that you can only get them in the South. We need mounts too.”

“Go buy a battle pet.” It was obvious from Velin’s tone that she felt no sympathy.

“But they are so expensive!” Mina’s eyes lit up. “Oh, that's right! Thorn, you got a battle pet, right? An Ailuridae, I think? Can you show us?”

“Sure, hold on a second. She should be somewhere around here.”

Calling Akira back from wherever she was exploring, Thorn explained how he had found her by accidently knocking over the tree that she called home. After a few moments Akira jumped out of a tree, landing on Thorn's shoulder. Shy, she half hid behind his head while peeking out at the girls.

"Try giving her some food." Thorn pulled out a few of Akira's favorite pastries and handed them to Mina who was practically drooling at the sight of the furry little creature.

"Master, who are these people?"

"These are friends, make sure you treat them well, okay? No stealing stuff from them."

"Come on little cute furry creature, come to Mina." Holding out one of the pastries that Thorn had handed her, Mina tried to entice Akira off Thorn's shoulder.

"You are so awkward that I am embarrassed for you." Velin covered her eyes with her hand. "Let me show you how to do this."

Watching the two girls play around as they competed for Akira's attention, Thorn couldn't help but smile. He could tell that the last bits of awkwardness in their relationship were disappearing and the girls were starting to feel more comfortable around him, which was a big relief. Mina was back to her chatty self and even Velin was starting to relax a bit.

After she had successfully coaxed Akira down from her perch, Velin left her playing with Mina and turned to Thorn, her expression becoming serious.

“I know we talked about it briefly before, but we need to do some digging before we take up any quests here. Because of the way Nova Terra is built, each quest you do has the potential to lock off other paths that could have been taken.”

“Every choice has a consequence, right?”

“Exactly. And if there are quests related to ownership of the valley, then we need to prioritize them.”

“Okay, say that you are right and there are quests related to controlling the valley. How do we go about finding them? So far, all the quests I’ve gotten have been a bit random.”

“Not random, focused. Every quest in the game is unique. Two quests could have the same overall goal, but how you get it, and the specifics of it, will always be tailored to the player or group that gets it. Take this situation for example. You have a quest for clearing the keep and recovering the statue of Hati for the temple in Greymane, but even if I go and talk to the village leader, I will not be able to get the same quest. I could get a quest for finding the statue, but the reward might not be the same and I will not be able to get it the same way.

“Where this gets complicated, is that any quest chain of significant value will generate contested quest lines. That means that if what I suspect is true, there are probably multiple quest lines that lead to this area and their ultimate prize has something to do with taking over the valley. Big guilds are always on the lookout for these sorts of quest lines. This means that if you have the quest, we can pretty much guarantee that there are other people here or on the way."

"So you are saying that we are on a time limit?" Thorn scratched his head.

"Yes. We need to find the proper quest line before anyone else does and complete it before anyone else can progress in their competing quest line. And to do that we need to find out the true history of this area. What we have now is pieced together from a few stories. I think we should start with Greymane and see if we can find anyone who knows the history of the valley. Hopefully, that will lead us to the right quest."

As Velin spoke, Thorn's mind was working furiously. While he had forgiven her and Mina and even hired them to his team, there was still some hesitancy in his heart about sharing information with them. But, if he was really serious about repairing their relationship, then hiding things from them was counterproductive. Taking a deep breath, Thorn strengthened his resolve and crushed the vestiges of resistance in his chest.

"Do you mean a quest like this?" Thorn opened his status window and shared his [Lord Greymane, the Moon Wolf] title.

Title: Lord Greymane, the Moon Wolf
Chosen of Hati, the Moon Wolf, you have earned the title of Lord Greymane, rightful ruler of Greymane Keep and the Lord of the Wolfkin. To take the first step in being recognized as the rightful ruler of the Fang Valley, you must take Greymane Keep back from the corrupted wolfkin who inhabit it.

Her jaw dropping open as she read the title's description, Velin stared at Thorn in undisguised astonishment.

"How..." the War Priestess' eyes grew even wider as she read it again. "Wait, Chosen of Hati? You are an avatar?"

Nodding, Thorn sat down.

"Yeah, after I was stripped of my potential, I ended up fighting off Karrandaras, the Betrayer, cleansing Hati's altar, meeting Hati, the Moon Wolf, and becoming an avatar."

"That sounds intense. But how did you end up with the Lord Greymane title?"

"Ah, earlier I killed a native named Gargish, the Blood Hunter. He dropped a ring that gave me the title." Thorn held up his right hand, showing the silver ring. "I mentioned it the first time we saw the wolfkin in the cave. He was part of a quest line called 'The Blood Moon' or something. This is the continuation of that."

"So you came here to try and claim the title? That makes more sense." Velin pondered for a moment. "You said you also got a quest for retrieving the statue of Hati to revive the temple, right? And the keep you have to take back from the werewolves is potentially related to Hati as well. We need more information, but I would say that there is high potential that finishing these quest lines will result in controlling this valley."

"Which means we need to expect to face some of the major guilds, right?"

"Correct. I know for certain that Ragnarok is looking for the valley. One of my friends in the guild dropped a hint when I talked to her yesterday. I'm not sure if there are any other guilds involved. This quest puts us ahead, as does the fact that you cleaned out the library at Davyos' Fall. Regardless, we should plan for a fight."

CHAPTER TWENTY-FOUR

"You know, Thorn, I don't know that I have ever encountered someone as lucky as you in this game." Velin tucked a strand of her hair behind her pointy ear as she looked at Thorn's seated figure.

"Haha, I told you." Mina stood up from where she had been playing with Akira. "Big guy has the best luck ever. And if we hang out with him, maybe some of it will rub off on us."

"That is not how it works."

"Says who? You told me that the gods were all dead too. But he met one. And now he is an avatar. I bet he has a rare race too."

"Unique, actually. I'm a Titan."

"What!" Mina and Velin both yelled, startling Akira, who

jumped up onto Thorn's head and squeaked angrily at them.

"Yeah, the system could not handle my size with any of the existing races so it gave me a unique race."

"I take it back. I have certainly never encountered anyone as lucky as you," Velin gave a sigh of defeat.

"This is so awesome! I bet Ouroboros will be so jealous when he finds out!" Mina danced around in excitement. "We should call him and rub it in his face."

"That is a terrible idea, Mina. Thorn, I don't know if I can handle any more surprises, so if there is anything else, keep it to yourself for now." Velin cracked a rare joke.

Laughing, Thorn led the girls to the cave where he fought against the corrupted wolves. He had explained how Akira had found the last few ingredients that they needed for the potions but he was simply too large to fit inside the cave to retrieve them. While this earned him endless mocking from Mina, Thorn did not mind. Her teasing was meant in good fun and did not bother him at all.

Velin had shown an interested expression when Thorn brought up the glowing stone that Akira found, but declined to comment when he asked about it, saying that it would be better to see the stone first. When they got to the cave, Akira affirmed that the logs had not been disturbed, so Thorn lifted them out of the way and the girls scrambled into the cave after Velin summoned a light.

Standing outside, Thorn looked around at the quiet forest while he waited, thinking about the fights that were coming. His encounter with Gargish, the Blood Hunter, had given him a healthy respect for werewolves, and it had only been reinforced by the fight with Amis. While he was much more confident in his fighting ability than he had been back then, his fight with the corrupted wolves at this very spot made him very aware that he could not take anything for granted.

Gargish had been one of the few enemies that Thorn had encountered so far that was able to knock him back. Combined with the werewolf's blistering speed, he had made for a nasty foe. Thinking about a whole castle full of enemies like that made Thorn shiver.

Mina and Velin took half an hour to collect all the Silverleaf in the cave before crawling back out to join Thorn. They had picked close to forty plants, giving them more than enough for the potions. Velin had also spent some time looking at the glowing stone that Akira had spotted. Unsure of what it was or how it worked, she left it in place.

The three players made good time on their way back to Greymane, arriving mid-afternoon. After delivering the last of the herbs to Charles, the girls explored the town while Thorn hung out with the alchemist. Since he had the books for it, Thorn figured that picking up some alchemy would not hurt. Reality, however, turned out to be much more difficult than he had anticipated.

Charles settled down on a tall stool at his alchemist lab in the back room of the inn. He explained that often, alchemist labs would be hidden in a basement, or somewhere underground, but that the inn only had a cellar and it was too small to use. Wiping away imaginary sweat from his brow, Thorn could only be grateful that he did not have to squeeze into a tiny space to watch.

The initial steps of the potions seemed reasonable. Charles crushed the Blue Bells and, carefully separating the plant pulp, poured the remaining liquid into little containers. The pulp was piled together in a large press that he used to squeeze out the last few drops of liquid. After clearing the press and washing all his tools, Charles repeated the process for the Silverleaf and Wolfsbane.

The Zimph root and the deer hearts were diced into tiny pieces, placed into separate pots and set to simmer over a low flame. While waiting for the cooking mixtures to finish, Charles began to carefully portion the Blue Bells, Wolfsbane, and Silverleaf liquids with a dropper. He paid special attention to the Wolfsbane, making sure to only get four drops in each container.

Watching Charles use the tiny dropper to mix the potions, Thorn immediately gave up the idea of becoming an alchemist. The closer he looked, the more tiny implements he saw. There were tiny spoons, knives, droppers, mixers, glass beakers, and countless other apparatus that he had no desire to handle.

That dropper was half the size of his pinky for goodness sake. Handling fragile glass like that? Forget it. At first Thorn was disappointed that he would not be able to become an alchemist, but the more he thought about it, the less of an issue it seemed to be. From the detail and care Charles was applying to his tasks, it was obvious that alchemy was a tricky, detailed occupation so it made much more sense for Thorn to hand the books to someone who would be able to focus on alchemy completely.

After watching for a few more minutes, Thorn excused himself and went to look for Mina and Velin. He found them sitting in the shade across from the inn, drinking lemonade and eating some cakes that Mina had brought with her.

“Hey Thorn,” Mina waved as Thorn’s large figure appeared.

“Find anything interesting?” After a skeptical look at the bench they were sitting on, Thorn settled for squatting next to them.

“Nah, this town is pretty desolate. Everyone is really down. Velin thinks it is the curse you mentioned.”

“Correct.” Velin meticulously licked some remnants of frosting from her fingers. “There is a curse over the whole village. I haven’t worked out the exact details, but apart from making everyone depressed, it seems to lower the effectiveness of most actions by at least 30%. This village will bloom should we be successful in returning the statue."

"What do you think about our chances of succeeding?" Thorn asked, swallowing the food he had gotten out.

"100%."

"That high?" Thorn raised an eyebrow at Velin's flat statement.

"Thorn, have you paid any attention to yourself recently?" Mina jumped in. "You are a walking boss. You beat an entire squad of Crimson Snakes to death with almost no effort. As long as you have a healer and someone to watch your back, there is no question about succeeding."

"Mina is correct. Our party composition is ideal. Though you are still classless you can operate as both a tank and as our main damage. Mina and I can support through crowd control and healing while handling any rogues or stealth."

"And me! And me!" Akira, mad at being left out, jumped up and down on Thorn's shoulder.

"And we cannot forget Akira, who can support all of us with healing." Velin smoothly continued, not missing a beat as she broke off a piece of her pastry and held it out. Akira, quite pleased, scampered down from Thorn's shoulder and took the piece of pastry in triumph.

“Once we have the potions, we should be able to mount ambushes on the werewolves which will help us clear Greymane Keep. We will want to be cautious. The werewolves are pretty tough enemies.”

“We burned through them pretty fast last time. What’s the big deal?”

“Those were not werewolves, they were wolfkin.” Thorn shook his head at Mina. “The difference is pretty substantial. Remember Amis? Imagine an army of him. After he hulked out.”

“Okay, that might be scary. Are all werewolves that big?”

“Actually, the first werewolf I faced was bigger. So I would assume that the current boss of the keep will be the biggest so far. We’ll have to move carefully so the potions will certainly help.”

As the three players hung out, chatting about their upcoming adventure, Charles emerged from the inn, looking tired.

“Hey, Thorn. Those potions are done but they need to sit overnight otherwise they will not be as potent. They should be ready to go tomorrow morning.”

“Thanks for your hard work, Charles.”

"It's my pleasure if you can wipe out those monsters in the keep. A couple things to note. The scent erasure potion works for you and anything you have equipped when you take it. If you get other things after that, it will not block their scents, so be careful what you pick up. Also, the attraction potion is quite potent, so only use a bit at a time. Splash it on a wall or something." The tired alchemist waved a hand and walked off, calling back over his shoulder, "Oh, if you haven't talked to Thomas, you should. He knows more about the keep than anyone."

"Thomas is?" Velin asked Thorn, watching Charles' back.

"Hm? Oh, Thomas is the village elder. Old guy, big beard, hangs out in the mayor's office? Or jail. I think it is both."

"We should definitely go talk to him." Velin perked up at the prospect of getting more information. Half an hour later, the group sat around a table in the town's makeshift mayor's office. Thomas, as grumpy as always, seemed secretly delighted to have an audience and began chatting as soon as they sat down.

"So, you want to know the history of the keep, do you?" Pausing to take a swig from the bottle of wine that Thorn had handed him, he coughed and wiped his mouth with the back of his hand. "It's a pretty dark tale. Not sure if your ears will bear the telling of it. Still, if you are going to go into that den of evil, you should know what you are getting yourself into.

Let me think now. It has been about twenty years since the curse of the blood moon appeared, but to get to the true heart of the story we must go back much further.

“In the Era of Gods, this land was prosperous. The forest kept to the mountains and the valley was filled with farms. Humans lived together with many other races here in Greymane. The land was peaceful, protected by the Temple of the Moon, a fortress monastery in the mountains. The warrior monks protected the valley, and in return were provided with food and other resources. Every generation, one of their numbers would be chosen to come down to the valley to lead the people of the valley, being named Lord Greymane. The other monks became Night Walkers, worshipers of Hati, the god who rules the night. The Night Walkers ranged far from the Temple, destroying evil wherever it was found.

“Yet, in time, a corruption set in. The Night Walkers grew stronger and fiercer, becoming a powerful force that many other gods feared. They ranged farther afield, leaving the valley defenseless. One day the army of another god came, overrunning the valley and destroying the Temple of the Moon. Furious, the Lord of that generation, a wolfkin named Davyos, led the few remaining wolfkin monks in a terrible ritual, producing the blood moon curse. Their act plunged the land into chaos and the valley was devastated.

“When the Night Walkers returned and saw what had become of the valley they blamed Davyos and cast him from the valley. The few remaining Night Walkers appointed a Lord Greymane from the village and chased after Davyos. Where he went, no one knows. Nothing was heard from the Night Walkers, or Davyos' descendants, until twenty years ago when a powerful werewolf returned, bringing with him the curse.

"Slaughtering his way into Greymane Keep, which had been built on top of the ruins of the Temple of the Moon, the werewolf turned the resident Lord Greymane, Gargish Moonclaw, into a beast like himself. Since then the werewolves have ruled the valley with the aid of their corrupted wolves, treating those of us in the valley as nothing more than vermin. The curse deforms anyone who remains in the castle past nightfall into a werewolf and binds them to the property except on the full moon when they come out and scour the land.

"If you are able, travelers, I beg you to save us from this cursed life." Putting the bottle of wine on the table, Thomas stood unsteadily and bowed his head to the three players. "The valley desperately needs a true lord, and if you can destroy the evil that plagues our land we will willingly serve."

ding

Quest Updated - Lord of Greymane
Elder Thomas, the Greymane Village leader, has asked you to break the curse hanging over these lands by

claiming your position as the Lord of Greymane. To break the curse you must sit in the Wolf Throne while wearing the Ring of the Wolf Lord. As an added requirement defeat all the werewolves in the castle.

0/100 Werewolves
0/1 Greater Werewolf

Rewards:
Title: Lord Greymane Unlocked
Area: Greymane Keep
Area: Fang Forest
Area: Greymane Village
Area: The Twins

“Well, the good news is that we know how many werewolves we have to kill.” Thorn said with a sigh, sharing the quest with the two girls. “The bad news is that there are a lot of them.”

“Sheesh. 100? No, 101. That is only a little bit terrifying.” Mina paled as she read the quest.

“It is alright. We’ll take it slow. Thomas, do you have any advice for us?”

“Hmm? Advice? For attacking the castle?” Thomas sat down and took a long swig of wine. “Go during the day. The werewolves seem to be more active during the night time so maybe attacking during the day would be the best."

"Thank you. We will accept this quest and will break the curse over the valley." Nodding to the headman, Thorn and the girls left the building.

"Thorn, is Oberlin going to be joining us?" Velin asked without lifting her head from her notepad where she was writing something down as she walked.

"I am not sure that he will make it back in time, so it will probably just be us. We should plan that way at least. Let's go get some sleep, we have a crazy day tomorrow."

CHAPTER TWENTY-FIVE

The morning sun rose in the valley, driving back the deep mist that blanketed the forest. Thorn watched with fascination as the mist retreated around him, melting under the warm rays of the sun. He looked over his shoulder at Velin and Mina. The elven War Priestess looked as unperturbed as always, poring over something in her notebook. Mina, on the other hand, was grumbling under her breath about everything that fell under her eyes.

Amused, Thorn turned back to look at the stone spire peeking over the trees ahead. They had left the inn before the sun was up at Velin's insistence. Thorn had been planning to sleep in, but Velin had argued that an earlier start would ensure that they would be able to complete their quest before nightfall. Truthfully, sleeping in was more of a habit than anything else as the time-dilation in Nova Terra made it easy for players to stay up for multiple days at a time, so neither Thorn or Velin took Mina's grumbles seriously.

“Summon Akira.”

With a blue flash Thorn’s furry battle pet appeared, chattering excitedly and jumping to his shoulder.

“Master, master! Where are we going today?”

“Hey Akira,” scratching behind her ears, Thorn stroked Akira’s head. “We’ve got a big day ahead of us and a lot of work for you to do, okay? You’ll need to be at the top of your game, alright?”

“Hah, of course.” Akira wiggled her three tails in excitement. “I am the best Ailuridae, so of course I’ll be amazing.”

Smiling, Thorn turned back to look at Velin who was still going over her notes. Rather than bothering her, Thorn pulled out the rest of his breakfast and began to eat it in earnest. He had found a virtual shop in Fantasia that sold breakfast burritos, so he bought three hundred of them. Kept warm and fresh by his inventory, he had been enjoying them for breakfast over the last couple days.

Watching Thorn eat a full burrito in two bites, Mina could only stare, her appetite disappearing. There was something off-putting about watching food being thrown into the bottomless pit that Thorn called a stomach.

"Don't you ever stop eating?"

Ignoring Mina, Thorn continued eating his breakfast burritos, only stopping after he had finished his tenth. Velin had finished what she was doing and walked over to stand beside him, her tall, slim figure only coming up to the bottom of his chest.

"This might be pretty tricky, but I think we have a good shot at completing this quest in one day if we can focus. It will depend on a few things. First, is this a dungeon or a field quest? A field quest is any normal quest. We can stop and start a field quest as we want, because the environment is not locked like a dungeon. If, on the other hand, this quest is in a dungeon, we will have to try and power through it in one go.

"Second, how strong are the basic werewolves? If they are all as dangerous as that Gargish you told us about then we are in a lot of trouble. However, I believe that Gargish, the Blood Hunter, was originally named Gargish Moonclaw, the former Lord Greymane. That would explain why you got the ring and quest from him. It would also indicate that we have some hope as it is unlikely that the regular werewolves will be as strong as he was.

"Still, we are going to have to pay careful attention to how many werewolves we pull at one time. This leads us to the third and fourth points, the two potions that we picked up from Charles this morning. The scent erasure potion will last for four hours, while the attraction potions can each be used five times. We have five of each potion, so we will have to ration them wisely."

"So each use of an attraction potion needs to attract four werewolves on average? Are we going to be able to deal with four werewolves?" Thorn asked, scratching his head.

"Given your track record so far, I don't think it will be an issue." Velin smiled. "The larger concern is the density of the distribution of werewolves and the layout of the castle."

"Are you two done yet?" From the side, Mina frowned unhappily at Thorn and Velin. "Why do you have to over-plan everything? Thorn, you smash them while Velin heals you. I'll slow them down or shoot them full of holes. What's so hard? I mean, this is a game, right?"

"Fair." Thorn shrugged. "Mina has a good point. We are probably better off rolling with whatever situations crop up."

"Agreed. I would, however, recommend that we use the scent erasing potion before we get any closer to the keep." Velin put away her notebook and withdrew four blue potions, handing one each to Mina and Thorn, and uncorking another for Akira.

Looking at the glowing blue liquid in the vial, Thorn had the strangest impression that his life was never going to be the same again. For so long his reality had plodded along, mostly unchanging. And now he was standing in a mist covered forest, about to drink a blue, glowing, magic potion before assaulting a castle full of werewolves in order to reclaim a giant wolf god's statue. How life changed.

Grinning, Thorn downed the potion in a single gulp.

ding

Scentless Potion
You have consumed a magical potion that erases your scent. For the next four hours, your body and anything you are wearing will not produce any scent. This potion can be consumed once every four hours.

Racial Trait: Titan's Endurance
Due to your natural resistance to physical conditions, the duration of the [Scentless] potion you consumed has been reduced to one hour.

"Well. That sucks." Thorn muttered, reading the second notification again.

"What's wrong?"

"I have natural resistance." Thorn sighed, sharing the second notification with the curious witch.

“Are you serious? Is that your racial trait? Gross.” Mina shook her head. “Velin, he has resistance to magic potions. Actually, it looks like he has resistance to most physical effects.”

“I have resistance to mental effects as well.” Thorn smiled smugly, sharing his [Titan’s Strength] racial trait.

“Literally disgusting.” Mina rolled her eyes at his boasting.

“If that potion is only going to last for an hour, we better get moving.” Velin started toward the keep, carefully writing down the descriptions of Thorn’s racial traits as she walked.

Within minutes of setting out they approached the road leading up to the keep. Built on the ruins of the Temple of the Moon, Greymane Keep was perched on the side of a mountain, a single dirt road rising steeply from the forest up to the mist shrouded castle. The keep was a gloomy gothic-looking place, overgrown with ivy and in complete disrepair. Despite the bright morning sun, the mist surrounding the keep seemed to be a permanent fixture, lending it a spooky air.

Climbing the rough switchback road, Thorn and the others soon found themselves in the shadow of its southern wall. Looking at the crumbling stone and weed-ridden gate, Mina could not help but shiver.
“Master, are you sure you want this place? It smells funny,”

asked Akira, jumping down from Thorn's shoulder and sniffing the fallen rubble.

"Eh, even if I don't keep it, clearing out the werewolves will be good for the village. And who knows, something good might come of it."

"If you say so."

The keep lacked a proper moat, but there was a deep pit at the edge of the wall running underneath an old wooden drawbridge that looked like it would snap with a stiff breeze. Nervous, Thorn tested it carefully before putting his full weight onto it. Though it groaned in protest, the bridge held fast so Thorn whispered a quick prayer and tried to walk as lightly as he could.

The four carefully crossed the rotting wooden drawbridge as a few shafts of sunlight broke through the heavy clouds, bathing the castle in a warm golden glow. Almost instantly Akira's mood brightened and she began to frolic through the tall grass and overgrown shrubbery. Thorn watched her with an amused look. He had never had a pet before and so this was a completely novel experience for him. An experience that he was quite enjoying.

While the sun did much to dispel the gloom of the castle it was evident that the gloom wouldn't give up without a fight. Seeping from the castle was a dark grey miasma that seemed to actively battle the sunlight, preventing it from reaching inside. Thorn walked up to the castle's gate and looked at it curiously.

Despite the age of the castle the gate seemed in relatively good shape, not showing the same rot that the drawbridge did. Pushing hard on one of the doors Thorn managed to get it open wide enough for the girls before the door caught on a rock.

"Hold on, let me see what it is caught on." Mina pushed Thorn to the side and squeezed in through the opening in the doors.

"Alright but be careful. Yell if there are any enemies."

"Umm, we may have some trouble." After a moment of silence, Mina called back through the entrance in a quiet voice.

"What is going on? Mina?" Not getting a response to her question, Velin squeezed through the small opening in the doors. Waiting outside, Thorn had no way of seeing what was happening in the courtyard of the keep.

"Watch out!"

Hearing Velin's yell, Thorn instantly sprang into action. Gripping the partially opened door, he heaved, the muscles in his shoulders and arms rippling as he exerted all his strength.

CRACK

With a thunderous sound, the thick, wooden castle gate splintered, shattering into pieces as Thorn ripped it from its hinges. Taking a large step past the ruined gate into the courtyard, Thorn saw a group of werewolves bounding across the yard of the keep toward Mina who was desperately warding off a werewolf in a tattered blue uniform. Near her, Velin struggled with another, similarly dressed werewolf.

At the sight of the werewolves a deep burning anger ignited in Thorn's chest, sending his brain into overdrive. Roaring a challenge, the titan crouched slightly and launched himself into the air, flying toward the charging werewolves. Easily clearing the struggling girls, Thorn summoned his [Avatar of the Wolf] ability. As he flew, silver light rippled around him, flowing like quicksilver around his hands and chest. Landing with a bang, the stone courtyard cracked and crumbled under his tremendous weight.

Still carrying a jagged piece of the keep's gate, Thorn roared out another challenge and threw the piece of the gate at the approaching werewolves. Dodging nimbly, the three werewolves all got past it without getting hit, but it still slowed them. Taking advantage of the drop-in momentum, Thorn charged into them, his large, clawed gauntlet taking a chunk of flesh from a werewolf who was still in the air, unable to dodge his swipe. Growling, the werewolves launched themselves at Thorn, entirely fearless, tangling him up in a furious melee.

“Akira, support Velin and Mina!” Thorn shouted.

Behind him, Velin was still struggling with the werewolf that had ambushed her while Mina blinked this way and that, leading the last werewolf on a nerve-wracking chase. Squeaking furiously, Akira ran around on the edge of the fight, making sure to stay clear of the struggling players and out of the werewolves’ reach.

Velin, dodging skillfully out of the way of a fierce strike, lifted her staff, chanting out in an arcane language. A bright glow burst from her staff, temporarily robbing her attacker’s sight. When the light faded it revealed the elven War Priestess clothed in thick platemail, made entirely from burning light.

No longer dodging, Velin accepted a strike from the enraged werewolf as she focused on the magic gathering at the tip of her staff. As if sensing the growing danger, the werewolf attacked as furiously as it could, smashing against the glowing armor that surrounded Velin. Unable to cut through the armor in time, the werewolf screeched. It looked down in horror, only to see its legs melting away under the intense light radiating from the end of Velin’s staff.

Across the yard, Mina was helplessly dodging and teleporting, barely staying ahead of the razor-sharp claws and snapping teeth of the werewolf that had ambushed her.

Her teleporting ability had a two second cooldown, so after teleporting she would summon a trail of ice and slide along it, occasionally flicking out ice spikes that would jab into her attacker, leaving thin bloody trails across his skin.

Knowing she could not keep it up, Mina gritted her teeth and looked around, her eyes lighting up as she spotted Akira who was squeaking at the side. Slipping closer, Mina yelled, "heal me!"

As an Ice Witch, the majority of Mina's spells were quick to cast but weaker in power and could be used in bulk to overwhelm her enemies. Unfortunately, in order to cast most of her offensive spells, she needed to activate her [Aspect of Winter] ability, which was going to be painful since she did not have the initiative in this fight. If she wanted to get her footing back she would have to bleed a bit. Gritting her teeth and hoping that Thorn's battle pet could understand her, Mina abandoned her defense and readied her wand, a string of arcane syllables falling from her lips.

Howling in triumph, the attacking werewolf ripped into her, sending her flying as its claws left bloody gouges across her chest. Gloating, it was about to pounce on her when the temperature dropped dangerously low, causing its motions to freeze up.

"[Sub Zero]." Her voice as bitterly cold as her spell, Mina rose to her feet, feeling the warm magic from Akira's Royal Grace ability closing her cuts. Finally ready to fight, Mina gripped her wand and pointed at the stunned werewolf. It was her turn.

At first, Thorn was worried that the werewolves would be too much for their group to handle, but he realized that they were similar to the five corrupted wolves he had fought in the valley a few days ago.

Large, hunched, and shaggy, the werewolves looked like overgrown, feral wolfkin. Knotted muscles covered in scars and mangy fur dominated their frame, broken only by their sharp claws and teeth. They were neither as quick or as strong as Thorn remembered Gargish, the Blood Hunter, had been and they were not particularly clever either.

Even though he was facing off against three of them, Thorn fell into a solid rhythm when he realized that he did not have to be afraid of their hits. Their claws had trouble with his armor, while his cut through them like a hot knife through butter. Growling furiously, one of the werewolves lunged forward, its maw opening wide. Sharp teeth glistened in the morning sunlight as its foul breath washed over Thorn.

CHAPTER TWENTY-SIX

Expecting to sink his teeth into warm, soft flesh, the werewolf was stunned when instead it got a mouth full of hard metal. Hard metal with claws on the end. Thorn caught the lunging werewolf by the open mouth, large fingers wrapping around its head, his meaty hand preventing its jaws from being able to shut.

Shocked at not being able to close its mouth, the werewolf struggled briefly until Thorn clenched his hand, ending its life. The two other attacking werewolves could not help but pause. While they were mostly fearless, watching the giant in front of them deal with their companion effortlessly put a damper on their aggression. Cautiously they circled, unsure how they were supposed to hurt him.

Sneering, Thorn threw the body in his hand at one werewolf

while drawing his tetsubo from his inventory and lunging at the other. His weapon hummed through the air, smashing into the side of his target, sending the unfortunate monster flying until the crumbling stone wall stopped it abruptly. The last werewolf, dodging out of the way of its companion's corpse, tried to take the opportunity to attack, only to feel an unstoppable pressure crushing down on its head.

Not bothering to check if the last werewolf he slapped down was still alive, Thorn turned to see how the girls were doing in time to see Velin burning the legs off her opponent. Wincing, Thorn reinforced his conviction to never get on the War Priestess' wrong side. Across the yard, Mina had taken control of her fight, stunning the attacking werewolf with her [Sub Zero] spell.

Seeing that Mina's ice spikes were not dealing a lot of damage, Thorn started over, only to see Mina wave her wand. The number of ice spikes abruptly increased, pounding down on the werewolf in an unending storm. Soon, the little that remained of the monster was buried under a pile of ice.

"You ladies alright?"

"Yes, thanks to your quick response." Velin looked around carefully before dispelling her magic armor. Obviously exhausted, she sat down abruptly.

"What happened?"

"When I first came in I saw some werewolves come out of the keep." Mina walked over, carrying Akira. "The three you fought. They did not see me so I was going to try and get closer but I was ambushed. Thankfully, Velin saw the two 'guards' as they jumped me and was able to pull one of them away. I'm sorry, I almost ruined everything because I wasn't prepared."

"Don't worry about it." Thorn waved a hand, wiping his other gauntlet off on one of the dead werewolves. Cleaning up the bodies while the girls rested from the adrenaline-packed fight, Thorn did not bother trying to skin the werewolves. Three of the werewolves had been crushed, burned, or ripped apart and the other two were pretty badly damaged as well.

After ten minutes Velin had recovered and they made their way into the keep itself. As they were resting Thorn had kept a close watch on the entrance to the keep, assuming that the loud sound he made smashing the courtyard gate open would have drawn other enemies, but no beasts appeared, leading Velin to mention that the keep might be a dungeon.

Sure enough, as they walked into the keep's entrance Thorn got a popup.

ding

Dungeon: Greymane Keep
You have discovered Greymane Keep. Built on the ruins of the Temple of the Moon, Greymane Keep has been infested with evil werewolves, spreading corruption to the surrounding area. Proceed at your own risk.

Curious, Thorn pulled up the quest that Thomas had given him.

Quest Updated - Lord of Greymane
Elder Thomas, the Greymane Village leader, has asked you to break the curse hanging over these lands by claiming your position as the Lord of Greymane. To break the curse you must sit in the Wolf Throne while wearing the Ring of the Wolf Lord. As an added requirement defeat all the werewolves in the castle. 5/100 Werewolves 0/1 Greater Werewolf Rewards: Title: Lord Greymane Unlocked Area: Greymane Keep Area: Fang Forest Area: Greymane Village Area: The Twins

Noting that the five werewolves that they had killed in the courtyard counted toward the quest, Thorn nodded in satisfaction. The burning desire to wipe out the werewolves grew hotter and he could not help but crack his knuckles.

“Whoa, slow down big guy.” Mina tugged on his arm ineffectually as he walked through the staging room at the dungeon entrance. “We need to come up with some sort of plan.”

“Weren’t you the one who wanted to deal with problems as they came up?”

Mina ignored his teasing, turning to look at Velin.

“Mina is right. We need a plan. We have the potions that will attract the werewolves and it would be a complete waste to not use them with these narrow hallways.”

Following her pointing finger, Thorn took in the dark stone hallway at the end of the room. Wide enough for him to pass through if he ducked, Thorn immediately understood Velin’s intention. It would be a relatively simple matter for him to block off the tunnel and deal with any werewolves that tried to attack him. Backed up by Velin and Akira’s healing and Mina’s ice spells and curses, Thorn was confident in being able to wipe out a thousand werewolves, let alone the 95 they needed to kill for the quest.

“Sounds good. But we will need to make sure we don’t let

any werewolves get behind us. We'll have to clear slowly." Lighting a torch, Thorn led the way, trying to stay as quiet as possible.

The flickering torch light reflecting off the dark grey stone that made up the walls of the keep set the tone of the dungeon expedition perfectly. As quietly as possible they moved down the dark hall way until Akira remarked dryly.

"Master, you realize that sneaking around while holding a torch is pretty pointless, right?"

Blushing slightly at his stupidity, Thorn put the torch out, explaining Akira's comment to Velin and Mina, causing them to chuckle. He continued to lead through the hallway, stepping over rubble and around deteriorating furniture.

Quite soon they came to a large room dominated by rotting tables and benches. The center of the hall featured a large fire pit, a rusty spit and roasting rack hanging over it. Moth-eaten tapestries hung from the vaulted ceiling and place settings lay scattered on the floor. Chairs were overturned and the sickening smell of rotten meat permeated the air. Thorn could only imagine how grand it had looked at one time.

However, what really drew Thorn's attention were the four werewolves who had been ripping apart a human body that lay on one of the tables across the room. For a moment Thorn and the four simply stared at each other, then with piercing howls they threw away their meal and rushed him.

Anticipating their movement, Thorn took a large step forward and hooked one of the tables with his foot. With a flick, the table tumbled through the air toward the oncoming werewolves, forcing them to dodge and granting Thorn and the girls a few more seconds. Across the room they bounded, jumping over tables and past chairs, their glistening teeth and claws enough to scare the crap out of anyone. Motioning the girls back, Thorn retreated until he stood in the hallway, outside the threshold of the great room.

Within less than a second the first werewolf reached him and pounced when suddenly everything seemed to slow down, like it had when Gargish jumped him. Feeling all his senses sharpen exponentially, Thorn blinked in confusion at the slow-motion pounce coming closer and closer. It was as if everything within the range of his senses came into sharp relief, categorized neatly in his head.

He knew the number of chairs in the room, could count the stones in the wall to his left and was sure where the leap was going to take the werewolf. It wasn't till he was halfway through counting the werewolf's teeth that he remembered that the monster was trying to disembowel him and the tetsubo in his hand shot forward in a straight stab.

Calculating the werewolf's trajectory, Thorn pushed himself back slightly and then stabbed up as fast as he could. Everything sped back up and the werewolf ran into the end of the tetsubo with a dull thud and a screech of pain. Rolling with it, Thorn stepped forward and thrust his tetsubo into the center of the werewolf's heart a second time.

Blood dripped to the floor as the struggling monster was thrown off to the side. Crouching slightly, Thorn got ready to take on the others. He barely had time to take a defensive stance before the next one came up to him, throwing a rapid series of slashes. Pushing into his opponent, Thorn managed to block most of the damage with his arms and shoulders but earned himself some deep slashes for his efforts. Seeing the werewolf trying to back up, Thorn helped it along by snapping a kick into its stomach, watching it as it blasted backward, crushing a table before it hit the stone wall.

Watching proved to be a mistake as the third and fourth werewolves hit him at the same time, one trying to bite into his shoulder as the other tried to gouge out his side with wicked looking claws. A cold blast raced past Thorn's side as Mina jumped into the fight, stunning one of the werewolves.

Seeing that the werewolf at his side had been dealt with, Thorn instinctively reached out and grabbed the head of the other werewolf and ripped it off his shoulder before throwing the startled monster at the wall so hard its skull shattered. As for the last werewolf, it only had time to gape in stunned astonishment before a fist smashed its head back, snapping its vertebrae like a twig.

Now bleeding profusely from his shoulder and side Thorn could feel the familiar weakness creeping in. Thankfully, Velin was quick with a healing spell and in no time warm energy filled him again.

“We seriously need to work on our coordination.” Velin’s voice was flat as she healed Thorn. “And you need to pay more attention. I noticed you looking away in the middle of the fight. While you have a lot of advantages, lethal strikes will still kill you outright.”

As Thorn continued to heal up, Velin explained that due to the realism of Nova Terra attacks did not deal a set amount of damage, instead health represented the state of the individual’s body. As damage accumulated so did fatigue, making it harder to act the more damage a person took. This didn’t mean that death would automatically come when an avatar’s health hit zero, instead, it would come when the avatar succumbed to its fatigue.

This allowed characters to launch devastating sneak attacks by targeting critical areas. A critical strike would overwhelm the target with a powerful burst of pain and fatigue, killing the player and logging them out of Nova Terra.

The encounter that Thorn had with the four werewolves took only a few seconds, but it showcased exactly how lethal Nova Terra was. Not only were all four werewolves dead but Thorn could easily have died as well. A bite to the shoulder was not that dangerous but if the same attack had landed on his neck or head, it would have sent him out of the game instantly.

“Healing is strong, but my casts are not instant. If you get hit with a critical strike, you won’t last long enough for me to get a healing spell off. Since you are not a traditional tank we need to set up some better patterns as my normal way of handling damage are not going to work with you.”

“Sure, what do you suggest?”

“Give me a moment.” Velin pulled out her notebook and started flipping through it while Thorn and Mina looted the bodies of the werewolves. After a few minutes, the elven Priestess snapped the book shut. “Here is the plan. Thorn, we are going to forgo the normal means of tanking. The hallways are too tight for you to swing your club around.”

“Tetsubo.”

“Sure. The hallways are too tight for you to swing your tetsubo so we need to stay in open spaces like this one. Additionally, since you can kill the werewolves with a solid hit, why not turn offense into defense? We are going to revisit our ambush strategy, using this hall. Using the attraction potions that we were given, we will draw the werewolves back here and then we will hit them. Preferably with a table or something like that.”

"Oooh, like a tower defense game!" Mina's eyes glowed with excitement.

"Sort of. We want to lure the werewolves into the center of the room and then ambush them. There are five entrances to the hall. We can ignore the one we came through, leaving four, which means we either need to block off one or someone has to handle two different hallways."

"How about Akira?" Thorn scratched his head as he looked around the room. "She could run down a hallway to attract the werewolves' attention."

"Can she outrun a werewolf?"

"I'm honestly not sure." Calling his battle pet over, Thorn stroked her fur as he questioned her. "Akira, can you outrun a werewolf?"

"Of course I can!" The little furry creature preened proudly. "I am the fastest Ailuridae ever!"

"Uh huh. Well, she says she can." Thorn shrugged his massive shoulders at Velin. "We can give it a try."

"We should not need to do much running, as the potion should do most of the work for us." Taking four of the potions out of her inventory, Velin handed them out. "Alright, the plan is simple. We will each walk halfway down a hallway and drop a bit of the potion. Try to get it on the wall. We'll then wait to see who shows up. If no werewolves show up we will move to the 75% mark and repeat the process.

“Remember to retreat as soon as you apply it. We don’t want to get separated. As soon as you have applied the potion, come back to that entrance.” Velin pointed to the doorway they had entered the great room from. “We’ll stay in that hall until we see the werewolves and then charge out to ambush them.”

“Sounds good.” Thorn nodded his head, holding a potion in his big hands. On a table, Akira crouched with a potion of her own.

“Haha, they won’t know what hit them.” Mina said, looking back at the others in excitement while she walked toward her hallway. Not paying attention, her foot caught on a rock and she tripped, stumbling forward. Barely managing to get her feet under her she finally stabilized and froze as the glass bottle slipped from her hand and landed on the floor, shattering into a million pieces.

An astringent, bitter smell rose into the air as the potion splattered onto Mina. A large puddle spread out on the ground as she stared in horror at the mess she had made. Hearing the shatter, Thorn and Velin looked at each other for a moment and began to run.

CHAPTER TWENTY-SEVEN

"Get back to the hallway!" Thorn yelled, his deep voice booming through the great room. As quickly as possible the three players ran back toward the hallway from which they emerged, Akira bounding ahead. Thomas had warned them to only use a bit of the attraction potion at a time since it was so potent, so Thorn could only imagine what dropping a whole bottle would do.

It was not long before he found out. Shortly after they made it to the entrance of the great hall, Thorn picked up the faint howls. From all around the castle the chilling sound echoed. Within moments Thorn could make out the grunts and growls of the werewolves as they began to pour into the large hall.

Werewolves bound into the room from three of the four other entrances, their noses twitching. Dressed in a ragged collection of armor and uniforms, it was obvious that these werewolves had, at one point, been guards of Greymane Keep. Now twisted into monsters, the werewolves rushed into the great hall, sniffing the air as they came.

Grey, black, and brown fur mixed together as the werewolves were drawn like magnets to the place Mina had tripped. Almost uncontrollably, they crowded around, pushing to be the closest to the puddle on the ground. Fangs and claws flashed in the light as the werewolves jostled for position.

Not wanting to let this chance go to waste, Thorn knelt and drew his arbalest, placing a pile of massive bolts against the wall next to him. The werewolves were so tightly clumped together that Thorn only had to aim in their general direction to guarantee that he would hit one. With a deep breath, he got ready to fire.

The City Defender series looked normal in Thorn's hands but standing next to it Mina was dwarfed by how absurdly large the siege crossbow was. Intended for use on a castle wall to defend against enemy siege weapons, the bolts were almost as tall as she was and the metal bow was almost five inches thick at the center.

Normally, it would take at least three men to handle it while it was mounted on the wall yet Thorn handled it like a normal crossbow. Due to Thorn's modifications the winch system was removed, making it impossible to draw without strength as insane as Thorn's.

About to pull the trigger, Thorn felt a hand on his shoulder and paused. Velin walked forward quietly, muttering a spell subvocally as her long, elegant fingers brushed over the tips of the bolts, infusing them with a golden glow. Once she had finished casting her spell, she nodded at Thorn and stepped behind him again, readying a healing spell.

With another deep breath, Thorn pulled the trigger on the City Defender, the powerful thrumm of the string rumbling in the hallway. Without looking to see if he hit anything, Thorn grabbed his next bolt and slid it into place, pulling back the metal string of the arbalest at the same time. Almost as soon as the bolt was in place he steadied the massive crossbow and pulled the trigger again, at the same time reaching for the third bolt.

Across the great hall pandemonium reigned. The werewolves had not missed the loud noise of the arbalest firing, but none of them had immediately spotted Thorn and the girls in the entrance to the hall. Instead, they looked around in confusion for a split second. Their confusion did not last long though, as they soon felt the massive crossbow bolt that Thorn had fired ripping its way through their crowd.

The first werewolf the bolt hit simply exploded into pieces as the force of the bolt hit its back. The second werewolf was luckier and only lost an arm and a chunk of skin from its side as the bolt deflected. Spinning with brutal force, the bolt smashed into another group of werewolves, breaking bones and throwing them to the floor. Furious howls of pain mixed with the cries of surprise as all the werewolves fixed their eyes on the bolt that had shattered against the floor after blowing through the crowd.

WHUUMMM

The sound of a second bolt shocked the crowd of werewolves out of their stunned state and instantly they began to scatter. Yet how could they be faster than the arbalest bolt? Two more unlucky werewolves were hit and died instantly.

Not stopping, Thorn drew and fired the City Defender like a machine. So long as he aimed at a werewolf and pulled the trigger, the poor monster would vanish in a puff of red as the bolt passed through its location. Scrambling to get out of the way, the werewolves soon discovered Thorn's figure kneeling in the entrance to the great hall, and with a furious howl, they began to charge.

"Mina!" Velin shouted, pointing to a clump of werewolves charging over from the right side of the hall.

"[Avalanche]," the witch commanded, summoning a massive swirl of snow and ice in the path of the charging werewolves.

"Thorn!"

Releasing one last bolt, Thorn put the arbalest in his

inventory and drew his tetsubo, launching himself forward into the large hall. Like a freight train he plowed over the werewolves who were leading the charge, his sheer weight smashing them to the side. Already he could feel the warmth of Velin's healing spells landing on his back.

Grinning ferociously, Thorn began to lay about with his tetsubo. With a whir, the large metal studded club cut through the air so fast that it almost disappeared. Even grazing a werewolf proved enough to draw blood and those that were unfortunate enough to be in the weapon's direct path simply ceased to exist.

Cutting his way through the werewolves in front of the hall, Thorn checked to make sure that the girls were alright before charging left with a roar. His glance had showed that the werewolves that Mina had tied up were struggling to get past her crowd control spells, giving him time to finish off the enemies on the other side.

Mina was casting icy spell after icy spell, slowing the charging werewolves to a crawl. Next to her, the elven War Priestess cast healing spells in succession, making sure that Thorn's health was staying topped up. This freed Thorn to attack with abandon, trading hits with the werewolves. The muted pain settings made even the most vicious cut feel like a sting, so Thorn's intimate experience with suffering allowed him to ignore the attacks entirely.

Within minutes he had cleared two thirds of the room and

turned to support Mina who was beginning to struggle to keep the werewolves back. Thorn helped by picking up one of the long tables and lobbing it through the air at them, forcing them to dodge backward. Charging forward, he smashed the last few werewolves and then walked back to where Mina and Velin were standing in the doorway. Akira, hanging on Mina's back, jumped up to Thorn's broad shoulder.

"Master! I helped the pointy hat lady!"

"Thanks, Akira." Thorn scratched his battle pet behind the ears as he talked to Mina and Velin. "How did it go on your end?"

"Great! Akira was a big help. Her heal is a full restore which allows me to cast without worrying about mana drain." Mina looked at Thorn's furry pet enviously. "Are you sure you don't want to sell her?"

"No way." Thorn shook his head as he fed Akira a treat. "Velin, you were totally right. I'm much better at offense than I am at defense. It was helpful to not have to worry about defending while fighting.

"Yes, that went much better. We'll keep this pattern for now. The only thing we will need to worry about is if we get surrounded, but as long as we don't let enemies get behind us we should be fine."

After resting for a moment, Thorn and Mina sifted through the drops while Velin meditated. With Akira using her healing ability on Mina, and Velin keeping Thorn topped up, they did not have to do much resting between fights. Velin, on the other hand, was using mana like water and needed almost ten minutes before she was ready to go again.

After picking up the loot that had dropped, Thorn checked the hallways one by one, starting from the three hallways that werewolves had come from. All three hallways led to empty rooms, abandoned in haste as the werewolves had picked up the smell of the potion. The last entrance had a thick, wooden door so Thorn carefully eased the door open, revealing a hallway filled with cobwebs. From the undisturbed dust coating the floor it was obvious that the hall hadn't been used in a long time, but soon the group came to a room with another werewolf in it.

The monster raised its head as Thorn opened the door. Seeing each other at the same time, it started to turn toward him. Without hesitation Thorn stepped up and, feet squared, jabbed out with his left hand as fast as he could, completely flattening the werewolf's snout and crushing its jaw. He followed up with wrapping his right hand around its neck, choking the rising howl of pain and then smashed his left fist into its head again, silencing the monster for good.

It evaporated into light, dropping a few coins and Thorn examined his left gauntlet that had been dented very slightly from the werewolf's teeth. Jabs worked quite well due to his absurd strength, but he didn't like the idea of harming his gear whenever he attacked an opponent.

Shrugging, since there was nothing he could currently do, Thorn and the girls continued their way. Apart from a close call when they walked around the corner into a three-werewolf patrol Thorn didn't have too much trouble swiftly killing the werewolves they encountered. Mina would obstruct them and Thorn would wade forward and stomp them into the ground, all the while healed by Velin.

There were no more large fights on the first floor and soon they had finished exploring it. Standing in front of the stairs to the second floor, Velin stopped the group.

"Before we go up to the second floor we need to prepare. It has been three hours since we took our potions, which means Thorn's has run out and ours have less than a quarter left. This means we need to prepare for waves of enemies since they will be able to sniff us out. We can set up a trap, but we will have to be very careful that we don't attract the boss. Based on the size of the keep, it is unlikely that the dungeon is more than two floors, so we will probably be facing the boss on the next level, as well as all of the other werewolves."

"Do we need to change up our approach?" Thorn asked, when Velin paused.

"No, I think we can maintain our current system, we need to

be ready to retreat if things start to go bad. These werewolves are not too dangerous because their defenses are weak. But if they do get hits in on me or Mina, we'll be in trouble."

"And this is why most people still run in the trinity formation." Mina chimed in.

"Trinity formation?"

"Tank, heals, damage." Mina rolled her eyes at Thorn's question. "There can be more than three in the group, but the roles are pretty locked when it comes to combat. On the other hand, we've got damage out the window but not having someone to control aggro is a major weakness. A tank's role is less about taking damage, and more about controlling where enemies attack."

"That is true. Ouroboros was really good at that." Thorn nodded. More and more he was feeling the effect of not having a class. Even though he had abilities granted through his Avatar title, he was missing a lot of the basic abilities that came with even the standard classes.

Resolving to make getting a class his priority, Thorn sat down with the girls and took a quick break. Getting out a few sandwiches that he had purchased in town and a large jug of iced tea, they ate and chatted. Thorn had gotten better at asking questions about the game and Mina was always happy to chatter on about anything so Thorn was able to put their breaks to good use.

After chatting for ten minutes, they were fully rested. Getting up, Thorn brushed some crumbs off his pants and called Akira who had been fighting with Mina over a couple cookies. Seeing that everyone was ready, he led the way up the stairs to the second floor of the dungeon. As they walked up the curling staircase, Thorn checked the status of his quest.

Lord of Greymane
Elder Thomas, the Greymane Village leader, has asked you to break the curse hanging over these lands in order to claim your position as the Lord of Greymane. In order to break the curse sit in the Wolf Throne while wearing the Ring of the Wolf Lord. As an added requirement defeat all the werewolves in the castle. 67/100 Werewolves 0/1 Greater Werewolf Rewards: Title: Lord Greymane Area: Greymane Castle Area: Fang Forest Area: Greymane Village Area: The Twins

Thirty-three werewolves and a greater werewolf left, thought

Thorn. Enough to provide a fatal challenge for the three of them should they not proceed carefully. Climbing up the dark stone staircase, Thorn could not help but marvel at the texture of the stone as he ran his armored fingers across the wall. Watching his fingers bounce along the slight inconsistencies, Thorn still found it hard to believe that all of this was a game. More and more, he was beginning to treat this world as real.

The more he learned about Nova Terra, the less it seemed like a game, or a way to pass his time. Intellectually he knew that his body was stuck in a giant tube, being treated by an advanced form of nanobots while his mind wandered around in this fantasy world. Yet every day he woke up and ate, talked and fought, growing more at home in this virtual space. He could feel his mind adapting to the new rules of his body and a small part of him was wondering if he would be able to adapt to life in his real body ever again.

Hearing the tink, tink, tink of his gauntlets on the stone blocks, Thorn felt a poke and suddenly realized that Velin was glaring at him. Sheepishly he took his hand back and walked as quietly as he could up the stairs. The top of the stairs led directly into a massive room and it didn't take the party long to realize that something was off.

CHAPTER TWENTY-EIGHT

The large room was divided into three rough sections, each marked out by iron pillars as thick as Thorn's wrist sunk into the stone floor. Attached to each pillar were three sets of heavy-duty chains suspending skeletons in various states of decay. Along the walls of the room dangled the corpses of prisoners and various instruments of torture. Directly in the center of the room a thick, rusty iron spike stood a full six feet tall with a skeleton impaled upon it.

Stepping into the room, Thorn focused his gaze across the room at a hulking brute of a monster, squatting on two back legs while it gnawed its way through chainmail armor to get at the flesh of the corpse it was feasting on. When Thorn and the girls came into the room the monstrosity looked up at them and then slowly stood, rising to a full eight feet of pure muscle and horror. Metallic-looking fur covered its body and its razor-sharp claws were easily as long as Mina's forearm. Saliva dripping from its maw, the greater werewolf grinned, its bloody muzzle creating a terrifying picture.

"Looks like we have a guest," slurred the creature, tossing the remains of the adventurer it had been chewing on to the side. Without warning it threw back its head and howled, a long echoing sound ringing around the keep. In response howls erupted from every corner of the second floor and the hurried sound of werewolves rushing over became quite clear.

Within seconds the room began to fill with werewolves, surrounding the group on three sides. As they pushed in, jostling for position, a large metal gate fell from the ceiling, cutting off the path back down the stairs and pushing them toward the center of the room. Their backs to a wall and with no escape, Thorn took a big breath.

Mina and Velin had started chanting as soon as the greater werewolf howled, and as the door behind them came down, Thorn sprang into action, decisively rushing forward, determined to keep the werewolves from gaining any momentum.

Surprised by Thorn's move, the greater werewolf roared out in anger, "Kill him!"

Jumping into the group Thorn began to lash out with his tetsubo as fast as he could, each blow containing as much force as could possibly muster. If he couldn't disable a large portion of the werewolves in this first rush, he knew that they would be in a lot of trouble. As the werewolves reacted and started to jump toward Thorn it became increasingly difficult for him to swing his weapon.

Monsters were tossed aside, skulls smashed and limbs bent, but as soon as Thorn managed to move one away, two would press into its place, their sharp claws reaching toward him. Thorn grimaced in pain as a claw caught his back, ripping through his leather armor and gouging his skin. Thankfully, Velin's warm healing light landed on him at the same time. Squirming slightly at the strange feeling of being injured and healed at the same time, Thorn spun. He threw out a sharp hook, blasting the werewolf that struck him into another, its mangled snout spraying blood and saliva through the air.

A snap kick drove another werewolf back, directly into an iron post but at the cost of another gash on Thorn's shoulder. The monsters were simply too numerous for him to avoid, especially if he wanted to attack, and as the brawl continued more and more cuts appeared on his flesh.

Back near the door, Mina was sending out a storm of snow and ice, trying her best to bog down the werewolves at the edges of the fight while using barrages of ice spikes to drive back the werewolves that approached her and Velin. Seeing a werewolf jumping for Thorn's neck, she pointed.

"[Sub Zero]!"

The pouncing werewolf froze solid and Thorn, feeling the cold air behind him, turned and backhanded it across the room where it shattered against the wall. As the struggle continued, Thorn swung his tetsubo with abandon, smashing down everything that came into its range. Finally, unable to bare the strain of the chaotic fight, his weapon snapped off at the handle. Tossing away the broken handle Thorn began to lash out with punches and kicks as fast as he could.

It was a deadly whirlwind of bone-crushing kicks and punches, razor sharp claws and snapping jaws. Countless werewolves fell, but no matter how many Thorn crushed into the ground, more jumped forward to strike at him. Additionally, the longer he fought the faster he seemed to lose his energy, despite Velin's healing. Sparing a glance down he could see blood soaking his armor, new wounds opening up even as others closed under the warm light. With the sight of the blood came the sure knowledge that unless the fight ended soon he would be experiencing his second death in Nova Terra.

"Thorn, I can't keep up!" Velin shouted, desperately trying to heal Thorn through all the damage. The bloody streaks appeared on his Thorn's massive form faster than her light could heal him causing his health to fall steadily. Every strike from the werewolves stacked a bleeding condition on to Thorn, and Velin's condition clearing spell was on cooldown.

While Thorn was struggling in the middle of the brawl, Akira was hiding behind Mina, trying to stay out of sight of the werewolves. As a support battle pet, she was no match for the monsters in a direct fight and thought it much safer to keep a distance. As she watched Thorn smash through the werewolves, worry began to grow. Thorn was slowing down and began to take more hits as his fatigue built up.

Akira rushed out and darted up an unsuspecting werewolf's back, launching herself through the air while calling up her most powerful support spell, [Majesty]. A spell unique to Royal Ailuridae, [Majesty] imbued a target with a majestic glow, drawing those around them in and providing various buffs to their stats. However most important was the fact that when cast it removed all negative status effects on the target while restoring them to perfect health, which, in this case, cleared Thorn's bleeding condition and put his health back to full.

Akira was so focused on casting her spell that she failed to notice the large black claw coming toward her side until it cut through her fur. With a shriek she fell to the ground, barely rolling out of the way as another strike came down at her head.

Thorn felt his fatigue suddenly vanish when Akira jumped, but it wasn't until he heard her shriek that he understood what had happened. Seeing her disappear under the roiling sea of monsters, his stomach jumped straight into his throat and a frenzy filled him.

[Wolf's Rage] triggered on its own, filling Thorn with a

savage power. Throwing his head back, Thorn instinctively activated [Wolf Lord's Howl], the shockwave of sound stunning all the werewolves. Still howling he sprang into the dense pile of monsters, blasting them away with a swift flurry of punches and kicks. Failing to move them fast enough he saw Akira surface again, bleeding from where she had been struck, desperate to get away from the werewolves, only to be struck again by a heavy claw, her battered body flying back toward the wall.

As she was about to hit the wall a bright light fell on her, its warm glow healing her wounds and waking her from her stunned state. Scrambling back to her feet, Akira quickly hid behind Mina who furiously blasted the werewolf that had been chasing the Ailuridae into a popsicle. Squeaking furiously, Akira shivered, scared by her close brush with death.

Never more thankful for teammates, seeing Akira nearly get mauled pierced Thorn's heart. Poking a hole in the thick wall that he used to shield his emotions from others. Like a dam bursting those feelings spewed forth, unleashing a wrath he had not known he possessed. A feral growl escaped his clenched teeth and a bloody glow rose in his eyes.

Grabbing a werewolf by the throat he began to swing it like a club, smashing into the other werewolves without any regard for defense. Large gashes began to reappear as the monsters slashed and snapped at him but Thorn paid them no mind, simply grinding any werewolves who got close into paste.

His eyes saw only the outlines of his enemies within a red mist and his hands sought them out without rest, gouging, crushing, striking and maiming. No matter how many werewolves came forward, Thorn pressed on mindlessly, slaughtering them however he could.

Within minutes a somber silence descended on the room broken only by the hoarse breathing of Thorn and the rasping breath of the greater werewolf who was staring at him in bemused astonishment. When Thorn had entered the room the greater werewolf had summoned the remainder of its kin from around the castle to deal with him, only to be surprised by the ferocity with which Thorn slaughtered them.

Behind Thorn, Mina stared in shock, her mouth open. Catching sight of Thorn's bloodshot eyes as he looked around for more enemies to shred, the Ice Witch could not suppress a shudder. Thorn had gone through almost thirty werewolves like a meat grinder and the raw savagery of it caused her to shake.

Velin stood behind Mina, her brow furrowed. Despite the worry that was evident on her face, she did not forget to heal Thorn, doing her best to bring him back up to full health. Sensing that Mina was about to call out, Velin grabbed her, placing a hand over the shorter girl's mouth.

"Shh. Don't draw his attention. Something is wrong." Velin

whispered, her eyes fixed on Thorn's broad back.

The greater werewolf wasn't concerned with the deaths of its kin, they would reappear if the curse continued. Rather, the greater werewolf was surprised that Thorn had managed to make it through all 33 of the werewolves it had called and remain standing. Bleeding from a dozen serious gashes, it was a miracle that Thorn hadn't collapsed long ago.

Thorn, for his part, still wasn't thinking properly. Having given into his anger all the sorrow, loneliness, fear, and worry that he had stored up in his heart throughout his life began to burn, serving as fuel for his rage. The 16 years of suppressed emotion was pouring out, feeding the flames of his anger until it was an all-consuming blaze.

Leaning heavily on the iron spike in the center of the room, the only things keeping him from sprinting forward were his iron self-control and his fearsome grip on top of the metal spike. Looking around at the corpses surrounding him, Thorn could feel the murderous drive trying to control him, telling him to rip into the greater werewolf.

His gaze eventually settled on the greater werewolf who was beginning to slowly make his way toward him from the throne. As the boss monster broke into a charge, one of the few remaining parts of Thorn's mind that possessed restraint recognized the danger and let go, sending him hurtling to meet the greater werewolf.

Issuing a roar of superhuman force, Thorn met the boss' charge. With an ear-shattering boom they collided, sending dust and blood flying. Smashing a fist into the greater werewolf's chest, Thorn felt a razor-sharp claw pierce his chest in return and only a desperate twist of his body prevented it from cutting into his heart. Still, the fury gripping him did not let him back down as he threw blow after blow at the greater werewolf, forcing it back.

Snarling, the greater werewolf slipped to the side, striking again. Its razor-sharp claws cut into him. Fiery pain erupted in his chest as blood spurted out, soaking the front of his body in gore. Darkness began to creep into his vision and Thorn could feel his strength draining quickly despite Velin's attempts to heal him. Yet in the haze of his fading consciousness a stubborn ember glowed, refusing to be extinguished.

Scenes from his childhood flashed across his eyes as the world grew dark. At three, already tall enough to look out over the window sill at the kids playing outside, unable to leave the house due to his condition. Age six, blowing out the candles on his birthday cake, only his aunt and nurse there to celebrate. The stark white walls of the hospital where the doctors finally put a name and description to his condition the day after his ninth birthday. The lonely hours that stretched into days, weeks, and months when his aunt was away on business.

All his life he had been alone, isolated and protected from

the world and anything that could harm him, protected from himself most of all. And now that he had the chance to experience true freedom the monster in front of him was trying to take it all away. Intellectually Thorn knew that giving in to his unbelievable fatigue would simply send him back to the spawn room, a simple rebirth of his avatar.

Yet, for whatever reason, Thorn could not tolerate the thought of it. The ember of resistance that burned in his soul ignited and his slipping hands tightened on the massive spike he was leaning on. Peering through the haze at the wavering figure of the leering werewolf who had stabbed him, Thorn grimaced in pain and his hand closed over the massive claw that impaled him, holding it fast as if letting go meant the end of everything. The ember burst into flame, a flame that raged through him, forcing a low rumble out of his chest as he straightened up from his slumped position.

The greater werewolf simply couldn't believe his eyes as before him the gore-slicked figure held on with a desperation that was out of this world. The fearsome grip crushed the bones in the werewolf's wrist, yet no matter how it struggled, it could not break free. In growing horror it watched as the monster who had walked into its lair began to straighten up.

Looking into Thorn's eyes it saw nothing but the mad promise of death and its instincts kicked in, forcing it into a mad scramble backward. The greater werewolf firmly occupied the highest spot on the local food chain, but right now it felt like nothing more than a rabbit being hunted. Or rather, the greater werewolf would have scrambled backward if his claw was not caught firmly by Thorn's hand.

Thorn, barely aware of his actions, continued to hold onto the struggling werewolf, his right arm straining at the firmly planted metal spike in the center of the stone floor. Heaving upwards with a herculean effort, the veins on his arm bulging, Thorn's strength overcame the spike and he ripped it from the floor. Thorn hoisted it like a giant club, bringing it down on the now whimpering werewolf with tremendous force that crushed its skull like an egg, blood and brain matter coating the impromptu weapon.

Ding

Greater Werewolf defeated: You have gained the favor of Hati. [Wolf Hide] Unlocked

Ability: Avatar of the Wolf
Because you carry the essence of the Moon Wolf, you have gained the form of the wolf. As you grow, you can adopt features of the Moon Wolf Form. Wolf Claws: You gain the Claws of the Moon Wolf Wolf Hide: You gain the Armor of the Moon Wolf Wolf's Rage: You gain the Strength and Speed of the Moon Wolf Wolf Helm [locked]

Wolf Form [locked]

CHAPTER TWENTY-NINE

Still caught in the grip of rage, Thorn's eyes fixed on the throne where the greater werewolf had lounged when they first arrived. Carrying the corpse of the greater werewolf in one hand and dragging the six-foot-long metal spike in the other, Thorn stalked to the throne. A warm golden light surrounded Thorn as he advanced, stabilizing his injuries and restoring his strength. Sitting down on the throne, Thorn gave off a barbaric air.

His ruined and bloody armor and the massive rusty spike resting against his leg presented a frightening picture, reinforced by the body of the greater werewolf dangling loosely from his other hand, its legs splayed across the steps leading up to the throne. Across the room, Velin kept Mina back, continuing to heal Thorn as she watched the blood in his eyes fade.

After a few minutes of frozen silence, Thorn woke from his rage, the day's last light peeking through the window and bathing the room in a soft glow. As he blinked the room changed, its dungeon-like air vanishing, replaced by decoration one would expect in an ancient castle.

Old but regal tapestries adorned the walls, faded and moth-eaten. A red carpet ran down the center of the room from the large double doors leaning precariously on their hinges all the way up to the platform where he sat in a large wooden throne. Around the outside of the keep, the thick, gloomy mist that had blocked out the sun slowly faded away. A ripple seemed to pass through the valley, lifting the silent, oppressive air that had once smothered the forest.

His mind still bleary, Thorn ran his hands over the chair, marveling at the detailed workmanship of the lifelike wolves that formed the arm rests. The corpse of the greater werewolf had disappeared from his hand and turned into a large black wolfskin carpet, its scarred head staring at the door from under the wolf throne. After blinking a few times a notification caught Thorn's attention and he clicked it open resulting in a torrent of messages blocking his vision.

By the door, Mina slowly calmed down the frantic Akira, stroking the Ailuridae's fur as she observed the changes in the dungeon.

“Boy am I glad we're his friends.” She mumbled. “He soloed a boss with no effort.”

“On that we agree. Apologizing to him was certainly the best idea you have ever had." A small smile grew on Velin's lips as she watched Thorn who was frowning on his new throne. "Come on, we should go greet the new Lord Greymane."

As they approached, Velin watched Thorn carefully. She had seen a frightening rage in his eyes as he ripped the greater werewolf apart and was slightly worried that rage still consumed him. Seeing that his eyes were clear, she gave a small sigh of relief and bowed her head slightly as Mina spoke.

"I can't believe you killed that monster by yourself!"

"Only thanks to your help." Thorn smiled, standing from the wolf throne and walking down the steps. "Velin, if it wasn't for you and Akira healing me I don't think I would have survived."

"Happy to help. Did you complete the quest?"

"Yeah, though we still have to go back to the temple in the village to unlock it as a respawn point."

"It looks like you unlocked your title though."

"Yup. I'm officially the new Lord Greymane." Thorn swiped through the notifications that had popped up after the fight.

[Wolf Hide]

A cunning wolf chooses to avoid the strikes of its enemy. But when they must take a blow, they rely on their tough hide to minimize the damage. Due to gaining twice the necessary favor, [Wolf Hide] has unlocked and you have cleared the penalty for unlocking [Wolf's Rage] out of order.

[Wolf Hide] increases the defensive capabilities of any armor you wear.

Quest Updated - Lord of Greymane - Complete

Elder Thomas, the Greymane Village leader, has asked you to break the curse hanging over these lands in order to claim your position as the Lord of Greymane. In order to break the curse sit in the Wolf Throne while wearing the Ring of the Wolf Lord. As an added requirement defeat all the werewolves in the castle.

100/100 Werewolves
1/1 Greater Werewolf

Rewards:
Title: Lord Greymane
Area: Greymane Castle
Area: Fang Forest
Area: Greymane Village
Area: The Twins

Lord Greymane (Unlocked)
You have defeated the previous Lord Greymane in battle and claimed his castle as your own. You are now known to natives in the surrounding area as Lord Greymane, ruler of Greymane Castle and the surrounding lands. +Strength +Dexterity +Constitution +Intelligence +Wisdom +Charisma Unlock Ruler Management Screen

Ruler Management Screen Unlocked
All good rulers need to be able to manage their territory. Access the [RMS] by saying RMS. As you gain areas they will be added to your [RMS], allowing you to manage them more effectively. Currently your [RMS] governs the following areas: Greymane Keep Fang Forest Greymane Village The Twins

Greymane Village has been unlocked as a starter village. Players who start the game as Wolfkin or become Wolfkin will start in Greymane Village. Return the statue of Hati to the temple in Greymane Village to enable it as a respawn point.

Due to the opening of a new starter village, Wolfkin has been unlocked as a playable race. New players, or players with a corresponding race change token will be able to select Wolfkin as their race in 14 days.

Sorting through all the various alerts took a while and by the time he reached the end, Thorn had a better idea of what was going on. By killing the greater werewolf and sitting on the Wolf Throne, he had completed both of his objectives. Not only had he lifted the curse for the quest that Elder Thomas had given him, but he had also unlocked his [Lord Greymane] title and now he was officially the Wolf Lord, ruler of Greymane Castle and the surrounding lands.

Mina and Velin had gone to explore the rest of the second floor of the keep while Thorn looked through the [RMS]. Opening it up, he began to scan its options. The basic menu was divided into four sections, each representing an aspect of governance. In the bottom right, there was a timer showing there were fourteen days before players would be able to select Greymane as their starting location.

The [RMS - Economy] tab-controlled things like taxes, trade

goods, guild rules, and various agricultural sliders that determined what seeds the native farmers had access to. After that came the [RMS - Citizen] tab that controlled various decisions related to the population of his land as well as containing statistics on the levels of happiness, wealth, health and other factors that his subjects currently enjoyed.

The other two tabs were the self-explanatory [RMS - Military] and [RMS - Diplomacy] tabs. All in all, the [RMS] was complex and as highly detailed as Thorn expected. The only things that took Thorn by surprise were the fact that the Diplomacy tab also contained a plethora of options for running an intelligence agency and that the Military tab already had several soldier natives listed as waiting to be claimed.

Curious, Thorn selected the name of a captain and pressed the button to claim his soldier. A moment passed and then, with a slight popping sound and a bright flash of light, a large wolfkin stepped out of the air.

Easily standing at 7’ 6” the muscular but lean wolfkin looked quite dashing in his brown and grey leathers, a massive longbow slung across his back and a sword by his side. Black fur, which covered him from the top of his ears to the end of his tail, except for a section around his neck where the fur was tipped with silver, created a striking contrast with his green eyes. About the same time he appeared so did his status and Thorn noticed that the native count in the [RMS] rose by one.

Name: [Del'har]	Race: [Wolfkin]
Health: [100%]	Mana: [100%]
Titles: [Vassal of the Wolf Lord]	Conditions: [None]
Abilities: [Wolf's Howl], [One with the Shadows]	

"My Lord." Said Del'har, falling to a knee, his right hand over his heart and his head bowed in a typical warrior salute. "I am here to serve."

"Oh, eh...rise?" Thorn coughed, embarrassed, at the Wolfkin's unexpected action.

"Thank you my Lord. Have you decided how I may best serve you?"

"Uh, no. How would I go about doing that?"

"Simply select the citizen tab in the [RMS] and select what role I should be assigned next to my name, my Lord."

"Oh, got it, thanks. What sorts of skills do you have?" Thorn asked as he fiddled with the [RMS] interface.

"My Lord, I am trained as a ranger, with a focus in using a bow and tracking. I am also trained as a leader and before my fall I was the leader of the Greymane's First Company."

Thorn mused for a bit, considering various options before finally deciding that Del'har would take up his old position. Like that, Greymane Keep gained its first captain. Going back to the military tab, Thorn found that the other soldiers listed were now grayed out. Seeing a symbol in the top right corner of the screen with a zero next to it, Thorn realized that he was out of the resource he had used to purchase Del'har.

Putting that aside for the moment, Thorn looked through the other tabs. As he did so, a couple of things really stuck out to Thorn.

First, the economy of the area was in shambles. Currently the castle required 300 gold a month to keep up, but since it hadn't been paid in years, there was a massive amount of work that needed to be done to restore the castle. On top of that the surrounding area brought in a bit less than 400g a month in taxes, but taxes hadn't been collected in years either which resulted in a completely empty treasury.

Second, Thorn currently only had one subordinate, Captain Del'har, and the whole region only had 65 people listed as citizens. The castle alone needed a minimum of 75 people to operate normally and while the surrounding lands could easily support thousands more, at least 50 people were required for Greymane Village to operate.

The first problem was easy enough as Thorn had incredibly deep pockets and could simply finance his new land indefinitely without any issue. The second problem was trickier. The lack of population meant that he couldn't throw money around and hope to succeed. While it looked like he could buy the currency he needed to hire native soldiers, he really needed builders, hunters, farmers and other skilled craftsmen which were much harder to find. Facing a massive shortage of people, there did not seem to be an immediate way to improve the situation.

The girls returned from looking around the keep. As they approached Thorn they were stopped by the tall wolfkin captain, who rested his hand on the pommel of his sword as he watched them warily. Seeing the protective gesture, Thorn smiled and waved him aside.

"Captain, these are my companions Mina and Velin. You don't need to stop them. Mina, Velin, this is Del'har, the Captain of the First Company."

His eyes still alert, Captain Del'har greeted the girls with a warrior's salute and stepped to the side, staying at the bottom of the steps leading up to the throne.

"Well, aren't you moving up in the world." Mina teased, laughing. "You have your own minions and everything."

"Came with this ruined castle and tons of debt. The whole region is an absolute wreck. I'm honestly not sure if this title is a good or bad thing."

"Definitely a good thing." Velin assured him, handing him a silver statue. "We found that in the lord's chambers. It looks like the statue you need to return to unlock the spawn point. So far, things have turned out as we planned. What are you worrying about?"

"The valley is in shambles and we only have two weeks until players start to show up."

"Sure, but if we can weather this first rough patch, controlling the region will bring a lot of money." Mina chimed in.

"Eh," uninterested by the earning potential of the region, Thorn shrugged. "It looks like the first issue we have to deal with is the lack of people. Rebuilding the castle, expanding Greymane Village, and harvesting the resources of the region are going to take a large population. Given what we know about how valuable controlling a region is, we will soon have people coming to see if they can wrestle this area away from us and we need people of our own if we want to stop them. But to support people we need infrastructure, which we need people to build. See the problem?"

"I do, but it is nothing that can't be dealt with." Velin nodded. "It seems like the biggest issue facing us is time. Do you know how long we have until the region unlocks?"

"Let me check." Pulling up the notification, Thorn looked at the timer that was counting down.

[13:23:56:43]

“Thirteen days and twenty-three something hours. So fourteen in-game days. Two day in the real world.”

“That is not much time.” Her brow furrowing, Velin thought for a moment. “Normally, situations like this are handled by guilds because of the need for manpower and financial resources. Honestly, the easiest route is to sell this information to a guild and let them deal with it.”

“Would they let me keep my position as Lord Greymane?”

“Probably not.” The elven War Priestess shook her head. “Not unless you joined them. And even then, they may not.”

“Then that isn’t going to happen.” Thorn smiled, his glinting teeth reminding Mina of a large wolf.

“My Lord, I might have some ideas regarding this situation.” The wolfkin captain said, dropping to a knee.

“Please stop doing that,” replied Thorn. “If you have to, salute or something.”

“Of course my lord.” The tall Wolfkin stood and crossed his right fist over his heart in a warrior’s greeting. “During my youth, the castle’s upkeep was the responsibility of the residents of Greymane Village. As Lord Greymane, you can assign them to work on the keep.”

“True, but honestly, they will have their hands full with rebuilding the village, so we cannot count on them for much.” Thorn rubbed his chin. “There is a lot to do everywhere, and not nearly enough hands to do it.”

“Well, uh.” Captain Del'har paused for a moment and looked like he was lost in thought. After a serious internal struggle the tall wolfkin looked at Thorn and spoke in a subdued tone, “My lord, we should take a trip to the lands beyond the valley.”

“You mean the mountains?”

“Yes, my Lord. There is a group of my people who used to live here but were forced to move after the curse twisted the former lord. Now that the curse has been lifted it might be possible for us to bring them back if you’ll accompany me to go talk to them.”

“Are they soldiers?” Mina asked, remembering the group that they had encountered in the tunnel leading to Davyos’ Fall.

“No, they are the descendants of the monks who used to live in the Temple of the Moon. They were once warrior monks, but due to the strength of the werewolves, they fled to the mountains where they have lived ever since. If you could bring them back to the valley, you would gain a strong workforce.”

“Are they still monks?” Thorn asked, curious. “Are there still Night Walkers among them?”

“Yes, my Lord, though there have not been many Night Walkers for the past few generations, ever since the last Temple was moved from the valley. These monks are a mix of the descendants of the Moon Guardians who were tasked with protecting the valley, and the remnants of the Night Walkers. Over time, as the memory of Hati, the Moon Wolf, faded, so too did their power. By the time the werewolf arrived and corrupted Gargish, the monastery was nothing but a shell of what it had once been and the few remaining Moon Guardians had no choice but to join them and flee.”

“What makes you think they will join us?” Velin cut in.

“The Wolfkin are a proud race, and we serve the Greymane.” The captain bristled at Velin’s question. “My Lord, as the one who freed the valley from the werewolf's curse and claimed the wolf throne, you are the only one the wolfkin will follow.”

“Excellent,” Thorn nodded. “Let's go tomorrow. I am going to head to Greymane Village. I’ll be back once I’ve had a chance to talk to Elder Thomas.”

“Should we come with you?”

“No, you and Velin can stay here. I’ll move faster by myself.” Thorn shook his head at Mina’s question. “Captain, please help these ladies take inventory of what in this dump is still usable."

CHAPTER THIRTY

After thinking it over, Thorn decided to go see Thomas in Greymane Village to turn in the quest and activate the temple as a respawn point. This way, should anything happen, he would not be respawning days away in Berum.

Leaving Captain Del'har and the girls to guard the castle, Thorn ran back through the woods. By himself, he covered distance at a fantastic rate, cutting the trip that had taken two hours that morning down to only twenty minutes. The village was quite different from when they had first arrived, and the loud sounds of a party could be heard spilling from the ramshackle tavern that stood near the center of town.

As soon as he ducked into the bar, Thorn was hit full force by the scent of alcohol and roasted meat and his stomach let out an involuntary grumble. The village leader, Elder Thomas, and Captain Charles noticed him at the same time and smiled happily. Yet, suddenly, their expressions froze and with a horrified look at each other they ran over, both bowing low and seeming quite nervous.

“My Lord!” The elder’s face was pale and white. “We were just celebrating your magnificent ascension to the throne. We were going to visit you first thing tomorrow to bring tribute.”

“Oh, that is great, uh. Actually I had a couple questions so I thought I’d come over.” Thorn looked around, totally oblivious to the terrified stares of everyone in the tavern. “Um, I’m kind of hungry, could I maybe get a plate of something?” he continued, absentmindedly scratching at his face.

“Yes, of course my Lord! Quick bring out something for his lordship to eat!” Thomas, trembling slightly, led Thorn to a nearby table, shooing the occupants away. Scrambling to their feet and bowing repeatedly they seemed almost eager to get away from Thorn who was finally starting to notice the deep silence in the tavern.

“Why is everyone so quiet?” Thorn whispered to Charles.

“Um... My Lord, have you seen yourself recently?” Asked the alchemist gently. “You look something awful. No offense your Lordship.”

Frowning, Thorn looked down at himself for the first time and noticed that his outfit was in utter shambles. The armor he had gotten in Berum was twisted and bent beyond recognition and his body was absolutely covered in dried blood, both his and his enemies. No wonder everyone was staring at him in fright; he looked like the main monster out of a horror flick. Disgusting flakes of dried blood fell from him every time he moved.

Blushing until his face was the same deep red as the rest of him, Thorn asked for a bath to be drawn up, and despite his hunger he spent the next 45 minutes scrubbing the evidence of his battle away. The warm water was soon filthy with blood and grime and Thorn had to replace the bathwater twice before he felt clean. As he scrubbed himself he thought carefully about all that had happened since he first logged in. In a way, everything that had happened to Thorn in the past few months was utterly unbelievable and he still hadn't fully wrapped his mind around it.

But a couple things he had certainly realized: first, he was currently the new Lord Greymane. Regardless of how he felt about it, he was stuck here in Angoril for the next fourteen years and the local population all now knew him as the ruler of Greymane Keep and the surrounding region, and second, he had no way to log out apart from going to Fantasia which, at this point did not interest him. A part of his mind worried that the role he had inherited would restrict his freedom, but at the same time there was an excitement in knowing he could be at the center of something grand.

Assuming, that is, that he could hold the castle. In the little bit of research that he had done, Thorn had read that towns, cities, castles, and even whole countries could be held by players if they had the strength and capital. The major issue was that Thorn, while he had plenty of capital, was only a single player. Compared to a guild his power was quite insufficient even with Mina and Velin.

Relaxing, Thorn's mind turned to Oberlin. He had sent the thief south after a long conversation and from Oberlin's last message, it sounded like the trip was going to pay off. Hopefully, he would make it back within the next week. If he took much longer, Thorn might be in real trouble.

Soon after, a refreshed and somewhat bashful Thorn made his way back down the groaning stairs and into the tavern's main room where the villagers were engaged in subdued conversation. Looking him over, the villagers got their first good look at their new lord and all were quite impressed with what they saw. While huge, Thorn was well muscled but not bulky, handsome but by no means a model. A gentle air emanated from him and his eyes were deep pools of brown that looked at the world with great calmness, a testament to having seen and survived great suffering.

Overall Thorn gave the impression of a stately mountain, solid and unyielding. Certainly a better option than the last Lord Greymane. Elder Thomas walked over to Thorn grinning.

"Feeling better m'lord?" he asked, chuckling at Thorn's

blush.

“Yes, I am. Sorry about that, had a lot on my mind.” replied Thorn scratching his head bashfully. “So, how about that food?”

“Of course, of course. Please be seated!”

And so the night passed. The villagers soon realized that Thorn wasn’t at all stuck up and got back to celebrating their new lord with copious amounts of alcohol, and it wasn’t until the morning dawned that the tavern finally emptied. As the man of the hour Thorn had been inundated with free drinks, all of which he consumed readily.

Despite his young age in real life, he had consumed alcohol before and while he was indifferent to the taste, it was practically impossible for him to get even the slightest of buzzes due to his abnormally large body.

The early morning light of Nova Terra’s sun saw Thorn supporting a staggering Charles while carrying a completely blitzed Elder Thomas over his shoulder as he walked them home. The evening had been intense and everyone in the town was going to get some rest. Like the rest of the town, the two men were soon in bed sleeping off the effects of their wild celebrating. Thorn, on the other hand, walked around greeting the few people who were up and getting a better feel for the town. As he made his rounds, he stopped at the rundown temple and placed the silver wolf statue in its proper place.

ding

You have unlocked Greymane Village's respawn point by returning the statue of Hati. You have gained Hati's favor.

Greymane Village was situated on a hill that at one time had been encircled by a large stone wall about a quarter of the way from the top. That wall had long fallen into ruin as the village had been sacked again and again. Instead, it was now surrounded by a fragile looking palisade that ran around the very top of the hill. The town itself had been reduced to a handful of stone buildings and wooden shacks with a barely functioning guard that was often away from the town hunting for food.

Merchants had long since abandoned the road that cut through the forest despite how long it took to go around because of it's dangerous lord and Greymane Village suffered as a result. The good news was that the forge was still in relatively good shape despite being rarely used over the last few years and the town had gained a rebirth point in its small temple.

One of the notifications Thorn had received said that Greymane Village was unlocked as a starting location once the shrine had been restored and opening a browser he looked for information on that process. After a couple minutes of hunting Thorn learned that the town would go through a countdown before opening up as a new start location option. During this time new natives would move into the area and set up, waiting for the incoming players.

A bit more exploring led Thorn to figure out that it was going to be important for the town to be a strong defensible location as beginner towns were hugely important. Each beginner town had a spawn point, allowing players to bind the town as the spot they would be resurrected if they died. If a guild or organization could hold on to a spawn point they would possess a massive advantage in the area as they could set the rules for using the rebirth shrine. In fact, that is why Thorn had to pay to use the respawn point in Embersplit. That money had gone into the coffers of the guild that controlled the city and they in turn paid for the guards and other city improvements.

Opening his inventory, Thorn looked at what sort of money he had available. Currently, his purse was woefully small, holding only a few gold. However, money was the last of his worries as Julia had set up an account in fantasia with a few million universal credits which, when converted, came out to 15 million gold. Surely enough to rebuild the town and castle.

The real issue was in finding enough people to help him hold the area. It would be maddening to sink tons of money into improvements only to have the town and castle snapped up from underneath him. Mulling over all of this, Thorn left a message for Elder Thomas and Charles to come see him at the keep and ran back with some breakfast.

The girls had logged out for a couple hours, so Thorn and Captain Del'har ate the breakfast Thorn had brought and then spent the morning demolishing the rotting parts of the castle while they waited for Thomas and Charles to arrive. Inside the crumbling wall of Greymane Keep were four other buildings besides the stone keep itself.

A few hours later, as Thorn was ripping the last of the rotten roof off the castle smithy, the village leader and the alchemist made their way into the yard, looking around in astonishment at how different everything was. All the buildings except for the keep had been reduced to their bare states or simply ripped down entirely if they were rotten. Del'har had watched in awe as Thorn leveled entire buildings in minutes with little more than his bare hands.

Seeing the two of them come in Thorn quickly finished snapping the wooden slats. Throwing them into the fire they'd built in the center of the courtyard he made his way over to the others. Instantly the two men dropped to their knees but Thorn stopped them and told them to cut it out. Already uncomfortable towering over others, he instinctively disliked when they saluted on one knee.

"Enough of that. If you must do something salute. Anyway, come on inside. We have a lot to talk about." Waving them inside the keep he introduced the tall Wolfkin as they entered. "This is Captain Del'har, he is the Captain of the

First Company and my second in command. Okay, grab a seat because this might take a while."

Getting comfortable in his throne, Thorn waved for the three natives to pull up some of the chairs he had moved into the throne room and then began to outline the issue as he saw it.

"First, let me lay out the problems. Problem number one, this castle and the surrounding areas are a complete and utter wreck. We have no economy, no infrastructure, barely any people and no money in the treasury. Given the number of people who will be coming the whole area is likely to turn into utter chaos soon."

"Uh, my lord? Who is coming?" asked Charles, confusion written on his face.

"Yeah, that's right, I forgot to mention. Greymane Village will be unlocked as a spawn point for travelers within two week and we have gained a respawn shrine. This means that soon you will have travelers and merchants coming and bringing new wealth, but also bringing new trouble. As it is, the town is woefully unprepared and unprotected."

"A spawn p.. point?" stammered Elder Thomas.

"Yes. I'm sure you know what that means? This whole area is about to be blasted wide open for exploration, trade and settlement. On top of that we will undoubtedly see an increase in banditry and other criminal activity if we can't keep a tight hold on everything from the get-go. This brings us to problem number two. Our second major problem is that once this area is announced as a new start location we will probably have guilds coming in to try to take the town and castle for themselves in a bid to control all the land. This means that apart from the normal issues we would face in developing this land, we are probably in for a war almost immediately."

Here Thorn paused to look over the others. Elder Thomas' face was pale, Charles' face was grim and Captain Del'har's face was unreadable, though that could have been the fur.

"This means that we need to do three things. Repair the city and castle, find people to settle, and find an army. And all this needs to be done before our two weeks are up. The captain has mentioned he might know where to find some other wolfkin who can help with the castle, any other ideas?"

For a moment they all sat in silence, thinking about the coming changes and all the ramifications of those changes. Finally Elder Thomas spoke up.

"My lord, we have tried to get new settlers to move out here in the past, but the werewolves and bandits kept them away. You have solved the problem of the werewolves, so more people might be willing to come. If you could deal with the bandits as well?"

"Talk to me about the bandits. Who are they and how many?"

"Quite a tragic story, m'lord." The captain spoke up, taking over for Elder Thomas. "They're mostly hunters and farmers and the odd soldier who at one time lived in these lands under the rule of the former lord. However, when the curse came they were slowly forced off their lands or forced to run from imprisonment, for one reason or another. As a result they have quite an enmity with the person who controls Greymane castle and live as bandits, preying on anyone who travels the area. It's why we see so few merchants these days."

"Hmmm, I'll have to go have a talk with them. Any idea where they might be based?" asked Thorn, scratching his chin as he thought.

"No m'lord, they stay pretty well out of sight. They're all woodsmen and can't be found when they don't want to be."

"Okay, deal with bandits, check. What else do we have?"

"We could advertise in a couple nearby cities for settlers if we had some coin to pay them." Elder Thomas looked thoughtful. "Actually, we might be able to pick up some older mercenaries as well that way. You know, give them a place to take their families and half retire?"

"Excellent idea, how fast can you do that?"

"Eh, should be able to get a message to the three closest cities within a day or so." Elder Thomas stroked his beard before remembering who he was talking to and added a hasty "my lord" to the end of his statement.

"I told you not to worry about that sort of thing. I'm not one for ceremony. I'll be busy for a few days dealing with the bandits and going with the captain to see about those wolfkin. We have six days till it becomes known that a spawn point is opening up, probably another three days till the first travelers get here. Doesn't give us much time so let's get to work. Elder, can you spend money for the town?" asked Thorn, rising from his chair.

"Yes my lord, I can. Thing is, we don't have any money to speak of."

"Not an issue." stated Thorn flatly, pulling out a massive pouch and setting it on the table, which creaked alarmingly. "10,000 gold in there, use it to rebuild the village, focusing on defenses and infrastructure. By the time I get back I want to be amazed. Now, please excuse me. I have much to do."

Ignoring the utter shock on the Elder and Captain's faces, Thorn left the throne room through a door in the back, motioning Captain Del'har to follow. The room they entered seemed to have, at one time, been a library or office, but the few books that remained were practically unreadable. Thorn sat down carefully in one of the chairs but sprang back up when it began to crumble under him. Swearing at the previous landlord he sat on a windowsill instead.

“Think we can trust them?” Thorn asked over his shoulder as he watched the two townsmen leave the castle from the window.

“You did give them a large amount of money, my lord.” replied the captain flatly. “You probably should have asked that question first.”

“Yes, I guess I did.” Thorn sighed. “Well, we’ll worry about that when we get back. Let’s go meet those friends of yours.”

CHAPTER THIRTY-ONE

"The village is over those ridges, my lord."

Taking a moment to look around the mountain range they had been winding through for the last three hours, Thorn couldn't help but take a deep breath. The clear air filling his lungs invigorated him. The captain had led the way into the mountains behind the keep and after three hours of hiking, they finally approached the village of the Wolfkin.

"Before we get there, why don't you tell me what I'll need to do to get them to come back with me?" Rather than beating around the bush, Thorn asked Captain Del'har bluntly. Unfortunately, the Wolfkin Captain shook his head.

"Sorry, my lord. I'm not quite sure. I have not met with them for a long time, so I don't know who is currently in charge. In the past, possessing the title of Greymane would have been enough. There is a possibility that is still the case, but I would not expect it to be that easy."

"Hmm. That is okay." Thorn smiled confidently, comforting the captain. "I'm sure I'll be able to handle whatever they throw at me."

Thorn and the captain continued their hike, climbing the mountainside at a swift rate. The girls had decided to stay back at the keep after hearing that the Wolfkin village was up in the mountains. Velin used the excuse of organizing the library while Mina flat out refused to go. Not expecting to be gone for more than a day, Thorn had asked them to come up with a plan for the valley's development. While he had a rough idea of what he wanted to do with the valley, he was not confident in his ability to handle the specifics of how to get there.

Velin, on the other hand, was both meticulous and a critical thinker. Even more importantly, she was experienced in coming up with plans, allowing Thorn the freedom to concern himself with the bigger picture while she handled the details. Mina, however, seemed to spend her time running around.

Constantly curious, Mina got bored quickly, causing her to bounce from one thing to the next. She was a good fit for Thorn's battle pet Akira and Thorn tasked the two of them with creating a detailed map of the whole valley, a task Mina accepted with relish. At first, Thorn was slightly worried as he watched them run off into the woods, but the detailed reports that soon started to arrive reassured him. Despite her scattered personality, Mina was an elite player and that shown through when it really mattered.

The mountains that surrounded Fang Valley were thickly forested with imposing, snow-covered peaks. The mountain range seemed to stretch into forever, carrying on until the peaks faded into the horizon. A large mountain stood between Thorn and the Wolfkin village, towering over the keep at the far end of the valley. After examining the [RMS], Thorn was surprised to find that the whole mountain range was part of the Greymane domain and fell under Thorn's control. Nestled between two high peaks was a hidden village of thatched huts that sat at the edge of a large stone ruin. From a ridge overlooking the village Thorn could see clearly into its center where a stone altar stood in the middle of a large dirt common area.

The huts looked to be in ragged shape, lending an air of poverty to the village. Wolfkin walked to and fro in the village, going about their business. All of them were dressed in the same grey pants and shirts with different color sashes, reminding Thorn of oriental monks. As he and the captain approached the village two guards saw them and gave a piercing call before rushing forward to bar their way.

Despite the shabbiness of the buildings, there was nothing shabby about the two spears the guards held in their hands. The afternoon sunlight glinted off the sharp steel spearheads, and the black metal bodies of the spears trembled slightly with suppressed tension as the guards blocked the way into the village.

"Who are you?" barked one of the Wolfkin. "How did you find this village?"

"Impudent!" Shouted Captain Del'har, his lips drawing back to show his sharp teeth.

"Calm down." Thorn commanded in a deep voice, resting a large hand on the captain's shoulder. "Let me talk to them." Taking a small step in front of the captain, Thorn looked down at the two guards. "We are here to see the village chief, or whoever is in charge. You can tell them that Lord Greymane has come."

"Lord Greymane?" Startled, the two guards looked at each other, slightly lowering their spears. For a moment they hesitated, conversing in low voices. Arriving at an agreement, one ran back to the village where curious Wolfkin were gathering while the other guard lowered his spear the whole way, saying, "I'm sorry, but you'll need to wait here."

Feeling the captain bristling at the disrespect the guards were showing him, Thorn smiled and kept his hand on the tall Wolfkin's shoulder. Wolfkin were fiercely loyal and treated their hierarchy very strictly so the sight of the guards questioning his lord made Captain Del'har seethe. Thorn could understand the guard's response, however, so after signaling the captain to bear with it he took out a large rock he had found in the forest while hunting for potion supplies and sat down. As they waited a crowd started to gather behind the remaining guard.

Within a few minutes the other guard could be seen walking back toward Thorn and the captain, an elderly Wolfkin walking slowly by his side. As they left the village, the gathered crowd separated, showing great respect for the elderly Wolfkin. His fur was a deep silver and he bent over as he walked slowly to where Thorn sat. Before he arrived, Thorn stood to his feet, storing his large stone seat in his inventory.

For a moment the old Wolfkin and Thorn looked at each other, each taking the other's measure. Despite his eyes being blurred with age Thorn could feel a faint pressure emanating from the elder wolfkin, causing the hair on the back of his neck to rise. Stifling the urge to summon his Wolf Form, Thorn gave the elderly Wolfkin a warrior's salute.

"Greetings, I am Thorn, Lord Greymane, the Moon Wolf." Normally reluctant to reveal the full extent of his title, the instinctive threat he felt made Thorn feel competitive.

"Welcome, Thorn." The elderly Wolfkin ignored the stir in the crowd behind him caused by Thorn stating his title. "I am Elder Havva. To what do we owe the pleasure of your visit?"

"This is Captain Del'har, leader of my guard." Ignoring the question, Thorn introduced the captain who was standing a step behind him. He looked at the crowd behind Elder Havva with interest. The crowd was mixed in age, though Thorn had a bit of trouble telling the differences between Wolfkin due to their features. After a moment of looking around, he looked at the elder who was still waiting patiently in front of him. “Aren’t you going to invite me in?”

“We don’t welcome travelers here.” The old Wolfkin shook his head.

Unable to contain himself, Captain Del’har snarled, his hand going to the sword at this side. In response, the crowd bristled as well, growls mixing with the ringing of steel as they pulled out knives, short swords, and hatchets.

“Stand down.” Thorn’s deep voice was calm, seeming unbothered by the tension. “I come with good intentions, there is no need for this conflict.”

“The elder has already said that you are not welcome here.” A large Wolfkin stalked forward from the crowd. Large muscles bulged under his brown fur and his piercing green eyes stared at Thorn menacingly. “You should leave while you still can.”

Ignoring him, Thorn kept his eyes on Elder Havva.

Infuriated at being ignored, the large Wolfkin drew his sword, crouching slightly as if he was about to charge. Sensing his increased tension, Thorn finally looked over, locking stares.

The big Wolfkin looked dangerous, but for some reason, Thorn felt that Elder Havva was a larger threat.

Just as the Wolfkin who stepped out was about to charge forward Thorn held up his hand, the Ring of the Wolf Lord glinting in the sunlight. The large Wolfkin froze, his instincts stopping him from attacking. Slightly panicked, he looked at Elder Havva. The silver-furred Wolfkin closed his eyes with a sigh, his shoulders drooping slightly.

"You better come in to talk." Not waiting for a response, Elder Havva turned and shuffled back into the village. Thorn and Captain Del'har trailed behind him under the wary gaze of the guards. Leading the way to a hut near the stone altar, the elder waved for Thorn to follow inside before entering himself. Squeezing in proved difficult, but Thorn managed to get into the hut without bringing the door frame down. Inside, the elder sat down on a small stool and beckoned for Thorn to join him.

Summoning his stone chair, Thorn sat down, ignoring the displeased glares of the other Wolfkin that squeezed into the hut behind Captain Del'har.

"May I examine your ring?" Elder Havva asked Thorn, his voice tired.

"Of course." Thorn handed it over, watching as the elder looked it over carefully, turning it this way and that. It took almost half an hour before Elder Havva was satisfied.

Slipping it back on his finger, Thorn smiled. “Are you satisfied that I am Lord Greymane?”

“Ha, you are not Lord Greymane,” spat the large Wolfkin who had seated himself near Elder Havva. “How can an outsider be Lord Greymane.”

Before anyone could respond, Captain Del’har’s sword was out of its sheath, its razor edge resting against the large Wolfkin’s neck. Stunned, the large Wolfkin could not even swallow for fear of cutting his neck against the blade.

“Speak disrespectfully again and I’ll have your head.” Captain Del’har barked, his eyes narrowed in a murderous glare. He had been restraining himself all this time but was finally unable to hold himself back.

Surprised as everyone else, Thorn stared at the captain. He had barely seen the captain move before the sword was out and pointed at the large Wolfkin. In fact, the move had been so quick that Thorn was not sure if he would have been able to avoid it. Glad that the captain was on his side, Thorn watched the rest of the crowd carefully, ready to draw his weapon as soon as someone made a move.

“Sir traveler, Gelish spoke rashly, but he is correct.” Seeming entirely oblivious to the drawn weapon, Elder Havva spoke to Thorn. “According to the ancient law, only a member of the Temple of the Moon can be appointed the position of Lord Greymane.

ding

The True Lord Greymane
The inheritors of the Temple of the Moon refuse to recognize any but the appointed representative as Lord Greymane. To convince them that you are the rightful holder of the Greymane title, you must pass their tests. Rewards: Varied

Scanning the notification, Thorn nodded. He had expected there to be some sort of challenge and while he did not know exactly what 'Varied' rewards were, he guessed that it would have to do with his performance.

"The ancient laws must be upheld." Thorn's deep voice rumbled around the hut. "Captain, stand down."

Pleasant surprise showed in Elder Havva's eyes as he heard Thorn's words. Normally, travelers were much more forceful about getting their way so Thorn's comment caught him off guard.

"Elder, I respect the ancient rules, but understand that I am here to claim the allegiance of the Wolfkin, as is my right."

Elder Havva held up a clawed hand, silencing the murmurs that broke out at Thorn's declaration.

“I will not deny that the title of Lord Greymane will grant you the allegiance of the Wolfkin race, but that assumes you can gain the title.”

“You mistake me. According to the Code of the Wolf, the Ring of the Wolf Lord grants the title of Greymane. As the possessor of the ring, taken through a challenge of combat from the last Lord Greymane, there is no question as to my legitimacy. As the Temple Elder, you have the right to challenge for my position, by direct combat or by proxy combat. You do not have the right to deny me my authority. The Greymane’s rule is unshakable.

“The ancient laws you speak of say nothing about Lord Greymane being a member of the Temple. Rather, it only gives the right of trial by combat to the Temple Elder. It matters not to me whether the Temple of the Moon nominates a challenger, but it must be understood that they are a challenger. I hold the title.” As Thorn’s deep voice echoed around the hut, a subtle pressure spread with it forcing down the raised hackles of the Wolfkin in the room.

The pressure was not heavy, but firm, an unquestionable authority that radiated from Thorn, suppressing everyone else in the room. Even Captain Del’har was forced back slightly, his grip tightening on his sword, as if it might slip from his fingers. Only Elder Havva was able to remain unmoved in the face of Thorn’s aura.

Looking around at the others in the hut, Elder Havva gave a strained smile. He had to admit that there was something to what this large traveler said, but more importantly, the way he said it carried obvious weight.

“How do you know the Code of the Wolf?” Gelish asked, his voice much milder than before.

“I read it.” Thorn retrieved the book he had picked up in Davyos’ Fall and held it up for all to see. “The ancient laws are quite interesting.”

“You went to the cursed city?” Excitement radiating from his eyes, Elder Havva stood up abruptly. “What did you find there? Are our people still there?”

“I did go there, but I’m sorry, the city is empty and looks to have been empty for years. The temple to Hati there had been overtaken by werewolves.”

“Karrandras.” The excitement faded away from the Elder’s face as quickly as it had come and he sat back down on his seat.

“Correct. The Betrayer had corrupted the temple and turned those inside into his worshipers.” Pausing for a second, Thorn looked around at the angry faces of the surrounding Wolfkin. The thought of the Temple being corrupted obviously upset them and suddenly he was surrounded by a lot of sharp teeth. Feeling slightly nervous, Thorn kept his face impassive and added, “The temple has been cleansed and restored to proper worship of Hati.”

At Thorn’s words murmurs arose from the others in the room, only stopping when Elder Havva held up his trembling hand.

“We stray from the main purpose. If you wish to hold the title of Greymane, you must pass the challenge of the Temple of the Moon. If you wish for the allegiance of the Wolfkin, you must convince us that you are worthy of the title.”

Thorn rose to his feet, towering above the seated Wolfkin. His head brushing the ceiling, Thorn’s face broke into a wide grin.

“I would like nothing better.”

CHAPTER THIRTY-TWO

The last few rays of the evening sun gleamed off the mountainside, falling finally on Thorn's broad shoulders, warming his skin. Stripped to the waist, his body adorned with countless runic motifs, he stood calmly in a large stone ring. Crowds of Wolfkin surrounded the ring talking quietly to each other as they waited for Elder Havva to announce the challenger. The old Wolfkin looked up at the sky, his eyes cloudy, lost in thought.

That afternoon, after agreeing to the fight, Thorn had been led away by Elder Havva to prepare for the ritual challenge. Behind the village was a small hollow with a short waterfall and a deep pool. Ice cold water streamed down from the snow-capped peaks that surrounded the village.

"Please wash yourself. I will return with your garments for the trial. It may take a little longer than normal as I don't know that we have anything in your size. Your clothing is currently being made."

"No problem." Thorn waved his hand as the elder shuffled off into the forest. On the way over, Elder Havva had explained how the ritual combat would work and the various rituals that had to be completed before the combat could start.

Wading into the pool after stripping down, Thorn washed himself. The water was so cold that it stung, but Thorn's physical resistance made it bearable. After cleaning his body, Thorn dried himself off with a large towel from his inventory and, wrapping it around his waist, sat down to wait for Elder Havva who had not yet returned.

As he sat, Thorn thought carefully about the plans that he had made. While the first half of his plan for the valley had gone well, Thorn knew that the real challenges were only beginning. According to the message he had gotten, Mina and Akira had almost finished mapping the valley and Thorn was starting to think about how he was going to make sure he kept control of it. Velin's source in Ragnarok said that the Crimson Snakes were on their way to the valley, which did not give him much time to prepare defenses. Still, if he could recruit the Wolfkin, Thorn would have a decent fighting force.

"My apologies for making you wait, sir traveler." Elder Havva approached, two female Wolfkin behind him. "We have procured clothing that will fit you."

"Um, thanks." Taking the pants and sash from one of the

ladies, Thorn was very glad that Nova Terra had an option for instantly equipping gear.

"Once you are dressed, please sit so we can draw the holy runes."

It was only now that Thorn realized that the other lady was holding a tray with various brushes and pots of pungent paints as well as a stone glowing with a pale light. Curious, he equipped the pants and sash, tossing his oversized towel into his inventory, and knelt. Even kneeling he was almost as tall as the two Wolfkin women. Elder Havva took a brush from the case and dipped it into one of the pots on the tray, picking up the glowing stone with his other hand. Tapping the end of the brush on the stone, a sliver of the pale light slipped from the stone to shroud the brush's bristles.

The old Wolfkin shuffled around Thorn, his blurry eyes scanning Thorn's body. Silence returned to the edge of the pool, the only sound the soft splash of the waterfall. Realizing that Elder Havva had stopped behind him, Thorn opened his eyes. The elder was frozen in place, his eyes fixed on the tattoos that ran across Thorn's left arm and chest. Curious, Thorn looked down, only for his own eyes to widen in shock.

At some point, the barbaric looking, but meaningless tattoos that he had added at character creation had changed. Among the lines of the tattoo were figures woven together in a wolf and moon motif. A full moon with the silhouette of a howling wolf dominated his chest, sitting over his heart. Moving left, the moon could be seen in various stages, surrounded by hunting wolves. The wolf tattoos were dark but held a metallic shimmer, reminding Thorn of Hati's fur, while the moons were a pale silver, almost glowing.

It took almost ten minutes before Elder Havva started moving again. When he did, his first action was to put the brush back on the tray and pick up another, thicker brush. Closing his eyes, Thorn waited for Elder Havva to begin drawing, completely missing the looks of shock in the eyes of the two women behind the elder.

The drawing of the runes took almost three hours to complete, completely draining the glowing stone in the process. When Thorn finally stood up, they covered his whole torso, so tightly drawn that they looked solid from a distance.

"What are these drawings for?" Thorn asked as he examined himself. In retrospect, he realized that he should have asked before the runes covered his body.

"They signify your status as the Greymane and call for Hati to bless the winner of the challenge." Elder Havva coughed. "They use the power of the moonstone to call the favor of Hati. Were you a Wolfkin, they would strengthen your abilities." His figure hunched even more than before, it was as if he had aged years in the last three hours. After a moment of rest, the old Wolfkin shuffled through the woods,

Thorn and the women trailing behind him.

The ring where the trial would take place was in front of the statue of Hati at the center of the village. Twenty-five feet in diameter, the stone ring was slightly depressed, sitting about four inches below the rest of the village common area. Thorn could not tell if that was by design or if time had caused the ring to sink down into the earth. The ring itself was not completely flat but it was clean and showed signs of having been swept that very morning, giving testament to how often the ring was used.

Standing on the cracked and uneven stone ring, Thorn idly wondered what stories the ring might be able to tell if it could talk. It had undoubtedly witnessed a large part of the history of the Wolfkin race, weathering the sunshine and rain of the changing eras, to mention nothing of the blood and sweat of those who practiced atop it.

At the far end of the ring stood the village altar. Made of dark, stacked stones it was four feet high with soft edges, worn by the wind and rain of countless seasons. Atop the altar stood a statue of Hati made of the same dark stone, meticulously polished. The statue was surprisingly lifelike, exactly matching the image Thorn had in his head of the giant wolf god.

After a few moments the murmurs fell silent and the crowds parted, revealing the large Wolfkin Gelish. Dressed in a pair of loose pants with a green sash around his waist, Gelish was well built and would have been imposing if he had not been standing across from a Titan. Seeing the Wolfkin warrior pad into the ring, Thorn stepped forward, standing a full head above his opponent.

“The ancient law grants the Temple Elder the right of trial by combat.” Elder Havva’s blurry eyes stayed on the sky, his quivering voice carrying over the silent crowd as he recited the rules from memory. “As the laws command, the trial of combat is a trial of skill, not a battle to death. As such, using any weapons but those that Hati has graced us with shall constitute defeat. The victor of the trial shall be the combatant who incapacitates their opponent. A combatant who kills or cripples their opponent shall be executed according to the law.

“As the laws grant, the Temple Elder will pass the right of trial by combat to their eldest disciple. I, Havva, Moon Temple Elder, hereby claim my right to contest for the position of Greymane. I will engage in combat by proxy, nominating Gelish, First Disciple of the Moon Temple, as the combatant in my stead. This trial shall be held under Hati’s all-seeing eye.”

As his voice faded away, the Temple Elder turned to the statue of Hati atop the altar and bowed, chanting a prayer under his breath. For a moment nothing happened and the crowd remained frozen in place. As Thorn was about to scratch his head, the statue’s eyes glowed silver, casting a pale light over the stone ring.

"The great Walker of the Night, Hati has agreed to stand witness to this trial. Should the rules be violated, Hati will punish the offender. May the challenger come forward." Shuffling out of the ring, Elder Havva stood next to the altar as he waited for Gelish to enter the ring.

"I, Gelish, First Disciple of the Moon Temple accept the honor bestowed on me by the Moon Temple Elder. I enter the ring of combat to challenge…" Here Gelish stopped suddenly, realizing that he did not know his opponent's name. He had been so caught up in denying the traveler's title that he had never paused to ask.

"Thorn." Thorn's big voice rumbled out encouragingly.

"Uh...Thorn, the current Greymane, for the title of Greymane." Gelish tried to finish strong, but the verbal stumble in the middle of his challenge had sucked the momentum out of it. Around him the murmurs grew again as the crowd began to whisper to each other. Taking a step forward as the now familiar excitement began to build in his chest, Thorn spoke, his deep voicing silencing the crowd as it echoed around the fighting ring.

"I, Thorn, Lord Greymane, the Moon Wolf, accept the challenge."

Fifteen feet apart, Thorn and Gelish stared each other down, the tension in the air growing thick. The large Wolfkin flexed his fingers, his sharp claws glinting in the last vestiges of twilight. Like Thorn, his fur covered torso was covered in dense runic lines that glowed silver in the fading light. As the sun finally slipped below the horizon the clouds faded away, revealing the bright silver moon in its full glory.

The light from the moon landed on the ring, bending around the two combatants, chasing their shadows away. The setting was barbaric, but there was an elegance to the picture as well. Two rune-covered warriors engaged in a contest of strength, using nothing but that which their god had granted them.

For a moment Thorn considered attacking, but then he recalled the words that Elder Havva had spoken as they walked back from the pool. The elder had assured him that he would know when the fight was to start and that he must restrain himself until that point.

Thorn had been very confident going into this fight, but now, standing on the moonlit ring, facing Gelish's razor claws and large teeth, Thorn was starting to get nervous. Along with that nervousness, burning excitement was building in Thorn's chest as well. Suddenly, a cloud passed over the moon, briefly blocking its light and for an instant, Thorn imagined the moon had turned into Hati's giant eye, blinking at him.

The moon's gaze returned and Hati's majestic voice echoed clearly.

[Begin.]

Gelish, waiting for the signal, sprang into action. Brandishing his claws and baring his teeth he dashed forward, slashing from the left. Thorn was no slower, settling into his combat stance and slapping out with a backhand to deflect the incoming blow. As their attacks connected, Gelish realized that going up against Thorn in a contest of strength would be a fatal mistake. Thorn's power was beyond overwhelming and there was no way the Wolfkin could confront it directly.

Jumping to the side, he slashed out with a low kick, cutting through Thorn's pants and leaving a line of blood on Thorn's shin. The giant responded by pressing the attack, stepping forward and launching a sweeping kick of his own. Ducking impossibly low, Gelish scrambled back along the uneven stone, trying to get out of Thorn's attack range. Unfortunately for him, Thorn's size made that almost impossible and with a single step, Thorn had once again closed the distance. As Gelish jumped back, Thorn caught him with a glancing blow that sent the large Wolfkin flying, tumbling head over heels across the ring.

The Wolfkin stood, his dusty fur bristling. Gelish was the head disciple of the Temple of the Moon and had never been so humiliated in his life. He could easily fight any three of his fellow disciples but now he was struggling against a single traveler. No matter how large Thorn might be, he could not accept that he was having so much trouble fighting him.

With a growl, Gelish flexed his clawed hands and raised them toward the shining moon. Silver streams of light gathered around his fingers, causing the rest of the ring to dim for a moment. The runes along his hands and forearms ignited, burning with a flickering silver flame.

The flames glimmered dangerously, causing Thorn to tense slightly as he recalled the magic flames that Bluefire had used in their spar. Without any armor, Thorn had no defense against the magical flames. His worry was reinforced as Gelish jumped forward, his flame covered claws accompanied by a dangerous whooshing sound as the flames devoured the air.

Thorn would have liked to abandon the thought of blocking the blow, but his large size, which had provided him with an advantage, now worked to his detriment. Knowing that he could not get away, Thorn abruptly surged forward, punching out with his large fist.

“Better to trade blow for blow and rely on my endurance.” Thorn thought as he struck out.

Thorn’s fist met Gelish’s flaming claws with a bang, the force of the blow sending a ring of dust and flame into the air. For a moment their figures were obscured from view by the explosion and the crowded Wolfkin could only wait with bated breath. As the dust and flames settled, the two combatants were revealed, their ragged forms separated by five feet.

Gelish looked like he had come out of the exchange on top. Though the flames on his hands had dimmed significantly, he was otherwise unhurt. He stood, gulping in huge breaths of air, his bloodshot eyes fixed on Thorn whose figure looked much worse for wear. Thorn's large body, still imposing, was fixed solidly where they had struck each other. As the dust cleared, a gasp rose from the crowd as blood dripped down to the ground.

Thorn's right hand was a complete mess, the skin ripped to shreds. Deep cuts and charred skin gave testament to the ferocity of the blow he had blocked. The steady drip of blood beat a rhythm on the stone ring. At the sight of the blood, Gelish's bloodshot eyes grew completely red and he threw back his head to howl up toward the moon.

A thick sense of bloodlust seeped out from the large Wolfkin and his figure swelled. Heavy, knotted muscle grew around his neck and shoulders and his fingers, already wickedly clawed, grew longer and sharper. Watching him carefully, Thorn could see the awareness fade from Gelish's eyes and a faint sense of disgust grew in his heart as Hati's voice echoed in his mind.

[See for yourself the corruption that has grown in my children. The influence of the Betrayer has hidden itself deeply in their hearts, twisting their thoughts until what was once known as an abomination is now treated as a boon.]

CHAPTER THIRTY-THREE

The long howl echoed through the mountains, a tinge of madness creeping around its edge. The crowded Wolfkin responded in kind, frantic cheers echoing after the fading howl. Out of the corner of his eye, Thorn caught Elder Havva's frown, reinforcing the discomfort in his heart. Something was off.

[Buried in the hearts of my children, the Betrayer's whispers have changed them. What used to be looked on with loathing is now held as a mark of pride. They have even taken to calling this bloodlust the Madness of the Moon and claimed that it comes from me. The first disciple of my temple has broken the prohibition. He has failed to abide by the ancient law, using the Betrayer's power in this trial.]

As Thorn listened to Hati, the silver moon in the sky above the ring pulsed, a wave of silver flowing down like a stream of mercury. As it touched the runes on Thorn's body they fused together, forming shining armor. The light healed the gouges on Thorn's hand as it flowed down his arms, thick armored bracers and gauntlets appearing a piece at a time, complete with claws.

[Champion, cleanse this corruption. Break the influence of the Betrayed. Show them the true path.]

Fully restored, Thorn faced the maddened Wolfkin, Hati's command ringing in his head. With a raging roar, Gelish stormed forward, emboldened by the cheers of the crowd. Once again the two warriors smashed into each other, shaking the stage with the force of their blows.

Standing toe to toe, Thorn and Gelish traded blows. Gelish's strikes were wild and filled with ferocity. Much more measured, Thorn warded the blows off, focusing on driving the raging Wolfkin toward the edge of the ring. Thorn could tell that the tall Wolfkin had been entirely consumed by madness. Despite the heaviness of Thorn's strikes, his opponent shrugged them off like they were nothing.

"You cannot beat me, impostor! I am the true Greymane!" Gelish screamed, veins bulging in his neck as he ripped into Thorn. A wild swing glanced off Thorn's armored forearm, forcing him to jerk his head backward to avoid a vicious claw. Annoyed, Thorn's eyes narrowed.

Abandoning his attempt to contain his opponent, Thorn lowered his shoulder and lunged, planting his wolf-head pauldron square into Gelish's chest. Not giving him time to rest, Thorn grabbed the enraged Wolfkin by the shoulder and lifted him up into the air. Swinging him around like a rag doll, Thorn smashed Gelish into the ground so hard the stone ring cracked.

The crowd, stunned by the sudden change in the pace of the fight gasped in shock. The cheering Wolfkin lapsed into silence at the sight of their champion being thrown to the ground. Gelish struggled to his feet, still caught in the grip of his bloodlust. The silver runes on his fur shimmered and warped, taking on a tinge of red. Roaring out in rage, his body swelled further as he called deeper upon the Madness of the Moon. The silver runes turned completely red and began to burn into his fur, searing bloody paths into his body. Warped arcane symbols rose around Gelish, forming a crimson cage.

Gasps rose from the crowd as the Wolfkin sensed that something was off. Near the statue of Hati, Elder Havva sighed, his head drooping even further. Inside the cage streams of bloody energy poured into Gelish causing him to scream in pain. His body writhed as the energy remolded him, causing sharp black spikes to grow from his spine and forearms. His form grew, quickly reaching Thorn's height as his muscles swelled.

Impassively, Thorn watched as Gelish struggled and grew in the crimson cage. The Wolfkin warrior had lost almost any semblance of his former self by this point. Gone was the self-controlled monk that Thorn had faced initially. In his place was a corrupted monster from a nightmare. As Gelish's twisted form reached completion, the cage warped again, sinking into Gelish's body. The crimson brand gave off the stench of blood, sickening and weakening those that smelled it.

Many among the tightly packed Wolfkin around the ring fell to their knees as the smell hit them, gagging and retching. The remaining Wolfkin shivered, their eyes turning bloodshot and their forms starting to twist and swell. Cursing, Thorn looked around, unsure what to do. All around the ring Wolfkin were either being consumed by rage or falling to the ground in pain.

As if in response to the spreading corruption, the silver moon in the sky pulsed again, sending down a wave of silver energy to land on Thorn. With a ringing sound it spread from him, purifying the bloody smell as it washed over the crowd. The Wolfkin who were being corrupted suddenly froze, their bloodshot eyes locking onto Thorn's shining figure.

"Well, this devolved quickly." Thorn muttered under his breath. Double checking that Captain Del'har was not turning into a corrupted monster, Thorn flexed his fingers.

The newly corrupted Wolfkin from the crowd had their eyes fixed on him and Thorn instinctively knew what was going to happen next. Sure enough, the moment the ringing sound faded the corrupted Wolfkin lunged forward, teeth bared and claws out.

Since the trial by combat was already ruined, Thorn did not hesitate to draw a weapon. Reaching for his tetsubo, Thorn only remembered that it had never been fixed when the massive metal spike he had ripped from the floor of Greymane Keep appeared in his hand. Dried blood and rust flaked from the spike's pitted surface as his gauntleted hand tightened around it. With no time to exchange it for an actual weapon, Thorn shrugged and threw back his head.

[Wolf Lord's Howl!]

The stunning effect of his howl stopped most of the charging Wolfkin mid-stride and Thorn took care of the few that managed to shake off the effect with a sweeping blow of his massive metal spike. The whistle of the spike cutting through the air caused the Wolfkin to pause, but the corrupting influence of the bloodrage was too strong and soon they surged forward again.

Near the statue of Hati, Elder Havva bowed his head, chanting a long prayer. As the words spilled from his lips they turned silver and hovered in the air, weaving together to form a semi-circular dome, covering everything within ten feet of the statue. The Wolfkin who were lucky enough to be inside the magical dome were not affected by the corrupting smell of blood and stood, waiting anxiously.

Captain Del'har, his face locked in a furious scowl, was

dragging two Wolfkin who had been curled up on the ground retching into the protected range of the statue. As soon as they entered the sphere, their symptoms vanished and they were soon able to struggle to their feet, joining the others. The captain panted for a moment, taking in large gulps of air, his body relaxing. After a couple breaths he gathered his focus and plunged through the ward, racing as fast as he could toward another set of fallen Wolfkin.

In the center of the ring, Thorn battled waves of corrupted Wolfkin, all the while keeping an eye on Gelish, who was still releasing the bloody scent. The large corrupted Wolfkin paced at the edge of the ring, his bloodshot eyes fixed on Thorn, acidic saliva dripping from his large maw. No reason was left in his brain, but the cunning instincts of a feral wolf kept him from charging straight in. Instead, he waited, looking for that moment of weakness.

Try as he might, Thorn could not help but hurt the attacking Wolfkin as he battered them back. Despite the cracking of their bones as they were thrown away, the Madness of the Moon made them all but immune to pain and they were soon charging back into the fray. Claws flashed and teeth snapped as Thorn was nearly drowned in furry bodies.

His mind working furiously, Thorn tried to figure out a solution that did not involve killing the attacking Wolfkin. While it would be easy for him to slaughter them wholesale, Thorn did his best to inflict as little damage as possible. The whole reason he had come was to bring the Wolfkin back as his subjects and killing their warriors was contrary to that goal.

Yet, it was apparent that without some means of cleansing them of the corrupting influence of the Madness of the Moon, Thorn had no way to beat them while keeping them alive. With a grimace, Thorn ripped a Wolfkin who had managed to bite into his shoulder from his back, swinging his massive metal spike in a circle to try and gain some space. His temper growing shorter, Thorn was about to activate his [Wolf's Rage] ability and crush the offending Wolfkin in his hand to pulp when a flash of light caught his eye.

Looking toward the end of the ring, Thorn saw Captain Del'har pull a pair of Wolfkin into the ward that Elder Havva had erected. As the two Wolfkin relaxed, no longer vomiting, a lightbulb went off in Thorn's head and without any further hesitation, he threw the corrupted Wolfkin in his hand at the silvery circle of protection.

The throw was strong and no matter how much the corrupted Wolfkin flailed he could not stop himself from flying through the air. Arms and legs waving the poor native drew a neat parabola toward the statue of Hati, dropping into the silvery circle. As soon as he got within ten feet of the praying elder, the eyes of the statue of Hati flashed with a silver light.

The corrupted Wolfkin let out a sudden scream and a boiling sound erupted from his body as a dark red liquid evaporated from his fur. The pain did not last long and the Wolfkin fell to the ground in a heap, unconscious.

ding

Cleanse the Corruption
The Madness of the Moon has taken hold of many of the Temple of the Moon disciples. As the Avatar of Hati, it is your job to cleanse the corruption, removing the influence of the Betrayer from the Wolfkin. You have chosen to remove the corruption instead of killing the corrupted. Corrupted Wolfkin Cleansed: 1/35 Source of Corruption Cleansed: 0/1

Hardly glancing at the notification, Thorn was ecstatic at the effect of throwing the corrupted Wolfkin near the statue of Hati. Putting away his weapon, Thorn lunged forward, grabbing two more of the corrupted attackers, tossing them toward the statue.

For the next few minutes a constant stream of flailing Wolfkin flew from the ring toward the statue, piling up into a heap of unconscious bodies. Captain Del'har watched in utter astonishment as the pile grew higher and higher, bodies falling out of the sky.

Across the ring, Gelish was still pacing. Growing more frantic by the minute, the source of the corruption could instinctively tell that his window was growing smaller. Thorn's reach and strength made it simple for him to grab and throw the attackers to the statue. Each throw reduced the number of attackers, making it even easier for Thorn to grab the next one.

Furious, the corrupted Head Disciple threw the last threads of caution to the wind and charged forward, howling out a challenge. The waves of sound washed over the ring, causing the few corrupted Wolfkin left to fall into a daze. As the howl reached him, Thorn could feel the sound trying to invade his mind and shake his spirit. The sound wave grew louder and louder, threatening to become the only thing in Thorn's world.

Shaking his head forcefully, Thorn broke away from the sound. He had only been shaken for the briefest of moments, but that was enough for Gelish to cross the ring. Despite the madness that had overtaken him, the Head Disciple of the Moon Temple had not forgotten his martial arts and he unleashed a furious flurry of kicks.

Six consecutive kicks smashed into Thorn, each stronger than the next. Grimacing in pain, Thorn could only raise his arms and legs to try and block the attacks. Gelish had not only grown bigger but stronger as well and while his attacks were not quite enough to force Thorn back, each hit left him shaken.

Having blocked the six kicks, Thorn threw out a palm strike, forcing Gelish to dodge backward. The corrupted Wolfkin jumped out of reach, taking his distance from Thorn's attack. Seizing the moment of reprieve Thorn grabbed two of the stunned Wolfkin and threw them onto the pile by the statue.

Like the others, they landed with a thud, agonizing cries spilling from their lips as the corruption in their bodies boiled out of them. Furious that his opponent was taking time to deal with the other Wolfkin, Gelish howled and rushed forward again. This time, Thorn was ready for him and lashed out with a kick of his own, barely missing the charging Wolfkin as he ducked.

Using the momentum of the kick, Thorn planted his foot and snapped out another kick, catching Gelish off-guard. Thorn's massive foot connected solidly, visibly compressing the Wolfkin's chest. Amid the snap and crackle of ribs shattering, Gelish went tumbling backward. Earning some breathing room, Thorn used it to throw the last few corrupted Wolfkin into the ward of purification.

Just as he reached the last one, the corrupted Wolfkin woke from his dazed state and attempted to bite Thorn's hand as it reached for him. Annoyed, Thorn's grab turned into a slap, sending the recovered Wolfkin right back into a stunned state. Hoisting him up, Thorn tossed him onto the pile.

ding

Cleanse the Corruption

The Madness of the Moon has taken hold of many of the Temple of the Moon disciples. As the Avatar of Hati, it is your job to cleanse the corruption, removing the influence of the Betrayer from the Wolfkin. You have chosen to remove the corruption instead of killing the corrupted.

Corrupted Wolfkin Cleansed: 35/35
Source of Corruption Cleansed: 0/1

Reading the notification, Thorn smiled in satisfaction. There was something really pleasing about completing quests. A quick glance around showed that all the affected Wolfkin had been dealt with, so his full attention settled on the source of the corruption. Thorn's eyes locked on Gelish who was still trying to regain his feet after taking the bone-breaking kick.

Unhurried, Thorn walked across the ring, his massive figure shining under the moonlight. His silver armor was scratched and dented and his body was wounded in multiple places, yet somehow the damage simply made him look more heroic.

Sensing his imposing presence approaching, the wounded Wolfkin looked up in alarm. He had barely made it to his feet when a massive hand reached out, gripping him by the neck and lifting him bodily from the cracked stone ring. Choking, Gelish's crazed eyes stared at the giant who held him up.

CHAPTER THIRTY-FOUR

The world fell still and Thorn felt as if he was frozen in a picture. Above the worn stone ring, the bright silver moon hung low in the dark, star-dotted sky. A light breeze kicked up a bit of dust, blowing past Thorn's silver clad figure. Held in his outstretched arm, a hulking, brutish monster wriggled with the last vestiges of his strength, unable to withstand Thorn's might.

Behind him, the statue of Hati stood atop the black stone altar, shining eyes fixed on Thorn. At its feet, countless Wolfkin warriors lay, groaning and cursing, their forms without strength. Next to them stood a tough looking Wolfkin in dusty armor, his hand resting on his sheathed sword, protecting an elderly Wolfkin mumbling prayers.

In the sudden stillness, Thorn heard the wind most clearly. It slid around the ring and wrapped around him, climbing from his feet to his head. With the wind a faint voice rose in

Thorn's heart, whispering quietly in his ear.

'Kill him. If you don't he'll recover and challenge your rule. Leading the Wolfkin is your right, ruling them is your destiny. You must crush anything that stands in the way of that. Otherwise those around you will make use of your weakness. You must rule them tightly or they will turn their backs on you.'

The whisper grew in volume, causing Thorn's hand to twitch, squeezing Gelish's neck until the bones in his spine creaked.

'That's right. One simple movement to smash out dissention before it grows. If you leave him alive he will not thank you. He'll lead his race to fight your rule. Kill Him. KILL HIM!'

Shivering, Thorn's hand started to tighten again when a thread of clarity bloomed in his mind and his body froze. His eyes, which had briefly flashed blood red returned to their normal color and Thorn woke from his daze with a start. Loosening his grip, he turned and dragged the defeated Head Disciple to the ward of protection around the statue.

As Thorn walked into the influence of the ward, a cool feeling washed over him, like a summer night's breeze. Thorn could feel it driving away another influence which had clung to him like thick, sticky syrup without him realizing it. Feeling much better, he held Gelish until the enlarged Wolfkin had been purified and had regained his normal size. Tossing him onto the pile, Thorn was happy to hear the sound he was waiting for.

ding

Cleanse the Corruption - Completed
The Madness of the Moon has taken hold of many of the Temple of the Moon disciples. As the Avatar of Hati, it is your job to cleanse the corruption, removing the influence of the Betrayer from the Wolfkin. You have chosen to remove the corruption instead of killing the corrupted. Corrupted Wolfkin Cleansed: 35/35 Source of Corruption Cleansed: 1/1 Reward: [Disciple] - Class

Reading the last line of the quest, Thorn was taken aback. A class? Why was he getting a class? Wasn't the point of the quest to gain the allegiance of the Wolfkin? What did getting a class have to do with it? His brow furrowed, Thorn stared at the pop up that followed his quest completion notice.

Class - [Disciple]
You have been chosen as a disciple of the Temple of the Moon. Unlike ordinary monastic orders, the disciples of the Temple of the Moon are warrior monks who serve Hati, the god of Night. Tasked with destroying evil and holding back

those who seek to disrupt the balance of the world, they work in the shadows as the counterpart to the Paladins of Skoll, the Sun God.

Accept [Disciple] Class?	
Yes	No

[Accept it, my avatar.]

Thorn was about to hit no, turning down the class, when a majestic voice echoed in his ears. Startled, Thorn paused and looked up. The statue of Hati that had stood frozen atop the black altar shivered with a silver light. As the light ran over the well-polished statue its fur began to tremble in the night breeze.

Warm eyes looked down on Thorn as the wolf came to life. After a few seconds, the wolf looked at Elder Havva, whose eyes were screwed tightly shut. The old Wolfkin had certainly heard the voice of Hati, but rather than look up he crouched even lower, prostrating himself in front of his deity. Next to the trembling elder, Captain Del'har fell to one knee, saluting with his fist over his chest, his head bowed. After a moment of staring blankly, Thorn snapped out of his daze and accepted the class with a shrug.

"In for a penny, in for a pound I guess," thought Thorn. While it was not what he had planned, everything Hati had given him thus far had served him well.

ding

Class - [Disciple]
You have been chosen as a disciple of the Temple of the Moon. Unlike ordinary monastic orders, the disciples of the Temple of the Moon are warrior monks who serve Hati, the god of Night. Tasked with destroying evil and holding back those who seek to disrupt the balance of the world, they work in the shadows as the counterpart to the Paladins of Skoll, the Sun God. Your journey to martial mastery has begun. Disciples practice one of the four martial forms of the Temple of the Moon and can use any basic monk weapon and any basic armor. Disciple Abilities: [Martial Form: Unselected] [Basic Weapons Mastery] [Pack Travel] Mastery Ability: [Form Mastery (locked)]

After Thorn accepted the class, the wolf turned its eyes back on him. Nodding its head in what Thorn could only assume was appreciation, the wolf stood still, its fur reverting to stone once again. As it changed, Hati's voice rang out once more.

[Thorn, Lord Greymane, Avatar of Hati, Disciple of the Moon Temple, has won the challenge. The ancient laws have been upheld and the winner of the trial has been determined. Thorn has shown wisdom, restraint, and martial skill, saving the lives of many of his fellow disciples. For this, let him take the mantle of the inheritor.]

ding

Title: [Moon Temple Inheritor]
You have been chosen as the Inheriting Disciple of the Temple of the Moon. Unless you lose this position, you will be treated by all Wolfkin as the next leader of the temple.

Slowly the radiance around the wolf faded leaving behind the worn stone statue. The bright moon in the sky lost some of its silver luster and the cloudless sky began to fill with dark clouds again. With a slight pop, the shining ward disappeared and Elder Havva lifted his head toward the sky with a sigh.

Fumbling around for his cane, he rose to his feet. Captain Del'har saw him struggling to stand and hastened to help the elder Wolfkin to stand. Around them, the collapsed Wolfkin struggled to get to their feet.

"Greetings, Lord Greymane." His attitude totally different,

Elder Havva bowed his head slightly as he faced Thorn. “We have much to discuss regarding the words the Great Wolf spoke.”

ding

The True Lord Greymane: Complete
The elder of the Temple of the Moon has recognized you as the appointed representative of the Temple of the Moon and as Lord Greymane. Through your trial by combat and the words of Hati, god of Night, you have convinced them that you are the rightful holder of the Greymane title. Rewards: Allegiance of the Wolfkin

Asking Captain Del’har to help organize the Wolfkin who were still trying to recover from the corruption the Madness of the Moon brought, Thorn and Elder Havva sat down for a long talk. Settling himself on his rock seat, Thorn tried to wait as patiently as possible for the elderly Wolfkin who was sitting in silence.

It was obvious that the Temple Elder was having trouble adjusting to what had happened. Thorn did not know if it was the fact that the temple’s Head Disciple had turned against the teachings of the temple, embracing Karrandras the Betrayer’s power. Or maybe it was the fact that Hati had manifested, speaking directly to Elder Havva. Either way, Thorn was on a tight schedule and was getting a bit impatient.

“Congratulations, Lord Greymane.” Thorn was about to start speaking, when the elder began to talk. His voice was strained, but as he continued his tone evened out and gained strength. “You have successfully passed the ritual trial and will be properly recognized as the Greymane. The Great Wolf has also granted you the mantle of the Inheritor.”

“What is that about?” Thorn scratched his head.

“To properly understand all of this, please allow me to give you an overview of the temple. That should make it easier to understand. The Temple of the Moon has a simple ruling structure. A single Temple Elder rules over the temple. In this generation, I am the Temple Elder. You might think of the Temple Elder position as an Abbot. I oversee the direction of the temple, help make executive decisions and approve rewards and punishments.

“Under the Temple Elder are the four Path Masters, each ruling one of the four courts. The courts are divided into the Dusk Court, Full Moon Court, New Moon Court, and Dawn Court. Inside the courts are the Chamberlains, Deacons, Night Walkers, and Disciples. Each court is responsible for overseeing one of the martial forms practiced by the disciples of the Temple of the Moon. When a new disciple is admitted to the temple, they choose a martial form and join the associated court. This determines what role they will take in the temple and what their training will be like.

“Your position in the temple is a bit different, since you are both the inheritor and Lord Greymane. The position of Inheritor is held by the disciple who is marked to succeed the Temple Elder as the next leader of the temple. For you to hold the title of Greymane as well as the title of Inheritor grants you significant responsibility and authority.”

“I meant to ask about that.” Thorn frowned lightly as he thought through what Elder Havva had told him. “What is the role of Greymane? I thought that Lord Greymane was the name of the individual who ruled the valley?”

“Really, the position of Greymane is comprised of two parts.” Elder Havva gestured to the ring on Thorn’s finger. “The first part is the appointed title, held by the bearer of the ring. The last temple appointed Greymane was corrupted many years ago and fled the valley, taking the ring with him. The second part of the position is the ruler of the valley, also called Lord Greymane by the people of the valley. To truly hold the title of Greymane, one must have both the ring and take possession of the Wolf Throne in Greymane Keep.

“Historically, the temple was divided into two sides. There was a public side and a reclusive side. The temple itself did not involve itself in any mortal affairs, sitting apart from the world. However, as part of their training, all disciples would spend a period of time in the world as Night Walkers. The Greymane was not only the public Elder, but also led the Night Walkers. Greymane Keep was the place the Night

Walkers lived while outside the temple and acted as the public temple. According to the ancient law, the Greymane is the public facing Temple Elder."

"Hold on, doesn't that mean that if I am both Greymane and Inheritor, I'll eventually be both the public and private Temple Elder?"

"Yes." Elder Havva gave a long sigh. "The elders are called the Full Moon Elder and the New Moon Elder. You are already the Full Moon Elder since you hold the title of Greymane. That is why only I, as the New Moon Elder, am able to challenge you."

"Huh." Scratching his head, Thorn was lost for words. For a moment silence fell over the hut where they were sitting as the two temple elders looked at each other.

"Regardless, we should now discuss the reason you came." Shaking his head, as if it could get rid of the depression that shrouded him, Elder Havva changed the topic.

"Sure." Thorn straightened and leaned forward slightly. "A few days ago I cleared the current Greymane Keep. From what I understand, the existing castle was built on the ruins of the Temple of the Moon. My goal in coming here is to gather the Wolfkin, leading them back to the valley to rebuild the temple. The valley will be gaining a spawn point and I think it is a good opportunity for the temple to rejoin the world. I have all the resources necessary to rebuild the temple apart from the workers and I was hoping that you would be able to help with that."

"Very well, we shall join you." Without pausing Elder Havva nodded his head.

"Uh." Stunned, Thorn could only stare at the Temple Elder for a moment. He had expected some sort of negotiation and had planned out numerous convincing reasons why it would make sense for the Wolfkin to join him. In the face of Elder Havva's calm acceptance they all fell flat, leaving Thorn tongue-tied.

"Don't be too surprised." Elder Havva shook his head with another drawn out sigh. "You are the Greymane, your words carry weight equal to mine. You have shown yourself to be a warrior beyond compare in the holy trial. That alone grants your voice power. You have joined the Temple of the Moon, an honor never before granted to one of another race. You joined by the command of our god no less, showing that you have Hati's favor upon you. You have taken up the mantle of the Avatar of Hati, becoming Hati's voice among us, tying yourself to our race with a bond that cannot be broken."

Slowly rising to his feet, Elder Havva made his way to the door of the hut, leading Thorn out into the main square. The Wolfkin had gathered into a group on the stone ring, standing before the altar in neat rows. The elder blinked his muddled eyes as he watched them.

"Our people have dwindled over time. There are less than six hundred of us left, with only three hundred warriors. The mountains are good for hiding but they do not allow for growth. Since you have cleared the werewolf threat, it is time for our race to venture out. We will either flourish, or we will die. Either way, we will follow you."

Taking in the crowd of Wolfkin, each standing over a large pack filled to the brim with their possessions, Thorn could not help but swallow. Everything they owned was on their backs. Even the statue of Hati that had watched over the stone ring was being carried with them. Bright eyes filled with excitement and anticipation stared at him from the crowd. Children peeked at him from behind their parent's legs and elderly Wolfkin bent with age smiled excitedly. Facing the clear expectation of the crowd, the importance of what he was doing settled on Thorn.

To Thorn, this was a game. A series of quests whose failure would not, ultimately, mean much. He could simply try his best and not worry about the result. His life was settled and secure. The staring eyes of the assembled Wolfkin told him that their lives were anything but. They were walking away from their homes, their lives, to follow him. Their hopes, their ambitions, were no longer their own. Instead, they were betting on him, pinning those hopes on the giant in front of them.

"Salute the lord." Captain Del'har's voice rang out. With a loud thud, all six hundred Wolfkin fell to one knee, saluting

Thorn together. "

"We greet Lord Greymane!"

CHAPTER THIRTY-FIVE

The voices of the bowing Wolfkin echoed off the mountain. Shaking his head slightly, as if to get rid of the weight, Thorn gestured for his new subjects to rise. Taking a small step forward, he summoned his armor. Streaks of pale silver covered his body as his armor materialized, the wolf motifs glinting in the moonlight.

"I am Thorn, Lord Greymane, the Moon Wolf, Avatar of Hati, Inheriting Disciple of the Temple of the Moon. Tonight, I will lead you back to Greymane Valley. Back to your home. Together we will rebuild the Temple of the Moon and reestablish the order of the Night Walkers. You have persevered through the generations, holding fast to the ancient laws, serving Hati faithfully. The work will be hard and we will face many enemies, but under the light of Hati's eye we will be victorious."

Cheering, the crowd shouldered their packs and turned to follow Captain Del'har who led the way toward the valley. Thorn marched among them, his tall figure sticking out above them. As they moved, Thorn realized that the Wolfkin were well suited to travel. Even the young children could run well, their long legs allowing them to keep up.

Rather than walk, the entire group jogged forward at a distance eating pace, reminding Thorn of marathon runners. The group accelerated and decelerated as one, spurring one another on. In the middle of the group, Thorn had no trouble matching their tempo, as if an unseen chord bound them all together. At the front, Captain Del'har led the way,

[Pack Travel]
Wolves can travel extraordinary distances with little energy. When you travel with other members of your order you only spend a tenth of the energy and can travel 50% faster, regardless of the terrain.

A little bit of searching soon revealed the truth. One of the abilities that Thorn had gained from his class granted him faster travel speed while moving with other disciples from the temple. Curious about the other abilities that he had gained, Thorn pulled up his status.

Name: [Thorn]	Race: [Titan]

Health: [100%]	Mana: [100%]
Titles: [Battle Mad], [Wolfsbane], [Lord Greymane, the Moon Wolf], [Friend of the Earth], [Inheritor]	Class: [Disciple] Mastery: [None] Allegiance: [Temple of the Moon]
Abilities: [Wolf Lord's Howl], [Avatar of the Wolf], [Call the Pack], [Blessing of the Moon], [Presence of the Wolf Lord], [Martial Form: Unselected], [Basic Weapons Mastery], [Pack Travel]	

On top of the [Inheritor] title that he had earned, the three abilities that his class had granted him were listed. Thorn also noticed that rather than showing his conditions, his status now showed his class instead. Under his class he also found a line listing his allegiance as [Temple of the Moon]. Making a mental note to ask Velin about how allegiances worked, Thorn turned to his new abilities.

The first ability granted by his new class was [Martial Form]. According to what Elder Havva had said, there were four martial forms taught by the temple. Each form corresponded to one of the four different courts of the temple and focused on a different set of skills. When a disciple first entered the temple they would be assigned to a court. After gaining proficiency in the skills of that court, disciples would graduate to be Night Walkers and would leave the Temple of the Moon to wander, beginning their fight against evil.

Selecting the ability, Thorn was not surprised to see four windows pop up. He passed the time as they hiked through the mountains by reading through them one at a time. [Disciple] was an interesting class because it did not belong to a single category. Instead, the category of the class changed depending on which Court, and form, the disciple chose. Each form taught a proficiency and an active skill and, upon mastery, led to a Two Category Class.

Dusk Form - Support
Disciples who learn the Dusk Form pursue the path of the scout. Fleet of foot, these disciples scout the enemy, setting ambushes and traps or flanking with deadly showers of razor tipped arrows. Few, enemy or ally, can match the wolves of the Dusk Form. Abilities gained: [Ranged Combat Proficiency] [Wolf's Speed] Mastery Path: Dusk Walker

Initially attracted by the [Ranged Combat Proficiency], Thorn could only laugh as he thought of himself setting traps or trying to hide for ambushes. While he really liked the idea of being a highly mobile archer, it did not seem overly practical, considering his size.

Full Moon Form - Combat
Disciples who learn the Full Moon Form pursue the path of the warrior. The main force of the Night Walkers come from the stalwart Full Moon Court. Trained in the use of armor and weapons, these tough as nails warriors drive their enemies before them relentlessly. Abilities gained: [Heavy Armor Proficiency] [Wolf's Toughness] Mastery Path: Full Moon Walker

Dismissing the window, Thorn frowned slightly as he scanned the side of the mountain, watching the steady stream of Wolfkin in front of him. Even though they were currently climbing a steep slope the group kept up a quick pace, only slightly slower than a jog. The Full Moon Form seemed to fit very well with his current abilities, though Thorn did not feel like he needed more toughness. Between his racial abilities and his size, Thorn felt pretty tough compared to most people.

Plus, as the Avatar of Hati, he already had magical armor that did not require any proficiencies. While he could not deny the appeal of the combat category, Thorn was confident that he did not need a class to be able to stand toe to toe with even the best warriors. Smirking at the memory of his most recent fight, Thorn pulled up the next form.

New Moon Form - Utility
Disciples who learn the New Moon Form pursue the path of the Assassin. Unseen and deadly, the disciples of the New Moon Court ply their deadly work in the darkest shadows. Trained to disrupt and demoralize, these lone wolves combine their excellent senses and stealth training to gather information and deliver fatal strikes to their enemies. Abilities gained: [Stealth Proficiency] [Wolf's Sense] Mastery Path: New Moon Walker

The opposite of the direct Full Moon Form, the New Moon form suited Thorn even less. After spending a couple fanciful minutes imagining himself turning invisible and popping out behind people, Thorn closed the window. As cool as it would be to take the path of an assassin, it was not his destiny.

Dawn Form - Leadership
Disciples who learn the Dawn Form pursue the path of the commander. Inspiring their allies with speeches and issuing commands on the battlefield are only two of the many ways that Disciples of the Dawn lead their fellow

disciples to victory. Disciples of the Dawn make the best diplomats, leaders, traders, and strategists.

Abilities gained:
[Oration Proficiency]
[Rallying Cry]

Mastery Path: Dawn Walker

The Dawn Form was the form with the greatest appeal to Thorn at the moment. He had been leaning toward finding a leadership class and this seemed to fit the bill nicely. Bonuses to speech and cognitive buffs would be helpful, not only in leading the Wolfkin, but in his efforts to put together his own team. It had become more and more apparent to Thorn that if he wanted to leave a lasting impact on the world of Nova Terra, he was going to have to gather others around him and taking the Leadership path would help with that.

The [Oration Proficiency] intrigued him so he opened the description.

[Oration Proficiency]
The tongue has power beyond even the sharpest of swords if applied properly. A single word can calm a turbulent wind or ignite a firestorm. Empires have risen and fallen through the words of their rulers.

You are an Orator, a practiced, experienced speaker. You know how to parry the strongest of strikes, to turn aside the most dangerous attacks, to avoid the tightest traps, and to steer through the strongest verbal storms. Others are more likely to take what you say seriously and to agree with you. At the same time, you gain increased resistance to verbal persuasion.

[Rallying Cry]
Power and speed are the hallmark of the wolf, yet physical prowess is not the wolf's greatest asset. The true strength of the wolf lies in its companions. You gain the ability to rally your allies, granting them increased stamina and health regeneration and allowing for the use of the [Pack Travel] ability in combat. This ability can only be used when at least one ally is present.

Both [Oration Proficiency] and [Rallying Cry] would only strengthen Thorn's leadership, so he selected the Dawn Form, watching as his ability changed to [Martial Form: Dawn]. With his form selected, Thorn looked at the last ability his [Disciple] class granted him.

[Basic Weapons Mastery]
You gain basic proficiency with the following weapons: Daggers, Short Swords, Long Swords, Staves, Clubs,

Axes, and Bows.

status

Name: [Thorn]	Race: [Titan]
Health: [100%]	Mana: [100%]
Titles: [Battle Mad], [Wolfsbane], [Lord Greymane, the Moon Wolf], [Friend of the Earth], [Inheritor]	Class: [Disciple] Mastery: [None] Allegiance: [Temple of the Moon]
Abilities: [Wolf Lord's Howl], [Avatar of the Wolf], [Call the Pack], [Blessing of the Moon], [Presence of the Wolf Lord], [Martial Form: Dawn], [Basic Weapons Mastery], [Oration Proficiency], [Rallying Cry], [Pack Travel]	

The trip back to the keep took a bit under three hours due to the [Pack Travel] racial ability that the Wolfkin possessed, an astounding feat considering the number of young and elderly in the crowd. When the spires of the keep came into view above the trees the jogging Wolfkin broke into cheers, increasing their speed.

Leading them through the gate, Thorn had them set up camp in the courtyard while he went to bed. Velin and Mina had logged out, leaving a message that they would be back in the morning so Thorn settled in for what was left of the night.

Staying up all night was not a problem, but some habits were hard to break.

The sun was shining brightly through the narrow stone window when Thorn woke up the next morning. Yawning, Thorn rose from the floor where he had slept and stretched his body, the yawn changing into a grumble as his arms hit the ceiling. Most of the keep's ceilings were barely over nine feet tall, which annoyed Thorn to no end. Opening up his friends list, Thorn saw that both girls had logged in so he made his way down to the courtyard.

Velin was chatting quietly with Elder Havva and the captain while Mina stood nearby entertaining some of the Wolfkin children by creating small creatures with ice. Akira, sitting on Mina's head, saw Thorn as he walked out of the keep's double doors. Chirping with excitement, she dashed over, bounding up Thorn's body and hopping excitedly up and down on his shoulder.

[Master! Master! You're back! Why'd you leave? Why didn't you bring me? I don't want to stay with that older sister! I want to stay with you!]

"Haha. Hi, Akira." Pleased to see his battle pet, Thorn fished out a pastry from his inventory. Stroking her fur as she chattered at him, Thorn walked over to Velin and the two Wolfkin.

"Greetings, Lord!"

Upon seeing him, the Wolfkin, who were standing around the yard dropped to one knee, shouting out together with one voice. Slightly taken aback, Thorn grimaced. Somehow, he could not get used to this. Seeing that the Wolfkin remained kneeling, he frowned.

“Rise.” Nodding to the Elven War Priestess, Thorn greeted Elder Havva and Captain Del’har. “We’ve got plenty to do, so let’s get started. Velin, have you filled everyone in on our situation?”

“No, I was about to start.” Velin shook her head, her serious eyes fixed on Thorn. “Would you like to?”

“No, go ahead.”

“Alright. As I was saying, we are in a precarious position, though it certainly is not as hopeless as it was. We have ten days until the shrine at Greymane Village is activated as a respawn point. Once that happens, the valley will be announced as a new player location. At the same time, we will see an influx of Wolfkin players. In fact, if trends hold, we will see at least five million Wolfkin players over the next year. Every time Nova Terra releases a new playable race we see large influxes of people buying race change tokens.

“We have three main considerations. One, holding the valley. We can treat this as two tasks. First, the keep contains a control point. Currently, the throne is set as the control point. If enemies hold the throne, they can forcefully take control of the keep. Second, the shrine in Greymane Village. Controlling the spawn point will grant an advantage to the team that holds it since they can allow their own forces to spawn while blocking others. This concern has to do with our immediate enemy.

"The guild Ragnarok operates in this area and has been looking for the valley for the last two weeks. It is highly likely that their scouts will find us within the next five days and that their main force will not be far behind. Ragnarok is a fairly large guild, but thankfully, the group operating in this area is no more than 1500 players and supporting natives."

"1500? That's a pretty sizable group." Thorn muttered, looking at the 200 wolfkin he had.

"Correct. 250 Crimson Snakes, 250 player guards, and approximately 1000 native guards. The force is not a cohesive army, though all of the players have a reasonable level of skill."

"Alright, continue."

"Apart from our approaching enemy, we have two other considerations. Infrastructure and population. I mention these together because they are so closely linked. Currently, the valley has been almost entirely reclaimed by the forest. This is to our advantage as it will prevent mounted troops and heavy siege weapons from being brought in. At the same time, this is a problem for us because we don't have the infrastructure to set up a profitable territory.

"A profitable territory needs food and money to operate, and the facilities to generate them. However, to build the facilities, we need population. To generate population, we need excess food, money, and time. As you can see, this is an issue for us. Because of our approaching enemy we do not have the time necessary to build defensive fortifications and we do not have the population to recruit guards or soldiers.

"This is our basic situation. We lack infrastructure and population and have an approaching enemy. However, we do have a number of things going for us." Velin paused and looked at Thorn. "First, we have absolute command due to your position as Lord Greymane. That cannot be underestimated. Second, we have about 200 combat ready disciples from the Temple of the Moon, courtesy of Elder Havva.

"Mina did not find the bandits, but according to reports from the village, they're a group of 100 former soldiers who are operating on the edge of the valley. Since they were once soldiers we might be able to absorb them and bring them back into our army. We also have almost 50 hunters from Greymane Village. While this combat force is not nearly as large as our enemy's, it is better than nothing. Third, we have guild backing of our own. If Atlas is willing to inject funds into this territory then we might be able to squeeze through."

CHAPTER THIRTY-SIX

Stepping over to one of the walls of the keep, Velin projected her map onto it, zooming in to show the valley. Three spots were marked out in red, eye-catching among the many other markings and notes on the map.

"The valley is a naturally defensive position with a single entrance, a pass between the Twins. This means we have three important locations. First, we have the keep which holds the control node for the valley, located at the far end of the valley. At the other end we have the entrance to the valley. This is the only known way into the valley. Close to the pass we have Greymane Village where the respawn point is located. We need a plan that will cover all three of those locations."

Stepping forward, Thorn examined the map. Mina and Akira had finished mapping the whole valley in the day he was gone. After a moment of thought, he turned to Elder Havva.

“Elder, is there any significance in the positioning of the old temple?”

“Hmmm? You mean here, where we stand?” The elder peered around as he thought about it. “No, not that I know of. The original temple was built on top of the village that our people originally settled. Over time, the village became the temple and a second village was started. That is where Lord Greymane and the Night Walkers were based. When the temple was destroyed, the Greymane of that generation built this keep.

“The temple will exist wherever the Wolfkin build the altar. Tradition has dictated that the statue of Hati watches over the valley, but when we fled the valley we moved it with us, carrying it to the village in the mountains. You would know better than I if Hati required the altar to be constructed in a specific place.”

“Good.” Thorn grinned. “I’m going to be moving the temple.”

“Moving the temple? What temple?” During the conversation, Mina had wandered over. Now that there was a chance to jump in, she did not want to miss it.

“Here.” Thorn’s large finger landed on the entrance to the valley. “We will place the Temple of the Moon in the pass that leads into the valley. I think it would make more sense to control the entrance then it would to try and control the rest of the valley. Frankly, if we can't control who gets into the valley then there is almost no point in trying to hold the keep. On the other hand, this will allow us to keep a firm grip on the resources we've discovered."

"Oh, did you see that we found more of those glowing rocks when we were mapping?"

"Yeah, I noticed that. According to Elder Havva, it sounds like those stones are moonstones. The Wolfkin use them to improve their racial abilities. They will be a great source of income if we get a lot of new Wolfkin players. Thanks for mapping everything." Thorn smiled at Mina and turned to look at Velin. "If we want to build a fortress monastery in the pass, what do we need?"

"Time, people, and money." Velin pulled out her notebook and began scribbling in it with a frown. "There are a couple ways to build new buildings in Nova Terra. The first requires the labor to be performed in game and, so long as the material is available, costs nothing but time and effort. This is by far the most popular way to build. The other, less popular way is to pay for the game to construct a building from scratch. This would automatically create the structure in-game according to a blueprint that the player inputs. While this seems easier than building by hand, it is not a good option for us."

"Yeah, it's a trap." Mina tossed in from the side.

"Trap? What do you mean?"

"The cost rises exponentially per feature you have the system build. It is much more cost effective to spend the money buying the materials and hiring workmen."

"But that takes time. Something we don't have the luxury of." Thorn's eyes locked on the Elven Priestess'.

"I don't think you are recognizing the depth of the cost. Building a house would bankrupt most people, let alone a castle. We should spend our effort on a defensive line. Or trying to negotiate."

"Negotiate?" Thorn's voice dropped slightly.

"Yes. Ragnarok is not unreasonable. While we currently hold the valley, there is little chance that we will be able to keep it once the Crimson Snakes find it. I could use my connections to help us negotiate a split. Then we would at least be left with something." Noticing that her surroundings had become silent, Velin looked up from her writing to find Thorn staring at her with a dangerous look in his eyes.

"Velin, I am going to assume that you are making that suggestion out of your concern for our group's wellbeing." Thorn's deep voice was not loud but it still sent a shiver down the spine of everyone who heard it. Slowly lifting his hand he planted a finger on the map. "We will not negotiate.

If Ragnarok wants to take something else from me they will pay for it in blood. We build the new temple here."

Palpable waves of force radiated from Thorn, causing everyone around him to instinctively cower. There was a bloody edge to him that had not been present the last time Velin had seen him. Rather than struggle against his aura, she bowed her head.

"I'm sorry, I spoke out of turn. I did not think through the issue properly."

Hearing her admit her mistake, Thorn's anger lessened, though a burning ember of discontent refused to be extinguished. Taking a deep breath, he did his best to soften his demeanor.

"Let's continue. Knowing that we lack time, what do we need to do?"

Finally free of the paralyzing aura, Mina was about to throw a fit until Velin caught her eye, giving a shake of her head. Biting her lip, the short Ice Witch scowled and stomped off. Ignoring her, Velin resumed where she had left off as if she had never brought up the idea of negotiating.

"Without time, we will need people and money. A lot of money. Nova Terra is not a pay to win game, even though money can be spent on an astounding number of items that grant advantage. Anything that can be purchased can be earned in game and the cost for purchasing through the store is beyond prohibitive. Building is a great example of that. A house costs a million credits base. Each room doubles the cost." Not seeing a response from Thorn, she sighed and continued.

"To top it off, there are no ready-made designs for sale. If we want to buy a castle, we'll need to buy plans. This will add expense as well. Prices for property blueprints are astronomical since it is assumed that only those who are too rich for their own good will bother paying the system to build."

"Money is not an issue. I'll handle that part. How do we submit the design?"

"If you've ever accessed the Fantasia shops from inside Nova Terra, it is the same. There is an office that handles building requests."

"Thanks. I need to deal with Greymane Village and the bandits. Please organize the Wolfkin here and move everything of value to the entrance to the valley. I'd like you to organize them into groups and have them patrol outside the valley. We need to know when Angdrin gets here. I'll meet you in the pass in two days." Not waiting around to see how she took his commands, Thorn turned and left, heading for the throne room.

Watching his broad back as he walked away, Velin closed

her eyes and sighed. Furious, Mina ran up to her.

"How could he do..."

Before she could continue Velin blocked her mouth.

"Leave it. We were the ones that disappointed him first. It is only reasonable that he be on his guard. Plus, I was overstepping my bounds so it is only right for him to chide me."

"What? No way! This isn't how you treat friends."

"It's more complicated than that, Mina." Frowning, Velin lifted a hand to rub her temple. "We're friends that picked our own interest first, friends who tried to take what was rightfully his. And now we're his employees."

"But."

"Leave it." Velin hugged her friend tightly. "I know he said that everything could go back to normal, but it will take time. Time and effort. No matter how much he wants to pretend everything is okay, there are bound to be wounds. And if this is the only cost to regaining his trust, it is worth it. Now, let's get these Wolfkin organized."

Inside the keep, Thorn was walking up the stairs glumly. His outburst seemed to have come from nowhere, blazing into existence before he could control himself. Even now, he could feel the uncomfortable burn of his anger, settled firmly in the pit of his stomach. He had not meant to take it out on Velin, but when she mentioned negotiating with Ragnarok he had almost lost it completely.

It had only been with supreme effort that he had not accused her of being a traitor right then and there. He had managed to hold the words in, but Thorn had no doubt that she had guessed exactly what he was thinking.

"So much for trusting," he sighed. Despite his nice sounding words and his best intentions, he seemed to have fallen at the first pass. Walking into the throne room, Thorn pulled up the [RMS], immediately noticing that the population count had shot up by 500. After hunting around for a moment he found the button to relocate the valley's control point.

<table>
<tr><td colspan="2">Relocate Control Point</td></tr>
<tr><td colspan="2">Selecting Yes will convert the control point for this territory into a [Control Orb] for 24 hours. Using the [Control Orb] will allow you to set a new Control Point for the territory. After 24 hours the [Control Orb] will expire and the Control Point will return to its original location. A Control Point can only be assigned once per week.

Would you like to relocate this Control Point?</td></tr>
<tr><td>Yes</td><td>No</td></tr>
</table>

Hesitating for a moment, Thorn finally punched the no button. His plan was to handle the village first before he built the new temple at the entrance to the valley. With three to four days left to go before the enemy arrived, Thorn was confident that he had time to move the Control Point later. Having decided to wait, Thorn took stock of what he still needed to do.

There were only a few days until the Crimson Snake scouts would start arriving, so he wanted to make sure that the important defenses were in place first. Not only did he have to relocate the temple, but he had to help rebuild Greymane Village, and deal with the bandits. Truthfully, Thorn was not confident that they would be ready in time for the influx of players, which would complicate things immensely.

Currently, the valley was largely unoccupied which made controlling it easy. However, if he could not fight off Ragnarok and consolidate his control before players started spawning it would become infinitely more complicated. Taking a deep breath, Thorn headed for Greymane Village. It was time to get to work.

The forest was quiet and cool. Tall trees filtered out the heat of the morning sun, as thin beams of light spotted the forest floor. Walking along with Akira in his arms, Thorn took a moment to appreciate the peacefulness. Soon this peace would be broken.

“How do you like our new home?” asked Thorn, petting

Akira's furry head.

“Master, it is so wonderful. The trees and places to climb and the trees! I love it. Master I am going to bring my whole family to visit! Can I?” replied the excitable furball, bouncing up and down.

“Haha, of course. Your family can visit any time. This is your home after all.”

“Oh, wonderful, wonderful, wonderful.” with a flick of her tale Akira flashed to a nearby tree where she scratched a little symbol into the bark. “This tree is mine! And this tree is mine! This tree is mine! I claim this tree!”

Startled Thorn watched as Akira bounced from tree to tree marking them with a small symbol while proudly claiming all the trees as her own. With a chuckle Thorn got down to thinking about how he was going to find the bandits.

Ultimately his goal was to keep them from preying on others in the area and based on what Elder Thomas had said he had a couple ideas of how to deal with them. As he solidified his plans Thorn idly pulled the large spike that he had gained from his epic showdown with the Greater Werewolf out of his inventory.

Six feet long and still covered in grime and dried blood, it tapered from eight inches in width down to a blunt point. The large end that had been buried in the ground still had bits of mortar on it but they soon crumbled off revealing a dark pitted metal underneath. Slightly less than halfway up the spike and right before the point there were thick rings that still held bits of chain hanging from them. Hefting the spike in his hands, Thorn decided to find a blacksmith who could refine it into an actual weapon.

Swinging it through the air created a very satisfying thrum and Thorn thought it a weapon particularly suited for his strength. Continuing to practice his swings according to the rhythm Master Sun had taught him, Thorn walked on through the forest until he got close to Greymane Village. Taking a break from swinging his spike, Thorn called for Akira again. It took a while since she was still frantically staking claim to all the trees they had come across but eventually Thorn got her to come over with the promise that she could have as many trees as she wanted later.

“Akira, Ailuridae have a pretty good nose, do you think you could find some humans for me that are not part of this village?” Thorn asked, gesturing to the town in front of him. “They'll be a big group. More than 100 people. And they will have weapons and armor as well.”

“Pretty good? Ha, Ailuridae noses are the best! And I'm the best Ailuridae!” Arching her back proudly, Akira turned up her nose at Thorn. “You watch how fast I find them!” And without another word she shot off to the village. Strolling in after her Thorn was pleasantly surprised to find that the village had already changed quite a bit. It had only been half a day since he had granted Thomas the money to rebuild the town but based on how busy everyone was they were not wasting any time.

CHAPTER THIRTY-SEVEN

Greymane Village was a total mess when Thorn strolled down the main street. Yet, despite the chaos a semblance of what the town would become was beginning to emerge. Most of the old buildings had been demolished and were now being reconstructed from massive piles of material that the elder had purchased. Additionally, the town's ramshackle wall had been pulled down and an old stone wall was being rebuilt further out.

Before, the town had only consisted of a few buildings, but now, in addition to the jail, tavern, and blacksmith's shop there was a large stable, three empty buildings that could be used for stores, a barracks, and a shrine covered in moon and wolf motifs. All of this was arranged around a new main street, complete with cobblestones.

Seeing the villagers running around like crazy, Thorn grinned and joined in the fun. At first it took a while to keep the villagers from stopping their work to salute him when he came by, but once they saw Thorn lifting massive stones to rebuild the wall by himself they jumped back in with renewed vigor. For Thorn it wasn't particularly hard work, but it was very satisfying. The warm sun beating down on him as he split, moved and fitted the stone reminded Thorn of the pleasant days he had spent in the quarry and he couldn't help but smile at the memory.

With Thorn they made astounding progress and had a good half of the wall complete by the time night fell. Akira had run off into the forest to hunt for the bandits and through his connection with her Thorn could tell she was somewhere northwest of the village. Joining the village for a meal, he was happy to hear that a message had been sent out to attract settlers and the village Elder had already left to recruit people from some of the local cities.

Waking the next morning completely rested Thorn had walked out of the inn when he spotted a small wagon being pulled by a slow-moving mule creaking into the village. Sitting in the driver's seat was an old man dressed in slightly ragged robes with a prominent wolf and moon symbol on his chest. Stepping out into the road Thorn raised a hand in greeting.

“Hello,” Thorn smiled as he walked in front of the mule, “welcome to Greymane. Not too often we get visitors, might I know who you are?”

"Thanks," replied the robed man, seemingly unperturbed by Thorn's size and confrontational manner. "I am Father Jansome, a priest of Hati, the Lord of the Night. I was dispatched to attend the newly built shrine in this... town?" Looking around, Jansome's statement morphed into a question.

"We're expanding." Grinning as he took in the changes taking place Thorn offered Jansome a handshake, "Welcome to town, priest. I am Thorn, the new Lord Greymane. I know a bit about Hati myself, but maybe you can help me turn that little bit into a bit more." Thorn's last statement earned him a quizzical look from the priest.

"I see." Jansome looked at Thorn with an appraising eye. "It is my pleasure to meet you, my Lord. I must admit I expected a Wolfkin, not a human as Lord of the valley. Though, given that this is a human town, I guess it makes sense." Jansome quipped.

"Don't think of it as a human town. We are accepting of all races here. Plus," Thorn pointed to the side of the road where a few Wolfkin disciples were helping to dig a foundation for a new building, "We'll be seeing an influx of Wolfkin before you know it. You are welcome to settle into the new shrine. If you need a place to stay talk to Charles, he's the captain of the town guard."

"Thank you, but I'll be fine staying in the shrine."

Thorn saw another carriage coming into the town, so pointing Jansome toward the newly built shrine he got ready to greet the next arrival. And so the morning went with carriage after carriage bringing new villagers and supplies. Altogether the town gained a priest, two merchants, a blacksmith and a large number of settlers with their families, bringing the total population up to 323.

About noon the wall surrounding the town was done thanks to Thorn's ability to shift stones and the new blacksmith started directing workers in building the gate while everyone else went to work on new houses for the incoming settlers. Between Thorn's muscle and the knowledge of the settlers it wasn't long before the house's frames were up and basic roofs were put on, ensuring that the settlers would at least stay dry for the first couple nights until they could get their walls built.

Everyone was sitting down for their evening meal at the tavern, when Akira bounded in, dashing up onto the table where Thorn was sitting and excitedly grabbing some bread off his plate.

"Master! Guess what! Guess, guess!" she chirped excitedly.

"You found them?"

"Oh yes, yes! I found all of them even though they were well hidden in the north. They hide in caves like moles! I call them mole people!" declared Akira with glittering eyes.

Sitting up proudly she started stuffing the bread in her mouth.

“Good job!” Hearing about the caves Thorn’s mind quickly revised his plan. It was one thing to approach an antagonistic group in an open area, quite another to try and deal with them in a fortified position. “Tomorrow you’ll have to show me where they are, okay?”

“Mph.” Clearing her throat Akira looked at Thorn curiously. “Why? The cave is dark and smelly. Only mole people live there. I don’t want to go in.”

“I need to meet with the... mole people.”

“Oh, that’s easy. They are on their way here.”

“What?” surprised, Thorn stood up. “How far away are they?”

“Oh, I don’t know. This bread is good!” having finished the last piece from Thorn’s plate Akira casually swiped another piece from the plate of the priest, completely ignoring his protests. “A few of them were hiding in the bushes and they saw you were rebuilding the town so they ran to get their friends. I’ve never seen moles run so fast.”

Explaining the situation to the others who couldn’t hear the mental communication between Thorn and Akira, Thorn gulped down his soup and then headed for the front gate. Keeping watch there, it wasn’t long before he spotted a ragtag group of men coming out of the forest. Heavily armed and dangerous looking, they looked warily at Thorn who stood in front of the new gate leaning on his improvised mace.

Each was armed with a bow, multiple blades and a short spear while broken armor and ragged clothing completed their bandit look. Even from this distance Thorn could see the mistrust radiating from their bodies. Soon there were almost sixty of them arranged in a rough half circle facing him. From their midst a large man stepped out, walking up until he was about twenty feet from Thorn. Dressed in a mostly complete set of chainmail and armed with a sword and shield, it was obvious from his bearing that he had once been an officer of some sort.

“Welcome to Greymane. What can we do for you?” asked Thorn as the man got closer.

“Depends. Who are you?” replied the man warily staring at the giant in front of him. The others, equally nervous, scanned the wall for an ambush.

“Isn’t it custom to introduce yourself first?”

“Not when you are outnumbered 60 to 1.” scoffed the bandit leader.

Thorn was surprised that despite facing so many armed men he felt no fear at all. Instead a faint excitement was starting to build in him as he stared at them. A faint hunger, as if they were a banquet waiting for him to feast. The bandit leader noticed this as he looked at Thorn's gaze and inadvertently took a small step back.

"I am Horvir Brightblade, leader of the Freemen." stated the bandit leader gravely, watching Thorn carefully for any sign of aggression.

"Well met Horvir. I am Thorn, Lord Greymane, the Moon Wolf. I am the current ruler of these lands."

Hearing this, the group of men gave sharp gasps and their hands tightened on their weapons. Having been driven into their current state by the last Lord Greymane they had little love for the bearer of the title. Angry murmurs grew as the hard-eyed men began readying their weapons. Waving his hand to keep them from doing anything rash, Horvir took a long look at the new lord.

"The Freemen have claimed the forest and mountains in the north of the valley. So long as you leave us alone we will not contest your claim as Lord Greymane. Otherwise you will find us a hard bone to chew."

"No." still smiling slightly Thorn took a small step forward. "I am the ruler of the forest and surrounding mountains and will not allow any challenges to my authority. You are free to become my subjects or leave, but I will tell you now that there are no other paths for you."

At this the murmurs grew into shouts as the motley collection of men grew angry with his ultimatum. The sound of ringing steel grew as swords were pulled from sheathes and arrows were strung on bows. Concerned that the situation was about to turn into a bloodbath Horvir wracked his brain for a way to stop the confrontation. The bandits were about to charge forward when a figure hurried out of the gate, holding up something and yelling for everyone to wait. Reaching Thorn completely out of breath, Jansome, the priest of Hati gulped in air and shouted for everyone to stand down.

“Brothers, there is no need for violence.” he said, waving his staff aloft. Mounted to the top was a small banner showing a wolf chasing a crescent moon. “Hati has once again blessed a shrine here in the village and upon this holy ground I humbly request that both sides come to talk this out. Surely as brothers of the wolf we can reach an agreement for the good of the pack.”

Hearing his words the bandits looked at each other in astonishment. Hati was back? Didn’t this mean that the taint of the werewolves was gone? The Moon Wolf would surely not grace a village corrupted by tainted blood, would he? Slowly lowering their weapons they looked to Horvir for his judgement.

Walking forward to get a better look at the priest, Horvir’s eyes widened. “Jansome?! You lived through the hunt?”

"It's good to see you too, brother." Smiling, the priest embraced the stunned bandit leader. "It was a close thing but Hati didn't let me fall. Come, come. Things have changed in the valley and I believe it is worth talking to our new lord." Pulling Horvir along by the arm, Jansome brought him into the village.

Soon Thorn, Jansome, Horvir and a few of the other bandits were seated in the inn around a table. Horvir and three other men had been allowed into the village and the others had been left outside the gate where Akira was keeping an eye on them. Taking a deep breath, Jansome began to explain what was going on to Thorn.

"My Lord, Horvir is my half-brother." Jansome's face blossomed into a smile, his gaze fixed on the still incredulous bandit leader. "Horvir used to be one of the captains for the previous lord. However, after he was corrupted, the lord instituted a hunt to drive out and kill all the followers of Hati in the valley. Refusing to go along with it, Horvir was added to the hunt and ended up fleeing with a few of the other guards. I was the priest of the village at the time and barely escaped with my life. Since then, I lived in hiding outside the valley, hoping to one day return.

"A week ago, Hati visited me in a dream, telling me to come back to the valley to resume my work at the shrine here in Greymane Village. It is with great excitement that I have come to serve again. Horvir, I know you have fought for the people's freedom for the last ten years, but I believe it is time to let that fight go. Our new lord has cleansed the curse from Greymane Castle and is doing much to restore the village to the way it was before the curse took hold. Please listen to what the lord has to say," entreated Jansome before turning back to address Thorn.

"Lord Greymane, please understand that my brother has been fighting and hiding for a long time now and is naturally distrustful. I know he has a good heart and is worried about the people under him so I beg you would be gracious."

"I understand." Thorn took a good look at those in the room. Not long ago they had no idea he even existed and now he had simply swept in and seized the power they had been fighting over for the last ten years. It was no wonder that they were not on board with him being their ruler. "Horvir, can I assume you speak for all the Freemen and their families?"

Horvir looked at the three men who had come with him and seeing their nods he said, "I represent the Freemen and have been given the rights to negotiate for them."

"Excellent. Then let me lay out my case for you and you can decide what you want to do. A few days ago I came to this valley with the express purpose of slaying the werewolf who was the last Lord Greymane. Having done so I assumed the position of Lord Greymane by force and merit." Here Thorn held up the Wolf Lord's ring for them to see. "As the Greymane, I rule the Fang Forest, the Twins and Greymane village.

“All of the valley and the surrounding mountains are my domain. I intend to rule them justly, but I will rule them. I am working to improve Greymane Village into a town and I intend to rebuild the Temple of the Moon as well. I intend to open the valley to all those who would live peacefully here and I will protect all that choose to do so. I will not, however, tolerate anyone who attempts to undermine my rule no matter their claim.”

“Hold on!” interrupted one of the men who had come with Horvir, standing and slamming his helmet on the table. “First I want to know how you took care of the last lord, and how we know this isn’t some sort of trick!”

Looking calmly at the rough man Thorn reached out and grabbed the metal helmet that the man had slammed into the table and, without a smidgen of effort, crushed it into a ball. Stumbling back over his chair the man’s face blanched white and everyone in the room broke out into a cold sweat seeing the iron ball in Thorn’s hands.

CHAPTER THIRTY-EIGHT

“Look. The main point is this,” Thorn’s tone was even as he tossed the crushed helmet onto the table, “I could really use some help in improving the valley and knowledgeable woodsmen would go a long way toward keeping people safe. I don’t have a problem with the Freemen so long as you work under me and not against me.”

Still staring at the ball of crushed metal, Horvir stammered, “Yeah, of course.”

“This is why I don’t like intimidation,” sighed Thorn. “How about this. You have, what, 120 family members back in your caves? And another 100 fighting men?”

“H… ho... how’d you know that?” burst out the man who’s helmet Thorn had crushed.

“Used my brain.” Thorn did not mention Akira’s nose. “I’m

guessing your food situation isn't so great and come winter it will be even worse. Why don't you move your families into the village? For any of you that want to, I'd like to employ you as rangers, patrolling the valley and keeping people safe. You'd be semi-autonomous, inside the command structure of my army, but tasked with keeping the roads safe, preventing banditry, and generally keeping the peace outside of town."

"Inside town, we'll be forming a guard. It will act as another part of the army we are establishing at the new temple to defend against any major threats from outside the valley. Both the guard and the rangers will be under the command of the army and may be deployed in the event of any major battles. The guard and the rangers will also be responsible for hunting down any remaining werewolves and killing them to make sure they never come back."

"I'll pay two silver a month plus a stipend for housing and food and you'll get free gear repairs so long as you are a ranger. Anyone over the age of 50 who has been a ranger for two years or more can retire with a pension of one silver a month so long as they agree to help train new recruits."

Silence settled over the room as the men thought about what Thorn was offering. Protection for their families, steady income and a place in the new society that Thorn was establishing sounded good. Especially the idea of being able to retire on a pension. A couple of the members of their group were already getting up there in years and would undoubtedly welcome the chance to settle down after two years of service.

Seeing they were seriously considering it, Thorn decided to give them one more little push. Tapping his chin like he was thinking out loud, he remarked, “Actually, it would be really nice to have a group with some autonomy around. This would help reassure people that I am being held accountable. I'm planning on forming a council to help manage the valley when I am not around and I could include a seat on it for the elected leader of the Freemen. This way you'll know what is going on and can watch for any signs of corruption. Anyway, think about it, I've got to check to make sure everyone is settled for the night. The four of you can feel free to spend the night here, but your men will have to camp outside.”

Leaving the men to talk over what he offered them, Thorn walked out of the inn and made his way to the shrine. Jansome had settled in quite quickly, adding some decorations to the otherwise simple affair. A low stone altar sat in front of the new banner bearing the wolf over moon emblem of Hati.

Thorn had never been one for religion but he knew that in old Norse mythology Hati was one of the sons of Fenrir, the wolf god. Supposedly Hati and his brother Skoll chased the moon and sun through the sky attempting to devour them. Never able to catch up they would continue to chase until Ragnarok, the end of the world, when they would finally be successful in eating the heavenly bodies. Obviously, Nova Terra was not using an exact match to real-world mythology, but many things seemed to carry over.

All the families that had shown up over the last couple days were under shelter and everything seemed to be settled down for the night so Thorn called Akira over and went to bed. The next morning he walked out to the street after breakfast and was startled to see the group of 60 bandits standing at attention in the street, obviously waiting for him.

“Present!” yelled Horvir, stepping to the front of the group. As one the group took a knee and placing their weapons across their hearts shouted together, “We pledge our lives to our Lord, our hearts to our people and our swords to the throats of our enemies!”

For a moment Thorn didn’t know what to do but a mental nudge from Akira snapped him out of his daze. Clearing his throat he stood tall and responded. “As your Lord I accept your pledge and make my own. My heart will be for our people, my blood will be for our land. You will be my fang and I will be your shield. You knelt as outlaws, rise as Freemen of Greymane.”

Cheers erupted from all around as the villagers celebrated the return of those who had been cast out so long ago. Tearful hugs were exchanged and Thorn commanded a keg broken open to toast the new rangers. Yet there was much to be done and it wasn’t long before 15 of the new rangers were headed back to get their families while the rest of the rangers helped around town. By evening all the houses were largely complete and Elder Thomas had been spotted leading a caravan of new settlers down into the valley.

Before the sun had gone down the new settlers arrived at the gates and after greeting them Thorn decided that it was time to head to the location of the new temple to meet up with Velin, Mina, and the Wolfkin. Elder Thomas and Charles had both been happy with the state of the town and were excited to see that the Freemen had agreed to join them again. The captain had hired a good number of older mercenaries to act as the town guard, and along with their families and the other settlers the total population of Greymane Village grew to over 900 people.

Making his way back to the keep took a little longer than usual due to the encroaching darkness, but unlike a week ago, the coming night did not seem sinister at all. Prior to the curse being broken a darkness had hung over the valley, muting the life that lived here and bringing a chilling fear into the air. Having been banished by Thorn, the oppressive darkness was gone and a peaceful air reigned, making the Fang Forest feel like any other old growth wood.

Strolling along, Thorn listened as Akira chatted about her kingdom and how many trees it contained. She continued to mark the trees they passed, jumping from branch to branch. It wasn't until she paused to mark a particularly tall tree that Thorn noticed the stillness that had fallen over the forest.

During one of the incredibly short pauses that Akira took in her stream of conversation Thorn suddenly realized that the regular night sounds had completely ceased. Not even the insects were making noise anymore, a good indication that something very dangerous was near.

Letting Akira continue to chat Thorn carefully looked around, trying to see if there was anything out of place. Just as he was sure that there was no one nearby, two yellow eyes appeared from the shadows in front of him and the form of a massive wolf stepped out into the moonlight. Covered in knotted muscle and with too many scars to count, the pitch-black wolf looked like it came straight out of a nightmare. An aura of monstrous strength radiated from its massive frame and a crimson tongue ran across giant fangs.

Eyes narrowing, Thorn took out his mace, holding it in a two-handed grip and letting the large end rest on the ground to his right while Akira shrieked and jumped to the branches of a large tree. Silence fell as man and beast stared at each other, each seeking the weaknesses in the other's form. As far as Thorn was concerned, the monster in front of him had none. With a back as tall as Thorn's shoulders and a head that, fully raised would dwarf him by feet, the wolf was impossibly huge and its tightly packed muscles and myriad scars were testament to its battle experience.

"Hmmm, you are the new Lord?" rumbled the wolf in a deep voice. "You smell strange. Like a weak blooded human and yet... There is something else. You will not do."

"Step forward and you'll see if I'm weak." Thorn spat back. Ever since his trial by combat with the former head disciple Gelish, Thorn felt an odd burning desire in his heart every time he thought about fighting. No matter how large the enemy, Thorn was confident in his strength.

"Ha, watch your words whelp. You are lucky that my master told me to give you a chance to flee. If I attacked you would never even see me coming. Weak senses, weak blood, weak abilities, you are not fit to be the Wolf Lord. Hand over the ring and flee this valley if you don't want to be hunted and killed like the prey you are." The massive wolf began to circle.

"Master?" brows furrowed Thorn turned his body to face the prowling beast. "Who is your master?"

"My master is the true ruler of this valley. Enough. Leave the ring and flee before my patience wears out. Otherwise I will destroy you where you stand and leave your body for the forest animals to feast on."

[Listen you stupid dog! My master is a hun.. a million times better than yours!] Akira cut in from her branch where she was jumping up and down in anger. [You're a smelly, mangy dog and you probably have fleas!]

Gaping at the exploding red furball in utter astonishment, Thorn was too shocked to move at the battle pet's sudden outburst. Akira, on the other hand was quite pleased with her effect and continued to throw insults and rude gestures toward the wolf who could only hear a loud burst of squeaks coming from the Ailuridae who was jumping up and down on a branch. Suddenly the absurdity of the situation hit Thorn and he burst out laughing, drawing an angry snarl from the wolf.

"You know where to find me if your master really wants the ring." Thorn said, wiping his eyes and grinning at the furious monster. "Unless you are going to try and get it now, I've got places to be. Come on Akira, let's go."

"Insolence!" growled the wolf, fury in its eyes. Dropping into a crouch it suddenly sprang, teeth and claws glistening in the moonlight! Thorn, however, was expecting it and had never relaxed his grip on his weapon. Seeing the wolf leap Thorn dropped his hips, bending his knees and winding up. A quick step forward with his left foot brought him closer to the slavering jaws of the wolf and with a twist of his waist he brought his mace up in a wicked arc from the ground to his left shoulder.

Reacting faster than should be possible the wolf somehow twisted its body in the air, avoiding being hit by the massive spike. Yet despite its agility it could not avoid the massive burst of air that accompanied the swing and it was thrown to the ground, lunging out of the way of Thorn's reverse swing.

Scrambling to its feet, the wolf jumped back. Unadulterated

astonishment blazed in its eyes as it stared at Thorn. If either of the blows had connected there is no way it would have gotten away without serious injury. Seeing Thorn rushing forward for another strike the beast jumped forward and swung a massive paw.

With a thunderous crash the two blows collided, the immense force sending both Thorn and the giant wolf reeling. Falling back, it took Thorn four steps to stabilize himself. Astounded by the force contained in the wolf's paw, Thorn dashed forward again as soon as regained his balance. Ducking a slash, Thorn jabbed out with his weapon, forcing the wolf to twist its waist to dodge.

Back and forth they struggled, ripping the ground to shreds. Blocking a bite with the haft of his metal tetsubo, Thorn roared, punching out with a rock-hard fist. The punch caught the wolf on the cheekbone, glancing off its iron hard fur and sending it staggering backward. His fury rising like a tide, Thorn gripped his long metal spike in two hands and raised it over his head, bringing it down with enough force to pulverize stone.

Sensing the power behind the strike, the wolf jumped back, moving impossibly fast. It gave a strange growl, melting into the shadows of the trees until all that was left were its yellow eyes.

“Interesting. You surprise me human.” snarled the wolf as it faded away. “I'll visit again.”

"Haha, that's right! You better run! Master we scared him off because he is a huge scaredy cat!" yipped Akira, jumping back down onto Thorn's shoulder. Sighing, he looked at the shadows where the monster had gone. Thinking back over the fight, Thorn could only shake his head. Even though it looked like he had the wolf at a disadvantage, Thorn knew better.

Not only had the wolf's awareness been way above his, but, despite being knocked back by the force of his blows, it had no problem avoiding his strikes when it chose. If he couldn't hit the wolf, he would have no way of winning. After careful examination of the fight, Thorn couldn't shake the feeling that this had been nothing more than a test and that if the wolf was serious, it could have slaughtered him where he stood.

And to think that behind the monstrous wolf was another and most likely stronger being. Its 'master'. Thorn had taken what he had from the hands of werewolves and had decided to try to hold what he had seized, no matter who came at him.

They would come, he knew that for sure. Without a doubt, the next few weeks would find people flowing into this valley in droves, looking for their hearts desires, taking what they could. Thorn had taken a pledge today to help those who lived here already prosper, and he intended to see it through to the end, no matter how much blood or sweat it took.

CHAPTER THIRTY-NINE

The keep was empty when Thorn arrived, stripped of anything of value that could be carried away by the Wolfkin. It had regained some of the palpable gloom that had shrouded it the first time Thorn had seen it. The crunching gravel under Thorn's feet echoed loudly in the now silent courtyard. Even Akira, normally chatty, had fallen silent.

Climbing the stairs to the throne room, Thorn ran his fingers along the uneven stone walls. Soon this derelict castle would join the old ruler of the valley, relegated to history. Thinking about it made Thorn wonder if someday he too would be overtaken, if the temple he was about to build would fall into disrepair, its original architect forgotten.

Shaking the depressing thoughts from his head, Thorn approached the throne, activating the familiar relocation option. Last time, his hesitancy came from the time limit on the [Control Orb] but after handling both the bandits and

Greymane Village he was confident that he would be able to finish everything he needed in time.

A bright yellow glow lit the room as soon as Thorn clicked the button and a glass orb appeared, hovering over the Wolf Throne. Like molten gold, rays of light poured over the back of the chair, melting it away as they fell. Once the throne had disappeared entirely the rays shot back up to the glass orb, filling it with swirling golden light. Floating gently through the air, the orb stopped in front of Thorn, allowing him to grab it.

You have acquired Greymane Valley's Control Point. Activate this [Control Orb] within 24 hours to select a new Control Point location. If a new Control Point is not assigned within 24 hours, the Control Point will return to its original location.

Stuffing the orb into his inventory, Thorn took one last look around the keep before leaving through the front gate. Taking in a deep breath of the crisp night air, Thorn called Akira and began to run toward the entrance to the valley. Passing quickly under the massive trees of the old growth forest, it did not take him long before the sight of the Twins entered his vision.

The entrance to the valley was dominated by two tall peaks, referred to locally as the Twins because of their symmetrical shape. With the pass between them being the only entrance into the valley, the Twins were a perfect natural defensive line due to their height. Thorn planned to place the temple squarely in the center of the pass, blocking the valley off from the outside world.

The map that Mina had compiled showed the valley to be rich in resources. Combined with the fact that the valley was going to be opening as a spawn point for players choosing to play as Wolfkin, Thorn had been thinking a lot about how to leverage his position as Lord Greymane. Less concerned about the monetary benefits of controlling a territory, Thorn had a different idea in mind and the first step was creating a place for his influence to grow.

Practically flying across the forest floor, Thorn soon made it to the foot of the Twins. Another ten minutes and he was standing in the pass. Campfires burned low and the soft breathing of the sleeping Wolfkin sounded clearly in the silent night. A sentry at the edge of the Wolfkin camp had nearly swallowed his tongue when Thorn rushed up the hill, but after patting him on the back and forbidding him from announcing Thorn's arrival, Thorn headed to the main tent.

The camp had been set up around a large central tent. Seeing a light still glowing from a crack in the tent's door, he pushed aside the flap and ducked his head as he entered. Leaning over a large map of the area, Velin was occupied in a low-voiced conversation with Captain Del'har. Hearing the swish of the flap, they looked up, stopping their conversation to salute.

"How many times have I told you not to do that?"

"Sorry, my lord. Old habits die hard." The Captain rose from where he had kneeled.

"And what is your excuse?" Thorn shot a glance at Velin before turning his attention to the map they had been studying.

"It seems the correct thing to do," Velin was serious, straightening from her half bow. Silence fell on the tent as Thorn stared at the map. As the atmosphere got increasingly stifling, Thorn sighed and shook his head.

"Velin, I'm sorry." Seeing that she was about to respond, Thorn held up his hand. "No, I am. I should not have snapped at you the other day. It is obvious that I am not as over what happened as I thought I was, and I let your comment get to me. Your suggestion was reasonable, but for whatever reason I took it badly. I know that it wasn't fair for me to shut you down like that. I'm sorry and I will try to do a better job in the future."

"Thank you, Thorn." Velin's normally cold face broke into a small smile as she looked down, adjusting her hair behind her ear. After a moment of warm silence she returned to her business-like attitude, obviously uncomfortable with such personal conversation. "Once it was clear that you are determined to control the valley I started planning. Take a look and let me know what you think."

Turning his attention back to the map, Thorn listened carefully as Velin outlined the situation. Crimson Snake scouts had been spotted less than a day's march from the valley, which meant that the army was going to arrive slightly ahead of schedule. Assuming the army was less than a day's march behind the scouts, the invasion was eminent.

"Our ability to defend the valley will rely on a few things. First, we'll have to be able to defend it physically. What I mean is that we are going to have to win the battle. The invading force is almost five times our number. They have as many player soldiers as we have native soldiers. Normally, this sort of battle will be unwinnable. Our only option is fortifications if we want to put up a fight. Thorn, I'm not sure what you have in mind yet, so I have not planned a defensive strategy.

"Assuming we can stop the army outside the valley, we're going to have to face the second issue. We don't have a way to make them leave. This is a game, so the players can respawn which puts us in a bind. There is nothing to stop the Crimson Snakes from camping on our doorstep until they wear us out. My only idea is to put pressure on Angdrin from inside Ragnarok, but to do that we would have to give up some control." Pausing, she looked at Thorn. "Both of these things are out of my hands. I'm afraid I'm not going to be much help in terms of planning."

"No problem." Thorn's gaze rested on the map as he

considered the two problems Velin had outlined. "I'm working on the second problem as we speak. For now, let's focus on dealing with the fight we have coming. I've got a plan drawn up for the temple that should help with our defense. It ended up going sort of a fortress monastery style. Big walls and that sort of thing which should allow us to minimize our disadvantage." Opening his interface, Thorn sent the design of the new temple to Velin and Captain Del'har. "I've never fought a war before, so I don't know if we need to make any modifications. Take a look and let me know what you think."

"This..." After looking over the design Velin was lost for words. She had expected a sketch and had instead gotten full architectural blueprints showing elegant buildings behind a towering wall. "Where did you get this?"

"Ah. I drew it a few years ago. Went through a castle phase and had a lot of time on my hands. Like, excessive amounts of time. This design is based on Punakha Dzong, a fortress in Bhutan. I thought it looked the most temple-like but it is also easy to defend. Though, this is a bit bigger because of the width of the pass. Anything jump out at you that wouldn't work?"

"No, my lord, this looks quite impressive." Captain Del'har shook his head.

Seeing that Velin was still speechless, Thorn nodded and stepped outside the tent. Knowing that Thorn was going to be building the temple in the pass, the Wolfkin had made camp away from the entrance. After making sure the area was clear, Thorn opened the store and uploaded his blueprints.

A few adjustments had to be made to allow the temple to fit in the space properly, but within less than half an hour the order was ready to go. Giving everything a once over to make sure he was not missing any of the details, Thorn smiled and hit the accept order button.

"Behold, the Temple of the Moon!"

bzzt

Error: Insufficient Funds due to account spending cap
Your order exceeds the fund limit set on your account. Please contact your guardian regarding raising the spending cap on the attached account.

Blushing with embarrassment as Captain Del'har and Velin stared at the empty pass, Thorn called his aunt.

"Xavier! How are you? Are you having fun?"

"Hi." Still bright red, Thorn got straight to the point. "Can you raise my spending cap on my account? I'm trying to build a building but the system says I can't because my spending is capped."

"Oh? Your limit is five million. What on earth would you spend more than five million on?"

Rather than trying to explain everything from the beginning, Thorn sent his aunt the blueprints and shared his vision through the call.

"Remember that valley I told you about? Well, it's mine and I'd like to keep it. I'm going to build a big fortress here to block the only way in." Thorn pointed to the entrance to the pass. "However, the cost is pretty serious. Sixty million."

"Sixty million credits?! Are you crazy?" Julia's eyebrows shot up when she heard the price. "What on earth could make it cost so much?"

"Well, I'm trying to make it both a temple and a fortress so it is a bit bigger than most castles. And there are two sub levels that can be used as extra barracks or storage, plus a mini shopping district. And some towers for ballista. And I might have added three heavy duty gates and a giant wolf head on top of the fortress with a waterfall coming out of its mouth. Oh, and I made the walls taller."

"Xavier, the base price for a system-built castle is twenty million. Twenty-five, tops. There is no way that stuff cost forty million credits."

"Well, this is more of a town than a castle."

"A town?!"

"Yeah. After all, people are going to need places to stay, right? So I added a large hotel and there are storefronts for people to rent. And I saw that I could add all sorts of different production facilities, so I did. This way, as our guild adds players with production classes we'll be set up already. Ah, and I bought a bunch of resources too. That was at least three million."

"You built a town? You better be mining gold out of that valley if you want to make sixty million credits back."

"Gold? Haha, I have something better. A race. The Wolfkin spawn here and their racial advancement quests are tied to the valley as well. So, anyone who wants to play a Wolfkin is going to be spending time here. There is also at least one ancient ruin in the mountains behind the valley, probably more than that. According to Velin, any time there is a new race there is a large influx of new players or people buying race changes.

"Even if it is not a popular race we can expect at least a million players. If each of them spends sixty credits in the valley our cost will be pretty much covered. To say nothing of the merchants that will come in to serve the new players. Add the other natural resources the valley possesses to that and whoever controls this valley will be making bank. I intend for that to be us."

"And here I thought that you were just playing around." At the prospect of making money Julia's eyes lit up. "I've adjusted your spending cap, you shouldn't have any problem. You're doing great, hun, I'll see you soon, okay?"

"Thanks! Love you." Closing the call, Thorn turned back to the empty pass and tried again. As he hit the button to accept the order the world shimmered, as if a wave of heat passed through the air. As the world stabilized, a familiar figure appeared.

"Greetings, traveler."

"Hello, Myst." Thorn smiled at the beauty in her shimmering blue dress.

"My system indicates that you have made a large purchase. I am here to ensure satisfaction. Please indicate that the details here are correct. If they are correct please initial at the six highlighted locations and sign on the last page."

"Thanks, what is the time frame on the build?" Thorn asked after flipping through the document on the pad Myst handed him.

"That is a great question, traveler. The time frame on the construction of your ordered building is forty-seven minutes and thirty-six seconds from the project's commencement." Accepting the pad back from Thorn, Myst tapped it a few times. "Thank you for finalizing your purchase. Would you like to give a name to your project?"

"Yeah. Let's call it Moon Wolf Citadel."

"Thank you, traveler. Your project is commencing, please standby until it completes." With one last smile, Myst turned and walked into thin air, disappearing as fast as she had appeared.

The air in the pass shivered again and froze. Curious, Thorn reached out, only to feel a smooth invisible wall blocking his hand. In the center of the pass a large blue box appeared with a large white zero on it.

[0%]

CHAPTER FOURTY

The new temple was laid out in a large rectangle, built to stretch from one side of the pass to the other. Walking with his hand on the clear wall Thorn found that it stretched the whole distance. Dropping his hand he returned to stand with Velin and the Captain, watching as a greyish blue fog rose from the ground, filling the space where the temple would be built. Suddenly, dirt fountained from inside the layer of fog, jetting up into the air where it disappeared.

[1%]

After thirty seconds the large number in the center of the wall climbed from zero to one. Shortly after, large stone blocks began to fall from the sky, vanishing into the roiling cloud. As time went on, other materials like timber, brick, and metal would appear and drop into the fog. Every thirty seconds the number would tick up and the fog obscuring their view would climb.

As they stood watching, Thorn looked around.

"Where is Mina?"

"She logged out."

"Is she mad at me?"

"Most likely. Please excuse her immaturity, she can be quite emotional and I think she is fairly sensitive right now."

"It is no problem. Would it be helpful if I sent her a message?"

"No," sighing, Velin tucked her hair behind her ear. "I think she needs time to think things through. Life has been moving fast since we climbed the tower with Ouroboros and she probably needs a bit of space to sort through the changes. Our relationship is not quite the same as it was, or as Mina hopes for it to be, and that is causing her some distress."

"Alright." Thorn nodded. "Let me know if there is anything I can do."

"Thank you."

After watching the gradually appearing temple in silence for a moment, Thorn changed the subject.

"I guess I don't actually know much about you and Mina. You live together, right? Have you lived together long?"

"That is true, I guess we've never really talked about ourselves." The corners of Velin's lips curled slightly, her small smile lighting up her face. "Mina and I have been friends for a long time. Since elementary school. We were roommates in college as well."

"Wait, that means you're in your twenties?" Asked Thorn, not bothering to conceal his shock.

"Yes. I'm twenty-five, Mina is twenty-four. How old did you think we were?"

"I mean, I would have guessed around that for you but I definitely thought Mina was sixteen."

"Haha, that is sort of understandable. Most people take her to be younger because of her height. How old are you?"

"Uh. Sixteen."

"No way." Velin smirked. Seeing Thorn's serious gaze, her smile faltered. "No way. You are sixteen? How…?" Trailing off, Velin held up her hand, as if she could measure Thorn's height.

"How am I so tall?" Thorn chuckled. "I grew fast. Thankfully, I've stopped growing." Seeing that Velin was distracted by his revelation, Thorn prompted her. “You were saying that you and Mina knew each other in college?”

“Hm, yes. That is right. We lived together in college. When we got out we joined Ragnarok. That was about two years ago. Since we were already good friends we got an apartment together. Since then we’ve been playing Nova Terra and trying to help Ouroboros grow his influence.”

“What did you study in school that got you a job with a guild?”

“I studied to be an information engineer. I was lucky that I was hired as an analyst almost right away. Mina studied communications but spent most of her time playing Nova Terra. She was hired as a combatant.” Seeing Thorn’s eyebrows rise, Velin defended her friend. “Don’t be fooled, Mina is an excellent player. She has great timing and her skill set is good in group fights. Wait until Ragnarok gets here. She earned her Ice Witch class by her own hard work.”

“Alright, I’ll pay attention. Both of you are great players, have you ever considered joining the Society of Roses?”

“Considered? What use would that be? They don’t accept new members. And even if they did, the application list would be at least twenty miles long.”

“Oh yeah? Are they pretty popular?”

“Popular is an understatement.” Velin pulled out her notebook and flipped to an empty page. “They are the most well-known group in the game. It doesn’t hurt that the Queen of Roses is rich and powerful in real life either.”

“Queen of Roses?”

“Ah, I forget how much you don’t know. The Queen of Roses is Athena, the leader of the Society of Roses guild. Her real name is Julia Lee. She is the CEO of Atlas.” As Velin finished speaking her eyes went wide and she shot a glance at Thorn who was watching the glowing number. With some effort she kept her voice from quivering. “She is strong, pretty, and rich. The envy of pretty much everyone in Nova Terra.”

“I can imagine.” Thorn rubbed the bridge of his nose as he diverted the topic. “Looks like the temple is about done. Let’s check it out.

ding

[100%]

As the glowing numbers reached one hundred, the invisible wall dissipated and the blue fog rolled back, revealing Moon Wolf Citadel in all its glory. A tall stone wall towered above Thorn’s head, easily reaching twenty-five feet high. Four tall towers stood at the corners of the walls, providing an excellent field of view of both sides of the pass. Lit in a soft, blue glow by magical ever-burning torches, the citadel looked like something out of a fairytale.

The fortress itself sat in the center of the citadel, aligned with the two large metal-studded wooden gates that controlled the entrance and exit of the Moon Wolf Citadel. Stone walls radiated out from the fortress like the spokes of a wheel, dividing the citadel into six sections. Two walls ran from the fortress to the sides of the gatehouses, forming a funnel leading from the gate to a tunnel running underneath the fortress.

To the sides of the fortress were the various areas that Thorn had built in preparation for the influx of players who would be arriving in the valley. Apart from the pathway leading through the citadel, the rest of the space was divided into four distinct districts. On the right side of the main gate was the merchant square, packed with empty shops and open areas for trade. Based on what he had observed in Berum, Thorn expected that most players would be spending their time in this area.

On the other side of the entrance, Thorn had placed the residential and training districts. While there, players would be able to arrange housing, visit inns, or get training in a variety of different basic skills. Purchasing a training hall had added quite a bit of cost to the citadel's price, but the fees Thorn would be able to collect from it made it an easy choice. Unlike the merchant area, Thorn had also left about half of the space in this section of the citadel empty to allow for future buildings to go in.

Behind the merchant area were the production buildings that Thorn had purchased. Much like the training hall, their cost had been high but Thorn felt that the expense was necessary in order to create a solid base for his guild. This area also had several residences that could be used by members of the guild and natives who settled into the Moon Wolf Citadel.

The last section of the citadel was the reconstructed temple. The area the temple took up was bigger than Greymane Keep and connected directly with the fortress in the center of the citadel. It had been expanded to include quarters for the disciples in training as well as four sectors for the different courts. Additionally, the temple was connected to a subterranean area containing a barracks and extra storage. Connected with tunnels to various sections of the city wall, the subterranean levels allowed for quick access to every part of the city.

Towering over the center of the pass, the fortress was an imposing affair. Sitting squarely in between the two tall peaks, it almost looked like a new mountain had been added. The fortress sat over a large tunnel that connected the front and back gates. Thorn had made sure that the tunnel was big enough to move two wagons through side by side but had also added six metal portcullises for a measure of defense. The inside of the fortress had the typical great room and ballroom, while the rest of the fortress was split up between the kitchen, a few offices, bedrooms, storage rooms, and even a wizard's tower.

After a quick tour of the citadel, the first thing Thorn did was head to the great room of the fortress. Taking out the [Control Orb] from his inventory, Thorn activated it, choosing to place the control point where the throne would go. With a flash of bright light the process that Thorn had witnessed in the Keep reversed. Seeing the [Control Orb] melting and reforming the Wolf Throne, Thorn had a hard time keeping a grin off his face. As he stood watching the throne being reconstructed, Thorn heard hurried footsteps behind him. Turning he saw Velin and Mina both rushing in.

"Thorn, the scouts have arrived! We need to get the army together since the main force will not be far behind. Wow, look at that view!" Distracted by the large balcony that ran the length of one side of the great room, Mina dashed outside, taking in the sight of the valley. Dark green forest stretched far into the distance, lying quietly under the twinkling stars. The soft breeze blew against Mina, causing her to grab her hat as she looked down. In the distance, the mountains cut against the sky, like jagged teeth under the bright moon.

"That is really pretty." Mina walked back inside and started examining the tapestries that covered the opposite wall. "This place must have cost a fortune. Looks like we picked the right side this time. Ah, I mean…" choking on her words, Mina blushed and looked away, her voice trailing off.

“It was expensive, but I think it is worth it.” Sitting on the newly reformed Wolf Throne, Thorn pretended he had not heard Mina’s last sentence to spare her embarrassment. “This will be our base of operations from now on. I was hoping to do this when Oberlin was back but we don’t really have a lot of time so I’ll go ahead and announce the official formation of our guild.”

“We’re starting a guild?” Mina looked at Velin and then Thorn, confusion written all over her face.

“Yes, I told you that, didn’t I?” Thorn scratched his head. A lot had happened recently and as preoccupied as he was with planning the valley’s defense he had been quite distracted. “Honestly, I can’t remember. Anyway, we’re starting a guild.”

“Hey, that is awesome!” Mina cheered. “But there are only three of us so far. How are we supposed to get more people?”

“We’ll be recruiting mostly natives, actually. Wolfkin disciples who become Night Walkers.” Seeing Mina’s expression revert to confusion, Thorn sighed and held his forehead in his palm. “Disciples from the Moon Temple become Night Walkers when they finish their training. Since we will be housing them and I am sort of their boss already, Elder Havva has agreed to allow them to join our guild.”

"Does this mean we will be getting players as well?" Velin asked, getting out her notebook to scribble some notes.

"Potentially. We have the right of refusal, obviously, but it is conceivable that any player who succeeds in joining the temple will be able to graduate into the Night Walkers, and therefore, into our guild."

"Oh wow, that is genius!" Mina's eyes were wide with excitement as she smacked her fist into her palm. "The Temple of the Moon is the primary way for new Wolfkin players to gain classes and advance which means that they are going to be walking right into our guild. It is like one of those spout things with water that goes straight from one place to your house!"

"A pipeline?" Velin's face didn't even twitch as she explained for Thorn's benefit.

"Exactly, a pipeline."

"Correct. My goal was to find a way to build a reliable pipeline for recruiting new members. We are not going to be exclusively Wolfkin, obviously, but since we are already in control of this region it makes sense to use that to our advantage. Plus, since we can recruit natives, why not do so in a way that consolidates our control?"

"So, what is our guild name going to be?" Mina was obviously much more interested in the answer to this question than she was in Thorn's schemes to consolidate his power.

"Nova Luna."

"Nova Luna? That is pretty." Mina considered it for a few minutes, before nodding her head sagely.

"It means New Moon." Velin tossed in without looking up.

"New Moon, right." Mina pretended she had known that from the beginning.

"I was thinking that we would keep it in line with our moon theme." Thorn said, trying to suppress a laugh. Opening his interface, Thorn clicked on his guild tab and activated it.

Guild Formed: Nova Luna
Congratulations! Your guild, Nova Luna, has successfully been formed. In order to grow your guild, the first step is to find members to join. Once you have found a new member you may add them to your guild from the guild panel. On the guild panel you will find everything you need to set the rules for your guild and to identify your guild's operating region. This will give your guild members the option to use that region's re-spawn point in addition to any other re-spawn point they have bound.

A [Region Management System] has been detected. Would you like to combine your guild tab into your [RMS]? Doing so will automatically bind this region as your guild's operating region.	
Yes	No

Immediately after Thorn selected yes, the guild tab he was staring at vanished, replaced by his [RMS] which had gained a new tab. Selecting it, Thorn made a mental note to spend some time figuring out what the countless options were used for as he scrolled down. Ignoring the questions asking him to set up the guild, Thorn found the spot for adding other players and sent invitations to Mina, Velin, and Oberlin.

"I've invited you to the guild. Alright, there we go." Seeing that Velin and Mina had accepted the invitation, Thorn looked at the elven War Priestess.

"Velin, when you have some time, can you set everything up? I honestly have no idea what most of these options are so I'm probably better suited to guard the gate than try and be the guild leader."

"Of course, it would be my pleasure. There is a role called administrator that will allow me to make changes with your approval. I'd be happy to show you how to do it as well."

"Thanks, maybe later." Thorn found the drop down next to her name and set Velin as an administrator, giving her control of the guild settings. Rising from the throne, Thorn summoned his silver wolf armor and drew his massive metal spike. “Right now, it is time to go greet those scouts.”

CHAPTER FOURTY-ONE

The morning sun was starting to peek through the trees when Thorn and Mina met up with the Wolfkin Dusk Walker that had spotted the advancing Crimson Snakes. Velin had deployed Wolfkin volunteers to be on the lookout for the advancing army and Mina had gotten the report as soon as she had logged in. Rushing to the hill where the Crimson Snake scout had been seen, Thorn and Mina were greeted by a Wolfkin dressed in leather armor and holding a bow.

“Greetings, my lord,” whispered the Wolfkin scout. “Hello, Lady Mina.”

“At ease.” Thorn replied, his eyebrow rising as he heard the way the scout addressed the Ice Witch. “Tell us the situation.”

“Yes, sir. The advancing scouts are moving at about half speed. They are holding a semi-circular pattern to increase the range of their search. The scout I spotted stopped on this hill about five hours ago and returned to the other world."

"Hmmm. They probably logged out to sleep. That means we should have at least a few hours before they are back. Did all of the scouts log out?" Checking his clock, Thorn realized that it was about midnight in the real world.

"It appears so, sir. We have been able to find tracks, but no enemy scouts."

"Excellent. Let's rotate south. Might as well use this opportunity to delay them." Bringing the Wolfkin Dusk Walker with them, the three rushed south, following the half circle path that the Crimson Snake scouts had occupied. Unsurprised by the Dusk Walker's ability to keep up with him, Thorn was a little taken aback when Mina refused his offer to carry her.

Shaking her head resolutely, the Ice Witch had muttered something about being perfectly capable in her own right and then, in a flash of icy wind, teleported forward. Each teleportation could take her fifty meters forward, allowing her to outpace the two runners easily. Constantly casting the teleportation spell was obviously taxing and Mina soon began to breathe heavily.

"Hey, Mina. Hold up." Thorn called for her to wait in between two teleports.

"What? Hey, what are you doing? Put me down!" Lifted off

the ground unexpectedly, Mina grabbed tightly onto Thorn's head as he set her on his shoulder.

"There is no need for you to waste your magic here. I need you fresh when we ambush the scouts."

"Hmph. Fine." Turning her head away, Mina lapsed into silence. Thorn could tell that she was still angry at him. Ever since she had logged in she had been much quieter than normal.

The group of three ran through the forests, occasionally seeing a Wolfkin Dusk Walker who would rise from their hiding places to point the direction to the next location. Within half an hour they had made it to the southern end of the Crimson Snake formation and met up with the Dusk Walker who was responsible for watching for the enemy.

"Let's wait here." After finding the spot where the scout had logged out, Thorn walked to a small copse of trees nearby. "Plan is simple, when the scout logs back in, we'll attack. Once we take out the scout, we will retreat a bit and watch for more scouts."

"How are we going to ambush them from here?" Mina asked, looking at the distance separating them from the tracks.

"Leave that to me." Grinning, Thorn pulled out his giant siege crossbow from his inventory. Resting the arbalest on his shoulder, Thorn made a shooting motion at the spot where the scout had logged out. “As soon as they log in, bam! Though, I will need you to back me up if I miss.”

“Sure thing, I got it.” Mina patted her chest confidently. “You know, I think we need a cool symbol for our guild. Like, something really distinctive.”

Used to Mina’s abrupt subject changes, Thorn nodded, happy that she was getting back to her normal talkative self. He produced one of the silver tokens with the mark of Hati that he had gotten in Hati’s Ascent, handing it over to her.

“What do you think about this? I am thinking of adapting the symbol of Hati. We’re already really closely tied with the Moon Wolf and the Wolfkin, so using it shouldn’t be an issue.”

“I think it is a pretty cool symbol, though I think it’d be better to use the citadel instead of the wolf head. Same idea, but with the outline of the citadel. Or maybe the citadel with the wolf head on top of it.” The longer she spoke, the brighter Mina’s eyes got.

“Yeah, that is a pretty cool idea.” Thorn nodded, his eyes fixed on the empty field where their target would appear.

For the next five hours they waited for the scout to log back in. Thorn used much of that time to compose messages and plan for the impending war, all the while lending Mina’s unceasing conversation half an ear. About half-way through the wait Thorn's stomach began to rumble, interrupting Mina.

"Really? Didn't you eat on the way over here?" Mina rolled her eyes. "You are ridiculous."

"Hey, there is a lot of me to maintain." Thorn protested, spreading a small blanket on the ground next to him. "It is time for a snack." He began to pull steaming hot dishes from his inventory, setting them on the blanket in preparation for his snack. After the sixth dish the two Night Walker's jaws dropped open. However, their shock at the amount of food Thorn got out for his snack paled in comparison to the horror they felt as they watched him swallow whole plates of food in a few bites.

Not wanting to be left out, Mina jumped in with gusto, desperately grabbing food to shove in her mouth before Thorn sent it down his throat into the bottomless pit that was his stomach. Practically choking on the food, Thorn patted her on the back.

"Slow down. There is plenty." Turning to the astounded Night Walkers, Thorn gestured with the large turkey leg he was holding. "Are you hungry? Please help yourself. Don't stand on ceremony either, I am not really into that."

After the four of them ate their fill and Thorn had cleaned up the plates, he picked up his arbalest again and aimed it loosely at the field. He was not completely sure where the scout would be spawning but he was confident that his giant bolt would be enough to take them out. After another forty minutes of waiting, one of the Night Walkers noticed a slight shimmer in the air and called it out in a low voice.

In the field a figure appeared as if they were stepping through a film of rolling mist. A young woman in the familiar crimson armor covered by a dark green cloak began to materialize. Looking around as she logged in, the female scout failed to notice Thorn and the others hiding in the nearby clump of trees. Her body broke through the last wisps of ether a giant crossbow bolt as thick as her wrist smashed through her crimson chest plate, blasting her body into shattered lights. Just as quickly as the scout had arrived she was sent out of the game.

“Alright, let’s retrieve the bolt and anything she dropped and retreat. We need one person to stay here and let us know if the army is moving this direction.”

“I’d be happy to that, my lord.” One of the Dusk Walkers stepped forward, his fist thumping on his chest in a warrior’s salute.

“Make sure you keep your distance. Absolutely no engagement allowed. Hide somewhere nearby and as soon as you spot the army, retreat to the Moon Wolf Citadel and report to Velin. We’ll need every possible fighter back at the pass, so prioritize safety over everything else.”

“Yes, sir!”

"Mina, I am going to head off the scout west of here and then retreat, you deal with the scout to the northeast." Thorn turned to the other Dusk Walker. "I am trusting you to keep her safe and back her up in case there is more than one enemy."

"Of course, my lord!" Giving a warrior's salute, the lanky Wolfkin gripped his bow tightly, his eyes shining with pride at Thorn's trust.

"Bah, I don't need help." Mina grumbled. "I don't lose one on one fights, ever."

"Mina, don't mess around. This is serious. We are trying to buy as much time as possible but if you go and get yourself killed we will have serious problems later."

"Okay, okay. I get it. Man, you're starting to nag like Velin."

"Alright, let's go." Patting the short Ice Witch on the head, Thorn gave an encouraging smile to the two Wolfkin and the group split up, heading to their respective jobs.

Thirteen miles northwest a large group of people wound their way slowly through the underbrush like a giant crimson serpent. At the head of the group, Telis and Korith, Angdrin's two lieutenants, talked quietly together as they led the way.

"That's what I'm saying. I feel like we're grasping at straws."

Korith grumbled in a low voice.

“Hush!” His crimson armored companion looked around to see if anyone could hear. “You know it is not going to end well if anyone hears you so stop talking about it.”

“Don’t pretend you feel any different about it.” The warrior spat on the ground. About to continue he was stalled by Telis’ raised hand.

“Hold on. I got a message from Jace.” Her eyes grew wide in excitement. “She was killed almost as soon as she logged in. Southeast of here, ten to fifteen miles away. Send the two nearest scouts to check what is going on. We’ll take a fifteen-minute rest and then adjust our direction if needed.”

“Hold march!” Bellowed Korith, causing the winding column of players and natives to stop. “We’re taking a fifteen-minute break so eat your rations if you have them but maintain march readiness!” Turning back to Telis who was still reading the message she had received from the scout, he frowned. “What is going on? What did Jace find?”

“Chill out. I’m still trying to make sense of this. She said that she spawned but as soon as she did she got hit by a giant spear and was killed.”

“A giant spear?”

“Yeah, the shaft was at least the size of her wrist.”

"Whoa, that is big. Sounds like an ogre's spear. I really hope it isn't ogres." Korith groaned, rubbing his bald head.

"We'll find out soon. I've dispatched Ellie and Silverflare to that position so we should have more information soon." The more even tempered of the two, Telis re-read the message while getting some rations from her inventory.

To the south, two scouts that had logged in nearby got a message and immediately changed their direction, heading toward the spot where their companion was killed. Moving carefully, the male scout smoothed back his silver hair with both hands, revealing sharp, pointed ears. As an elf, he had a natural affinity for moving through nature and made good time getting to Jace's last known position.

Studying the empty field from afar, a slight prickling along the back of his neck told him that there was something off. Thanks to his class he could sense the danger in the air, though he could not pinpoint exactly where the danger was originating. Concerned, he was about to retreat when he heard a sound and the temperature around him plummeted, reaching zero degrees in less than a second. Shocked, he tried to throw himself backward but his feet would not move. As an arrow cut a path through the back of his neck his brain caught up to his ears.

"[Sub Zero]."

Watching as the elven scout vanished into sparkling lights, Mina stood up out of a bush and stomped her way to where the scout had fallen, grumbling under her breath the whole way. She was confident that she could have beaten the scout in a one on one fight, but Thorn obviously did not trust her so he had sent a Wolfkin along to help. Kicking the grass aside, her mood brightened when she found a small hand crossbow that the dead scout had dropped. Hugging it to her chest, she waved to the Dusk Walker and the two of them sped off.

Back at the Crimson Snake camp, Telis was putting the last of her rations in her mouth when she received two messages at the same time. Reading the first line, she choked, sending crumbs of bread, cheese, and dried meat all over Korith.

“Ugh, gross. What was that for?” Wiping his face off, the large warrior stepped over to pat his partner on the back only to have her dodge away and wave him off. Once she had gotten her coughing under control she straightened, a dangerous look in her eyes that caused Korith to backup warily.

“On your feet, we move now!” Enraged, Telis yelled, causing the army to burst into action. Rations were finished or put away and within two minutes the army was lined up neatly, ready to go.

“Hey, what is happening? What’s wrong?” Korith asked as Telis began to lead the way to the south.

"Silverflare and Ellie both died. They sent me messages. It looks like someone doesn't want us going that direction."

"Are you serious? Both of them? What happened."

"Yes. Ellie said she died because she got hit by a tree? What? That is what the message says. A whole tree. As she was approaching the spot where Jace died, a tree suddenly jumped up in the air and smashed her."

"Uh. What?"

"I have no idea. And frankly, from what the letter says, neither does she."

"Then what has you so steamed?"

"Before Silverflare died he was hit with [Sub Zero]."

"You mean that spell that Mina uses? No way. Why would she be attacking us? She got kicked out of Ragnarok by Ouroboros. If she was going to be attacking someone, shouldn't it be the Blood Guard? Why would she be killing our scouts?"

"Maybe she was never really kicked out? I have no idea. The point is, that witch is killing our scouts and I'm going to beat her into a pulp." Telis fumed.

“Whoa, slow down. I know you don’t like her but remember why we’re here.”

“I know, I know. I won’t let my personal issues with her get in the way. My main concern is that Ouroboros dispatched her and Velin to find the valley first. We’re going to have a lot of trouble if that is the case.”

Drawing in a quick breath when he heard the elven War Priestess’ name, Korith turned to the army behind him and bellowed, “Get a move on, we’re marching double time!”

CHAPTER FOURTY-TWO

Thorn met up with Mina and the Dusk Walker that had accompanied her shortly after he accidently threw a tree at another Crimson Snake scout, crushing her directly. He had intended to use it as camouflage but had tripped in his rush to hide, dropping the tree and killing the scout. Mina reported that they had discovered and killed an elven scout as well so the three of them left, traveling back to the citadel.

Without a good way to track the enemy army, they had to rely on their own scouts to detect and report movement. Unsure if their plan to misdirect the enemy had worked, Thorn and Mina arrived at Moon Wolf Citadel and regrouped with Velin who had been organizing the defenders. Gathering everyone together in front of the fortress, Thorn looked them over.

The Wolfkin who had come down from the mountains numbered three hundred in total. Of those, two hundred were disciples who were trained for combat. Divided into fifty groups of four Wolfkin, the Temple of the Moon disciples looked disciplined and dangerous. Each group contained a member of each court and was led by a dual category Night Walker. While the rest of the disciples were still in training, they were all skilled and shouldn't be underestimated.

Next to them, attempting to imitate the neat, cohesive appearance of the disciples stood one hundred and fifty humans in assorted gear. The rag-tag group looked more like bandits than soldiers, though there were a few who were obviously veterans. Armed to the teeth and clad in whatever armor they could scrounge; the Freemen presented a wild and eclectic look. The only thing uniform about them was the longbow that each carried on their back. Six feet long and made of a variety of material, every single bow was well polished by years of use.

The last group was composed of the hunters from Greymane Village who had doubled as guards. With the influx of new settlers over the last few days, the group had grown to almost four hundred. However, as Thorn looked them over, he could not help but give a mental sigh. Even more poorly equipped than the Freemen, the village guards barely had a single weapon each.

The Crimson Snake scouts that Thorn had killed had been dressed in full leather armor, armed with bows, swords, and knives, every weapon shiny and like new. Undoubtedly, the army that followed behind them was similarly well-equipped.

The difference between the two forces was almost laughable, though Thorn was in no mood to laugh at this point.

Had he not built Moon Wolf Citadel, the Crimson Snakes would have undoubtedly crushed their defenses without any trouble. As it was, the large walls should give them pause, though Thorn had no real hope that it would stop them. With another sigh, Thorn tossed aside his concerns and started to organize his troops.

The attacking force was, at last estimation, 1500 players and natives. Considering that the pass was being guarded by half that number, Thorn knew that they were in for a tough fight. Thankfully, the walls compensated for their deficiency in numbers. In the coming battle, the attacking force would be the one forced into action, while Thorn's force could simply wait behind their large walls.

"My lord, what are your commands?" Captain Del'har saluted, bringing Thorn's wandering mind back to the present.

"How would you arrange them, captain?" If Thorn had not been watching closely he would have missed the sliver of disappointment that flashed across the Wolfkin captain's eyes.

"The most common tactic would be to use the hunter units to clog the top of the wall during the assault while the Freemen and disciples are held back as a counter strike."

"Hm. Casualties will be too high that way." Thorn shook his head, immediately rejecting that idea. "Let's split the hunters into two groups. Get one group to cut long poles with forks on the end. Make them seven to eight feet long. The second group is to build some simple shields. Six feet high, four feet across. They'll need six-foot poles as well. Two per board.

"They'll hold the wall in rotations along with the Freemen. Our armory is well stocked so send them over to find armor and weapons. I've ordered extra arrows that we'll need to put out on the wall as well. Hopefully our diversionary tactic will give us a few more hours. We don't have long so we should get to work. Oh, and send the leaders of the Night Walkers to talk to me."

"Yes, my lord!" Executing another crisp salute, the captain whirled around and began barking orders, sending the army into a flurry of action. The Freemen began transporting bundles of arrows from the sub-level up to the wall, placing the stacks five feet apart the whole length of the wall.

Imbued with a sense of urgency by the captain's commands, half of the hunters from Greymane village rushed out of the Citadel to cut long poles from the forest while the other half began to hammer together simple plank platforms. After setting the two human groups into motion, the captain called over the leaders of the temple forces, meeting Thorn at the gatehouse.

“Hello everyone.” Thorn looked up from the map he was studying. “Please rise. We don’t have a lot of time, so I am going to keep this short. The main bulk of the fighting on the wall will be handled by the Freemen and the hunters. That said, I’m going to be putting a lot of weight on your shoulders. The Dusk Court has already been deployed, feeding us information about what the enemy is up to. They’ve been given strict orders to retreat before the enemy arrives, so I expect most of them will rejoin us.

“Once they come back, I’ll be deploying the Dusk Court in the towers. Disciples of the Dawn Court will be joining me atop the wall. You will be responsible for passing my orders among the army and maintaining morale. Remember that your fellow fighters are not trained combatants, so pay close attention to anyone that is starting to panic. You’ll be responsible for determining when the Freemen and hunters rotate off the wall.

“The Full Moon Court will be held in reserve in two groups. You can decide how you split, try to make it even. You’ll be stationed here in the gatehouse and will be responsible for clearing the wall if the enemy makes it up. You will also be the first line of defense should the gate be breached.” Pausing for a moment, Thorn looked over the determined faces of his subordinates. The thought that some of them might not live past the coming battle was beginning to weigh on him. With a deep breath, Thorn pushed the feeling aside and turned to the last group.

"Those in the New Moon Court will have the most difficult job. We will be using the beheading strategy, aiming to kill as many of the enemy officers as we can, specifically targeting the native officers. Don't bother with the travelers initially, we want to cripple the enemy's native support as much as possible. I want to split you into three units. Two groups will leave the citadel before the enemy arrives. If the chance presents itself I'll give a signal and they'll assault the enemy headquarters, aiming to take the heads of the enemy generals and destroy any supplies the enemy camp has. The last group will stay in the citadel and will ambush any leaders that come to fight against me or any of our other leaders."

After talking through the details of their deployment, the Wolfkin left the gatehouse to organize themselves, leaving Captain Del'har, Velin, and Thorn alone above the gate. Mina had run off with Akira to supervise the hunters who were cutting the long poles. Seeing Thorn's furrowed brow, Velin started to pat his shoulder and then hesitated, her hand hovering in the air for a moment before it dropped back to her side.

"What are you worrying about?" she asked instead.

"This is going to be tough. The wall is a huge advantage since they are not expecting it. In fact, I think surprise is our biggest advantage. My main concern is how to delay them. We need to hold out for three days but I'm worried that we are not going to be able to survive a direct confrontation."

"Correct. To breach the walls or the gate, the Crimson Snakes will need to build ladders or a siege tower." Velin nodded, pointing at the forest outside the pass. "They have ample supplies as well, so I don't expect it to take more than a day for them to construct something. We can use the poles to deal with the ladders, but siege towers will be a problem."

"We will have to do our best." Thorn felt more and more was slipping from his control, a feeling he did not like.

"My lord, the scouts are back." Captain Del'har spoke in a low voice.

Striding over to the parapet, Thorn looked out over the entrance to the pass. Rushing from the forest, the sixteen Dusk Walkers that had been deployed to track the enemy army headed directly for the front gate. The Wolfkin were naturally tall and lean in form, making them suited to cross distances quickly, but this was the first time Thorn had seen them moving that fast. In the time it took him to arrive at the edge of the wall, they had already crossed half the distance to the citadel.

One side of the massive gate opened a crack, enough for the Dusk Walkers to slip inside. Captain Del'har had hurried down to meet the scouts and soon returned with the two scouts that Thorn had worked with when he and Mina had gone to try and distract the enemy army.

"My lord." The Dusk Walkers saluted, their hands over their chests.

"I'm glad to see that everyone made it back." Thorn smiled warmly at them, equally happy to see that they followed his directions to retreat. "What did you find?"

"The enemy is still progressing toward the southeast, though I expect that they will turn back toward this direction within half a day."

"When should we expect them to arrive?"

"A conservative estimate would be within four hours. However, the army moves much slower than we do, so there is a chance that it will take them longer."

"Let's stick with the conservative estimate. Captain, please pass the word that we are to be finished with preparation within three hours. The sooner the better. I want everyone to be in place within the hour. Organize a squad of hunters to pass food out to everyone at their stations."

"Yes, my lord." With a crisp salute, the tall Wolfkin officer bounded out of the gatehouse to give his orders.

"What else did you find?"

"The closest count we could get of the enemy army was around 1700, sir. The first fifteen hundred were as we expected. We counted 250 travelers with the Crimson Snake guild symbol, 250 other travelers who looked like guards, and 1000 native soldiers, with standard equipment. In addition, there were 200 other travelers, who wore a different symbol." The Dusk Walker handed over a piece of paper with a sketch of the symbol.

Drawn on the paper Thorn saw a snake, drawn in a figure eight, its mouth holding its tail. Through the center of the figure eight was a sword, its pommel shaped like a dragon's claw. Handing the sketch to Velin, Thorn raised his eyebrows.

"Blood Guard," the slim elf said quietly.

"Ouroboros' group? Why would they be here? Didn't you say that his territory is further south?"

"Yes, he holds the region below this one. I'm not sure why he would have sent soldiers to support Angdrin. As far as I know they are in direct competition." Velin pulled her notebook out and started to thumb through it. "Give me a few minutes to think about it."

"Sure." Thorn dismissed the scouts after hearing the rest of their report. Once they had left, he leaned on the stone parapet, looking out over the entrance to the pass, a feeling of disquiet bubbling up in his heart. Over the last few weeks,

Thorn felt as if he had been barreling along, tossed ever quicker by the momentum of things outside his control.

As his eye ran over the woods that had been cut back by the hunter squads, he idly wondered if the citadel below him had been a subconscious attempt to place down something immovable. There was so much going on in Nova Terra that it was honestly overwhelming.

“Ah, it is the Wolfkin!”

“Pardon?” Shaken from his musings by Velin’s exclamation, Thorn straightened up and looked at the elf who was scribbling furiously in her notebook.

“The Blood Guard are here because of the Wolfkin. Ouroboros’ new class is tied to the Wolfkin race, like your title is. It is highly likely that his advancement requires him to increase the corruption of the race as a whole, since his backer, Karrandras, the Betrayer, has been trying to do that.”

“If that is true, doesn’t that mean that I am destined to have to fight against him?”

“Certainly. Though it would be more accurate to say that you are destined to battle his influence. It looks like you are two sides of a scale, seeking to draw the Wolfkin to your side. He is trying to bring out their bestial nature through the influence of Karrandras, while you are trying to bring out their civilized nature through the influence of Hati.”

"Well, I'd say I'm winning so far."

"Correct. However, you have yet to face him directly." Pausing slightly, Velin stared into the distance, as if remembering something difficult.

"Even if I do, I'm confident in my combat ability."

"I'm not worried about your combat ability." Velin's eyes met Thorn's, taking him aback with their intensity. "However, you will not only be competing to see who has the hardest fist. Your entire being will be weighed against his. Winning this conflict will require you to face off against his charisma, his leadership ability, and his influence."

"You don't seem confident in me." Thorn joked, trying to lighten the mood.

"Thorn, you are a gifted individual, but you are going up against the soon to be leader of one of the largest, most influential guilds in the game. It is not a matter of being confident or not. Please understand that I am on your side completely. However, that doesn't mean that I am going to pretend that you have the advantage in this coming conflict. Ouroboros is smart, careful, an outstanding player, a charismatic leader, and he wields serious influence in this game through his position in Ragnarok. You are in for a difficult fight."

As Velin talked, Thorn grew quiet, his head bowed. She was right, it was going to be a difficult fight. Yet, was he really that disadvantaged? Slowly, Thorn had begun shedding many of the mental restrictions that he had brought into the game. He had begun to lose some of the social constraints that he had been raised to follow, shaking himself loose from their hold. More and more, he was feeling comfortable leveraging his advantages without worrying about what was fair.

“It may be difficult, but I will win.” Raising his head, Thorn took a deep breath, his already large form seeming to grow and fill the whole room. “Let them come. What is mine will stay mine, and no matter how impressive Ouroboros is, he will gain nothing more from me.”

CHAPTER FOURTY-THREE

“And you did not think that it might be a distraction?” Furious, Angdrin glared at his two lieutenants. “You lost two scouts so you redirected the whole army? Are you kidding?”

Abashed, Korith and Telis stood in front of their raging commander, avoiding his burning gaze. Korith started to speak up, to point out that they had lost three scouts, but Telis tugged on his arm, silencing him. The motion did not escape Angdrin’s gaze, causing him to break out into another string of curses.

Angdrin had caught up with the army a few hours ago and immediately made them pitch camp. They had chased Mina for hours but failed to find her or the valley. By the time the leader of the Crimson Snakes had arrived they had wasted the whole day, causing him to fall into a towering rage.

“I told you where the valley is! What in Gaia’s name made

you think it was a good idea to change directions? Now we won't get to the valley till tomorrow, putting us behind. And worse, you make me look like an idiot." As he was about to start cursing again, the sound of footsteps approaching the tent made him swallow his words.

The tent flap was pushed back and a heavily armored player entered, removing his helmet to reveal his handsome face. His well-formed features held a pleasant expression, naturally drawing in those who saw him and immediately defusing much of the tension in the room. Yet the perfect picture was somehow ruined by the trace of ruthlessness lurking in his eyes.

"It looks like you are having some trouble."

"My trouble is none of your concern, Ouroboros!" Angdrin spat, turning his attention away from his disappointing underlings.

"This concerns the future of the guild, Angdrin. Of course I am concerned." Ouroboros smiled at the two disgraced lieutenants, indicating for them to leave with a slight tilt of his head. Thankful for the chance to escape, Telis and Korith left the tent as quickly as possible, their gratitude evident in their faces.

"I have it under control." Doing his best to control his fury, Angdrin sat down on a chair, and poured himself a glass of wine. Tossing back the full cup, he filled it again, not bothering to offer any to his competitor.

“I’m glad to hear that. Look, I’m not here to fight with you over this achievement. I know you probably don’t believe me, but I really do want you to succeed. Sylith is too strong for either of us to fight so our only chance is to support each other.” Walking over to the table, Ouroboros took the jug of wine and filled up Angdrin’s now empty cup. “We gain nothing by constantly being at each other’s throats. I heard you encountered some of my old companions, so I thought it would be appropriate for me to come and help you deal with them. And maybe mend a few bridges along the way.”

Staring into Ouroboros’ handsome face, Angdrin could not help but begin to waver. There was a certain magnetism to Ouroboros’ words and actions that made him want to go along with what Ouroboros said. The words of agreement were about to escape his lips when he growled, slamming his cup down on the table, sending wine splashing everywhere.

“Ha, don’t try tricks on me! I’m warning you. They will not work.”

“Hmm?” Ouroboros appeared taken aback by the outburst, his brow furrowing. “Oh, right. I’m sorry. I’m still having trouble controlling my aura. It wasn’t intentional.”

“I’m sure.” Angdrin stared at Ouroboros through narrowed eyes. Ever since the former Holy Guardian had gained a quad category class, his influence in Ragnarok had exploded. In part, it was due to the potential that his new class afforded him, attracting the attention of the elders who truly ran the guild. However, even more dangerous to Angdrin was the alluring aura that Ouroboros now carried.

A devilish air hovered around the Exalted Devil Blood Berserker, lending a coercive strength to his every word. Ideas that used to be easy to ignore now wormed their way into the listener's mind, slithering past defenses and common sense. The effect was subtle, hard to spot, and even harder to resist. It was only when Angdrin received a message from Velin, Ouroboros' old advisor, that he was able to understand his competitor's swift rise to power.

"Look, Angdrin, let's put our cards on the table. I see you as a valuable ally and I don't think there is any good reason for us to be in competition." Ouroboros smiled disarmingly at the leader of the Crimson Snakes. "Let's talk this through. And, if you're not happy with it by the end of our conversation, we can go our separate ways."

"Fine. You have five minutes." Knowing that he could not escape the conversation, Angdrin drained his cup again and placed it on the table, fixing his stormy eyes on Ouroboros' handsome face.

"That is fair. Look, you are in a bit of a bind. From what I understand of the situation, you lost some important items to a thief. We're all familiar with Mr. Oberlin Danihoff, the third, but what was out of my estimation was that he somehow connected with Thorn, one of my old party."

"A companion that you betrayed," spat Angdrin.

"A foolish player who was at the wrong place at the wrong time." Ouroboros corrected. "Now, to top it off, it seems that some of my old companions have rejoined with Thorn and Oberlin and are competing with you for control of a valley with quite a few natural resources and a respawn point for a new race. To make matters worse, they seem to have found the valley before you."

"Thanks for the summary. If you're here to rub this in my face then you can leave. Now."

"No, I am here to help. To help you, to help myself, and to help Ragnarok. Look, I don't care about the valley. It is in your region so if I gain control of it I'd have nothing but trouble. I came here because I can help you deal with Mina, Velin, and even Thorn."

"You can deal with them? Are you kidding me? Have you ever seen that guy?" Angdrin scoffed, pouring himself more wine.

"Yes, I have. I'm confident that I can take him down. Size is not everything, and I've spent enough time with him to know his weaknesses."

“Haha, I don’t know if you are cocky or an idiot.”

“Why are you so cautious about him? He’s a giant noob. You should be much more concerned about Velin and Mina.”

“Oh, sure. Both of those girls are quite dangerous. Mostly thanks to you, might I add?” Angdrin shot Ouroboros a pointed look. “But they are nothing compared to the walking tank. I watched him throw a wagon at five of my men, crushing them. A wagon. Did I mention that he popped my bubble with his bare hands? If Telis had not burned a finishing blow, he would have popped me with it!

“That ‘giant noob’ killed almost thirty of us without breaking a sweat. I don’t know what you did to him, but whatever it was created a monster. An absolute monster. He is literally a walking boss. And I mean that in every sense of the word. He has crowd control, a rage ability, ranged and close combat attacks, and insane defense. If I didn't know better, I would have assumed that he was a native. You can fight him all you want, but I don’t want a single piece of him.”

“You make him sound much scarier than he actually is. Believe me, I spent quite a while with him.”

“Whatever you say.” Since Ouroboros did not want to listen, Angdrin abandoned his attempts to communicate how dangerous Thorn was. “What do you get out of this? If you are not here for the valley, what are you after? I don’t believe you’d help me for free.”

"Of course not." Ouroboros ran a hand through his hair, flashing a smile. "I want your trust. I want you to see that we don't have to be enemies. That we can work together."

"And?"

"And, I want you to work with me against Sylith and the Silver Guard." Holding up a hand to stop Angdrin from interrupting him, Ouroboros continued. "I know, we are both trying to become the guild leader of Ragnarok. But hear me out." As the sun set, painting the tops of the trees in pink light, the two commanders continued to talk, negotiating the details of their cooperation.

The same pink light shrouded Moon Wolf Citadel in its soft glow, reminding Thorn of the massive cakes that his aunt would buy him for his birthday when he was younger. Currently, he was sitting on the balcony of the great room of the fortress, looking out at the last vestiges of light disappearing behind the mountains at the end of the valley. Sitting next to him on the wide balcony, Mina was feeding bits of pastry to Akira who seemed determined to eat every pastry in the game. Joining them, Velin shook her head when Thorn looked at her. Sitting on the blanket on the other side of Mina, the elven War Priestess frowned.

"We still have not seen them. I almost suspect your diversionary tactic worked."

“You say that as if it may not have.”

“I mean no disrespect, but it was honestly a foolish idea.” Velin rolled her eyes. “Any intelligent player would have ignored the distraction and continued on their route.”

“But was it? It worked, didn’t it?”

“Sure, but even a broken clock is right twice a day.”

“Haha, that is true. Hey, it was worth a shot and it paid off. We only need to hold on for two more days.”

“Why two days? What happens after two days?” Mina asked, looking between Velin and Thorn. Seeing the elf shrug, she turned her attention to Thorn.

“We’ve got friends on the way.”

“Friends? What friends?”

Towering over her, even sitting, Thorn smiled and patted Mina’s head. Ignoring her grumbles, he asked Velin how the preparations were going. According to Velin’s report most of their forces were now relaxing as they waited for the Crimson Snake army to arrive. After finishing his meal, Thorn called Akira, who climbed up his large frame to sit on his shoulder. Together, Mina, Velin, and Thorn toured the citadel, looking over the defenses.

Large wooden shields had been constructed and hauled up onto the wall, raised to defend against arrows. Each shield was supported by two poles and contained a few angled openings to allow for firing arrows at anyone who attacked the wall. Velin had been astounded to see a small groove built into the inside of the wall designed to take the weight of the shields off the soldiers.

Similarly, special grooves were cut into the top of the wall to allow for the long poles to be secured, making it difficult to lean a ladder up against the wall or to place a siege tower right up against it. When designing the citadel, Thorn had poured countless hours into making it as easy to defend as possible, not sparing a thought for how long it would take to complete such an intricate set of instructions.

Ultimately, the system simply did not care how intricate the design was. So long as the money and resources were there, the system would build it. On top of the wall, Freemen and hunters from Greymane Village sat between bundles of arrows, eating and laughing together. Scouts stood every fifty feet along the one-thousand-foot-long wall, watching the dark forest at the entrance to the pass for any sign of the approaching enemy.

Seeing that the forest was quiet, Thorn instructed them to come wake him up if the enemy army arrived and went to bed. He had ordered a custom-built bed through a carpentry shop in Fantasia and collapsed on it with a contented sigh.

The next morning, after a big breakfast and checking on the wall, Thorn decided to spend what time he had following up with the class he had gotten from Elder Havva back in the village. Figuring he should start with finding the other Dawn Court disciples to ask them, Thorn headed for the Temple district of the citadel.

Most of the disciples were either practicing their forms in front of the statue of Hati in the Temple district or chanting together to complete the morning lessons. The chanting caught Thorn's attention so he walked over to see what was going on. Thorn had joined the temple as a disciple and even chosen to study under the Dawn Court, but he had yet to attend any lessons or find out what his responsibilities were. The Temple Elder was leading the chanting class so Thorn stood nearby, waiting until the chanting had finished.

"Disciple pays his respects to Temple Elder."

"There is no need for you to greet me that way." Elder Havva shook his head. "Simply calling me Elder will suffice."

"Elder Havva, I am a disciple of the temple now. I should follow the protocol."

"Forget the protocol. Unless of course, you want me to call you Lord Greymane, the Moon Wolf, Avatar of the Great Night Wolf, every time I speak to you," chuckled the elderly Wolfkin, clasping his hands behind his back. "Of course, I also need to get on one knee when I say it."

“Please, please don’t.” Thorn recoiled in mock horror, waving his hands.

“Then call me Elder. Now, what did you need from me?”

“Certainly, Elder.” Thorn walked beside the Elder Havva as they made their way toward the fortress. “I was hoping that you could help me to understand the courts a bit better and that you could tell me more about how I am supposed to advance my class.”

“You chose the Court of the Dawn, hm?”

“Yes, I thought their abilities would come in handy in my other roles.”

“It was a good choice. You have natural presence which helps immensely with things like oration. The courts are relatively simple though not all their rules apply to you. You may study under any Dawn Walker who is interested in teaching you. Normally, a disciple would need to seek out a teacher and convince them to take them on as a student. As you are the current Greymane and the avatar of the Great Wolf, I imagine you will have the opposite problem.

“Thankfully, the Dawn Court fights more with their words than their weapons, so there shouldn’t be too much blood shed when the teachers are determining who will take you on as a student. Once this situation with the valley is resolved, take some time to familiarize yourself with the various teachers and they will let you know what you need to know regarding advancing your class."

"Thank you, elder. Hopefully we can resolve this fight quickly." Thorn smiled calmly.

"I'm sure you will. Remember, your enemies are not only those you see in front of you. Karrandras, the Betrayer, has long sought to dominate and enslave the Wolfkin race and your defeat of him in the trial should not make you complacent. In fact, it should make you even more wary of his attack. He excels at twisting desire to achieve his purpose and will not rest simply because you beat one of his minions."

As Elder Havva finished speaking Akira rushed over.

"Master, master, the enemies are here. They've arrived!"

CHAPTER FOURTY-FOUR

The morning shone bright on the Crimson armor of the army standing in neat rows in front of the Moon Wolf Citadel. It would have been a peaceful, artistic scene, with the army and the citadel presenting a sharp contrast against the wild mountains to the sides if it wasn't for the steady stream of loud swearing spewing from the commander's mouth as he stared in abject fury at the citadel wall.

“Is that Angdrin?” Mina nudged Velin.

“Yes, at least I think so.” The elf nodded, examining her notebook. “Though he is normally much calmer than this.”

Standing atop the gatehouse, Thorn watched the raging leader of the Crimson Snakes with interest. The enemy army had arrived almost an hour ago but had not sent anyone forward to negotiate. Instead, Angdrin had exploded with anger, swearing and throwing things as he raved. Thorn had not been exposed to much foul language growing up, so he was finding this episode quite instructive.

After a few more minutes another figure came forward, putting a hand on Angdrin's shoulder. Dressed in heavy black armor, with a full helm, Thorn could not identify who it was, though he felt immediate revulsion at the sight. Talking together, the two were far enough from the wall that their voices could not be heard, but it wasn't that difficult to figure out what they were talking about. After talking to the black armored figure, Angdrin stepped forward, his crimson cape billowing behind him.

"Greetings. I am Angdrin, leader of the Crimson Snakes, vice leader of Ragnarok. We wish to speak to the ruler of this castle."

"Steady, Thorn." Velin appeared at the giant's side. "He is trying to subtly threaten us."

"Don't worry. I know what to do." Thorn nodded to Captain Del'har who stepped forward.

"The valley is closed, traveler. Please go back where you came from." The tall Wolfkin leaned over the parapet, shouting down to Angdrin.

"We come in peace and bring many benefits. Consider well before you reject us."

"Peace? Then why do I see an army?" Scoffing, the Captain laughed at the Crimson Snake commander. "You are not welcome here. Take your soldiers and leave."

"You are making a huge mistake." Veins in Angdrin's neck bulged briefly as he struggled to keep his anger under control.

"Don't worry about us. The valley is closed."

Watching the captain disappear from the top of the wall, it was all that Angdrin could do to keep himself from rushing forward to smash the gate. With a visible effort he took deep breaths, calming himself.

"Was this part of your plan?" Despite all his restraint, he could not stop himself from snapping at the black armored figure as he walked back to the army. "A twenty-five-foot-high wall? Where did this castle come from?"

"I'm not sure, but it is certainly a mixed blessing."

"A mixed blessing? Are you serious? How could having a massive fortress blocking me off from my land be considered a good thing?"

"Sure, it is in your way now. But what about after you conquer it? It won't disappear, right? That means you will have a massive fortress. Imagine people's faces when you speak to them from atop that wall." Ouroboros' voice drifted softly around Angdrin, cooling his anger and hardening his determination.

"That is true. Per our agreement, the land and everything on it is mine." Angdrin looked at Ouroboros from the corner of his eyes. "That includes the fortress, right?"

"Of course it does. Like I said, I'm only here to prove myself trustworthy. The spoils will all go to you this time around."

"If that is the case, then we attack."

"You don't want to try negotiating one more time?"

"No." Angdrin was determined. "You know how stubborn natives are. The only way they will listen is with a sword through their gut." Lifting his hand, he was about to command his army to advance when the hair on the back of his neck rose and a sense of danger swept over him. "[Blood Shie…]!"

Whump

Angdrin had almost finished summoning his [Blood Shield] when a massive bolt from a siege crossbow ripped through the air, glancing off the half formed red orb in front of him, sending him tumbling to the ground. The bolt smashed into the ground, showering the area in dirt. It had come without warning and would have skewered Angdrin through his chest if he had not been instinctively moving to the side.

Even with his defensive ability, the sheer force of the attack glancing off his shield knocked him from his feet. Rolling over, Angdrin scrambled to his feet, looking around wildly. For a moment, the only sound in the pass was his ragged panting.

Creak

The clear sound of a crossbow being reloaded drew all eyes to the top of the gate where Thorn stood, his arbalest loaded and leveled. Silent, he stood there, his armor glinting silver in the morning light.

At the sight of the giant, Angdrin took an instinctive step back, watching him warily. It took him a moment to realize that the bolt was not even pointed at him. Thorn's arbalest never wavered, his large hands holding it as still as stone, fixed firmly on the player in black armor.

"The valley is closed." Thorn's deep voice brooked no argument.

"Thorn!" The fury that Angdrin had been trying so hard to restrain burst forth like a river through a breached dam, completely erasing any restraint he had possessed. "Charge! Kill them all!"

Responding with a roar, the Crimson Snakes surged forward into the pass, weapons drawn. A block of archers drew their bows, sending arrows flying toward the top of the wall to try and provide cover for the charging warriors. Behind them, healers began casting buffs on the warriors, trying to minimize as much damage as possible.

“Shields up!” Bellowed Captain Del’har, sending the top of the wall into a flurry of action. Lifting the large wooden shield, the soldiers rested one end in the slot cut in the wall and propped up the other end with the wooden poles that had been cut from the forest.

“Return fire!”

The Freemen archers stepped forward, their well-used bows drawn to the fullest. A sharp hiss rose as the arrows shot forward, falling on the charging warriors. Groups of four arrows targeted the same warrior, causing casualties immediately. Each group of archers contained four Freemen and two hunters. The leader of each group would call a target and all four archers would fire on the target, usually causing instant death. Next to them, the two hunters from Greymane Village would have arrows ready to hand them.

Wave after wave of concentrated fire poured from the wall, cutting down the Crimson Snake fighters. Ouroboros, seeing the shields go up, instantly knew that things were going to go poorly for the Crimson Snakes and called his forces back. Angdrin, oblivious to the damage being caused to his army, charged blindly forward, his elite squad surrounding him.

Seeing them run forward, Captain Del'har commanded four squads to focus fire on Angdrin's group. Twelve arrows shot out with deadly accuracy, each aiming for one of the warriors around the Crimson Snake leader. Almost instinctively, the four targeted warriors lifted their shields, knocking aside the arrows with ease. Seeing that the arrows would have no effect, the Captain commanded the archers to resume firing at the regular soldiers.

Thorn had kept his arbalest aimed at the black armored enemy who had not moved a single step from his original position. The black armored warrior gave Thorn a dangerous feeling. Seeing that he was still standing there, Thorn swung his arbalest toward Angdrin, watching for movement. Still, the black armored man just stood in place, watching.

Tearing his eyes away, Thorn aimed at Angdrin's advancing party and fired, sending the large bolt through the air. This time, Angdrin was ready and a quick chant raised a red swirling shield over the group. Splintering on the shield, the bolt exploded into shards, peppering the surrounding fighters with slivers of wood and steel. A second and third bolt soon followed the fate of the first, hardly slowing their advance.

By this point, the warriors had reached the wall and began to toss out grappling hooks, trying to gain purchase on the wall. As fast as they landed on the wall, the hunters would dash forward, severing the ropes under the cover of the archers. Back and forth, the two forces fought in a mad scramble to control the top of the wall. Near the front gate, Angdrin and his group stopped, the warriors keeping their shields up. Angdrin began to chant, his voice growing in power as the chant came to a climax.

“Velin, what is that?” Thorn asked, his voice carrying over the din of the battle.

“A movement spell, they’re coming up to the top of the gate.” Velin calmly pointed to a growing red dot in the air near them.

“Everyone retreat.” Thorn waved for the Wolfkin disciples that had crowded around to move away. “I don’t want to reveal any more strength than we need to. Mina, can you help me handle them?”

“Of course,” excited to be asked, Mina began to mutter under her breath, cold air beginning to surge around her.

The red dot expanded suddenly, sending out a rippling ring of burning heat. The area inside the ring rippled and Angdrin appeared, surrounded by his five guards with their shields up. Instead of the wall of weapons that they expected to see, they found themselves in a largely empty space, facing a charging giant and a metric ton of icy snow.

“[Avalanche!]” Mina’s spell created an abrupt snowfall over the group, slowing their movements and trapping them in three feet of snow. The burning temperature around them plummeted, reaching freezing in a matter of seconds, causing their weapons and armor to creak alarmingly as the temperature change strained the metal.

"[Burning Blood!]" Not to be outdone, Angdrin responded instantly, sending out a wave of heat to melt the snow, following it up by summoning three large fireballs, only for them to be pierced by a barrage of ice spikes. Seeing his fireballs fizzling out, Angdrin gritted his teeth. "Mina!"

"Hey, Angdrin? How is it going? Enjoying yourself these days? I heard that Ouroboros has been walking all over you. That can't be very comfortable." Somehow, the Ice Witch managed to keep up a steady stream of small talk as she summoned endless waves of ice spikes, forcing the Blood Mage into a defensive position.

"Shut up!" Angdrin squeezed the words out from between his clenched jaws as he maintained his shield. About to call for assistance, he felt a movement at his side and looked over in time to see one of his elite guards being blown off his feet.

As Mina had engaged Angdrin, Thorn charged forward striking out with his metal club. The warrior in his path smashed his sword on his shield, creating a thick red barrier on his shield's face. Tensing his muscles, he got ready to absorb the blow, planning on creating an opportunity for his teammates to counter-attack. Without needing to communicate verbally, the other warriors rushed forward, intending to strike as soon as Thorn's momentum was halted.

Unfortunately for the Crimson Snake warriors, nothing went as planned. Thorn continued to charge forward, his blow connecting with the blood colored shield. With a sharp crack that rang over the battlefield, the shield shattered and the force of the blow continued forward, blasting the warrior off his feet and over the parapet. Flying straight backward, the warrior did not begin to fall to the ground for almost twenty feet, going straight over the heads of the Crimson Snake army. Smashing into the ground, his body cut a furrow in the battlefield, tumbling over and over before exploding into particles of light.

Awestruck, the army looked up toward the top of the wall and witnessed two more of the elite guards following the same fate as the first. The last two guards looked at Thorn with horror, their minds trying to catch up to the fact that he had completely obliterated three of them. Before they could react, he was on them, cutting them down with a single sharp swing. Turning his head, Thorn's eyes landed on Angdrin, who flinched.

Taking advantage of the Blood Mage's distraction, Mina summoned a larger ice spear that thrust forward, punching through the blood shield. Wincing in pain as the ice spear scraped along his ribs, Angdrin panicked at the sight of Thorn striding toward him.

"[Blood Escape!]" With a shrill yell, the commander of the Crimson Snakes disappeared in a bloody flash.

"[Sub Zero!]" A split second late, Mina tried to stun Angdrin, causing the temperature where he had stood a moment before plunge to arctic levels. A large blob of blood that had not yet disappeared froze instantly, dropping to the ground where it shattered into countless pieces.

On the battlefield below, Angdrin appeared, stumbling to the ground. A large wound formed in his stomach, caused by the blood he left behind. Groaning with pain, he struggled to get up, staggering toward Ouroboros who still stood calmly in the same place that he stood since the beginning of the attack.

Mina, rushing to the edge of the wall grumbled. She had hoped to kill Angdrin in one blow but had been a split second late. Still, forcing him to retreat was not a bad result. Turning to Thorn who was looking quite impressed, she beamed.

"Ha, see that? He did not stand a chance."

"You were very impressive." Thorn had to admit that he had underestimated the short witch. Up to this point, he had only seen her fight as supporting ranged damage. However, in this fight she had stepped up and acted as a direct combatant, dueling Angdrin directly.

"See that you remember it the next time you assign tasks." Mina nodded smugly. "Hey, look over there. Something is happening with that armored guy."

At the entrance to the pass, Ouroboros finally moved. Stepping forward, he supported Angdrin who was about to collapse, while waving for a healer. Putting his arm around Angdrin's shoulders to steady him, Ouroboros led him away from the castle wall.

"A healer is coming. Rest up for a moment and you will be good as new." Ouroboros' voice was calming, causing Angdrin's tension to bleed out of him. Opening his mouth to speak, he suddenly choked, coughing up a mouthful of blood. Unable to see the smile on Ouroboros' face because of his helmet, Angdrin struggled to speak, his hand landing powerlessly on Ouroboros' chest plate. Losing strength, his hand dropped, leaving a bloody streak as it fell.

"His wounds are too grievous. It looks like they used a powerful poison." Ouroboros spoke with sorrow in his voice as he laid the now powerless Blood Mage on the ground. The approaching healer cast her spell, but to no avail. She could only watch, helpless, as her leader disappeared into particles of light.

"Collect his belongings and sound the retreat. We need to regroup." Ouroboros looked at the citadel blocking the entrance to the valley as he slipped the dagger in his hand back into his inventory. "But fear not, I will lead us to victory on Angdrin's behalf."

CHAPTER FOURTY-FIVE

Like a crimson wave, the attacking army pulled back, retreating out of range of the arrows that continued to rain down on them. Watching them go, Captain Del'har began organizing the defenders, taking stock of the wounded and ordering more arrows brought up onto the wall. After settling everything, the tall Wolfkin met with Thorn and the girls in the gatehouse where they were watching the remains of the Crimson Snake army.

"My lord," the captain saluted, "we eliminated approximately two hundred of the enemy. We also managed to kill the Crimson Snake leader and a group of five elite guards."

"What were our losses?" Velin asked from the side, ready to jot down the numbers.

"Two dead, fifteen wounded, Lady Velin."

“Hmmm, that's not bad.” Thorn turned around to look at Mina. “It seems that you took a bigger chunk out of Angdrin than you realized.”

“No, I don’t think so.” Surprisingly, Mina did not take the credit like she normally would. Her eyes remained fixed on the tent that had been set up outside the pass for the black-armored figure. “My spell did not hit enough of him to be lethal. He should have gotten healing before he died. That black-armored guy must have done something.”

Taken aback by the uncharacteristic seriousness in Mina’s voice, Thorn followed her gaze to the tent.

“Why would someone harm their team...” Thorn’s voice stopped abruptly, but he couldn’t stop his last words from echoing. As the deep voice faded away the gatehouse grew quiet. “It was a stupid question.” After an awkward moment Thorn chuckled. He knew exactly why someone would conspire to harm their teammate.

“It is not a stupid question, though it is a bit silly.” Velin walked up next to Thorn, pushing her hair behind her ear. “Rather than ask why, we should ask, ‘for what’ would someone harm an ally. That would undoubtedly depend on who their ally is.”

“Point taken. If Angdrin is a member of Ragnarok, the only person who would be willing to betray him would be someone of equal standing. And, given his pretentious nature, the only people that he would consider of equal standing with him would be the other leaders of Ragnarok. That is Ouroboros, isn't it?"

Hardly able to breathe because of the stifling air that had settled over the gatehouse, Mina poked Thorn in the side with an ice spike.

"We are not your enemies, big guy. You don't have to crush us." She complained.

"Hmm? Oh, sorry." Thorn took a deep breath and the atmosphere lightened considerably. "I'm not sure why that keeps happening."

"What are you going to do if it is Ouroboros?" Velin asked, her eyes carefully watching Thorn's face.

"You know? I don't know yet. Probably hit him. Maybe a couple times. But I don't know. I guess we'll find out when we confirm who that is. Until then, let's keep defending."

"Speaking of defending, I have some bad news." Velin flipped closed her notebook, storing it in her inventory. "It is highly unlikely that we will be able to maintain this sort of kill to death ratio moving forward."

"Yeah, I'm aware." Thorn nodded.

"Well I'm not," Mina pouted, glaring at Velin and Thorn. "I

hate it when you talk in code."

"No problem, we can dumb it down for you." Thorn grinned at her and then immediately ducked to avoid an ice spike. Laughing, he explained, "That was an anger fueled attack. No plan, no purpose other than grinding us away. Add to that their lack of ability to get up the wall and it makes sense that it was so one sided. Maybe if Angdrin and his squad had been able to break through and open the gate it could have worked."

"Correct. That is the primary method that the Crimson Snakes employ. Angdrin and his team do the heavy lifting while the rest of their forces act as slightly above average fodder." Velin chipped in.

"Too bad for them, they met us." Mina gloated, giving Thorn a high five. "But what does that change? We still have a really defensive position."

"That is true, but if you look out past their camp you can see they are starting to clear trees." Thorn pointed toward the entrance to the pass. "Chances are that they are building ladders as we speak. Possibly even siege towers. The next time, their goal will be to move the fight from the bottom of the wall to the top of the wall. Our defenses will not allow them to achieve that goal easily, but if they do, they will have an absolute advantage.

"They not only have a larger number of soldiers than we do,

but they have a solid core of players who are better than almost any force we have. Expect the next fight to be bloody and difficult. The only plus side is that it will probably take them at least a day to finish building the siege weapons, which gets us a day closer to our goal. Honestly, as long as we can make it through tomorrow I think we should be okay."

"Have you figured out a way to get Ragnarok to back off?" Velin's normally impassive face lit up.

"Yeah, I think so. It is a bit of a gamble, but I'm pretty sure it should work. We will find out tomorrow night, though for it to work we need to maintain control of the valley, which means keeping the control point. So, let's make sure we keep them out." Taking a deep breath, Thorn had a hard time keeping the smile off his face.

Tomorrow would be the final showdown, the final fight for the valley. If he could keep control of it, he would be paving his path in Nova Terra. If he lost, everything he had worked for so far would evaporate. "All the cards will be played tomorrow, we will have to wait and see how they fall. But I'm getting ahead of myself." With a wave, Thorn left the girls and went to find Elder Havva. There was much to do.

Later that night Thorn stood on the wall with the Elder, the captain, and both girls. He had been trying to explain to Mina why she was not coming with him to raid the enemy camp.

"Mina, you are not stealth based." His attempts were not

going well.

“Oh, like you are? Look Velin, it is a super sneaky giant. Don’t worry, if he stands still people will mistake him for a tree on account of his giant head. He can blend right into the forest.”

“Mina, Thorn is in charge so if he says you are not going, then you are not going.” Velin did her best to keep the corners of her lips from curving up.

“Mina, I need you here so you can help me get back into the citadel without having to open the gate. I’ll need you to create stairs or something for me to climb. This is serious so stop messing around. If you can’t do it then I’ll come up with a different plan.”

“But why does Velin get to go?”

“So I don’t die. You will see plenty of action tomorrow, but right now I need you to follow directions.”

“I…” Thorn was trying to be as patient as possible, but the rough edge of his annoyance must have peeked through his slow speech because the response on Mina’s lips died out and she looked away. “Fine, I’ll stay here.”

“Thank you.” Thorn rubbed the bridge of his nose as he thought through the plan. “Velin, you’re with me. We might need to make a quick getaway, so my apologies if I pick you up without your permission. Captain, you are in charge of the wall until I get back. If something goes wrong and I don't make it back, hold for as long as you can. Alright. Let's go."

Grabbing the slim elf around the waist, Thorn placed a hand on the edge of the wall and casually hopped over the edge. Keeping his grip on the wall, he waited until he was hanging fully before he let go, sliding down a few feet and then pushing off to land on the ground. As he put Velin down he couldn't help but wonder if he would be able to completely encircle her waist with two hands. Shaking away the errant thoughts, Thorn walked toward the Crimson Snake camp.

From the flurry of action at the camp, it was obvious that the sentries on night watch spotted him. The flurry of activity only expanded when Thorn unrolled a giant white cloth, waving it above his head. Soon, a couple hundred Crimson Snake soldiers and players had circled him, holding weapons. Thorn was amused to see that they stood at least thirty feet away, well out of reach, and even maintained that distance as he advanced.

Holding the white cloth, Thorn strode toward the Crimson Snake camp, slow enough that Velin did not have to run to keep up. The jostling crowd of players and natives that surrounded them struggled slightly to maintain the proper distance from him as he moved, causing him to smile. By the time they arrived most of the camp had been woken up and was gathered to watch as Thorn and Velin entered.

"Hold. Are you here to surrender?" One of the Blood Guard held out his hand for Thorn and Velin to stop.

"I would like to speak to your leader. Please take me to him." Thorn made no effort to control the volume of his voice, and his deep rumble woke those who had not yet gotten up.

"There is no..."

"Take me to your leader." The full weight of Thorn's presence fell on the Blood Guard, causing him to shrink back slightly, his face paling. Before he could fall back more than a step, a hand fell on his shoulder, steadying him. Stepping out of the shadows, the black-armored figure gestured for Thorn and Velin to follow and made their way to the tent in the center of the camp.

"Be careful." Velin whispered as she watched the figure in front of them, a note of fear in her voice. "I'm almost 100% certain that is Ouroboros. His quad category class is incredibly powerful. We need to avoid a direct fight if possible."

"Relax, we are here for a chat."

"I'm afraid that we will not be the ones deciding that soon."

A crimson tent sat in the center of the Crimson Snake camp. The golden symbol of the Crimson Snakes adorned the tent flaps but it was two Blood Guard players that stood outside guarding the entrance. Not bothering to see if they followed, the black-armored figure walked inside. Ducking to follow them into the tent, Thorn was surprised to see how comfortably furnished the tent was. Much larger on the inside than the outside, the tent was divided into multiple richly furnished rooms.

A thick carpet covered the floor of the tent and elegant furniture dotted the main room. A large, throne-like chair with the symbol of the Crimson Snakes carved into the back dominated the far end of the room and the black-armored figure walked toward it, taking off his helmet and tossing it onto a small table. Sitting down, Ouroboros stared at Thorn and Velin, his face glum.

“Please, have a seat.” Sighing, he rubbed his face, as if he could rub away his frustration. “Would you like anything to eat or drink? I believe there is some wine around here somewhere.”

“No, thanks. And it may be better for your furniture if I stay standing.” Thorn chuckled.

“Eh, suit yourself. It isn’t my furniture.” Ouroboros shrugged. “If you are not here for a drink, what are you here for? Only a fool would believe that you are going to surrender, but only a fool would walk into their enemy’s camp alone. So I must admit, I’m at a loss as to what to think about you.”

“Haha, that is a pretty fair assessment.” Nodding, Thorn

examined Ouroboros closely. He had been torn about how he would feel facing the person who had orchestrated his betrayal, but he found that he had been entirely wrong. Thorn had been sure that he would have trouble controlling his anger when he finally met up with Ouroboros. Instead, Thorn felt a strange apathy, as if Ouroboros was a stranger. The anger was still there, but it was slow, deep and burning.

"Look, I don't mean to suggest that we have to be enemies, but it would certainly seem like we have fallen on opposite sides in this conflict." On the large chair, Ouroboros leaned back, one of his fingers tapping his arm rest. "I took over this operation until Angdrin returns. And it is hard for me to give up guild business like this. Why don't we work something out that will work for both of us? Once everything with the valley is arranged, we could reform the team. I miss playing with all of you."

"That's it?" The coldness in Thorn's heart solidified into ice.

"What else is there?" Ouroboros spread his hands, confused.

"Disappointing." Somehow, Thorn's deep voice pierced Ouroboros, causing him to lower his hands, a flash of desolation crossing his eyes. His hands dropped to grip his armrests tightly, opening his mouth as if he was going to say something. Seeing his hesitation, Thorn suddenly felt a wave of fatigue wash over his soul. Shaking his head, Thorn spoke.

"We are here to discuss terms on behalf of Lord Greymane, the Moon Wolf, Lord of Moon Wolf Citadel. And to deliver a present." All friendliness was gone from Thorn's voice. "You are to take your army and retreat, as your current actions are unlawful. Per the ancient and just laws of the empire, you have intruded on the sovereign ground of a native race. Withdraw or face the wrath of the empire.

"Penalties range from paying reparations to execution of all participants. If you continue, your full guild will be forfeit. Given your lack of awareness of the laws, we will agree to not pursue any reparations for the damage your army has caused to this point, should you choose to withdraw. If you choose not to withdraw, we will prosecute Ragnarok to the furthest extent of the law.

"You have until nine o'clock tomorrow morning to pull your army back, taking nothing from the land that you did not bring, but removing everything you did. We will welcome a diplomatic group at the beginning of next week, but any other forces will be met with appropriate force. Those are the terms. And this is the present." Thorn placed the white cloth on the table, covering Ouroboros' helmet. "Given your history of making the wrong choice, I think it is likely that you will need this."

CHAPTER FOURTY-SIX

“Are you serious?” Ouroboros broke the silence that had fallen over the tent, his quiet voice cutting through the tension like a hot knife. “Why must you be so serious about this? Is there really no room to compromise? Look, I don’t know how you connected with Lord Greymane, but the ownership of the valley isn’t something that can be resolved like this. Ragnarok has invested a significant amount of money in this corner of Nova Terra and we cannot afford to give up on resources just because a native said we should.

“Believe me when I say that you don’t want to put yourself on the wrong side of Ragnarok. Not just because of the influence that the guild has in game. I know we talked about this before, but you don’t seem to have taken my words to heart, Thorn. This game is way more than a place to run around and complete fun quests. There are serious business interests tied into the economy of the game and behind the guilds are major businesses.

“They are not going to step aside because some NPC wants them to. This is even more true of the top ten guilds. Ragnarok has immense sway in the real world and it is not wise to try and stand in the way when they want something. I know our last interaction was not pleasant, but please have some understanding about your position in all of this. For guilds like Ragnarok, players are there to be used or run over. I’m choosing to be useful, and I hope that you will make that same choice. It is the only way for people like us to survive.”

Rising from his seat, Ouroboros walked closer.

“There are forces at work that are beyond your understanding. Forces that will not hesitate to apply pressure in the real world. Unbearable pressure. Don’t throw away your life simply because you had a negative experience. There is still time for you to join the right side, the side of progress and growth. There is always a place for strong players in Ragnarok and both of you are among the strongest. Why not join me? Give up this pointless struggle and join the Blood Guard. I can guarantee the best treatment, both in game and in the real world.”

“I…” Velin, who had been standing at Thorn’s side opened her mouth, a haunted look in her eyes.

“Velin, you left before we had a chance to have a good conversation.” Turning his attention to the elven War Priestess, Ouroboros held her gaze, his eyes full of sincerity.

"I am sorry I was so preoccupied, but you understand how much work building a faction is. Please don't throw away what we had because I was being stupid. I know I was not including you enough. I was stupid to think that I could do everything on my own. Since you and Mina left I realized how important you are to me. Please give me another chance." Staring into her eyes, Ouroboros stretched out his hand, pleading. "Please."

"I…" Velin's words caught in her throat, her emotions turbulent. Slowly, she lifted her hand, reaching for Ouroboros. A moment before they touched, a massive hand closed over her slim palm, enveloping it. The huge palm covering her hand was warm, causing Velin to realize how cold her own hand was. With a shiver she woke up from her daze, the warmth cutting through her confusion.

"Try to bewitch one of my people again and I will remove your head. Permanently." Thorn's deep voice was mild, yet somehow that made his threat all the more scary. There was an absolute conviction in his words that was as firm as stone.

Stepping back, Ouroboros stared at Thorn, his eyes hard. The soft, persuasive air that had surrounded him was replaced with a sharp, cold aura.

"That is your answer? You are going to put up a pointless struggle? You are going to willingly bring suffering on yourself and your companions in both the game and the real world? Your choice condemns them to death."

"I choose a life of my own. I choose not to be another's dog. And I choose to grant that to my companions." Thorn chuckled mirthlessly. "However, I would appreciate it if you would pass on a message for me. Tell your masters that they should keep the game in the game. Let real life be real life. Let Nova Terra be Nova Terra. You would do well to remember that as well. Lord Greymane's message has been delivered to you, and by proxy, your guild. You can make your choice accordingly. Either retreat and this whole thing will be written off or fight and pay the consequences." Still holding Velin's hand, Thorn turned to leave.

"If that is the case, why should I let you go?" Ouroboros' tone had taken on a dangerous edge. "What stops me from cutting you down where you stand?"

Stopping, Thorn looked over his shoulder and smirked.

"You will let me go because if I start a fight here you will have no chance of taking the citadel. Tomorrow, you will rely on your siege weapons, and we will rely on our wall. And we'll see whose is better." Without waiting for a reply, Thorn strode out of the tent, easily pushing aside the guards that stepped up to stop him.

Stumbling to the side the guards looked at Ouroboros who stood in the entrance to the tent, staring at Thorn's large back, his face inscrutable. Since their leader did not make a move the guards stood to the side as well, letting Thorn pull Velin out of the camp. Enemy soldiers gathered to either side, but they did not impede Thorn's path and soon Thorn and Velin reached the edge of the camp.

"That went better than I expected." Thorn muttered, his voice so quiet that Velin had to strain her ears to hear it. "But we're not out of the woods yet. Velin, I'm going to start moving quickly in a second. Be ready to heal."

Nodding mutely, Velin's mind couldn't help but stray, returning to what she had just experienced. When they entered the tent with Ouroboros, she had been on guard against him. She knew firsthand how easy it was for him to twist the truth, reversing black and white with a few words. Yet nothing had prepared her for how invasive his words were. It must have been a new class ability. His words had deadened her resistance, slipping past all her defenses and muddling her ability to think. Emotions that she had buried started to surface, casting her into an illusory world. Causing her to believe that he was telling the truth.

She shuddered. If Thorn had not been there... If he had not been able to withstand the corrupting influence of Ouroboros' words, she could not even begin to imagine what would have happened. Tightening her grip on Thorn's big hand, she was grateful for the warmth it brought.

"Hold on." His deep voice sounded and Velin found herself swept from her feet.

Lifting the slim elf, Thorn launched himself forward, instantly accelerating. Behind him, he could hear shouts of anger and panic. Not bothering to look back, Thorn summoned his armor and fixed his eyes on the wall of the citadel, focusing on nothing but reaching the wall. Behind him, a furious shout rang out.

"Thorn! Kill them!"

Ouroboros had watched until Thorn was almost out of the camp when a commotion caught his attention. Walking around the tent, Ouroboros looked toward the back of the camp where licking tongues of flame leapt into the sky. His eyes going wide at the site of the siege equipment they had spent all day constructing burning up in flames, Ouroboros lost it. Screaming out in rage, he roared out.

Thorn paid the shouts no mind and focused on running. This was the first time that he had truly tested his top speed since the game started and, as his stride lengthened the land under his feet flashed by. Velin, held to his chest, found herself having trouble catching her breath as the wind whipped by. Behind him the Crimson Snake camp had erupted into chaos as half of the camp rushed toward him and the other half tried to put out the burning siege weapons.

The pursuers raced after him as fast as they could but were unable to close the distance no matter how fast they ran. Soon a strung out line of Crimson Snake soldiers trailed

Thorn, trying to slow him with spells and attacks. Arrows pelted Thorn as he ran, most bouncing from his armor, spent after their long flight. Others stabbed into his back, chipping away at his health.

Chanting softly, Velin rested her hand on Thorn's chest, continuously healing him even as his health drained away. Soon the citadel's wall appeared in the charging army's sight and they noticed that Thorn sped up.

"Keep charging! We can break into the city when they open the gate!"

No one knew who yelled it first, but the cry was soon taken up by the rest of the pursuing force and the group plunged onward toward the wall. If the gate was opened to let Thorn enter it would never close fast enough to keep them from fighting their way in. And even if the gate was not opened, they would be able to cut Thorn down as he tried to climb the wall. Drawing their weapons they rushed forward with abandon.

Thorn started slowing down as he approached the wall. Moving as fast as he was, he thought that he could probably jump and reach the top of the wall if he kicked off it, but he was not about to take the chance. Who knew if his foot would go right into the wall at this speed? By the time he had managed to curb his speed the enemy army was almost right on top of him.

"Mina!"

"On it! [Ice Wall!]"

Rising from the ground directly next to the citadel's wall, a thick wall of ice shot upwards. Timing it so he stepped onto its rising top, Thorn launched himself upwards, grabbing onto the edge of the battlement. Below him the ice wall shattered, unable to bear his colossal weight. Hanging by a few fingers, Thorn grit his teeth. Lifted in his other hand, Velin was able to scramble up over the parapets and onto the wall.

Thorn groaned with the effort, but by swinging himself to the side he was able to get another hand on the wall and then pull himself up, all the while being pelted by arrows and spells. Three Dawn Walkers took over healing him from Velin, who had been healing him the entire chase. As he ducked down, below the edge of the wall, Thorn lifted his hand.

"Cut them down."

Freemen, Dusk Walkers, and hunters alike stood from where they had crouched below the edge of the wall, lifting their bows. Arrows tipped with rags covered in pitch were raised and set aflame, bathing the wall in a blaze of light. Crying out in shock, many of the Crimson Snake soldiers started to retreat only to see the flaming arrows arching over their heads. As the flame illuminated the pass the retreating players and soldiers were startled to see that the ground was still dark.

“Pitch! There is pitch on the ground!”

“Run!”

Pandemonium ensued as the arrows landed, igniting the ground that had been soaked in pitch. The fire spread quickly, helped by the low piles of brush that had been scattered across the entrance to the pass. As the flames grew they rapidly spread across the entrance, creating a solid wall of flame blocking the Crimson Snakes from their camp. Tendrils of flame reached out to caress anyone who tried to get near and thick black smoke filled the air. Soon the flames started following the ground, approaching the high wall of the citadel.

“Fire at will!” Captain Del’har’s voice rang out over the field, followed by the hiss of arrows cutting through the air. Screams of pain rose as the enemy soldiers tried their best to defend, but with fire approaching from one side and a rain of arrows from the other, they had few options. Gazing down on the chaotic field, Thorn was surprised to see that several players had formed small groups and were reacting well to the situation.

A few players guarded against arrows from the wall while the rest dug into the ground, trying to create a space free from pitch. Narrowing his eyes, Thorn drew his arbalest and focused, aiming carefully at one of the players who was guarding the others.

"Mina, I'm going to crack that group. Do you have range?"

"Yes, yes I do." The short Witch was currently standing on a box to help her see over the wall.

Waiting until Mina's chant was almost complete, Thorn took his shot. The bolt flashed through the air, smashing squarely into the shield held by the Crimson Snake player, nearly taking his arm off. Tumbling backward, he smashed into three other players who were digging as fast as they could, knocking the whole group down in a heap.

"[Blizzard!]"

Razor sharp icicles and snowflakes swirled into existence over the group of players, slowing them and cutting into their exposed skin. Taking advantage of their disarray, countless arrows showered the group, turning them into pincushions.

"Excellent, let's do that again. Captain, organize a squad to come with me and Mina and another one to help Velin. Velin, will that laser spell you have crack their defenses?" Seeing her nod, Thorn grinned. "How many can you shoot?"

"I can do five before I run out of mana."

"That should be good enough. Try to knock out healers and

any other casters. Mina, we're going to be moving up and down the wall, so jump up."

"Whoohoo!" Excited, Mina clambered up onto Thorn's broad shoulder, holding on as he made his way down the wall toward the next group of players. Between the attacks of the Night Walker groups on the siege equipment while he was talking to Ouroboros and the trap that they had set here, he was hoping to slow Ragnarok down for another day. Yet, despite how well both plans had gone, Thorn could not shake the feeling that tomorrow would be a bloody day.

"Let's focus on one thing at a time." As if sensing his distraction, Mina patted Thorn on his head, bringing him back to the present. "We need to cut down as many of the players as possible before they realize that they can retreat through the wall of flame."

"Yes, ma'am." Giving a sloppy salute, Thorn raised his arbalest as Mina's chanting filled his ears.

CHAPTER FOURTY-SEVEN

Dawn rose over Moon Wolf Citadel, the clouds painted a bloody red. The night had been long and the light revealed how much damage had truly been done. His face impassive, Thorn stared out over the scorched field that lay in front of the citadel wall. According to the scouts, the Crimson Snake camp was in shambles after the night time raid. Between the trap in front of the citadel wall and the chaos caused by the Night Walkers, the enemy had been reduced from 1700 down to 1100, with over 600 enemy soldiers falling.

The trap had taken down over four hundred and fifty soldiers who had died to arrows and spells. But the truly surprising thing had been the devastation caused by the Night Walkers who had claimed a full one hundred and fifty enemies through assassination during the chaos. Confused about how they had been so effective, Thorn had talked to Elder Havva who had showed him the poisoned dagger that all the

Night Walkers used.

A simple cut was enough to drop a player, especially when left untreated, and ingesting the poison only made it work faster. The Night Walkers had slipped through the crowds, ambushing players they found alone and wounding as many as they could. By the time that they were discovered, it was too late to save most of their victims and they slipped away into the darkness.

While the night had gone as well as Thorn could have hoped, he was still concerned. He had a nagging feeling that something was going to happen today. The Crimson Snake camp was still there, and the ringing of axes floating from the forest sounded the preamble to a bloody day of fighting. The sound had not stopped since the night before and siege towers were starting to rise at the edge of the pass.

“I guess we know what Ouroboros’ answer is.” Thorn remarked, to no one in particular.

“Was that ever in any question?”

Hearing Velin’s voice, Thorn glanced at her before turning back to watch the Crimson Snakes hurrying around.

“No, I don’t think it was. He made it clear where his priorities lie. And they are not with us.”

“They are not with Ragnarok either. Which is why he stood

by while Angdrin lost. This is the curse of power. Once you have it, you must keep it. And to keep it, you have to get more of it." Velin sighed, pushing a wisp of hair out of her face. "He was not always like this, you know."

"No?"

"No. He used to be quite gentle. But between the pressure from his family and a few key disappointments, he grew cold. Hard. He raised walls around his heart and learned to manipulate others into doing what he wants." Velin shivered, remembering Ouroboros' magnetic voice from the night before. "It seems like his class has added to his abilities. Be careful of him, Thorn. He gives me a really dangerous feeling."

"Yeah, me too. And it is highly likely that we have used up any possible goodwill that he had toward us last night." With a shrug, Thorn straightened up and stretched. "Time to eat some breakfast. I have a feeling we'll need quite a lot of energy today."

It was almost ten in the morning by the time the remnants of the Crimson Snake army marched on the pass again, this time with Ouroboros at their head. He had not bothered with a helmet this time and had replaced the Crimson Snake flags with his own Blood Guard flags. Of the remaining 1100 soldiers, two hundred of them were members of the Blood Guard, forming the most elite group in the army.

Dragging four hastily constructed siege towers with them, they stopped outside of arrow range. On the wall, Thorn, Mina and Velin stood with Captain Del'har, Elder Havva, and Horvir, the leader of the Freemen.

"This is going to be tough." Thorn pointed toward the siege towers. "The last attack was anger driven, without thought or plan. In fact, it is highly likely Ouroboros instigated it in order to get rid of Angdrin. Our raid last night went well, but we've only cleared the chaff. The true elite core of the enemy force is still there. Our advantages remain what they were previously, but those siege towers will be a problem.

"Thankfully, they were put together pretty quickly so they should not be that sturdy. Let's focus our attention on destroying them as fast as possible. Captain, we need four teams to target on the towers. Please organize those. You'll be leading one and Mina, Velin, and I will each lead another. Elder Havva, we will be committing our whole force to this battle. Please organize the remaining disciples that have not yet participated in two groups. I'd like to deploy them in the towers on the front wall to provide help clearing the wall should the enemy make it up.

"Our strategy will be fairly simple. We will do our best to ensure that the enemy does not get a solid foothold on the wall to try and delay them as long as possible. I don't have any illusion that we will be able to win a direct fight against their forces, so we should avoid direct combat as much as possible. However, if we can delay until this afternoon, we should be able to pull out the victory."

"We have reinforcements coming!" Mina's brow had been furrowed, showing how much effort she was putting into thinking about Thorn's words. As realization dawned, her face lit up with a smile and she shouted, as if she had discovered the greatest secret in the world. Seeing her so pleased with herself, the rest of the group burst into laughter.

"Correct, Oberlin is on his way." When the laughter had subsided, Thorn continued. "Alright, everyone has their orders. Let's take our positions. Horvir, please stay, I have a couple things I want to talk to you about."

"Yes, my lord." The leader of the Freemen saluted as the others split up to take their positions on the wall.

After a hushed conversation with Horvir, Thorn took his place on the wall with the others. Like the day before, the Freemen were spread along the wall in teams of four with hunters standing by to help. Today the disciples of the Temple of the Moon had also been deployed, hiding behind the large wooden shields.

"Steady!" Captain Del'har's voice rang out across the wall as the siege towers began to rumble forward. Unlike the mad rush of the last attack, the enemy army moved slowly forward. The first two rows of the army held shields in front of them, trying to provide the army with some cover against the waves of arrows that were sure to come. Behind them, the siege towers were being pushed toward the wall.

Due to their hurried construction, the towers were simply frames with three sides covered, leaving the back completely open. Each stood at thirty-five feet tall, ten feet higher than the wall and contained a drawbridge opening on the top. Built almost entirely of wood, the towers were effectively a one-use item, but should the attack succeed in breaching the wall, that would be enough.

“Steady!” Still, the captain did not give the order to fire, his eyes locked on the advancing troops. While the enemy had entered the maximum range of the Freemen longbows, the arrows would be spent by the time they had traveled that far and would deal little damage to the shield wielding soldiers.

Time seemed to slow and crawl by at an agonizingly slow rate. Despite the day being cool, Thorn felt a bead of sweat roll down his cheek. Unblinkingly he kept his eyes on Ouroboros’ dark-armored figure at the back of the enemy force.

Across the field, Ouroboros frowned. He had been hoping to waste some of his opponent’s arrows by baiting them into attacking his shield warriors but they had not fallen for it. The mysterious Lord Greymane had a competent military commander.

“Tell the vanguard to advance at normal speed. Our goal is to breach the wall as soon as possible, so hold nothing back."

"About time." The leader of the Blood Guard, a heavily scarred half-orc nodded, bloodlust rising in his eyes. "Advance! For Ragnarok!"

"For Ragnarok!" The shout echoed out over the pass and the whole army accelerated abruptly, sweeping across the field.

"Steady! Steady… Fire!" At the captain's command, hundreds of arrows arced over the battlefield. Immediately after the first arrow the archers reached down, taking a second arrow and sending it flying at the enemy. Sacrificing accuracy for volume, the defenders rained arrows down on the battlefield as fast as possible.

Thorn watched the enemy streaming toward the wall, a slight smile curling the corner of his lips. The arrows were not dealing much damage to the advancing soldiers, but really, that was not what they were there for. Thorn's slight smile blossomed into a grin.

The soldiers at the front of the charging army lifted their shields to ward off the falling arrows as they sprinted forward. In the real world, charging like this in full armor was a death sentence as they would be too tired at the end of the charge to fight, but in Nova Terra, their armor weighed almost nothing, enabling them to rapidly cover long distances and still operate at full fighting capacity.

Running forward at full speed, the first few soldiers felt something strange under their feet but were moving too quickly to shout a warning. With an echoing crack, a long trench, jaggedly cut, appeared underneath their feet, sending them plunging down into the earth. The soldiers behind them tried to stop as well, or if they couldn't, tried to jump over the pit, throwing their lines into disarray.

"Focus on the shields!" Captain Del'har shouted, directing the archers to target the shield warriors trying to cross the wide pits. Thorn had spent much of last night after the army's retreat quietly digging out a trench that spanned the width of the battlefield. Due to his strength and endless stamina, Thorn could move earth better than an army of diggers and it had only taken him six hours to litter the battlefield with traps.

The Dusk Walkers and hunters from Greymane Village had showed him how to stretch thin cloth over the trenches and scatter dirt and ash over them to make them blend in to the burnt ground. As soon as any significant weight was applied to them, the cloth would collapse, sending the person who stepped on them tumbling into the pit.

If he had the time, Thorn wanted to add spikes or something dangerous like that, but he had barely been able to finish before the plain began to grow light so he had to put that part of the plan aside. Still, he felt quite proud when he saw the enemy army falling into the deep trench. Six feet wide and eight feet deep, the trench zig-zagged this way and that, making it quite hard to determine where it began and where it ended.

The Crimson Snake army slowed to a crawl, the momentum of their charge stopped by the deep trench. While many of the soldiers who fell into the pit lost a good amount of health, few died in the trap, and soon a ragged line of shields formed on the far side of the trench, trying to block the arrows streaking in from the wall. With the added layer of protection, more and more soldiers climbed their way over the pit.

Almost one hundred shield warriors had fallen to arrows as they tried to climb out of the trench, but once the shield wall was re-established, the number of casualties began to fall. On the wall, Mina glowered. The trench had been her idea and she had hoped that it would take more enemies out.

“It was well worth it.” Thorn was all smiles. “The first trench will slow them down, the second will slow them down even more. Both were great ideas. Remember, our goal is not to kill them all, we need to slow them down.”

“Killing them all would slow them down.” Mina glared at the enemy army, her voice heavy.

Thorn looked at Velin, slightly concerned. The elf, catching his gaze, nodded and stepped forward, putting her arm around Mina’s shoulders. Giving her a squeeze, Velin pulled her away.

"Let's get ready for the fight. They will be here sooner than you think."

On the battlefield, the shield warriors had begun to push ahead again to make room for the rest of the army. Walking instead of running, they tested the ground for more traps, making detours around them when they were discovered. The large siege towers stopped before they reached the trench, pausing while soldiers began to collapse the sides of the trench to create a large bridge for the towers to be pushed over.

The ringing of axes graced the battlefield again and the bridge was soon reinforced by newly cut trees. Balancing the towers precariously on the bridge, they were pulled over. Spreading out again, the towers resumed their advance, pushing toward the citadel.

Ahead of them, curses began to ring out, mixed with laughter from the wall. Only fifty feet from the wall, the shield warriors had discovered another deep trench, though this one was a bit different. Rather than dropping straight down, this trench featured a long, sloped side that dropped more than ten feet down into the earth, ending abruptly with a ten-foot wall of dirt.

Short enough that the tower's exits were too high to be easy to use, the wall of dirt would require the ladders to climb. However, if the ladders were being used to climb up the wall of the trench, they could not be used for climbing up the citadel's wall until the whole army finished getting over the trench.

On top of that, the endless rain of arrows had not let up for even a moment and once they were within fifty feet of the wall, the shorter distance would make the arrows more dangerous. Not to mention, the whole army had heard about the magic from Mina and Velin the night before and fifty feet was perfect range for the Ice Witch and War Priestess' spells. Looking at each other in frustration, none of the officers wanted to be the one to order their forces to breach the dirt wall. Without a doubt, the group that did would get obliterated.

"Let our glorious leader decide." A grizzled looking native officer spat on the ground. Already upset by how many of his men had fallen, he had no interest in sending the rest to their death. Nodding, the others agreed and sent a soldier to call Ouroboros up to the front.

A few moments later, staring at the newly appeared obstacle, Ouroboros began to swear.

CHAPTER FOURTY-EIGHT

Without any other good option, the Crimson Snake army got to work trying to breach the dirt wall. Due to the height, Ouroboros commanded his army to focus on a single section, cutting into the dirt wall so that it would collapse. Packing the fallen dirt down, they dug into it again. As they repeatedly dug into the wall, a path began to emerge for the siege towers.

At the same time, a section of warriors was sent to each side of the battlefield, using the ladders to climb up in a bid to distract the defenders. The shield warriors, who had borne the brunt of the arrows as the army approached the citadel, had been greatly thinned out and the other soldiers quickly found themselves at the mercy of the archers on the wall.

Mina, running back and forth on the wall, dropped ice storms on the attackers trying to climb up the ladders. The swirling ice and snow slowed them down as they tried to organize a defense, making them easy targets for the archers on the wall.

Standing in the center of the wall, above the gate, Thorn and Velin discussed quietly what to do about the siege towers. Between fifty and sixty feet away, the path that was currently being opened for the siege towers would be finished within the hour, at which point the superior combat ability of Ragnarok's forces would begin to take effect.

Without the wall to keep them away, Thorn knew that his forces would not last long. If they wanted to win this fight, they would need to keep Ragnarok at a distance, which meant finding a way to destroy the siege towers.

"What do you think?"

"We need to destroy at least three of them." Velin scribbled furiously in her notebook, calculating the odds of success. "I would say that if we can destroy all of them, Ragnarok's chances of victory fall to below twenty percent."

"Still that high? What about if we don't destroy them?"

"One hundred percent. If we take out three of the siege towers, their chances of victory should be at around sixty percent."

"What makes you so confident in their success?" Thorn asked, curious.

“Ouroboros has not pulled back.” Velin sighed, putting away her notebook. “He is a cautious general and must have something that is giving him confidence. He would not stick around for this fight if he did not have a backup plan. But without an idea of what that backup plan is, we can only push forward and try to draw it out.”

“Then we better start. Fancy helping me start some fires?” Thorn smiled and patted a barrel next to him. Ten barrels lined up under the edge of the wall, dark, pungent smelling tar oozing from their tops. Thorn lifted the first barrel, carefully aiming at the closest siege tower. Drawing his arm back, he breathed out, steading his nerves. More than anything, this would determine their victory or defeat.

Offering a little prayer to Hati, Thorn hurled the first barrel. Turning over lazily in the air as it flew across the battlefield, the barrel fell slightly short. Whether from excitement or nervousness, he had not put quite enough power into the throw, and with a crack, the barrel landed on the edge of the dirt wall, spraying the ground that enemy soldiers were trying to smooth out.

“Close. Let’s try that again.” Thorn muttered to himself as he hefted the second barrel. The next throw hit the tower squarely, coating the side of the tower in thick pitch. “Haha, that’s what I’m talking about!”

With four towers to take down, Thorn’s goal was to hit each tower with two barrels. However, reality was not so kind and despite the initial success of his second throw, Thorn was only able to hit three of the towers. Vowing to himself to practice throwing in the future, Thorn stepped back with a sigh, motioning to Velin that the stage was set for her.

The War Priestess moved forward to the wall, lifting her staff up above her head. Muttering under her breath, Velin focused her attention on the three towers that had been covered in pitch. The Crimson Snake soldiers were trying to spread the towers out again, but it was proving difficult since they had to move them one at a time. As they pushed and struggled, a clear voice rang out from the wall.

“[Flame Storm!]”

Horrified, the soldiers scattered, running from the towers as fast as their legs would take them. Instinctively they knew what the target of the incoming spell was and none of them wanted to bear its wrath. Above the middle tower the clouds gathered into a vortex, spinning into a fearsome thunderstorm.

Yet instead of rain, large fireballs began to fall, impacting the tower and everything within forty feet of it. Smashing into the ground, the fireballs ignited the pitch, causing pitch covered towers to erupt into hellish infernos, burning so hot that the wood glowed white. With a series of bangs the towers bust apart as the abrupt change in temperature caused the water in the freshly cut wood to boil and expand rapidly.

"Oh, wow." Thorn stared, wide-eyed at the mass destruction caused by Velin's spell. Throwing a quick glance at her, he noticed that her face had become paler than normal. Concerned he stepped forward and took her trembling hand. "Are you alright?"

"Yes." Velin took deep, calming breaths. "I just overdrew my mana. I'll be fine in a couple minutes. But I probably will not be able to cast another [Fire Storm] for a few days."

"Not a problem." Glancing at the inferno burning in the middle of the path that the Crimson Snakes had been carving through the dirt wall, Thorn smiled. "One looks like it is going to be enough. We are in really good shape."

ding

"Haha, speaking of angels." Throwing a glance at the message he had just received, Thorn was so happy he almost started dancing in place. "Mina, get over here! Captain! Get ready to give the signal." Snapping out orders, Thorn supported Velin to the edge of the wall.

Below them, the battlefield was in utter chaos. Thick plumes of smoke rose from the burning towers, forming a haze over the whole field. Along the edges of the battlefield, the Crimson Snake soldiers struggled to climb the ladders and attack the wall under the endless torrent of arrows from the defenders.

Behind the burning towers, Ouroboros stood in front of his private soldiers, a strangely still island amid the chaos. Considering what sorts of countermeasures would allow them to breach the wall now that the path to the wall had been blocked, Ouroboros could only curse under his breath.

“Sound the retreat.” The Exalted Devil Blood Berserker’s voice was hard enough to sever iron.

Taking a horn from his hip, one of the Blood Guard blew three short blasts, signaling the end of the battle. Relieved soldiers streamed back, away from the wall, desperate to get out of arrow range. Watching his forces pull back like a tide, Ouroboros’ jaw tightened under his helmet.

“We regroup at the camp. As soon as the fires burn down, we assault again. This time, we’ll take the vanguard.” Sending a final cold glare at the figures on the wall, Ouroboros turned to go back to the camp when screams began to ring out.

The Crimson Snake soldiers had retreated as fast as they could back to the camp where they had collapsed on the ground. The assault had not gone well and those of them that had made it back were exhausted, physically and mentally. Yet their dreams of a rest were not to be. Moments after they made it back to their camp and sat down, two groups charged out and began to slaughter them.

From the forests an army of almost two hundred charged

out, cutting down anyone unfortunate enough to be in their path. Leading the charge were a hundred Wolfkin who sprinted forward in heavy armor. Crushing through the Crimson Snake soldiers, they opened the path for an even more brilliant group of fighters who followed right behind. As the attackers reached the center of the camp a brilliant figure flew over the heads of the charging Full Moon Walkers. Landing with a crash, a ring of blue flame burst out from them, cutting through the nearby enemies.

"Roses, charge!"

Under the cold eyes of the Full Moon Walkers, part of the force behind them suddenly accelerated, overtaking them in an instant. Sixty players pounced on the Crimson Snake army, wreaking havoc. A mystical light swirled around each of the women, connecting them together and giving them an ethereal air. Each had unique equipment and weapons, yet their movements were strangely coordinated, allowing them to cut down their enemies with ease. Within minutes the camp had been completely decimated as the Society of Roses killed off the remaining soldiers.

"Keep moving, ladies." The Queen of Roses strode through the camp, wisps of light tying her to all the other Society of Roses players. "We're not done yet." Above her head the flowing light solidified into a blooming rose.

Ouroboros, reading a message sent from one of the players at the destroyed camp, paled.

"Why are they here?" Unable to stop himself from losing his cool, Ouroboros shut his eyes, trying to calm himself down.

Hearing their normally unflappable leader mumble to himself, the Blood Guards looked at each other, concerned. With a deep breath, Ouroboros turned to look at the citadel.

"Well, gentlemen. It looks like it is time to attack." Ouroboros' voice was cold and bleak, yet the magnetic charm still ran under the surface, convincing those who heard it of the rightness of his words. "We have a seemingly impenetrable fortress before us, and certain death behind. I don't know about you, but I'd like to kill some people before I die, so we're going after the fortress."

"Sir, what..." One of the Blood Guards pointed at the camp that had fallen silent.

"The Society of Roses are here." Ouroboros cut him off, keeping his eyes fixed on the figure standing above the gate. Despite the distance, Ouroboros felt like he could see the giant's calm face.

"Society of Roses? Sir, there are two hundred of us. We should be able to defeat them."

"All of them. They are all here. Not a squad, not a group of them. All of them are here." Ouroboros pointed toward the blooming rose appearing above the smoking camp. "The only way to survive this is through the fortress."

"Oh…" The Blood Guard fell silent and then turned resolutely toward the Moon Wolf Citadel.

"Let's go." Not bothering to try and help the struggling remnants of the Crimson Snake forces, Ouroboros led his Blood Guard toward the citadel, even as the Society of Roses and Full Moon Walkers closed in from behind.

Standing in the gatehouse, Thorn watched the approaching force, his eyes lighting up as he spotted Ouroboros' black-armored figure. Next to him, Mina was pestering him with questions.

"Who is attacking Ragnarok? Where did you find players crazy enough to do that? Are these the reinforcements you talked about? Wow, check out those fireworks. Hey, is that…?" Trailing off in shock, Mina pointed a trembling finger at the decimated Crimson Snake camp where an ethereal rose had bloomed. Next to her, Velin nodded, her heart beating wildly. "AHHH! You know the Society of Roses!"

"Hmm? Yeah, I guess." His eyes fixed on Ouroboros, Thorn was having a lot of trouble keeping himself from jumping from the wall to attack. Holding tightly to the battlements, he breathed deeply, driving down the burning excitement in his chest that had grown almost unbearable.

"You guess? What do you mean, you guess?!" Mina was

hopping up and down in excitement. "That is the whole guild, too! Do you know how hard it is to get the whole guild to move? AHHH!"

"Mmhmm." Thorn was barely registering her voice at this point. It wasn't until he heard a crack that he realized he had manifested his claws, leaving thick gouges in the stone wall he had been gripping.

ding

Alpha Challenge
A powerful threat to your pack has appeared. You have identified the enemy in front of you as particularly dangerous to your budding family. Per the ancient traditions, you are responsible to face the challenger, or appoint a champion to face the challenger. Should you lose, you will lose your position as Greymane. Fight for the glory of Hati, for the glory of the Wolfkin. Failure: Decreased Wolfkin Loyalty Loss of Title: [Lord Greymane]

The quest served as the final push and without another thought, Thorn leapt the battlements. Startled by his sudden move, Mina and Velin dashed forward, their hands resting on the wall as they watched him jump down from it. With a massive boom, Thorn landed on the battlefield, sending a cloud of dirt and ash billowing. With a wave of his hand his massive metal spike appeared in his hand, leveled at the approaching Blood Guard.

Climbing over the wall of dirt, Ouroboros stopped in front of the gate, staring at the silver giant who stood in his way. Behind him, the Blood Guard gathered, spreading out into a half circle to surround Thorn.

“You’ve lost, Ouroboros.” There was no gloating in Thorn’s voice, just calm finality.

“Not quite yet.” Ouroboros’ voice was also calm. “There is one chance left.”

Striding forward until he was within twenty feet of Thorn, Ouroboros pulled a large, double-handed sword from his back, sinking it into the ground in front of him. Hanging his helmet on the pommel of the sword and flashed a winning smile at Thorn.

“I must admit, it never crossed my mind that there would be a wall here. When I found out that Angdrin had discovered the location of a new spawn point for Wolfkin I could not help but be tempted to seize it.” Slowly removing his gauntlets as he spoke, Ouroboros hung them on his belt. “When Karrandras whispered to me that this was a chance to control the Wolfkin race, how could I resist? But imagine my surprise when I arrive to find the valley that should have been open for plucking was hidden behind a giant fortress.

"And, only serving to deepen my surprise, who do I find guarding the fortress but my former companions? Poetic in a way. I used you and threw you away, yet you persist in a futile effort to stand in my way. I must admit, your spirit is commendable. Your spirit will not, however, help you here. Regardless of your struggle, as heroic as it might be, the valley will be mine. Not only will the valley be mine, but this fortress will be mine, and the Wolfkin will be mine."

Before Thorn could react, Ouroboros pulled a dagger from his belt, slashing open his palm.

"[Exalted Devil's Contract of Blood]."

CHAPTER FOURTY-NINE

Bright, crimson blood sprayed from the cut, swirling into the air as the ability activated. Gathering together, the blood began to sway, as if it was burning. With a flash of red light, the blood collapsed, revealing a shining parchment hanging in the air in front of Ouroboros. Spidery writing filled the parchment, yet when Thorn looked at it he was unable to see what it said because the words seemed to skitter to the edge of his vision. The feeling that the parchment gave Thorn was one of deep evil, sending a shiver down his spine.

"I, Ouroboros, initiate the sacred trial of combat under witness of the supreme contract." Under Thorn's gaze, the cut on Ouroboros' hand healed as he reached toward the floating contract. "Under the ancient laws, this trial of combat shall be carried out without interference from any third party. The penalty for interference is death." Ouroboros' words manifested themselves in blood red letters as he spoke, hanging in the air threateningly. “The wager shall be the life of the loser and free passage into the valley for the winner, without any interference from a third party. The stage shall be this battlefield. The weapons shall be the armaments of the participants.”

The words hanging in the air pulsed and separated, copying themselves. Shivering, they danced gently in the air, stopping in front of Thorn, as if to give him a chance to read them. As he began to look over them the world seemed to freeze for Thorn and the words morphed, turning into crimson chains that seeped into his body.

ding

The Cursed Life and Death Contract
You are the target of an ancient cursed contract created in the Lost Era, before even the gods walked the land. Due to the curse attached to it, this contract may not be refused and the terms of the wager are absolute. However, should the one who initiated the contract lose, they will pay double the price. Given the strength of your bloodline, you have the opportunity to change a facet of the contract. You may choose to increase the scope of the stage or increase the wager. Should you choose to increase the wager of the contract and win, the loser of the wager will pay double the

price.

Wager: Life and Death
Winner: 24 hours of safety while in Fang Valley
Loser: Death (normal penalties apply)

A cursed contract that could not be avoided. Thorn was almost upset by how game breaking this ability seemed, yet when he thought about his abilities he could not find it in himself to be perturbed. As one of the very few four category class holders, it made sense that Ouroboros would have incredibly powerful abilities.

His mind working furiously, Thorn examined the details of the contract. Its basic form was simple, a trial of combat, like the one he had faced in the Wolfkin village. With two participants, the trial would end when one of them died. Technically, they could surrender, but since the loser would die, it was effectively the same.

The prize of the trial of combat was simple, safe passage into and around the valley. That section was a bit confusing because of all the detailed terms, but as far as Thorn could understand, players would not be able to attack the winner of the trial in the pass or valley while their opponent was dead. This sort of immunity was very powerful as it would allow Ouroboros to escape from being surrounded and killed by Thorn's reinforcements.

Despite knowing that Ouroboros would be locked out of Nova Terra for 48 hours if he lost the fight due to the double penalty, Thorn wasn't satisfied. Ouroboros had achieved his current abilities by stepping on Thorn and being kicked out of the game for two days simply was not enough for Thorn's tastes. Making his decision, Thorn blinked, the world around him resuming its normal flow of time. Smiling grimly, Thorn stepped forward.

"By my rights under the ancient law, I, as the challenged, wager more than my life and safe passage. I, Lord Greymane, the Moon Wolf, wager my title, my possessions, my land. Winner takes all."

Thorn's deep voice had no problem carrying over the battlefield, eliciting gasps from those on the wall. Looking up at Thorn's wide smile, Ouroboros paused, his mind racing.

"Why bother with such a lame bet? If we are going to throw down, why not make it worth it? What do you think Ouroboros? If you win you can get everything. The valley, the citadel, even the allegiance of the Wolfkin. All you have to do is walk over me again." Spreading his arms, as if to take in everything around him, Thorn took another step forward. "Why are you hesitating? Don't you have the confidence to grab what you want here? All you have to do is beat me."

Behind the Blood Guard, a flickering, ethereal rose approached swiftly. As the flower apparition came closer the heavily armored guards shifted, facing outwards, their fidgeting revealing their nervousness. Rushing over to the wall, the Society of Roses stopped and their leader stepped forward, her sword raised. Just about to order the attack, she paused, as if she was reading something.

“Stand down, ladies. No fight quite yet.” Her brow furrowed, Julia turned her eyes on Ouroboros and Thorn. After a brief consideration she ordered her troops to move to the gate and strode forward, pushing past the Blood Guard who hesitated as if they did not know whether to try and stop her.

“Get out of the way,” her voice was ice cold, sending shivers down the spine of the Blood Guard in her way. For the briefest of moments it seemed as if the Blood Guard would not move and blood would be spilled, the air growing even tenser.

“Let them through.”

Looking gratefully at their commander, who ordered them to step aside, the Blood Guard stepped back, letting the Society of Roses pass by Ouroboros and Thorn and walk to the gate. Everyone who had entered the area had been notified that a trial by combat was about to take place and the commander of the Blood Guard saw no reason to fight until it was resolved. Besides, while the commander was confident in the group of players he had trained, he had no desire to face up against sixty of the best PvP combatants in the game.

Walking past Thorn, a few of the Society of Roses smiled and waved, greeting Thorn. The rest looked at him with unabashed curiosity, whispering to each other. Hearing the giggles and seeing the pointing fingers, Thorn shuddered internally. Only Julia stopped next to Thorn, bumping fists with him, the gentle tink of their gauntlets ringing across the battlefield.

At the sound, Ouroboros' pupils shrank and his smile faded. The motion was such a simple action yet somehow it managed to convey the depth of the relationship between Thorn and Athena, the Queen of Roses. As the sound echoed in their ears, the Blood Guard trembled and Ouroboros sighed, knowing that he had gotten himself into serious trouble.

When his investigation into Thorn's background had not revealed anything he had assumed that Thorn, though giant, was simply a player. Yet now the Society of Roses had committed themselves fully to the fight and it was obvious that Athena had a close relationship to Thorn. Cursing mentally, Ouroboros could not believe that his investigation had missed that piece of information.

While Ragnarok was one of the top guilds in the game, no one wanted a piece of the Society of Roses. The elders of Ragnarok had warned him numerous times not to get on Athena's bad side, not that he would have challenged her anyways. Suddenly, Ouroboros' breath caught in his throat as he stared at Thorn. He knew who Athena was in the real world, which was why Ragnarok did its best to stay out of her way and seeing her bump fists with Thorn triggered a memory in his head.

“Come, Ouroboros. You challenged me, I set the wager. That is all there is to it. There is nothing to consider as the trial of combat has been set.” The giant stepped forward, the force of his presence commanding all the attention on the battlefield. “Let us begin.”

“You are Xavier Lee.” Ouroboros spoke numbly, his voice was quiet but certain. His posture sagged slightly as he looked down at the ground. “You are Julia Lee’s nephew, the owner of Atlas.”

Silence fell over the battlefield as every one of the Blood Guard froze, any remaining fighting spirit draining from them.

“So? Right now, I’m Thorn. Let the real world stay in the real world and Nova Terra stay in Nova Terra.”

At Thorn’s words, Ouroboros’ gaze which had been directed at the ground snapped up, his eyes searching Thorn’s face. Seeing no deceit, the black-armored warrior shook his head in disbelief.

“I don’t know if you are heroic or simply foolish, but I agree. I’ll accept your terms.” As his words faded, Ouroboros slipped his hands back into his gauntlets and picked up his helmet. "The contract is established."

ding

The Cursed Life and Death Contract - Updated
You are the target of an ancient cursed contract created in the Lost Era, before even the gods walked the land. Due to the curse attached to it, this contract may not be refused and the terms of the wager are absolute. However, should the one who initiated the contract lose, they will pay double the price. Through the strength of your bloodline, you have changed a facet of the contract. You have chosen to increase the wager to include your combined title, [Lord Greymane, the Moon Wolf], your position as Lord Greymane, and the land you currently rule. Wager: Life and Death - Winner Takes All Winner: Gains everything lost by the loser Loser: Loses Title [Lord Greymane, the Moon Wolf] along with associated positions and areas (Position of Lord Greymane, Area: [Greymane Keep], Area: [Fang Forest], Area: [Greymane Village], Area: [The Twins]) or equivalent titles, positions, and resources

His chest burning with excitement, Thorn summoned his claws, flexing his hands as the silver light condensed around the end of his fingers. Gripping his large metal weapon, Thorn dropped into his stance, taking in his opponent's every movement. While he had never fought against Ouroboros, he had watched the former Holy Guardian carve his way through countless mobs and he knew how skilled his opponent was.

Ouroboros had traded his shield in for a much larger, two-handed sword that he wore across his back. He had retained his full suit of plate armor, but the style had changed from that of a paladin to something sleeker with spikes on the shoulders. Ouroboros fixed his helmet in place and pulled his sword from the ground in one swift motion, leveling it at Thorn.

“Come, let’s settle this.”

“Haha, that is my line.” Thorn wasted no time in dashing forward, his mace swinging through the air.

Avoiding the strike with a neat dash to the side, Ouroboros returned a slash of his own, his sword cutting toward Thorn’s side. Blocking with his club, Thorn stepped back, creating a bit of distance. Normally, both fighters would want to be at an arm's reach to give them room to swing their weapons, but with Thorn’s larger size, distance benefited him more.

For a tense few minutes they traded blows, testing each other with probing strikes. Thorn’s attention focused on his defense, his attacks quick, meant to try and poke out

Ouroboros' weakness. Ouroboros did the same, never quite committing fully to any of his strikes. Back and forth they pushed, their weapons dancing.

Cutting at Thorn's feet with his blade, Ouroboros suddenly accelerated, putting his full weight behind his attack. Sensing the danger, Thorn jumped back, throwing out an overhead strike. Before his attack could hit, Ouroboros sidestepped and slashed up with his sword.

"[Blood Strike!]" As his sword swung toward Thorn's stomach, blood seeped from between the plates in Ouroboros' gauntlet. Joining together, the blood congregated on the handle of his sword and shot up the blade, staining the edge with a crimson glow. The tip of the sword clashed against Thorn's armor, scattering sparks into the air. With a roar, Ouroboros stepped forward as soon as his blade made contact, trying to stab it into Thorn's stomach.

Grunting at the impact, Thorn found himself staggering backward as the blood infused attack drilled into him. Gritting his teeth, he shifted his body to the side, and smashed down with a palm attack, hoping to break the blade by trapping it between his palm and body.

As if he had a sixth sense, Ouroboros jumped back as soon as he saw Thorn's body start to shift, quickly getting out of Thorn's reach. Separating, neither warrior moved forward to re-engage. Instead, Thorn took a small step back, his hand pressed to his stomach. Silence had fallen over the battlefield and when the ringing sounds of their combat died down, all that could be heard was Thorn's labored breath.

"Whew. This might be harder than I thought." Thorn murmured, gulping in air. He could feel the spot that Ouroboros' sword had stabbed into his side and while it had not managed to pierce through, the strike had deformed his armor quite badly. No doubt he would have a significant bruise. Twisting his body a bit to make sure there was no impairment to his movement, Thorn glanced down to see what damage had been done.

"Your defeat is inevitable, Thorn. Why bother with this useless struggle?" The hypnotic undertones of Ouroboros' words slid through the air, poking at the edges of Thorn's will.

"Haha, you mistake what I'm saying, Ouroboros." Thorn looked up from inspecting his side, his eyes glowing with excitement. "I'm pleased that I will not be able to flatten you with a single strike. You must understand how frustrating it is to rarely have a solid fight. But here you are, presenting yourself to me." Thorn stepped forward, his aura deepening as he did so, his words taking on a slightly hoarse tone. "Thank you for offering yourself up!"

"[Wolf Lord's Howl!]" As Thorn threw back his head and howled, sound waves pulsed from him, covering the battlefield. For the briefest of seconds, Velin, watching from the wall, felt like she could see them spreading out from

Thorn. The sound battered against Ouroboros, ringing in his head as the long howl grew in volume.

Distracted by the ever-increasing waves of sound, it was as if he was being tossed around without knowing which way was up. Ouroboros shook his head and focused his attention on feeling his surroundings. The dirt and ash of the battlefield under his feet, the firm handle of his sword. With a low shout, he broke free of the stunning effect of Thorn's ability and looked up, in time to see Thorn's mace flying toward his chest.

CHAPTER FIFTY

Abandoning any pretense of defense, Ouroboros threw himself backward as the head of the mace grew larger in his sight. It did not take a genius to know it was pure suicide to try and block one of Thorn's full-powered strikes, so his only option was to dodge. Tumbling, Ouroboros did a backward roll, coming to rest in a crouch, his sword held in front of him.

Thorn, unperturbed by his missed attack, shortened his grip and swung his mace around his head, maintaining the momentum of his strike. Bringing it down with increased force, he smashed it into the ground where Ouroboros had rested a moment before, blasting a crater in the already mangled battlefield. With a roar, he launched his mace sideways, hoping to catch Ouroboros before he could regain his balance.

Feeling the mace slide over his head with millimeters to

spare, Ouroboros broke out in a cold sweat. If any of the whistling swings were to connect, he knew with certainty that he would not survive. Gritting his teeth under his helmet, grateful that his armor hid how difficult he was finding the fight already, Ouroboros activated one of his skills. In a flash of dark power, his armor blurred and he appeared twenty feet away.

“What was that?” Her eyes locked on the fight taking place in front of the gate, Mina asked Velin who stood at her side.

“Looks like Power Charge, or something similar. Probably a corrupted version of it. Possibly with an evasion effect? The Holy Guardian Power Charge skill had a micro-invulnerability effect but evasion would make more sense considering the devil aspect of his new class.”

“With a quad category class, how many skills does he have? I don’t think this is going to go well.”

“Don’t give up hope yet,” Velin put her arm around Mina’s shoulders, pulling her in close. “Remember the greater werewolf in Greymane Keep? Thorn is only just getting started.”

Down below, Thorn had stopped his attacks and turned to face Ouroboros.

“Running away? Not what I expected from a berserker.” His tone faintly mocking, Thorn pointed his weapon at

Ouroboros. “Why don’t you show me that power that you got for betraying me. Or is this all you have?”

“You want to see my power? Alright, I’ll show it to you. [Blood Rage].”

CRACK

With a sharp sound, the plates on Ouroboros’ smooth black armor shattered, revealing crimson cracks that oozed blood. Like veins pumping, the red lines pulsed with a demonic glow as if Ouroboros had stepped straight out of the underworld. A disgusting stench drifted from him, spreading out over the battlefield, causing those caught in its grotesque embrace to feel nauseous.

Feeling the familiar distaste welling up in him, Thorn’s eyes narrowed. He had fought the Wolfkin Disciple corrupted by Karrandras in the Wolfkin village, but this feeling was on another level. Ouroboros’ corruption was so complete that for a moment, Thorn felt like he was in the presence of the Arch Devil himself.

“You wanted to see how powerful I have become, right?” Ouroboros’ voice dripped with the promise of power, his calming words at odds with the murderous vibes radiating from his bloody figure. “[Blood Strike!]”

His armor pulsing with crimson light, Ouroboros dashed forward. The red light from his body streamed across the edge of his sword, granting it a barbaric aura. Rather than try and dodge the attack, Thorn stepped forward, smashing out with an attack of his own, determined to beat Ouroboros in a contest of strength.

BOOM

With a thunderous sound, the weapons met, sending sparks flying. Without pausing for even a moment the two warriors threw out another strike, their weapons smashing into each other again. With each earthshaking swing, they clashed, sending out shockwaves that sent ash and dust into the air, blurring their figures. They were completely hidden by the cloud of debris when Ouroboros roared out.

“[Blood Splits the Earth!]”

Under the horrified gaze of the defenders, Thorn’s massive body flew backward out of the cloud of ash and dust, the force of Ouroboros’ strike blasting away the flying dust. Tucking his body, Thorn rolled over on the ground, coming to a stop on one knee. A bloody mark crossed his chest where the attack had connected, the gash showing in stark contrast to his silver armor.

In front of the gate, Athena took a step forward, the murderous aura that had been growing around her suddenly spiking out of control. Just as she was about to act, Bluefire grabbed her arm, stopping her in place.

"Don't. You can't interfere. Besides, even if you could, he doesn't need help yet." The Society of Roses officer pointed her tonfa at Thorn who had already started to move.

Before he had come to rest, Thorn was already changing directions. Sliding backward on one knee, Thorn planted his right foot and launched himself back into the fight. Strength surged through his leg, propelling him through the air toward Ouroboros who had given chase. With a low roar, Thorn unleashed his massive strength in a full powered strike, his massive metal mace ripping through the air with a piercing whine.

"[Blood Strike!]" Meeting the attack with a full powered strike of his own, Ouroboros tried to match Thorn with force. As their weapons collided, it was Ouroboros' turn to go flying. The power behind Thorn's attack was simply too much to overcome and Ouroboros could only deal with the remaining force by throwing himself backward. Despite his attempt to neutralize the power of the strike, Ouroboros struggled to maintain his balance as he tumbled through the air, staggering as he landed.

Charging forward, Thorn roared, his eyes turning red as his [Wolf's Rage] activated, granting Thorn a boost in his speed and strength. The increase in Thorn's speed was abrupt and terrifying, carrying him right up to Ouroboros.

Still off balance, Ouroboros barely had time to get his weapon up when another brutal strike from Thorn landed on his side, sending him tumbling head over heels. Relentless, Thorn chased after him, forcing Ouroboros to use another of his skills.

"[Blood Break!]"

Still in midair, Ouroboros forcefully righted himself, a red ring bursting from him. The ring expanded, bouncing Thorn backward, allowing Ouroboros a precious second to land on the ground and stabilize himself. But a second was all he got before Thorn was back on top of him, his mace swinging.

Watching Thorn rampage like an unstoppable beast, murmurs arose among the Blood Guard. They had never seen their leader so hard pressed before. His quad category class put him in an elite tier matched by only a few players and his skill in combat was among the best in the game. Yet Thorn seemed to bat him around like a rag-doll.

"What is going on? Is the commander going to lose?" Clenching his fists, one of the Blood Guard asked the player next to him. Unable to muster up a response, his companion shook his head mutely as again and again Ouroboros was driven back by Thorn's powerful strikes. Cheering broke out along the wall as the defenders watched their lord battling the enemy commander. Only Velin was silent, her face grave.

Noticing that the elven War Priestess was not cheering with the rest of them, Mina frowned, her enthusiasm dampening.

It only took her a moment to see what was causing Velin such concern and when she spotted it, her mood fell even further.

Ouroboros was being tossed around the battlefield, looking for all the world like he was seriously struggling against Thorn's massive strength, but both Mina and Velin could tell that appearances were deceiving. Having spent countless hours fighting alongside him, they understood how accomplished Ouroboros was at tanking and they could see him putting those skills into practice against Thorn. The angle of his blade, the way he moved around Thorn, the timing of his dodges, and his counter-attacks all worked in concert to create a rhythm that ensured he took the minimum amount of damage while expending as much of Thorn's strength as possible.

Already, Thorn's boosting ability, [Wolf's Rage] was starting to wane and his attacks were starting to slow down. It was here that Ouroboros' experience began to shine. Slowly, even though he was being knocked around, Ouroboros was taking control of the fight's rhythm. As Ouroboros dodged a strike for the fourth time, Thorn realized that he was slowly being drawn into repeating patterns.

Exhaling, Thorn jumped backward suddenly, causing Ouroboros to start to charge forward after him. As if he sensed the impromptu trap, the black-armored warrior suddenly stopped and stepped backward.

“You are really good.” Thorn shook his head, resting his mace on the ground as he caught his breath. “Most enemies would have been crushed into pulp by now. I’ll admit that you gained a lot from your choice to stab me in the back and steal my destiny points for a quad class. But I feel like the weakest part of you is these crappy abilities. When we go head to head, you lose every time. If you were not such a good tank you would have died already. That means that you don’t need Karrandras or this quad class to be strong, Ouroboros.”

“Shut up.” Ouroboros’ voice had taken on a raspy quality ever since he activated his [Blood Rage] ability. The grating sound did nothing to remove the hypnotic element in his voice and even served to enhance it. Thorn was quite thankful that his [Oration Proficiency] ability helped him resist his enemy’s verbal bewitchment. Without it, he was not sure that he could have resisted falling prey to Ouroboros’ lulling words.

The disgusting smell had faded from the battlefield, a sure sign that Ouroboros’ rage ability had run out of time. Unlike [Wolf’s Rage], the [Blood Rage] ability had an infinite duration so long as the player who used it killed other players or natives, making it ideal for a messy group fight. Unable to show off its strengths against a hard to kill enemy like Thorn, Ouroboros found himself running out of juice with nothing to show for it. The veins in his armor continued to pulse, but each second the glow faded.

"You do not get to judge me." Ouroboros said, his voice carrying despite how quiet he was. "You have no idea what sort of power I've gained. You think that you understand? You understand nothing. Blood Guard, sacrifice!" Ouroboros' voice grew in volume until his last words thundered across the battlefield, echoing from the citadel's walls.

Without hesitating, the Blood Guards each pulled out a long, wickedly curved, forked dagger. Turning, they stabbed them into their companion's bodies under the shocked gazes of all the defenders. Too late Athena realized what was happening and, unable to stop it, she could only watch as gouts of blood streamed from the grimacing players.

Each wicked blade, enchanted with a bleeding effect, caused blood to splash to the ash covered ground, pooling under the feet of the Blood Guard. One by one, the player's lives drained and they disappeared into sparks of light. Within moments all two hundred players had been sent out of the game, leaving a massive pool of blood running in rivulets across the battle-scarred ground.

"You wanted to see my power? The power of Karrandras? Let me show you what real power looks like, Thorn."

As if drawn by a magnet, the blood began to ripple, moving toward Ouroboros' feet. Defying gravity, it surged toward him at increasing speed, bringing with it the ash and dirt of the battlefield. Swirling around underneath his feet, the blood seeped into his armor's cracks, climbing the red veins and bringing with it a fresh crimson glow. The scent that had faded returned suddenly and in full force, cloying the air with a disgusting stench.

More and more blood rushed over, getting so high that the swirling maelstrom at his feet soon reached his knees. Faster and faster it was sucked up by his broken armor, as if it was drinking from the life essence of the sacrificed. At first Thorn was not sure if it was a trick of his eyes, but he imagined that the blood pumping into Ouroboros was causing him to swell. Soon, however, he knew it was not a trick of the fading daylight as Ouroboros suddenly grew three inches all at once.

The red glow running in veins around Ouroboros' armor had been growing and expanding, and with an abrupt cracking noise, the veins expanded, causing Ouroboros to grow larger and larger. The more blood he absorbed, the bigger he got until he was standing a full foot taller than Thorn's 8 feet nine inches. Ouroboros presented a truly frightening picture, his hulking form dripping with the glowing crimson plasma that he had absorbed.

His armor, once smooth and sleek, was now comprised of cracked and broken plates floating in a sea of crimson, causing him to appear to be a giant elemental made of blood. Gone were any human features, and instead long, jagged blades grew from his arms. A tail tipped with a wicked looking barb formed from a piece of broken armor swiped from side to side behind him, seeking an opportunity to impale Thorn. As the last vestiges of the pool of crimson fluid was drawn into Ouroboros' armor, it revealed his legs, reformed into the legs of a goat, only adding to his new, devilish look.

"Well? What do you think?" Obvious pride could be heard in Ouroboros' voice as he stepped forward, showing off his devil form fully. "The power granted to me by Karrandras is the greatest this game has ever seen. With this [Blood Devil] form, there is nothing, player or native, that can stand against me. With it I will crush everything and everyone in my way, starting with you. Thorn, you are powerful, but against a true devil, you can do nothing. Give up. This fight is hopeless. Give up and you can join me. You can gain power like this. Power to stand alone atop the world."

For the briefest of moments, Thorn's eyes wavered, dropping to the ground at the giant devil's feet. The words of Ouroboros ate away at his mental defenses, urging him to give up, to lay down his weapon. Then Thorn's eyes snapped back up, cutting through the bewitching air that Ouroboros' words had woven.

"I don't need your power." Thorn mumbled, his burning eyes fixed on Ouroboros' figure. "I have plenty."

CHAPTER FIFTY-ONE

As each moment passed, Thorn could feel the force of Ouroboros' devil form pressing down on him, eating away at his consciousness. The fact that he could still think at all was due to his unnatural resistance to mental effects, granted by his class. A quick glance back toward the wall showed that the others were not so lucky. The greater devil's form carried a natural suppressive force that pulled those who encountered it into a passive state, making them unable to resist.

Thorn could feel that suppressive force clearly, and if he could not figure out a way to break it he knew that it would only be a matter of time until he too fell into a stupor. His wounds seemed to respond to the aura, and the blood that had been trickling from them increased, winding its way in thin streams toward Ouroboros' grotesque figure. Even gathering his thoughts was growing harder by the second so

Thorn decided to stop thinking.

"[Rallying Cry!]" A long howl poured from Thorn's throat, echoing around the pass, the eerie tones bouncing from the stone of the citadel and reflecting from the Twins. On and on the call went, powered by Thorn's seemingly endless breath. Elder Havva was the first to respond from where he stood, slumped over on the wall. Unconsciously, he struggled to straighten and, with a shuddering breath lifted his head and joined in the long howl. Slowly, the other Dawn Walkers joined in, throwing back their heads to howl along with Thorn.

At first, the call was scattered, disorganized. Yet as it continued, it grew in strength and intensity, the varied voices combining into a single harmonious voice. As more and more Wolfkin joined in, the corrupting power of Karrandras began to collapse, eroding at the edges. The bloody scent that had dominated the battlefield began to clear, and those who had fallen under the natural stupor effect of the greater devil began to awaken.

"What? Impossible!" Ouroboros growled, droplets of acidic spit flying from his slavering maw as he spoke. Hate grew in his eyes as he stared at Thorn. All his troubles stemmed from this giant figure in front of him, blocking his path. Determined to remove Thorn once and for all, he strode forward, lifting the blades on his arms to strike.

With a roar, the greater devil slashed at Thorn, intent on

cutting him down where he stood. Thorn, seeing the blow approach, cut off his howl, sliding back on his feet and dropping naturally into his taijiquan stance. It felt like it had been a lifetime since he had used the martial arts that he had learned before coming into Nova Terra. His training had been largely useless due to the size difference between him and most enemies.

The greater devil form that Ouroboros had revealed was as big as he was, making it a perfect target for him. Seeing another strike coming in, Thorn shifted his stance by sliding his foot back, moving outside the range of the attack. Ouroboros, growing increasingly furious that he had missed both his attacks rushed forward, his devil's tail stabbing forward.

Thorn lifted his hands, holding his mace like a broadsword, deflecting against the barb on the end of the whipping tail, and bringing his feet together smoothly, stabbed forward with the end of the mace. Taken back by the smoothness of Thorn's transition from defense to offense, Ouroboros was unable to react in time and took the main force of the blow, and staggered backward. With a ferocious roar, the greater devil surged forward again.

"Your puny attacks cannot stop me, Thorn! This form is invincible!" Raving, Ouroboros rained down attacks on Thorn, slashing and gouging with the blades on his arms while his tail whipped this way and that, seeking every opportunity to stab forward.

Weathering the storm of attacks, Thorn felt as if he was a boat being tossed in a gale, threading through the waves and wind, ever in danger of capsizing, but somehow staying upright. At first his reactions were slightly jerky as his body tried to remember the forms and paths from his training. Despite the bloody gashes that began to appear on his body, Thorn persisted, emptying his mind of all distracting thoughts and focusing on the enemy in front of him.

Slowly, his moves began to become smoother, his reactions slightly faster. The transitions between his deflecting moves and his attacking strikes began to blur until they merged together, forming a weaving net of intermixed offense and defense with no distinction.

Ouroboros could feel control of the fight slipping from his clawed fingers as Thorn's moves became smoother and smoother. Furious, he redoubled his efforts, striking with as much power as he could muster, yet his attacks were deflected to the side or redirected into empty space, wasting his strength. Each time he swung his blade Thorn seemed to be out of reach, moving outside the range of motion of his attack. About to explode with fury, Thorn's smooth, slippery motions suddenly changed and Ouroboros barely registered a silver blur before something hit him in the ribs, hard.

CRACK

With a sound so sharp it cut straight through the air, Thorn's mace impacted the greater devil's side, crushing the remnants of armor that floated in the crimson plasma that made up its body, sending it plunging to the ground.

Thorn had let himself go, clearing his mind to focus on the fight and allowing his muscle memory to guide him as he fought. Slowly, the years of training he had received before coming to Nova Terra had been unearthed, allowing him to keep himself from being overrun by Ouroboros' greater devil form. As his movements had grown more natural, they had begun to unconsciously merge with the tetsubo training that Master Sun had given him in the gorge of the earth elementals, combining defense and offense into one smooth action.

As he deflected the last attack, Thorn had instinctively felt an opening in his opponent's defenses, and without hesitation he had stepped forward, planting his feet solidly as he struck out, smashing his mace into the greater devil's ribs, driving it into the ground. As soon as he connected, Thorn could tell through the feedback of his weapon that he had dealt significant damage.

Flipping the giant metal spike around, Thorn stabbed the pointed end down, putting his full weight behind the blow. The sharp spike pierced through Ouroboros, pinning him firmly to the ground, and eliciting a shriek of pain from the greater devil. His arms flailing, Ouroboros struggled to free himself, only to feel a massive weight clamp down on his body, forcing him further into the ground.

Thorn, loath to give up the advantage he had seized, dropped a knee onto Ouroboros' chest, pinning one of the greater devil's arms to the ground with his other leg. The dwarven trainer from Berum's words echoed in his head and he began to throw fist after rock hard fist down at the greater devil's head, battering it into an unrecognizable shape.

Each furious hit smashed into Ouroboros, sending blood flying, yet the greater devil simply regenerated, his head reforming after each strike. The whipping tail plunged toward Thorn's back, stabbing into his shoulder. Roaring with pain, Thorn grabbed the spiked end of Ouroboros' tail and, with a furious pull, ripped the talon right off, plunging it into the neck of the greater devil.

Ouroboros' scream of pain turned into a gurgle as the barb pierced through his throat and for the first time, he began to know fear. His furious attempts to dislodge Thorn from on top of him gained an edge of hysteria, yet no matter how he struggled, he could not move the figure on top of him. Thorn's weight was like a mountain, sealing him to the ground. Again and again, Thorn smashed down, his strikes getting faster and faster, raining down blow after blow on the greater devil. The burning ember of fury that Thorn had been suppressing for so long suddenly burst forth, igniting into a raging flame.

Ever since the events in the dungeon, Thorn had been doing his best to keep a tight lid on his feelings, but now the dam had broken. The frustration and anger Thorn had bottled up inside poured out in a storm of strikes, imbuing his rock-hard fists with even more power than normal.

Watching from near the wall, her eyes wide, Athena turned to look at Bluefire

“Don’t look at me. I didn’t teach him that.” The Society of Roses fighter shook her head and held up her hands. “I thought you said that he had a peaceful childhood? That doesn’t look very peaceful to me.”

“I...” Unsure what to say, Athena fell silent, watching as Thorn pummeled the greater devil into a pulp.

Soon the angry bellows of the greater devil were silenced and the body below Thorn evaporated into shining particles of light. Utterly drained, he knelt on the battlefield, too tired to even move. As he gulped in air, he could hear Mina’s screams of excitement approaching. A warm golden light fell on him, removing the weariness from his limbs, healing his wounds.

ding

The Cursed Life and Death Contract - Winner
You are the target of an ancient cursed contract created in the Lost Era, before even the gods walked the land. Due to the curse attached to it, this contract may not be refused

and the terms of the wager are absolute. However, should the one who initiated the contract lose, they will pay double the price.

You have won the trial of combat

Wager: Life and Death - Winner Takes All
Reward: You have gained the following items, abilities, and resources.

Items: [Nobility Upgrade Token], [Asha's Vambrace], [Asha's Boots], [Asha's Greaves]
Abilities: [The Devil is in the Details], [Shadow Dash], [Language Proficiency: Abyssal], [Intercepting Strike]
Resources: [Legacy Deed: Imperial Mansion], [Legacy Deed: Imperial Mine] x2, [Legacy Deed: Imperial Town]

Alpha Challenge - Completed

A powerful threat to your pack has appeared. You have identified the enemy in front of you as particularly dangerous to your budding family. Per the ancient traditions, you are responsible for facing the challenger, or appointing a champion to face the challenger.

You have succeeded, maintaining your position as Greymane.

You have gained the favor of Hati.

Greater devil defeated: You have gained the favor of Hati.

Thorn's jaw nearly hit the floor when he looked at the rewards for defeating Ouroboros. He had expected to be rewarded well considering that he had bet practically everything he owned, but four items, four abilities, and four resources were out of his expectation. Especially when he started looking at their details.

First were the three pieces of named armor that Ouroboros had dropped. Each piece was part of the smooth black armor set that Ouroboros had been wearing. Never having seen a named item in his time playing Nova Terra, Thorn was curious as to what advantage they would have.

Asha's Vambrace - Heavy Armor
The legendary holy warrior Asha fell to the darkness, becoming the champion of the Devil King Malros'Tharn. For countless years he waged war against the forces of good, crushing them in direct combat thanks to his formidable hellplate armor. Marked with the symbol of Malros'Tharn, Asha's Vambraces grant the wearer increased physical strength as they kill their enemies. Set Bonus:

[2 pieces]: +Constitution
[3 pieces]: [Devilish Aura]
[4 pieces]: +Constitution
[5 pieces]: [Summon Helfiend]
[6 pieces]: +Strength, +Constitution

Asha's Boots - Heavy Armor

The legendary holy warrior Asha fell to the darkness, becoming the champion of the Devil King Malros'Tharn. For countless years he waged war against the forces of good, crushing them in direct combat thanks to his formidable hellplate armor.

Marked with the symbol of Malros'Tharn, Asha's Boots grant the wearer increased agility as they kill their enemies.

Set Bonus:
[2 pieces]: +Constitution
[3 pieces]: [Devilish Aura]
[4 pieces]: +Constitution
[5 pieces]: [Summon Helfiend]
[6 pieces]: +Strength, +Constitution

Asha's Greaves - Heavy Armor

The legendary holy warrior Asha fell to the darkness, becoming the champion of the Devil King Malros'Tharn.

For countless years he waged war against the forces of good, crushing them in direct combat thanks to his formidable hellplate armor.

Marked with the symbol of Malros'Tharn, Asha's Greaves grant the wearer increased endurance as they kill their enemies.

Set Bonus:
[2 pieces]: +Constitution
[3 pieces]: [Devilish Aura]
[4 pieces]: +Constitution
[5 pieces]: [Summon Helfiend]
[6 pieces]: +Strength, +Constitution

Immediately, Thorn could see how important having a named armor set was. Just the double increase in constitution that came with wearing four pieces was enough to give a player a huge advantage, to say nothing of the full six piece set bonus. Curious about the other two bonus abilities that the set gave, Thorn opened them up. The [Devilish Aura] added a fear effect to the player's aura, while the [Summon Helfiend] could summon lesser Helfiends to the battlefield. Thankfully for Thorn, both only activated after killing an enemy, making them useless in the one on one fight that Ouroboros and Thorn had.

While the set would not fit him, Thorn instantly thought of his follower, Captain Del'har. Remembering the Wolfkin Captain's lightning fast sword draw at the Wolfkin camp,

Thorn could only imagine how strong the captain would be while using a set of named armor like this.

The other item that Ouroboros dropped was a simple, golden token. Rectangular in shape, the token was embossed with a castle and seven stars arranged in a half circle. The token was four inches tall and three inches wide and less than an inch thick. Despite its small size, Thorn found it surprisingly heavy, as if the game's automatic weight reduction did not work on it.

Nobility Upgrade Token
Once controlling the entire continent of Angoril, the Holy Empire has fractured, splitting in two. Despite the split, these ancient tokens are still honored, granting an instant upgrade to a noble's rank. To apply this token to a title, it must be turned in at the administrative office of one of the existing empires.

The description for the token was brief, but Thorn could immediately see the immense value it held. In his study about the game he had come to realize that the natives saw themselves as different from the immortal travelers who came from another world. This manifested itself in numerous ways, but one of the most obvious was the difficulty that players faced when trying to gain noble positions or raise their noble rank. Ouroboros must have planned to use this token to bypass that restriction.

His brow furrowing slightly, Thorn skipped over the abilities that he had gained and looked at the [Legacy Deeds] in the resource portion of the reward. As soon as he read through them a clear picture of what Ouroboros had intended emerged, causing Thorn to chuckle. It was obvious how much effort Ouroboros had put into this plan, only to have Thorn benefit.

Legacy Deed: Imperial Mansion (Human)
Once controlling the entire continent of Angoril, the Holy Empire has fractured, splitting in two. Despite the split, these ancient deeds are still honored, granting the bearer control of an imperial asset. This deed allows the bearer to select one property in the imperial city, as determined by the bearer's noble rank. To redeem this deed, please proceed to the administrative office of the human empire.

Legacy Deed: Imperial Mine x2 (Human)
Once controlling the entire continent of Angoril, the Holy Empire has fractured, splitting in two. Despite the split, these ancient deeds are still honored, granting the bearer control of an imperial asset.

This deed allows the bearer to select one mine and its surrounding area within the human empire, as determined by the bearer's noble rank. To redeem this deed, please proceed to the administrative office of the human empire.

Legacy Deed: Imperial Town (Human)
Once controlling the entire continent of Angoril, the Holy Empire has fractured, splitting in two. Despite the split, these ancient deeds are still honored, granting the bearer control of an imperial asset. This deed allows the bearer to select one town and its surrounding area within the human empire, as determined by the bearer's noble rank. To redeem this deed, please proceed to the administrative office of the human empire.

Exactly like the [Nobility Upgrade Token] that Ouroboros had dropped, the four [Legacy Deed] papers that Thorn received would grant him official status in the eyes of the empire. Should Ouroboros have been able to control the valley, he could have applied for official noble status and then used the four [Legacy Deeds] and the [Nobility Upgrade Token] to instantly elevate his rank.

Yet now, all his hard work had come to naught, and instead it was Thorn who was benefiting. With a sigh, Thorn could only shake his head and wonder if the game had planned this.

CHAPTER FIFTY-TWO

Putting the items aside, Thorn looked through the four abilities that he had taken from Ouroboros. The first was a non-combat ability that seemed like it was tied to Ouroboros' devil class.

The Devil is in the Details
Common wisdom says to never make a deal with a devil. Experts in the manipulation of rules and legalities, devils are known for their convoluted contracts and misleading agreements. You have learned to spot details that are not to your advantage in contracts and agreements to which you are party. You have gained the ability to skirt around the letter of the law, operating in the grey areas between the lines without incurring the penalties of the contract.

Curious about how he would know that this sort of ability was active, Thorn made a mental note to ask Velin. Many of his abilities, like the language proficiencies that he had picked up, simply worked unconsciously, but he was not sure if this was the same. The last three abilities were straightforward, so after looking over them he closed the windows and stood up.

Shadow Dash
Borrow the power of shadow to shroud your form as you dash forward. While you are moving, you gain the [Evasive] condition. Your next strike causes the [Bleeding] condition.

Language Proficiency: Abyssal
You have gained proficiency in speaking Abyssal, the language of the Abyss.

Intercepting Strike [level 1]
Swing your weapon in a wide arc, blocking incoming projectiles.

"Thorn!" Running over, Athena was smiling and shouting, ecstatic that Thorn had won. Behind her, streaming from the fortress, Mina and Velin led the Wolfkin and human residents of the valley, everyone cheering loudly.

"Whew." Thorn breathed out, the tension from the fight draining from him. "It was a close thing, huh?"

[Master, master! That was amazing! You totally beat up that evil blood giant guy!] In a streak of red, Akira zipped past Thorn's aunt and climbed up Thorn's bent and scratched armor, jumping around excitedly on his shoulder. [But next time why don't you bring me? I could have helped you and we would have smashed his smelly face into the ground!]

"Thanks, Akira. Next time I will, okay. Thanks for cheering for me." Rising to his feet, Thorn removed his helmet and greeted the cheering crowd, holding up his hand for silence. It took a few minutes before everyone calmed down, but once they had, Thorn's deep voice carried over the battlefield. "Friends, we've won." An explosion of cheers erupted from those gathered, forcing Thorn to wait until they died down.

"Our valley is safe, thanks to your efforts. Yet now is not the time to relax our guard. Very soon we will see an influx of new Wolfkin arriving in the valley. With them come opportunities and challenges. We have much to do before they arrive and I will need your continued dedication and hard work if we are to grow and improve our land. We have a battlefield to clean up, supplies to restock, building to do, and some rules to organize. Tonight, however, we feast! In honor of our first victory together, let us celebrate by eating and drinking to our hearts content!"

Gesturing for Captain Del'har to lead the cheering masses back into Moon Wolf Citadel to get ready for the celebration, Thorn turned to his aunt. Canceling his armor, Thorn enveloped her in a big hug.

"Thanks for coming." Thorn whispered, gratitude heavy in his voice. While the Society of Roses had not fought all that much, their arrival had forced Ouroboros into a dead end.

"Of course, kid. Wouldn't miss it for the world." Athena patted him on the shoulder. "Though, judging from that last fight, I don't know that you actually needed any help. You've gotten quite impressive, Xavier. Quite impressive indeed."

"Thorn! You..." Mina was so excited she was breathless.

"Congratulations on your victory, Thorn." Placing a hand on Mina's shoulder, Velin smiled. "That was an impressive display of combat."

"Seriously, are you sure that you are not actually a native boss?" Oberlin's voice cut in. Grinning, the thief appeared from among the Society of Roses who had crowded around. "Haha, hey boss. That was something else."

"Thank you, everyone." Thorn smiled, a slight blush creeping up his cheeks.

After he had greeted Bluefire and the rest of the Society of Roses, Thorn invited them all into the citadel's fortress where Captain Del'har and Elder Havva were waiting. Massive tables had been laid out in the entrance to the fortress and many of the valley's residents were running back and forth, piling food on them. Two huge barrels of wine were rolled out and tapped, and the smell of roasted meat soon rose into the evening sky.

While the food was not fancy, it was hearty and plentiful and, above all, delicious. Thorn, famished from his fight, swept an entire table clean by himself, to the utter astonishment of his subjects. His aunt, used to his eating habits, kept up a steady stream of conversation with the others at the table, entertaining them with stories and funny anecdotes while her nephew polished off two whole roast boars, countless pieces of bread, a whole bucket of mashed potatoes, and a massive amount of fruit.

When she had first met Velin and Mina, Athena had been rather cold, but after talking with them for a bit she gradually warmed up. Despite Thorn's assurances that his relationship with the girls had been repaired, Athena was skeptical until she saw it with her own eyes.

When he had finally eaten his fill, Thorn leaned back in his chair with a satisfied sigh. The tables were cleared and most of the residents had turned in for the night in preparation for the work that had to be completed over the next week. Noticing that Mina had a sliver of worry in her eyes and was not her normal, excited self, Thorn asked her what was wrong.

“Ah, it is nothing.” Mina smiled stiffly, waving her hands. “I’m really happy about our victory.”

“She is probably worried about what is going to happen when Ragnarok comes back.” Sitting next to Mina, Velin played with the stem of her wine glass. “Even with the Society of Roses here, Ragnarok has a lot of people.”

“Oh, that's right. I completely forgot.” Thorn tossed one of the nuts he had been snacking on at Oberlin to get his attention. “Hey, do you have that thing I asked you to get?”

“If, by ‘thing’ you mean the territory appointment, yes.” Rubbing his head with one hand while he got a stack of papers out of his inventory with the other, Oberlin wondered why the peanut had hurt so much. “Here you go. Just needs your signature to be official.”

“Excellent, thanks.” As Thorn got a pen from his inventory and signed and initialed the papers, Mina crawled over the table to look at the top sheet. Laughing, Thorn pushed the papers to her while he explained to the rest of the table that was looking on with interest. “Before we came to the valley I sent Oberlin down south to act as a guide for the Society of Roses. However, he also had another job.”

“This is an enfeoffment!” Few things could shake Velin’s calm, but when Mina, unable to make heads or tails of the paper, handed it to her, her eyes widened in shock.

“That is correct. The Wolfkin and other inhabitants of this valley have officially applied to be members of the Northern Empire. They have recognized the title of Lord Greymane and granted the holder the rank of Baron, with control over the valley. We’ll be paying taxes to the Iron Fist Duke who oversees this dutchy.”

“Wait a second. You are a Baron?” Mina was skeptical.

“Yup.” Grinning, Thorn shared the notification that had popped up for him.

Title Amended: Lord Greymane, the Moon Wolf [Baron]
As the ruler of Fang Valley, your position has been recognized by the Northern Empire. You have gained the landholding rank of Baron and the responsibilities associated. For a complete list of the privileges and responsibilities associated with your rank please refer to the Imperial Codex of Law.

“Wait a moment, you did not have the title yet when you sent Oberlin to the capital. How did he apply for citizenship?” Velin pointed out the hole in Thorn’s explanation.

“Haha, let's just say I’m a very talented individual.” Oberlin grinned smugly from his seat.

“Ah. I see.” Velin nodded.

"I don't see." Mina exclaimed, her pouting expression causing everyone around the table to laugh.

"He probably wrote the documents before Thorn arrived here. By the time Thorn cleared Greymane Keep, the documents he forged were no longer forgeries, which allowed Oberlin to file them immediately after getting them checked."

"Exactly." Thorn nodded, taking over the explanation from Velin. "At the end of the day, the empire wants taxes and so long as we pay them, they are not too concerned with a small baronage. We agreed to pay a higher than normal tax rate for the first two years as well as a special tax to the Ironhold Duke. While the empire is not concerned with us, our new position means that a player guild like Ragnarok will have to be cautious about attacking us since we are vassals of the Ironhold Duke and any challenge to us is a challenge to him."

"Leave contacting Ragnarok to me." Sitting next to Thorn, Athena looked up from feeding tidbits of fruit to Akira. "I'll let them know what the situation is and negotiate a settlement."

"I don't mind handling it."

"No, I insist." Athena smiled, though her eyes carried a cold look. "You focus on what you are good at, like punching people. Let me take care of the things I am good at."

"Like taking a layer of skin off business rivals at the negotiation table," cackled Bluefire from the other side of the table before ducking a piece of fruit that Athena threw across the table.

"Trust me Thorn, I'll handle it appropriately." Athena shot a warning glance at her chuckling guild mates.

"Thank you, aunt. I know you'll do a great job." The look in his eyes was soft and full of love as he watched Athena fool around. She had always taken wonderful care of him and it seemed that nothing had changed now that they were in this new world. Standing to his feet, Thorn looked around at the gathered players and natives. He could read many thoughts and feelings in their faces. Some looked to him for security and stability, some looked to him with their ambition. A few even looked at him with a burning flame in their eyes that he could not quite place. Regardless, their eyes were fixed on him, and for the first time in his life, it was not because of his abnormal size.

"Thank you all for celebrating this victory with me. We have much to do in the coming days so I want to thank you now for your hard work. A few things to note. Per our agreement with the Society of Roses, a branch of their guild will be established here as a mark of the alliance between Nova Luna and the Society of Roses. Additionally, Elder Havva has agreed to open the Temple of the Moon to those who want to walk the path of the disciple. He will be responsible for overseeing the temple and the training of new disciples. We expect a large influx of new players.

“Velin has been tasked with negotiating with the merchants who are interested in establishing themselves in Moon Wolf Citadel, so if you hear anyone asking around, please refer them to her. Diplomatic questions go to Oberlin, who will be assisted by the disciples of the Dawn Court. He will be handling our representation as part of the Ironhold Duchy. Mina has kindly agreed to work with Horvir and the Freemen to explore the surrounding mountains and categorize the different resources the valley possesses. She will also help train our soldiers and will be assuming command of the magical combat squad we hope to build.

“If you have questions or concerns regarding security, please see Captain Del’har. For any guild business regarding Nova Luna, please come and see me. We will be opening guild membership to players and natives alike and the ladies of the Society of Roses have agreed to assist us in setting up the guild structure and helping us process applicants. I know you all probably have a lot of questions, but it has been a long day. Tomorrow morning we will have a meeting at eight o’clock. You can raise your questions then.”

As he finished, Captain Del’har and Horvir, the leader of the Freemen both stood to salute. Following them, Velin rose to her feet. Oberlin joined the elven War Priestess in giving Thorn a half bow. Mina, seeing the others do it, bounced up as well.

Taken aback, Thorn looked around in surprise as those around the table stood and bowed to him. Unsure how he was supposed to respond, he fumbled around for a moment until he felt a pinch at his side. Looking down, he saw his aunt poking him.

“Stand up straight, Baron Thorn. They are simply giving you the respect you are due.” She whispered, fighting to keep the smile off her face.

After everyone else had gone to bed or logged out, Thorn climbed to the top of the fortress and walked out on the protruding wolf head, sitting on the nose as he watched the water running from the mouth fall, unbroken, down to the pool below. The stars had come out in full effect and gazing across the dark valley brought peace to Thorn’s heart. The last couple months had been full of ups and downs, full of pain, betrayal, and suffering. But for the first time in his life, he didn’t feel trapped in his own skin. He felt free.

Tomorrow, more people would come and more problems would have to be addressed. Conflict loomed on the horizon, and Thorn knew without a doubt that it would dominate the coming years. Others would come to this place and try to take this land from him. And beyond the mountains that ringed the forest before him were countless other mysteries and problems waiting to challenge him. Yet for all that, for the first time ever, true contentment reigned in his heart.

Here, now, in this quiet, peaceful moment, he was free.

Afterword

I really appreciate the time you have spent with me in Nova Terra. I am working on Book Four right now and cannot wait to share it with you. Before I tell you how to get a peek at what that looks like, please spend a few moments and leave me a review. Reviews are so important to indie writers, like me. Knowing that you are out there, reading and thinking about Nova Terra, is what keeps me writing.

Now for the good stuff. After you leave a review, head on over to my Patreon to learn how you can see up to 7,500 words *per week* of brand new material. There are lots of different levels of participation, all with various cool benefits, including being first to read new stuff, guiding the story line and character development, having a character named after you – lots of possibilities.

On a personal note, like some of you, I'm sure, I insist that coffee is the best food group and a proper substitute for stamina potions, though I'm excited to switch when someone finally gets around to making them. In the meantime, coffee gets me through to dinner time, which I share with my lovely wife and family.

I'm a Monday – Friday member of the #5amWritersClub on Twitter, so if I sleep in, you have my permission to send me disappointed gifs. I've been fortunate to participate in panels at various conferences, so please sign up for my Patreon and/or follow me on Facebook to get announcements of new material and where I am speaking. I'd love to meet you and hear your thoughts about Nova Terra, writing, and world building in general.

WWW.PATREON.COM/SETHRING

WWW.TWITTER.COM/SETHRING

WWW.SETHRING.COM

Acknowledgments

A huge thank you to my friends and family who encouraged and supported me on this wonderful journey.

Thank you to my Patrons, who make my writing possible. A special thank you to the following Patrons who have been especially generous in funding this story:

Barry Rucker
Berzerker
Brandon Nichols
BrangorTheSecond
Craig Macker
David Moran
Emmett Ord
Igor Dolas
James A Ring
Jermey Anselmi
Joshua Knapp
Kyle Gravelle
Matthew Bennett
Max Lambon
Robert Zelensky
Sean Amy
Tricky402

If you are interested in reading more GameLit or learning more about this or related genres like LitRPG, there are a couple cool communities on Facebook where you can find new books and get recommendations for old books.

https://www.facebook.com/groups/LitRPGsociety/
https://www.facebook.com/groups/LitRPGGroup/

Made in the USA
Lexington, KY
18 December 2019

58748548R00387